Praise for Pride

"Bob's *Pride's Puget Sound* is a rattling good read. His hero, john. ollows closely in the footsteps of such classic private investigators as Chandler's Philip Marlowe and MacDonald's Travis McGee, but updated to the modern world of the Internet, violent ecological protest, and the vested interests of big business and the genetically modified food industry."

"Anyone who likes fast action, twisting plots, and exotic locales to say nothing of flashbacks to a subplot of Scots and the naval War of 1812 cannot fail to be taken in from page one and kept turning the pages to see what happens next."

Patrick Taylor - *New York Times* and *USA Today* bestselling author of the *Irish Country Doctor* series.

"I have known - and shared - Bob and his passions for life and adventure - for more than three decades. This book is but another chapter in the journey."

W. Brett Wilson - author of *Redefining Success*, co-founder FirstEnergy Capital Corp., chairman of Canoe Financial and Prairie Merchant Corporation, entrepreneur, member of the Order of Canada, innovative philanthropist, *Dragons' Den* co-star and adventurer.

"Pride's adventurous, clever, but, better yet, he comes with flaws."

Ted Bell - *New York Times* Bestselling Author of Alex Hawke Thrillers

"In *Pride's Puget Sound*, Bob evokes the landscape and ambience of North America, through his descriptions of the beauty of the Pacific Northwest and his flashbacks to the War of 1812. Yet this is also a thoroughly modern novel, with cyber crime that stretches across continents and eco-terrorists who know no boundaries. In the midst of the hero's entertaining hunt for the culprit, we also get a glimpse into the moral dilemmas facing those who flirt with terrorism, and how the desire to change the world can lead to unforeseen and destructive consequences."

Jennifer Welsh, Professor in International Relations,
University of Oxford, England and
Lumsden Beach, Saskatchewan

"Take notice Grisham and Turow - things are happening in Puget Sound! Financial crime has never been so exciting, as John Pride steps in to assist the FBI and RCMP in an international thriller. Fast boats, fine Scotch, and Caribbean Islands keep the pages turning, almost as quickly as the elusive wire transfers circle the globe. Attention to detail is superb, and Pride is just the man we would hire if our firm was fortunate enough to have an exciting case like this- deal me in for an adventure."

Bill T. - Senior Partner,
International Law Firm

Dedication

This novel is dedicated to several very special family members.

Mum - Tanyss taught me my first lessons in economics and ecology. I can still remember you stopping to pick up a piece of litter long before the word sustainable was commonplace.

Dad - RHD (Bob) showed me the value of well-written words and the importance of family discussions around the dining room table.

Peter, my brother, spent many weeks helping shoulder the load on numerous mountains, rivers, lakes and portages.

Bree, my wife—always there and more than she really knows it—the real love of my life, and our two children:

Robert David, we love you for your strength and ability to make true friends wherever you go.

Genevieve Tanyss Pride, you have the beauty and confidence to do anything, and I mean anything, you want to do.

Thanks for all your support and encouragement.
The future is for you.

> *"Don't keep forever on a public road…*
> *following one after the other like a flock of sheep.*
> *Leave the beaten track occasionally and dive into the woods. Every*
> *time you do so you will be certain to find something that you have*
> *never seen before."*
>
> *Alexander Graham Bell*

"Out of my last fifty-three cases, my name has only appeared in four, and the police have had all the credit in forty-nine."
Sherlock Holmes in *The Naval Treaty*
—*The World's first Forensic Accountant*

"Genetic engineering involves taking a gene from one species and splicing it into another to transfer a desired trait. This could not occur in nature where the transfer of genetic traits is limited by the natural barriers that exist between different species and in this way genetic engineering is completely new and incomparable to traditional animal and plant breeding techniques. Genetic engineering is also called biotechnology. Another name for genetically engineered crops is genetically modified organisms (GMOs)."
Genetic Engineering, Food and our Environment
Luke Anderson, Chelsea Green Publishing Co.,
White River Junction, Vermont

PRIDE'S PUGET SOUND

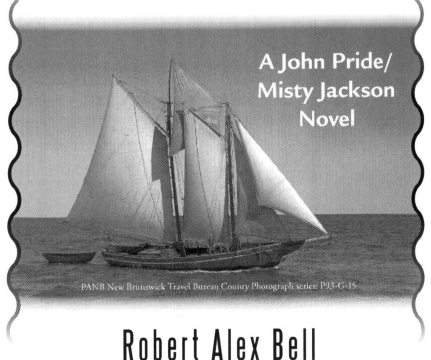

A John Pride/
Misty Jackson
Novel

PANB New Brunswick Travel Bureau County Photograph series: P93-G-15

Robert Alex Bell

iUniverse, Inc.
Bloomington

Pride's Puget Sound
A John Pride/Misty Jackson Novel

iUniverse books may be ordered through booksellers or by contacting:

iUniverse
1663 Liberty Drive
Bloomington, IN 47403
www.iuniverse.com
1-800-Authors (1-800-288-4677)

Cover Picture is provided by Thinkstock. Stock imagery © Thinkstock.
Photographs used with permission, as noted, by Provincial Archives of
New Brunswick (PANB) and McCord Museum, Montreal.
Alfred G. Bailey poems used with permission from the
Bailey family, and Quebec Chronicle-Telegraph.
Jack Whyte poems used with permission.

Phillips, Robert Alexander Bell, 1955-
Pride's Puget Sound / Robert Alex Bell

(The Pride trilogy; bk 1)
ISBN: 978-1-4759-8290-9 (sc)
ISBN: 978-1-4759-8292-3 (hc)
ISBN: 978-1-4759-8291-6 (e)

Library of Congress Control Number: 2013906164

Printed in the United States of America

iUniverse rev. date: 5/30/2013

CHAPTER 1

"Of all the fire mountains which, like beacons, once blazed along the Pacific Coast, Mount Rainier is the noblest."

John Muir

TWELVE HOURS IS NORMALLY a short period of time and it is hard to believe that twelve hours can change one's life as much as mine had been changed. Just yesterday I had been relaxing on the deck with a new Jack Whyte novel, nursing a cold Rickard's Red beer, when my phone rang. I had spent a thoroughly enjoyable morning on my Hobie Cat sailboat trying some new maneuvers around the island and planning how to win the annual sailboat race, to be held in a few days. This was the end of July, normally the two-week period when I try to relax at my cottage. I turn off the phone and ignore work but I had been expecting a call from Misty. Over the years I had learned that when Misty wants to get you, you better be available.

It wasn't the love of my love. It wasn't even Misty.

"John, you are going to want to see this personally. I need you to fly into Seattle immediately and meet with Blake Kingsley. He will fill you in and take you to the lab." I recognized the voice as belonging to Francis Letourneau from the Seattle office of Computer Law Enforcement of Washington (CLEW). CLEW is a new organization, which includes the Washington State Attorney General's Office, U.S. Attorney's Office, FBI, Washington State Patrol, Washington Association of Sheriffs and Police Chiefs, and the Washington Association of Prosecuting Attorneys.

I had been doing some forensic accounting work on exciting and complicated fraud cases during the past four years. My expertise was investment fraud and I usually got involved long after the dust had settled and the perpetrators had fled. It was rare that I got to see the scene of the crime until someone complained they had lost their retirement nest egg or a financier turned out to be a low class swindler.

"I didn't know you had a lab in the Seattle area, Francis," I mentioned.

"You are going to be up at the University of Washington's laboratory. They have been doing some genetically modified organic research on soybeans and there has been an accident, or I should say terrorist action," said Francis. "We think your skills may be of benefit in investigating the cause and Blake needs you today."

"You have my attention, I will be there within the hour. Tell Blake to expect me."

Normally I receive a full dossier on upcoming projects with all the financial data and a complete rundown on the players. This call had my interest and without waiting I grabbed my computer, threw some clothes into my flight bag and headed down to the dock. Before leaving I had already checked Freedom's water and food dishes. He was used to staying on guard on the island for the day and if I was away for longer the neighbors on the other side of the island would drop by and look after him. It gave me some sense of security to know he would be on hand to greet all guests and discourage curious passersby. He's a Nova Scotia Duck Tolling Retriever, sometimes called a toller, and had been with me since the accident. One of the few true Canadian breeds—he was an excellent water dog.

Two years since the accident. My mind drifted back to a time of turmoil and pain. What was I thinking? Oh yes, Freedom had been with me for the past two years. Since just after the time that had brought me pain and then more pain. Freedom was the one thing that brought me back into the workplace of international wire transfers, unbelievable investment returns and broken financial promises. It was hard to believe that an animal and other peoples' broken dreams could bring stability into one's life.

I did a quick walk around my yellow turbo Beaver floatplane checking all surfaces and testing the fuel for water, called for the weather and prepared for takeoff. Most people around here are weekend or summer residents who come over on the ferry, but I live here year round and when necessary have a quick mode of transport to get into Seattle or north to Vancouver. Everything was ready and within minutes I was in the air, high over the Puget Sound islands on the way to Seattle.

My Beaver floatplane was manufactured by de Havilland Canada and cruises at 157 mph with a range of six hundred miles. It gives me the ability to move quickly and has been of use to me on several cases when I had been able to fly into remote areas and see people who were difficult to arrange to meet in the city.

I could see the Cascade Mountains and was flying almost directly towards Mount Rainier with Mount Baker to the northeast. It was a bright sunny day, a relief from the past few weeks of rain and low lying fog. I imagined the orcas and salmon below and quickly thought about the coming weeks, which would be filled with sailing and fishing.

My home in the Puget Sound is part of what is known as the Island Region, which includes the islands of Whidbey, Fidalgo, Camano and the rest of the San Juan Islands. Its many islets are what I really call home. The ones away from the multitude of tourists who have started to change the charm of the islands. Now the visitors look for gift shops and quaint restaurants. You will find neither on Lumsden Island, one of those almost forgotten islets scattered across the Sound.

My mind was drifting. Soon, I would have to concentrate on the new business.

Blake met me at the harbor pier and within minutes I was settled into his Jeep headed for the university campus, northbound on I-5. On the way he filled me in on what we were doing, but nothing would have prepared me for what I was to go through the next day. The lab would just be the start of my week.

"This is an unusual case, John. It has all the makings of one that will take us out of the country for answers to find the culprits. It appears to be more than a random case of terrorism by a small group against big corporations."

"What happened? All I know from Francis is that the university lab had an accident and people were injured and some killed," I questioned him.

"It was definitely not an accident."

"Francis mentioned something about a terrorist action. What kind of terrorist group targets a university in the Pacific Northwest? It is not as if there are any nuclear reactors being built here. The last time I remember any public demonstration was when the federal government considered removing the nuclear powered submarines. The navy has always been good for this region," I stated.

"You are right about the navy's image but this has to do with big business and in particular big corporate agriculture. The university has been involved with genetically modified organism research and it has attracted the attention of some nasty internationally-based characters," Blake explained.

"So, how do I fit in? It sounds like a job for your anti-terrorist squad, not a fancy accountant."

"Your job is to find them. We'll bring them to justice. Our preliminary check of the terrorist database in Arlington has drawn a blank, not even a shadow of who they might be. Although they appear to have a public image in Europe, we are not able to get a handle on the main players."

"I am still puzzled by my selection." I tried to get more information from Blake.

It was noon by the time we arrived and it was quiet–almost too quiet on the campus. I expected to see a scene out of a crime mystery book or the 11 o'clock news with yellow tape and police cars and sirens. It was quiet. It had an unreal feel to it. I had been told that there had been a big accident in the agricultural lab with several people killed and a few others injured. I expected my job would be restricted to reviewing and making copies of associated financial computer files.

We walked down a long sterile hallway with offices on either side. There were nameplates on all the offices but it reminded me of a prison. All the doors were closed tightly and it appeared as if they could be opened on sliding tracks. Each office had a small window from the hall but all were covered with notices or cartoons. I could not see into any of the offices and assumed because it was July many of the professors and lecturers would be away from the campus. We turned to the left and although I asked Blake several questions, he remained silent and just pointed ahead as if all would be answered as we moved forward.

Three more turns into corridors that got smaller and smaller until the last one was so narrow that it could have made me claustrophobic if I had to use it regularly. Here, breaking the silence were several people talking quietly as if to raise their voices would disturb whatever evils had already been loosed. Blake motioned to the two officers at the lab door and they moved aside looking as if they were relieved to see someone else in charge. One look in the lab was enough to make me happy I had not had a large lunch.

There would be no ambulances taking any of these workers away for medical assistance. Any help they needed had come and gone and it was left to the experts to explain what had happened. I could see that the coroner and photographer were busy in the far northeast area of the lab and we moved to the left.

"Why am I here?" I asked Blake. "You don't need me for this. I don't know who you need, but it isn't me."

"Actually, we think you might be the only one who can stop this from happening again," Blake replied. "You have a successful history of tracking down people through their computer trails and that is all we have to go on. This is only the start. We have a manifesto with demands and you may be able to help us stop them before they go to their next step. They have involved several banks and investment houses in their plan of terror and it appears as if your experience with the Internet Crime Section will be of bearing here."

It was hard to tell what color the walls had been. They now had an almost abstract splattering of human blood and brain material. Nothing can prepare one for the first time that you see the end of a human life and although I had been involved with crime fighting agencies for over ten years, this was the first crime scene I had visited with dead victims.

I think I always thought of dead people the way they are usually portrayed in novels, a white chalk line or a body, lifeless with some blood or perhaps a bullet hole. This was not at all like that.

It looked like the lab had been busy with people all over the room. It was a relatively large room with windows overlooking the ocean and new long lab tables with experimental equipment. At least I think they were new, it was hard to see because it looked like a cyclone had hit. Blake had explained the process—the experimental machine, which had been booked for use in the genetically modified organic (GMO) experiments, was tampered with and two things had happened. The first was the explosion, which ripped through the lab, had flung all the exposed technicians against the west wall. The second thing that happened was the technicians who were protected from the force of the initial explosion were then slashed to pieces by metal shards which tore though the wood and metal tables as easily as through human flesh and bones. One minute was all I needed to come to the conclusion that this case was going to move faster than the one I was presently working on with the Royal Canadian Mounted Police (RCMP).

"There were twenty three people in the lab when the explosion occurred," Blake explained. "Of those, thirteen were killed outright with another two dying on the way to the university hospital. The remaining eight technicians were all injured; luckily only two of them appear to have serious injuries."

I was drawn to a sight, which was to stay with me for many months, and in fact woke me up several times in the coming week. In the middle of the lab there was a circular table with one technician sitting in what used to be a chair. I was told later that this was the senior technician who had been responsible for running the experiments. He had been hit from two directions – directly from the explosion and from what appeared to be a more localized explosion under the desk. It was the under the desk explosion which caused the most damage to him. Some sort of timed explosion had gone off and what looked like more than a thousand pens had been propelled upward. The pens passed though and some simply pierced the technician, and his body was now riddled with over a hundred pens.

I reached down and picked up one of the pens, which hadn't hit the technician. It was a low quality pen, the type you might see any day with a cheaply engraved corporate name. *Humans for Untouched and Unmodified Foods – Milan.*

> *"There are a thousand hacking at the branches of evil to one who is striking at the root."*
>
> *Henry David Thoreau "Walden" 1854*

CHAPTER 2

"An ecosystem, you can always intervene and change something in it, but there's no way of knowing what all the downstream effects will be or how it might affect the environment. We have such a miserably poor understanding of how the organism develops from its DNA that I would be surprised if we don't get one rude shock after another."

Professor Richard Lewontin
Professor of Genetics, Harvard University

Two very different sets of victims and two very different types of cases. Occasionally I lecture at the University of Washington and recently I have been doing an interdisciplinary spring class at the University of British Columbia for their law and accounting faculties. This year several Vancouver RCMP officers attended the class as part of a Canada-wide effort to stop white-collar crime before it attracted any more Internet interest. As a direct result I became involved in an ongoing sting operation to shut down corrupt Internet Websites promoting online personal ads.

The case involved a shell company, which started advertising cheap travel holidays for singles with a promise of meeting other interesting and interested singles. I didn't get involved until over $15 million had been swindled. It looked as if most of the money had already been spent and the victims would receive little if anything in compensation. We were still trying to track down the principals involved and stop the fraud.

But the terrorist bombing would clearly have the higher priority.

"We need to get some initial answers within hours," Blake said. "If it is alright with you I would like you to take a look at some of the material we have compiled in the last few hours."

We walked next door to what I assumed was the administrative office for the lab.

Seated in a leather chair behind a large wooden desk was a man who appeared to have lost hope. He was staring at an empty computer screen and it was obvious that he was distraught. Seated at a chair over to the right was another federal agent.

"John, I would like you to work with Dr. Frank Hillier," said Blake. "Frank is the Executive Director of the GMO Research Project and can give you the background on our situation."

No one made any move to introduce the second man. He made no motion to get up or introduce himself.

I waited for Frank to make some sign of recognition or movement towards the two of us, but he remained seated and focused on his thoughts. Finally he made eye contact and said, "This is all my fault. If I had just paid attention to their threats none of this would have happened."

"Please tell me what you know and I'll try to help you," I offered.

Blake added, "John is a special consultant whom the government calls upon when we get highly technical computer links to crimes. Please tell him what you told me earlier."

"I have been working on GMO research for over ten years and am just at the point where we are garnering significant financial interest from several large multinational agricultural companies," Frank started. "We have been able to attract several well known researchers from the University of Missouri and the University of California. Not only have we been able to develop several weed resistant grain varieties but we are also on the threshold of announcing a breakthrough in drought resistant corn. Two months ago one of our researchers, Geoff Dodson, was approached in Milan at an Agricultural Conference. This was after a paper he had presented on the benefits of GMO foods and how third world countries could increase crop yields by embracing the new technology. It appears this individual was a member of a little known group called Humans for Untouched and Unmodified Foods."

"Geoff spent several minutes trying to explain to him that the history of humans has also been the history of food production. How with new techniques of cultivating and handling grain and other foodstuffs, man was able to move from an agricultural society to a technological society. How with new varieties of grains we are able to produce more and how we are winning the ongoing battle against disease and insect infestations with improved strains," continued Frank.

"At the end of the conversation they both agreed to disagree and exchanged business cards. Geoff thought nothing of the meeting until he started to receive emails when he was back in Seattle. At first the emails were innocuous, just looking for summary information about what our team was working on. Then over the past month we have been receiving darker messages from them with references to doomsday scenarios from out of control genetic experiments. By the time I got involved it had progressed to outright threats against property and researchers and I felt it was time to get the local police involved. After they reviewed the emails, a conclusion was reached that it appeared to be a fringe group that had no resources to carry out any of their threats. We were warned to keep an eye out for any strange goings on around the lab and I proceeded to forget about the whole incident."

"Last week we received another email mentioning our upcoming experiments and I put it down as another idle threat." Frank handed me a printed copy of the email.

> From: The Caretaker, Humans for Untouched and Unmodified Foods
>
> To: Geoff Dodson, University of Washington – GMO Research
>
> Subject: Upcoming GMO Research
>
> This is your last warning. If you do not issue a press release stating that the University of Washington is stopping all further GMO research we will take steps to physically shut down your operations. We take no responsibility for any loss of life or damage to research property. Last chance.

He had started his story slowly and by the end of the hour I was not sure whether I was more fascinated or terrified.

"Can you explain what makes a food genetically modified?" I asked.

"Genetic modification can be achieved using nature or biotechnology to affect the transfer of genes from one organism to another. The result is a genetically modified organism with a desired characteristic. Quite often with traditional breeding methods this would be impossible or extremely difficult to obtain. When you bake bread or make wine, microorganisms in the yeast provide the starting block for the process. A good example of what we are doing here at the university is our research into a disease resistant variety of soybeans. Using traditional methods it might take us years to achieve what we can now do in months. What we would call the first generation of genetically modified crops involves altering crops so they are virus or insect resistant or herbicide tolerant. This is widespread and well established with over forty million hectares of grains under cultivation around the world."

Frank continued, "Some other examples of what our colleagues have done in the past few years has been their research into reducing the fat in potato chips and fries. By genetically improving potatoes with more starch and less water they absorb less oil during cooking. Cooking oils made with modified corn, soybean and canola have reduced saturated fat levels. The genetic alterations are becoming more complex and have more genes involved. We are trying to modify the plant's physiology and growth and introduce new plants. Sometimes this involves increasing the vitamin levels or making them grow faster like the Atlantic salmon which can grow up to six times faster."

"We are trying to make the world a better place and what thanks do we get?" he lamented.

I ended the afternoon reviewing the known facts and starting a data trace on my laptop computer. The facts were slim and I could see my job would be complicated by the fact that the original threats were not taken seriously. There was no tracing software installed at the university and I would have to work backwards and try to find the originating computers. I was not very confident an actual Internet Service Provider (ISP) address would be of much help to us. The guilty would not have wanted to publicize their whereabouts and I thought I might have to bring in some more sophisticated resources.

The search yielded several badly written articles, which appeared to be little more than a general dislike of all things global and change in particular. There were several mentions of global domination spearheaded by international trading companies along with the willing encouragement of the US government and many of the European governments.

Based in Milan, Italy, the public image of the group Humans for Untouched and Unmodified Foods didn't show anything related to terrorist activities, but it was apparent from researching the email correspondence that there were some unstable characters within the organization.

The most chilling words were not in the final threat but in something that had been sent a number of months ago. The university had received an email from the group.

From: Humans for Untouched and Unmodified Foods

To: Geoff Dodson, University of Washington – GMO Research

Subject: Inquiry about GMO Research

Further to our discussion in Milan, can you please consider the following? One of our researchers would like to join you in Washington to review the status of your research. We believe it is important to consider all your options before continuing with your unfortunate area of research.

I would like to offer Dr. Michael Hoffman of the University of Milan.

Now is the time for action.

It took me less than ten minutes after being hooked up to the University of Milan's database to realize that these initial contacts should have been taken more seriously. Dr. Hoffman had died two years ago in a highly suspicious mountain car accident. Long before the email campaign. At the time he had been working on GMO research and although Geoff Dodson would have had no contact with him, the case was well known within the research community. And surely Dr. Hillier would have seen the cruel reference to a dead colleague as a warning note.

There was a connection and it was important to find it quickly.

"It's not what you look at that matters, it's what you see."
Henry David Thoreau

CHAPTER 3

"But we realize that with any new and powerful technology with unknown, and to some degree unknowable—by definition—effects, then there necessarily will be an appropriate level at least, and maybe even more than that, of public debate and public interest."

Bob Shapiro, Chief Executive of Monsanto

"Misty, what do you have on your planner for the next few weeks?" I had just dialed her on my mobile phone. Actually I hadn't dialed anyone in years. I just pushed one memory button and there she was, almost in the flesh. Sorry—wrong train of thought and I didn't need to be hit by that train.

"I need your undivided time."

"Your house or mine, tall dark stranger?" she sexily purred. "I have always wanted to give you my undivided attention. What did you have in mind?"

"Misty—not now, this is serious. We have a case, and I mean a real case which requires all your talents."

"I'm all ears, boss, or should I say sailor." Misty Jackson occasionally joined me when I headed north for cruising on a friend's forty-foot Benneteau sailboat. She enjoyed playing part time cook and full time mate, and was always alluding to a long lost lust of yours truly. Although we came close to an intimate relationship years ago, we had now settled into the comfortable roles of friends as well as working partners.

"This case is right up your alley. It has murder and more murder written all over it and as a further bonus you will get to work with the FBI. I know you love to interact with them." She was a little stubborn to put it mildly and was known for forcefully getting her point of view across. Her saving grace was that her hard work usually paid off and when she was on a case you had better be on her side.

"I'll meet you at the Seattle pier and we can discuss our plans on the island. Plan to stay for a couple of days and bring your computer and all your electronic toys." Misty had been one of Seattle's finest until the combination of the bright lights and drugs got the best of her.

As Blake's Jeep pulled onto the harborfront I didn't have to look far to find Misty. That wasn't her real name but rather her effect on most men and quite a few women. She was tall—over 5' 10" with a slim, well muscled body along with long auburn hair and green bedroom eyes. Sitting by the floatplane, feeding a friendly harbor seal what looked like the remains of yesterday's sandwich, she had attracted a number of young rollerblading enthusiasts.

"I'll give you a progress report by noon tomorrow," I promised Blake. "Have the Internet Crime section in DC contact me in a couple of hours and we'll coordinate our activities.

"Good luck, John. We'll all need it. The last thing we need is more terrorism on American soil. Homeland Security will be going nuts with trying to figure out what type of threat this poses. Not to mention having to change the color of alert."

I responded, "At least we now have some of the resources we need. Perhaps this will finally change some of the people who think 9/11 is a once in a lifetime event and we remain safe in North America."

As I got out of the car Misty got up and as we met she gave me one of her wet, somewhat less than professional, kisses. My knees went wobbly and I almost lost my well-known restraint and made love to her on the pier beside the floatplane. I have always been a sucker for a beautiful body and a wet kiss but I didn't want to upset the seal. The kiss was enough to discourage the rollerbladers and we didn't waste any time getting our ride ready. I stowed her travel bag and computer case. It would be a little harder to stow my lust.

In a few minutes we were cleared for takeoff from the harbormaster. Misty playfully grabbed my knee and jokingly asked, "How is your love life? Do you have any new additions to the cottage or is it just Freedom and me?"

Last month she had tried to line me up with one of her friends from college days but as usual I was less than an interested participant. She had also started a special file she called The John File from some of the more interesting women - Sparkling Eyes, Future Plans, Fit and Ready for Nature - and several others with tantalizing nicknames and bios who had been posting to the Internet Personal Websites we had been investigating.

She was trying but I was happy with my present single status. Well, maybe not happy, but at least resigned for now.

"No new surprises, but I have a couple of interesting leads we should follow on the Web Shadow Personals Website. I have tracked down two of their largest investors through an offshore company in the British Virgin Islands. One of us will need to go down there and check it out. I am at a roadblock as far as getting any more helpful information from this end."

"Great, and now what is so important you had to pull me away from Seattle on a Thursday evening?" Misty asked.

"Let's wait until we are set up in the spire. Sit back and just enjoy the flight. The morning has been draining and although I know you are used to seeing human carnage, this was my first real exposure to that side."

I concentrated on flying. The flying was almost second nature to me. I could see the various islands that I would be passing over before heading down to home. Home—that was a strange concept for a single man. I had always equated home with a house full of family members, and here I was in my 40s all alone with one dog. This is not what I had envisioned when I thought of my mid-life period.

I looked over at Misty and saw she was staring at me.

"What are you thinking about, Pride? You have a far-away look on your face."

I answered her, "Just thinking that it will be good to have you on the island for a couple of days. It has been lonely the last little while."

"It will be good to be of service."

I asked her to look out her window for boats on the water as I started to concentrate on the task at hand. The next few minutes would be busy. We were almost ready to land and I had to check the water for debris and boats.

This was the trickiest part of flying a floatplane—the landing. One would think the landing would be easy, but landing on water was more difficult than it looked. Some days it was hard to see just where the sky ended and the water started. Then I would have to make a few passes and ensure that the water was churned up enough for me to have a good definition. Today there was a little chop, the sea had some good motion so it would be straightforward. I could see exactly where we were going to come down.

I increased the flaps to twenty degrees and controlled the rate of descent to about a hundred feet per minute. The last ten to twenty feet is always the trickiest for a new pilot or a novice floatplane passenger. It looks like you have lots of height above the water, but that is usually a deceptive phenomenon. You are looking through the water at the bottom of the lake. Today this would not be the case.

Just a quick fly by and we came in for a short landing and a quick taxi over to the dock. I shut the single engine down, hopped out and secured the floatplane to the dock. Misty joined me on the dock.

Freedom was waiting for us. I knew he would enjoy having Misty for a day or two. He loved the extra attention.

Half an hour later we had retired to the spire, at the top of the cottage. This was my point of operations and reached through a hidden opening bookcase and up the spiral staircase from the first floor study. I didn't go overboard when it came to security but I had a lot of expensive computer equipment and didn't like keeping it out in the open for prying eyes. I also did sensitive government work and they insisted on locked and secured cabinets. So it was easy to justify the spire when I did the renovations several years ago. In addition to the security I now had the best view of the Sound from up in the spire.

"We don't have long to crack this case," I said after we had reviewed the facts for two hours.

"I would like to see what type of connections can be made between the terrorists and the various researchers," Misty suggested. "There might be a way to get one step ahead of them and monitor their activities before they strike again."

"You should get started right away and I'll talk to the Internet Crime Section. They will be calling any moment."

"Good plan of action, boss. But before I put my brain in action, I need lunch. Do you still have some of your smoked salmon and sourdough bread I enjoyed the last time I was here?"

"Help yourself. There is some fresh bread on the counter and the salmon would go well with some split pea soup I made yesterday," I offered. "If you don't mind I'll stay here and get ready for the call."

I could hear Misty and Freedom moving around downstairs as the secure satellite telephone connected.

"John, it's Dale Hanson and I have the Internet Crime team with me in DC. I am sending our initial work on the Humans for Untouched and Unmodified Foods group. I must say it is very sketchy and may be of little use to you. Our take on this is that the group itself is not responsible for the terrorist action but someone else may have used them. We have looked at their past and although they have some rather radical views on food and research we can find no links to any violent actions."

"Dale, do you have any idea who might want to carry out an action of this magnitude?" I asked, thinking it would have needed resources and manpower to bring it this far.

"We don't have any leads but we are looking at some of the other anti-globalization groups which might want to use them as a cover. One of the interesting things we have been able to uncover is a partial computer address from the Chicago area on one of the emails from the Milan group. Other emails were routed through the Milan area and in fact some actually were forwarded from or through the group's mail server."

"Send me what you have and we'll try to find out where it is originating from," I suggested.

"All yours, John. You should have it within seconds. Looking forward to hearing something encouraging from your end."

"We are working as fast as we can and I'll let you know when I have something."

After running the encryption program I was able to view the subject email. The government provided me with a regularly updated encryption system, which allowed them to send me files without the worry of anyone intercepting and reading them.

Misty joined me and between bites of salmon, fresh sourdough bread and split pea soup we started to tackle the problem of identifying the source computer.

> *"Part of the secret of success in life is to eat what you like and let the food fight it out inside."*
>
> *Mark Twain*

CHAPTER 4

"Men occasionally stumble over the truth, but most pick themselves up and hurry off as if nothing has happened."

Winston Churchill

"THIS DOESN'T MAKE ANY sense, John. Why would one email originate from Chicago when the rest came from Milan?" We had finished the excellent meal and were concentrating on the job at hand.

"My guess is they came from several computers and the idea was to forward them to the Milan mail server to give the impression of coming from that organization. Why this one from Chicago, I have no idea. There doesn't appear to be a link and I can't get any closer than the metropolitan area of Greater Chicago.

The phone rang.

As I picked it up movement outside the window momentarily distracted me. Two adult bald eagles were taking what appeared to be an early training flight with a newborn. This was one of the main reasons I had stopped working downtown. That and the fact I enjoyed being able to step outside my office nude and go for a quick dip in the ocean!

"John, they have struck again," Blake shouted without introducing himself. "Another pen bomb and this time in Vancouver at a local Starbucks Coffee outlet. No one was injured but we are getting all kinds of pressure to get some results."

"What do you have?" he demanded.

"Hello, Blake, how are you? I have just been on the case for a few hours. Miracles take a little longer."

"Can we give you any resources?" Blake offered. "I don't want you to depend on your Misty."

"She is not my Misty and despite your lack of respect for her results, we are a team and one which works." Blake and I had had this conversation many times since Misty's fall. She was known as a conscientious officer and had been responsible for cracking the Hillside Murderer case shortly before she got involved with unsavory characters from the drug culture.

"Understood, John, stand by for Cameron," Blake responded.

"Two cases with you at the same time." The friendly voice of my Scotch drinking RCMP buddy intoned over the secure line.

Cameron Fraser runs the Internet Crime section of the Royal Canadian Mounted Police (RCMP) based in Vancouver, British Columbia. With a limited staff of fifteen officers he doesn't have the resources needed to deal with all the new Internet based crime and he had been working with me whenever there was an accounting or financial spin to a crime. We were presently working on the Web Personals case. I was on retainer with both the FBI and the RCMP and would be sending invoices at the end of the month.

"Cam, are you ready for an evening of Aberlour? It is a great new find for me, fifteen-year-old single highland malt with a sherry finish. You should come down here for the sponge races next week."

"The races will have to wait for another year I'm afraid," Cam said. "I will have my hands full with this GMO group. There may be a tie in here besides the small explosion at the Starbucks. Our group did some research and found that a local chapter of the Humans for Untouched and Unmodified Foods group is going to be exhibiting at a festival this weekend."

"What does Starbucks have to do with this case?" I asked.

"After the explosion Starbucks gave us a copy of a threatening email they received from the same group. Only this time the group was targeting a Starbucks Coffee shop in downtown Vancouver."

"Starbucks the small coffee chain! I can understand the university and big business, but not my coffee shop."

"Actually, John, Starbucks is big business," Cam said. "They have over 3,300 locations with most of the stores being company owned. Starbucks has locations in Japan, Thailand and China as well as all over North America and in the air on your local airline."

"This case is getting away from us. What do you have?"

Cam explained the situation. "Earlier this year Greenpeace and the Organic Consumer Association started a national leafleting and pressure campaign in over a hundred and thirty cities around the world against Starbucks. We don't think either of these groups is related to the threat but they have been demanding Starbucks remove genetically engineered ingredients from its foods and coffee drinks. They also want Starbucks to raise the wages and improve the working conditions of coffee plantation workers around the world."

He continued, "In response, Starbucks has started to provide hormone-free milk and has said they are committed to offering products without genetically manufactured organisms if they can be made at a reasonable cost. They have also confirmed that its core products, coffee and tea, are not genetically modified and have completed a review of their other products and said the majority are GMO-free. Monsanto and other companies have accused the company of caving in to the pressure campaign."

"What was the threat?" I asked.

"The email says that Starbucks must pay a coffee fee and promote the fact they are completely GMO free. If they don't agree to the demand, the group promises that they will be targeted for action."

"Did they say what the action would be?"

"No, but I don't want to find out. Do you? The explosion was just a homemade small bomb but it did have a couple of their pens. It went off in the early hours of the morning before any of their employees had arrived for work."

"There goes my pleasant early morning coffee. What other foods are bad for me?"

"Did I tell you about your eggs and butter?" Misty offered.

"Don't start with that."

"Cam, can we get into Starbucks and try to get their cooperation on this?" I asked.

"I'll see what we can do from this end. Their initial corporate reaction has been to say it is an isolated local action and they don't want to give it any media prominence in the States."

"I can understand their thinking, but we know it is related to the university bombing and they may be able to help us stop it."

"Send me the details. We should get together and discuss this," I said.

Cam emailed what he knew and we planned to meet the next morning.

As I piloted the floatplane up the coast I remembered my last trip north. We had just had a big break in the Web Personals case and had located several young women who were prepared to talk about their experiences. They had been looking for love in all the wrong places. After corresponding with what to them seemed like interesting matches they were drawn into a financial fraud that we were just starting to unravel.

The consistent mode of operation was for the men to arrange an initial harmless meeting at a coffee shop or restaurant. We hadn't been able to identify any of the men but it appears there are at least three. They were all relatively good looking with the appearance of wealth. After suitably impressing the lovelorn women, a quick romance is kindled. After a couple of weeks of meeting in hotel rooms and bed and breakfast establishments, a surprise vacation is the next step. Each of the women joined their new lovers on a flight to Belize, just south of the Cancun area of Mexico, on the Yucatan.

In what appeared, to the women, to be a coincidental meeting at the bar in the resort, the three couples were introduced. One of the gentlemen, and I use that term loosely, told them he was a successful resort developer and asked if the group would like to see his proposed destination resort. The next day they all set out for an enjoyable afternoon along the coast. They were introduced to the Ambergris Caye area and went by boat out to the outer reef area. After snorkeling and seeing some great schools of fish followed by an excellent picnic lunch with rum drinks, they were given the pitch.

The developer talked about the financial opportunity and asked if any of them were interested in investing along with him as a seed investor. He explained he had secured the property and needed $500,000 to build and promote the first ten villas on the beach. Both of the other men appeared to jump at the opportunity and one of the women was very enthusiastic about owning a Caribbean villa. Later that evening the three women talked and decided it looked like a good idea and as new friends, all from the Vancouver area, this property might be a great investment and certainly wouldn't hurt their budding relationships with the men.

It had been explained to them that they would not have to put up much money. Each would contribute $50,000 up front with the balance when the villas were completed. Paperwork was finalized within days of returning to Vancouver, funds were transferred and before they knew what had hit them they were not getting any returns to their calls to the new lovers and could get no answers from the budding developer. The three of them called Cam's department and I was soon involved. We had no idea how many other women had fallen for the fraud but we were working to put a stop to it. Before the GMO case came up I was scheduled to make a visit to Belize to see if I could get some results from that end.

This case was going to be more complicated.

> *"Sometimes I wonder whether the world is being run by smart people who are putting us on or by imbeciles who really mean it."*
>
> *Mark Twain*

CHAPTER 5

"GM crops really do carry theoretical dangers that could be ironed out, given time, but will not because the companies that develop them cannot afford to wait. It is entirely unsurprising that GM crops could be toxic. Most domestic crops have poisonous relatives or are descended from poisonous ancestors. The modern crops may still contain the genes that make the toxins: not lost, but merely dampened down."

Colin Tudge, Research Fellow,
London School of Economics

I FLEW OVER THE Spanish Banks area, just off the University of British Columbia. I could see Wreck Beach below with all its lovely delights and was quickly flying past Stanley Park and by Lions Gate Bridge.

Up Burrard Inlet with Vancouver on my right and the North Shore Mountains on the left, I could see several cruiseliners leaving for Alaska along with the hustle and bustle of the busy port city.

I was headed back in time to the small town community of North Vancouver. Nested between the mountains and the Deep Cove area, it was the site of the Under the Volcano festival. Held every summer, the festival was named after local squatter and author Malcolm Lowry.

I was to meet Cam on the waterfront to see if we would find any interesting facts about the local activists. I banked left and came into a well-watched landing not far from the beach. The pier was free of boats and Cam was standing at the end watching us. He helped us disembark.

"I see you brought your trusty partner."

"Yes, Freedom needed some exercise and he is always great in the plane. You look a little rough around the edges."

"I'm undercover," Cam laughed. "I thought I wouldn't stand out as much if I had a couple of days of growth. I'll shave tonight."

"What can you tell me about the Humans for Untouched and Unmodified Foods group?"

"We haven't been able to get a good handle on the local participants. It appears that this is the first time they have been at the festival. Under the Volcano has the reputation of attracting every type of alternative living group and fringe protest organization along with several of the long time green environmental organizations."

I left the Beaver at the pier and we walked past the tarot card reader, the vendors selling tie died clothes and veggie burgers, and entered the grounds. This smelled and looked like the 60s. I noticed the Earth First booth and was surprised at the long lineup in front of the Philippines Woman's Center food stall.

The music was loud and it was hard to hear what Cam was saying about the local scene but I gathered the only real concerns he had were with the anti-globalization crowd. Food and production of food hadn't really come up on his radar screen.

I filled him in on what we knew about the industry and the group. "Where do we go from here?"

"There they are, John, under the red tent with the large picture of a field of grain. Let's walk by and I'll see if I know anyone."

As I stopped at the Young Communists League table, Cam got a good look at the organizers behind the local anti-GMO group.

I strolled over to the red tent and listened to the end of a lecture on genetically modified foods. The speaker looked like one of my professors from the 70s. He had a neatly trimmed beard and horn-rimmed glasses. Speaking with a British accent he was telling us all the evils of big business.

"Big business is behind the drive for genetically modified foods. Genetic engineering is a radical new technology, one that breaks down fundamental genetic barriers between humans, animals, and plants. By combining genes of unrelated species it alters their genetic codes and new organisms are created."

"Just talking about crops, big business is altering plants to resist viruses which means the viruses will mutate into new forms which can attack other plants. Genetically engineered plants will endanger us and will reduce biological diversity. We have seen what happens when the farm-grown Atlantic salmon are put in pens up and down our coast. They are getting loose and they are competing with Pacific salmon for food and habitat. What is going to happen when we get genetically modified salmon out in the wild?"

I exited the tent and was still trying to make eye contact with a young lady selling hat feathers when Cam returned. I was no longer hungry.

"We are meeting with an informant in a few minutes. He might have some information for us."

Twenty minutes later walking along the shore we were met by a middle aged man with long hair and a bad sunburn.

"Call me Standler."

"Standler, John is a friend from Seattle."

"Cam, I heard about the explosion and as far as I know the local group is scrambling to find out what happened. I don't think they are involved. I know the local chapter president and he is an old school protestor who was with Greenpeace at the beginning. I am sure he wouldn't be involved with anything violent."

"We need to get some information about their contacts around the world," Cam said. "In particular we would like to see if they have any European links."

"I know they are headed up the canyon after the festival and you could join us and see where it goes," Standler replied.

We spent the next few hours trying to get more information about the local protest community. Other than finding out that there was a core group, which went from protest to protest depending on what was in town, we were unable to gather any real intelligence.

Cam and I drove up the canyon and hiked across the suspension bridge. If this were in the Seattle area, there would be a tollgate with Starbucks Coffee on both sides. Here it was just a narrow footbridge a couple of hundred feet over a spectacular rush of water. Tall cedar and Douglas fir trees towered above us. I could see several waterfalls and lots of pools. There were people lying on rocks and I could hear shouts in the distance.

"You are hearing the jumpers," Cam explained. "This is a local hangout for teenagers and young adults along with being a popular place to bring tourists. The water is cold, being fed from mountain runoff. The shouts and screams are adventurers jumping or diving from the cliffs into the pools. There are several safe places where the water is twenty or thirty feet deep and the cliffs are straight down."

"I think I see Standler. Wait here and I'll see what is going on."

I sat on the rocks, removed my hiking boots and socks and soaked my toes in the cold water. As I looked around I could see more people than I originally thought were in the area. There were several pools within view and I could see up the gorge towards a waterfall where a number of people were lying on a large boulder enjoying the last rays of afternoon sunshine. One of the things I liked about the Pacific Northwest was the long summer days. And this was really noticeable once you were in Canada.

Cam rejoined me and motioned me to stay quiet.

"Standler has a short range microphone on him and if we move over towards the west cliff we should be able to hear what is going on with his group. We will not be able to see them but if we need to know he can tell us who said what later."

"What about the water?" I asked. "Won't it affect the electronics?"

"You may not have seen these," Cam said as he handed me a disc player. "They have been modified for underwater use and he has a completely waterproof system built into his backpack."

I put the earphones on and we listened to several minutes of banter about the festival, who was there and who didn't make it up the canyon. I could make out Standler's voice and it sounded like there were at least three other voices.

"What's next?" Standler asked. "Do we do a press release saying we had nothing to do with the explosion?"

"We don't know what to do. Something is happening and it is sure going to attract a lot of attention on the whole issue of genetically modified food production. My thought is to stay silent for a few days and see what happens. Perhaps we could grant a couple of interviews."

Another voice stated, "Chicago will know what to do."

The first voice said, "Don't mention them again. We're not sure they know anything but we don't want to send them any unwanted attention."

Standler said, "You never mentioned anyone else before."

The first voice replied, "I'll call them and get a definitive answer tonight."

A few minutes later I told Cam about the Chicago connection. This was getting interesting and I would have to redouble my efforts to tie down the computer link.

We went for a quick dip and then headed back to the cove. Within the hour I was back in the Beaver and on the phone to Misty. Freedom had spent most of the time in the water and climbing the cliff. Ready for a quiet ride, he settled in the back of the floatplane and was asleep by the time we were airborne.

> *"It is better to have your head in the clouds, and know where you are… than to breathe the clearer atmosphere below them, and think that you are in paradise."*
>
> *Henry David Thoreau*

CHAPTER 6

"I see worries in the fact that we have the power to manipulate genes in ways that would be improbable or impossible through conventional evolution. We shouldn't be complacent in thinking that we can predict the results."

Colin Blakemore, Waynflete professor of physiology
Oxford University
President, British Association for the Advancement of Science

FLYING SOUTHWARD, LOW OVER the western edge of Vancouver, I had Misty on the phone. "What's new?"

"It has been busy. You have several Internet intercepts to translate and I think I am getting somewhere with the Milan messages. It looks like this is related to the protests in Milan at the recent G8 Meetings. Some of the wording is almost identical to a threat Interpol received before the clashes between the police and the protestors which led to a death and several injuries."

"Good work, Misty. I think we should pursue the Chicago angle." I told about her what I had learned.

"We can be in Chicago by lunch tomorrow."

"Let's book a couple of flights and depending on what I can confirm tonight we can get the local FBI agents in Chicago to help us out. Francis wants to throw all his resources our way."

"Are you hungry?" Misty asked. "Your neighbor dropped by this morning and brought a couple of blackberry pies I thought would go well with your barbequed chicken."

"I am now! Get the barbeque hot, I'll be landing in twenty minutes."

Over an excellent dinner accompanied by a local Washington cabernet wine, we talked about our next steps. It was agreed Chicago looked interesting but before we headed east we would need a concrete lead. Misty volunteered to talk to the FBI about radical groups in the Chicago area and I would get to work and try to do some computer magic.

Three hours later I was still hard at work on the emails trying to get closer to an answer when Misty burst into the office.

"I think we have something we can use. One of my contacts in Chicago mentioned a local radical who has been in and out of court for several crimes including unlawful storage of explosives. He talked for some time and one thing led to another and we found out he has been corresponding with several groups on the Internet. He has been providing groups with explosive advice."

"How does that get us closer to the solution?" I asked.

"When we mentioned the explosion at the University and the fact there were pens involved, he realized he might have given someone advice which led directly to the deaths. He had been told it was for a non-violent demonstration. He doesn't know who they are but he did give us a copy of all his emails with them. We are contacting the Internet service provider right now with a court order and expect to know momentarily who is behind the nickname."

A few minutes later Misty brought me what I had been looking for—the missing piece from the email address. What most people don't realize is that almost all email is not private and is readily available for review by a variety of people and organizations. This group had been using a forwarding service and that was giving them a sense of security. I had been able to get close to the originating site of the data but I couldn't get the computer or user. What I needed was a clue as to the individual user and this would give it to me.

The data source showed that our Chicago contact had corresponded with the same group but he also received one email from them through a Hotmail account and it was here I would be able to get our answers.

We stopped for a nightcap. While drinking my Scotch I looked over at my Scottish heritage bookcase. I could see the pictures and wooden ladle from our Scottish farm and thought about the last time I had been there. It would soon be time to return. Memories—

Through the night the legal system worked its magic and by the time the two of us had awakened and gotten back from a quick kayak trip to the rocks and back, we were ready to head to Chicago.

Two hours later, high above the Midwest watching the grain fields below, I logged into my FBI account and confirmed our surprising lead.

"Misty, we are going to have to bring ourselves up to speed on Cargill," I said. "We don't have an individual but we know they work for one of the world's largest agricultural companies. With over 90,000 employees in fifty-seven countries and revenues of over $40 billion, this is one big company. They are a big supporter of GMO research and have released several new GMO grain varieties. Their link to the University of Washington is a $4 million grant for multi-year research related to soybeans. It looks like someone related to them is trying to sabotage their work."

"You are going to have to use your charm and talents to find our terrorist."

"I wonder whether Cargill knows they are harboring a criminal?" Misty asked. "We may have to get their head office's approval in Minneapolis. Chicago is just the GMO office."

"What do you know about the local scene?"

"Cargill has an excellent reputation as a well run private company but I am not able to get any real financial statements. Because of their size they seem to attract the majority of the anti-GMO protests and just last week there was a major rally in downtown Chicago."

"Can you get any information about the organizers of the rally?" I asked.

"Yes, we are going to be briefed by the local FBI. Evidently they have been trying to get someone inside the radical groups for years and have had no success," Misty said. "They are looking at this as a breakthrough and think they have persuaded the contact to become an informant."

It was a hot and humid afternoon as we cleared the terminal. It appeared as if we had joined the rush to Chicago as there were hundreds of conference goers. I was relieved to hear my name being shouted.

"John Pride, over here," said the man who was clearly a FBI agent in the unmarked car at the curb. "Francis gave me the details and we are looking forward to working with you. I'm Dave Isbister with the New York office and I used to work in Seattle with Francis. And you are Misty," as he moved towards Misty.

"Stay away from me, Dave," she demanded. "I had enough of your antics in Seattle."

"Whoa guys, I don't know what happened but we have to work together," I said.

"John, this is one of the guys I told you about who set me up when I was having my problems."

"Misty, I was just there. I didn't have anything to do with what came down, and between you and me, I think it could have happened to anyone," Dave said.

"Let's leave it at that," I suggested. "Why's a New York agent in Chicago? I thought we were going to be briefed by the locals."

"Things are moving fast and I have been involved with a similar group for the past year," Dave explained. "This is not just an isolated action. We have found four other related actions in the past couple of months. We need to get some answers and it appears like your work might prove promising."

On the drive downtown I noticed the improvements to the inner city since the last time I had been in town. We pulled in front of the Tribune Tower at 435 North Michigan Avenue. The Gothic revival building was modeled on the Butter Tower of Rouen Cathedral with great flying buttresses. It was faced with Indiana limestone, and I could see several inset stones from famous structures around the world. Right in front of me were contributions from Westminster Abbey, the Taj Mahal, and the Great Wall of China. WGN Radio Studios was at hand and through the front doors I could see the offices of the Chicago Tribune. They had sponsored the international competition for the building in 1922.

We all rode to the twenty-eighth floor in silence. I could see Misty really did not like Dave and, although she was usually tricky to work with, we would have to deal with her feelings as soon as possible. I really didn't know all the details of her problems but I knew some of them were unresolved.

I looked at her but she didn't return my look. She was obviously upset. So the three of us rode upward in silence. Towards the last century and perhaps the next. This building gave me the feeling of having seen much history over the past eighty or so years. And if what we were to learn about GMOs proved helpful, the old building would live up to her reputation as a place of crossroads between the past and the future.

> *"Get your facts first, and then you can distort them as much as you please."*
>
> *Mark Twain.*

CHAPTER 7

GREAT ARCHITECTURAL DETAIL ADORNED the elevator and as we exitedI could read Cargill's prime goal on the facing wall.

"Cargill's vision is to raise living standards around the world by delivering increased value to producers and consumers."

A Cargill Researcher joined us.

"John and Misty, this is Eleanor Johnson who heads the GMO Research Group at Cargill. She might be able to help us," said Dave.

"We have been monitoring the anti-GMO protests for the past three years and it's just within the past few months we have become concerned," Eleanor said. "We have a full security department and thought we could handle any problems which came up. I think we need assistance. Our expertise is handling internal theft and the occasional farmer who illegally plants some of our seed. We are not organized to handle murder."

"The resources of the company are all yours," she continued. "We want to stop this terrorism as soon as possible. This is the file with all the threatening letters and email. We don't have any indication any of them are related to our staff."

"All we know is that John has been able to track at least one email to this office," Dave explained. "We need to try to narrow down the possibilities."

Eleanor left us and within minutes we were joined by some of Dave's co-workers.

"John, since you left Seattle we have been able to get a few more details about our phantom group," Dave was talking to a group of eight of us. Six members of the anti-terrorist squad had joined Misty and me in the Cargill conference room overlooking the river.

"I'll get right to the point, John. We have no leads and Washington is on our collective asses to produce now," Dave said.

"I wanted you to meet the local team to show we are ready to move quickly."

"Misty, can you coordinate your plans with the team while I try to get a better lead on who we are dealing with?" I asked.

I spent the rest of the afternoon meeting with the chief security officer, discussing options and then accessing the main Cargill intranet. Cargill had received several emails from the same group and had a policy of ignoring them. These emails had suggested a stop to the protesting in return for $100,000 wired to a Caribbean account. Cargill assumed it was just a prank and hadn't even forwarded it to the police.

I was still reviewing the outgoing email log when I realized I hadn't even thought about dinner. I had just completed running a search using some of the words that we had found in the threatening emails when Misty joined me.

"Local cuisine or do you just want to grab a hotdog on the street?"

"I need to clear my head. I have been at the computer for too long. Let's go for a walk and find a good restaurant. We can discuss next steps."

We walked towards the river and stopped at the first inviting street-side restaurant. Over fresh Italian linguini pasta and a dry white wine we talked about leads and possible contacts.

"I think we need to focus on the people who made contact with the Humans for Untouched and Unmodified Foods group," I suggested. "At Cargill there were four individuals who dealt with their email. Why don't you try to find some answers while I continue to track down computer trails?"

"That sounds like a plan, John. This afternoon I was able to find out that the FBI really doesn't have much of a case so far. They are definitely up the creek and I think the press is starting to get to the bureau. They like to manage the news and this anti-GMO stuff is way ahead of them. Dave is clueless and I don't know how he got involved in this case."

"What is your history with him?" I asked.

"Don't ask."

"Misty, you've never really explained what happened when you left the Seattle police. I know what I read in the local papers but it never seemed to be the whole truth."

"It's in the past and I'm not bringing it back for you or anyone else." Misty clearly didn't want to elaborate.

After dinner we headed back to the Tribune Tower. Misty headed off to do some snooping around the four potential leads and I jumped back on the computers. Usually by this time in a case I would have a good idea of what I was looking for, but today I seemed to be at an impasse. I wasn't getting anywhere with any of the emails I had so far. I leaned back in the comfortable chair and knew that before long I would be asleep. Ever since the accident I would take short naps. They seemed to refresh my mind and provide new insight into whatever problem was at hand.

Drifting into a state of relaxation, I was roaming over the high hills overlooking the inland sea. I could smell the heather and see the highland cattle. My friend Gregor and I had been out all day and could feel the sun on my face as we headed down towards town. We had spent the day looking for several missing cows and calves. I didn't mind the hike, if that is what you could call it. We had been all the way up the glen towards the neighboring Graham farm site and finally found the missing cattle down in their valley. After herding them and a couple of new additions, which happily joined the migration homeward, I thought that it was a good day had by all. Father would be happy with the additions, especially when I mentioned that they might have been Graham stock at some earlier point in the day. Although the Prides and Grahams were neighbors, there was history to be remembered. Both families had links to the Border Reiver families of Scotland and England, and had moved northward in the hard times. Although we didn't raid or ride as Reivers anymore, no one would complain about a few new cattle–at least no Pride would complain. It was in this happy state of mind that I distractively ambled towards our home pasture. Relaxed after a good day in the hills. Not a care in the world.

A while later, back in town after dropping the cattle off at the farm, we wandered. When suddenly there was someone in my side vision, someone heading towards us quickly. Then my heart started to race uncontrollably as I quickly realized the danger. There was a gang of them, four or five, running hard. The press gang, the dreaded press gang. We were alone, near the docks, with no one to help. And I knew better. Just last night, while we downed a pint or two, there had been a rumor of English in the area looking for able sea-going men to press into service in his Majesty's British Navy. And here I was...

A loud noise, I awoke quickly with Misty barging into the computer room all out of breath.

"What happened?"

I felt as winded as she looked. She obviously has run up a few flights of stairs. I had been trying to outrun the press gang.

After she had settled into one of the nearby chairs I got her story. She had spent an unfruitful couple of hours going through several of the suspects' offices when she headed down to Cargill's library to check on a few facts. Taking the old staircase she had the feeling she wasn't alone and carefully entered the library. She interrupted a tall man in the stacks and before she could say anything he fled out the door and onto the elevator.

"I caught the next one but by the time I was on the ground floor he was down the street," Misty continued. "I ran down the street and followed him into the harbor district before losing him."

"That was close. I wonder what someone was doing in the library so late at night."

"I think I might be able to recognize him," Misty said.

"History... is a nightmare from which I am trying to wake."
James Joyce "Ulysses"

CHAPTER 8

"At the moment, as is so often the case with technology, we seem to spend most of our time establishing what is technically possible, and then a little time trying to establish whether or not it is something we should be doing in the first place."

HRH the Prince of Wales
19th September 1996
Royal support for genetic food withdrawn

THE NEXT MORNING I was talking to Dale Hanson in DC. "The FBI has been able to track down four universities which had been shaken down by the same scam tried with Cargill. All of them are involved in GMO research and they were all recipients of Cargill funding. I have some information that you can review."

"Why didn't any of them report the scam to the authorities?"

"They had multi-year research projects on the go and reasoned that if there was a concerted protest against their research they would have to forgo any future grants. They just put it down to a cost of doing business and went on to the next conference or to generate the next paper."

"Is there any link between the various universities?" I asked.

"The FBI has developed an interactive spreadsheet I sent to your system. The only common factor that I'm able to see is they all received Cargill grants. I asked for a complete list of Cargill backed research with the idea that we may be able to get one step ahead of the terrorists. Perhaps we can set ourselves up with an alias to lure them into a trap."

"What did you have in mind, Dale?"

"I have been talking to the University of Missouri and they had been approached last week. The group was looking for a "contribution" to the group so they could evaluate the GMO research. They made it clear that if the university paid them some money, and they were asking for $75,000, their evaluation would take several years. This is similar to the approach that was successful with several other universities. The universities would pay the money and the problem would go away. It appears they thought this was the lesser of two evils."

"You mean to say our own universities have been funding a terrorist group within the United States?"

"It gets worse. Not only have they been financing the group but they have also have been providing them with information which could be used against other universities. Evidently they got the information about the University of Washington's research from two researchers at other universities."

"Let's look at what you have."

Hours later I had filled in a few missing pieces. We were going to try to see if we could lure the terrorists out into the open with an offer they couldn't refuse. Up until now it looked like our anti-GMO protest group had been coercing money from universities. Something had changed to add a level of violence and it was up to us to try to get to the bottom of the problem. We needed to find the missing piece to lead us to the leaders of the terror.

"I need to get the Cargill executive on side in order to try to get to the leader. We will offer a small amount of money in order to get them to stop all activities," I explained to Misty.

Late at night, I lay down in bed for a minute and closed my eyes. I could see the explosion again and when I opened my eyes I called my Cargill contact.

"Everything is set up for you tomorrow."

"I'll need to use the Cargill email system to contact our group and see if we can make a deal," I said. "What was the last demand?"

"They have promised to stop all violent actions for a payment of $10 million. They want it transferred to a Caribbean bank account. Our Board of Directors met this afternoon and there was a real heated discussion about the whole problem. It appears only two of the directors knew about the problem and the rest had been in the dark. Our CEO had tried to solve the problem by ignoring it. Now some of the directors want nothing to do with your idea. You will have to sell the board tomorrow on the merits of using the Cargill infrastructure to catch the terrorists. I have been talking to the local FBI contacts and they don't hold much faith in your proposal and I think one of them has been talking to the CEO."

"I'll talk to the CEO before the meeting and try to get him onside before I meet the full board."

The next morning after walking over to The Tribune Tower I met with the CEO. When I joined him in his large corner office overlooking the lake I was surprised to see Dave Isbister already comfortably sitting in a chair to the left of the CEO.

"John, I have just been bringing Harrison Donnelly up to speed on where the FBI is on this case," Dave explained. "I might be able to help you with your meeting this morning."

"I thought your group had run out of leads. Has anything come up?"

"I just explained to Harrison we should go slowly with this group. The FBI doesn't want to spook them. We have a great lead with the University of Missouri and the FBI is prepared to front the $75,000."

"I am not sure we should get another university involved. Perhaps we can just have Cargill deal with the problem and hope to get a handle on who they really are."

Harrison had been quiet up until now. "Cargill does not negotiate with terrorists. We are a private company and we don't want the publicity that is coming with this problem. We were not going to pay the original $100,000 they were asking for and now we are not going to pay $10 million to a group of thugs."

I suggested, "Perhaps if this had been handled by us in the beginning we could have avoided the bloodshed. I have a plan that involves no money and just tracking the terrorists by their electronic traces."

"John, we want to get some fast results," Dave raised his voice. "The FBI is ready to act. We should just pay the money and capture them later."

"We know they are using offshore accounts and if we monitor the accounts we may be able to catch them in action," I suggested.

"What do you have in mind?" Harrison asked.

"I would like to use the Cargill network to set up an arrangement where we trace their email back to the real source. If we can locate them we may be able to stop this without any more damage."

Harrison thought for a minute. "I like the idea of fast action. Let's put this to the board."

We walked down the hall and up a large staircase to a glass enclosed boardroom that was already in action. I could see there were several heated discussions taking place as we entered.

"I would like everyone to meet the FBI agent and their consultant." Harrison took quick control of the meeting. "We talked about our problem yesterday and the FBI thinks they have a solution. John, you have the floor."

"Thanks, we want to see if we can track the terrorists using the resources of Cargill. This means we will try to set a meeting or transfer with the group and through our electronic systems we will find out who is involved."

After a few more minutes of questioning they left me with a hollow promise. "We will have to discuss your idea and decide what is best for the company."

That afternoon Misty spent several hours with the security department reviewing human resource files. I pulled up the files on the four suspects I wanted to deal with and started to gather information on each of them. I was not getting anywhere fast when Misty looked over my shoulder.

"That's him. I recognize the profile."

We rounded up the security officer and paid a visit to one of our suspects, the midnight librarian. He was not very cooperative. He was tall, gaunt and dark eyed. He looked like he hadn't slept last night. Twenty minutes was all it took to realize our suspect was in over his head. Finally I explained the murders and he broke down and told us what little he knew.

Evidently a cousin of his who needed some inside information about the status of Cargill's research was using him. He had been promised that it would just be some harmless background info but one thing had led to another and now he was heavily involved.

"What were you thinking when you released private information?" I asked him.

"I was just trying to help my cousin. We have always been close and Christine needed me."

"You are going to have to help us get in contact with her," I stated.

We finally arranged for him to call his cousin and arrange a meeting for later that afternoon. The last I saw him, the security guard was leading him away. The FBI would be dealing with him before the day was over.

The cousin did not want to meet with us but when she realized her actions had put her cousin in legal jeopardy she relented.

Her condition for a meet was I come alone and not involve the FBI. She wouldn't come into the city and insisted I head out on Route 66. She had my cell phone number and agreed to call me at five o'clock that afternoon.

An hour later I was cruising southwest on Route 66. If I had a few more days the road would take me all the way west to Los Angeles. I was pretty sure I wouldn't have to drive quite that far.

I had just arrived in Lincoln and was admiring the view when she called. "Where are you?"

"I assume this is the mystery cousin," I said. "I have just reached Lincoln. Where to next?"

"I still don't feel right about meeting with you, but if we have to meet turn right just after you go through Elkhart and follow the red car. You should be there in a few minutes."

Christine, the cousin, was where she said she would be. Sitting in a red Morgan sports car at the side of the road as I passed through another small scenic town. She didn't look my way but pulled out and headed west. Three turns, over a narrow bridge and we stopped at the side of the road beside a meandering creek.

She was alone and looked harmless enough. No smiles but then I wasn't expecting any.

"We are trying to change the world," Christine said by way of introduction. "We are not terrorists. None of this would have happened if they had just listened to us."

I didn't respond. She was an attractive woman but she had a look about her, which said she had made up her mind about many things. I didn't think I would be able to alter her worldviews today.

"All I need is some information about the group," I said. "If you don't deal with me you will be dealing with the FBI."

She looked at me but said nothing. Both of us looked at the creek without a word for several minutes. Finally she looked at me and said one word, "Yes."

"Yes, I knew it would come to this at some point. The choice between what I thought was right and what I would be prepared to fight for. I am not a fighter. I can't see myself fighting alone for what I believe in. Alone."

We just stayed like that, quiet for several more minutes. The creek was beckoning. I got up and wandered over, giving her space in which to make the right decision.

Quietly she joined me. She looked into my eyes and I thought she might start crying. But no, she just started talking.

Before long we left our place on the bank of the creek and I had our deal. She would help us and I would try to keep her from going to jail forever.

We agreed to meet that evening at the Pumping Station in Chicago and she would bring me the material we needed to get access to the terrorist group.

Returning to Chicago I thought about bad decisions and nowhere to go. This was a classic case of someone getting in over her head. She didn't consider herself a terrorist but one thing had led to another. Now she would be faced with having to work against the very group she supported.

The rest of the day I was locked in battle with my computer. The sun was down before leaving the building. The afternoon and early evening were spent in a networked computer search along with a colleague in the Seattle CLEW office. We were trying something new. We thought we would use the cousin's email alias to try to get a response from the group. Nothing we tried worked. I was hopeful we would be able to get her assistance this evening.

Walking down Michigan Avenue I could see the old Water Tower before reaching Chicago Avenue. It looks like a medieval fortress and I can almost imagine archers lying in wait at the top. I looked for the Chicago Avenue Pumping Station and recalled that I had read earlier these two buildings were the only public buildings to survive the Fire of 1871.

The Pumping Station was dark and Gothic and all the vendors had closed up and gone home. I walked past an empty pizza oven and through the large archway and into the pumping room where I could see the above ground water pipes. They are huge with a walkway all around the immense room and windows that look out on the street. The only noise is the pumping of water.

Shadows played against the walls with the outside lights moving through the pumping station. I walked along the walkway and thought about what Misty said. She wanted to join me but I thought she should remain in the Tribune Building and wait for something from Dave's group. He was promising some information from the New York office and thought we might be able to get together tonight.

Although the rush of daily Chicago was absent, the Pumping Station was not quiet. The longer I waited the louder the rush of the water became. It must be a trick of the brain as my focus increased; the background noise seemed to be to magnifying. All I could hear was the water. And as I pondered my mind raced back...

Behind me something moved, and then nothing. I felt this crashing pain and then white light followed by nothing.

> *"I do not know how to distinguish between waking life and a dream. Are we not always living the life that we imagine we are?"*
>
> *Henry David Thoreau*

CHAPTER 9

"No man will be a sailor who has contrivance enough to get himself into a jail; for being in a ship is being in a jail, with the chance of being drowned…A man in a jail has more room, better food and commonly better company."

Samuel Johnson

1809, I knew it was the year 1809 because Dad kept saying it's ought nine. I hadn't seen either Dad, or Mum or for that case any of my family for over a month. I can still see that last breakfast together. Hot porridge with warm cow's milk, freshly delivered. I could almost taste it, even now after a month of terrible rations.

A month of cramped quarters below deck on an overcrowded five-sailed Indiaman sailing ship. I wondered if I would ever see Bo'ness, Scotland again. A month of adjusting to the life of a pressed sailor on the way to the British Navy, I had resigned myself to my changing fortune. Gone forever would be the fishing life of coastal Scotland, and now would begin the hardship of naval training. Another voice sounded in the chorus of unwanted sounds, this one friendly.

"Pride, join me amidships," Gregor called. The two of us had been caught up, in the wrong place last month a group of sailors spotted us high above town. They captured us and dragged us down to the dock and onboard their merchant ship. We had become part of the local sweep for new British Navy recruits and became one with the rest of the pressed or kidnapped locals. I joined Gregor watching the activities in the Indian Sea's Madras harbor. The captain had told us what to expect. Our voyage from Scotland was just the beginning and we were resigned to our future. We could see the activities underway and knew that we would be transferred to the naval ship. The H.M. (His Majesty) Ship *Russell* had arrived nearby last evening and we were part of over one hundred others who were being pressed into service. I learned later that the H.M.S. *Russell* was a third rate ship of the line, smaller than the first and second rate ships, but built for fighting. It had seventy-four guns and had been launched forty-five years ago. The British Navy would pay our bounty and we would start our military training. What did we know about ships and fighting?

"What do you think, Pride? Are we bound for adventure?" Gregor asked.

I responded, "Anything which gets us away from this ship and the conditions we have endured will be a blessing, adventure or not."

"They are starting to transfer us. I can see that it will take a few hours. We might as well try to get to the railing and see when we are getting off."

We jostled our way closer to the railing. I noticed that in the past few minutes a couple of British Naval officers had come aboard and were now examining some of our fellow sailors. It appeared as if they were doing some sort of selection. I couldn't see the final decisions but not all of us were headed into the navy.

As I watched the activity around the bay, my mind started to wander. I couldn't focus and felt lightheaded. I lay down, and before I knew what was happening I realized I had been daydreaming about my long ago relative. I didn't want to wake up and face the present day. I wanted to stay right where I was and try to keep the daemons away.

A crime scene surrounded me. I opened my eyes and saw yellow crime tape all around. I closed my eyes. My head felt like a thousand little jackhammers were all trying to get through my skull. I could feel my blood pounding through the back of my head. I just lay there and waited for the world to refocus. I didn't want to move and at the time I couldn't think of any place I had to rush off to in a hurry.

"John, can you see me?" Someone called out from far away.

"Pride, Pride, wake up." Another voice joined in the chorus of unwanted sounds.

I was in no rush to rejoin the land of the living. Damn, I was just thrilled to be back close to the land of the living. And I was certainly in no hurry to rush to stand up until my head stopped throbbing. I wasn't sure whether I wanted to rejoin this century. Perhaps the past with the sailing ships would have been a safer choice.

"Make way, that man is under arrest." Someone was in trouble.

It took me a few more minutes to realize that someone was yours truly. I felt terrible. Actually I felt worse than terrible but no one was giving me enough time to really understand how bad I felt. Nobody seemed to want me to do what I wanted. I just wanted to go back to sleep, or whatever state I had been in before all the commotion.

"We are going to take you to the hospital," said a voice attached to someone who was maneuvering a stretcher under my aching body. It had been a long time since I had felt this bad. And that previous time had been a lot worse, but I didn't want to start thinking about back then.

I was loaded on the stretcher and within minutes I was feeling better. I should have stayed on the stretcher and gone to the hospital but I shook off the dull weight of the concussion and rejoined my friends and enemies.

"I'm getting off this slow boat of a stretcher."

"John, we thought you were dead too." Misty threw her arms around me as she kissed me. "What happened?"

"Misty, stand away from Pride," commanded Dave. "He is under arrest for the murder of Christine Duforth. Come with me, John. The Chicago police want to talk to you."

I thought I had come back to the land of the living but evidently someone had taken me away from my world and I was about to enter the world of the condemned.

Taken by squad car, I was fingerprinted and stripped of my belt, pen and shoelaces. Still wearing my suit I was segregated in a cell with seven other men. I learned later I should have gone into a single cell away from the general prison population. Instead I was put into the special case cell. I was segregated from the regular drunks and drivers who had forgotten to pay a few parking tickets. Instead, I joined the transferees. I joined the prisoners who were in transit from prison to court to answer a new charge or to appeal a sentence.

"Are you a cop?" big gut asked.

"What are you wearing a suit for?" another asked.

I looked away and reached inside. They take my belt and leave me with my suit and a full wallet of cash! Here I am with a bunch of real characters who look like they would roll their mothers for twenty dollars and I stick out like a sore thumb.

I was seated on the long metal bench. Bars all round, and not a drink to be found. There were empty cells on both sides, and an observation desk manned by a lone officer about thirty feet away. By the time the officer reached me I could be down with a boot in the face or a knife in the stomach.

"You look like you have some money. Can I have some?" big gut asked.

"I'm an accountant and no, I don't have any money," I said.

"You sure look like someone who has a bundle of cash."

"No cash, just a few bruises and a hankering to get out of jail real quick," I replied.

"Why are you here? Did you steal your boss' money?"

"I don't know why I am here. And no, I didn't steal anyone's money."

They moved in around me and one of them reached behind me and grabbed my suit jacket while big gut stuck his finger in my face.

They were a few inches away from my money. I stepped back and all of a sudden I felt my feet going out from under me. They grabbed me just before I would have smacked my head on the cement floor.

"What's going on in there?" the guard asked.

"Nothing." They remained standing around me and I asked, "Where are you guys going?"

"Two of us are just being remanded and we will be back in jail this afternoon. If you need anything on the inside talk to Jake. Everyone will know how to get to me."

By showing no fear while my heart felt like it was pounding away at a mile a minute, I had defused the situation. Funny how there is such a short distance between disaster and just having an interesting afternoon with new friends. I guess this is part of what my father once told me you have to live through in order to have something interesting to tell your grandchildren. Grandchildren— I'd be glad just to be able to have a happy ending to tell Misty.

"Pride, you're out of here," said the guard.

I spent another two minutes saying goodbye to my new friends and was escorted out of hell by two of Chicago's finest.

"What the hell were you doing in with that gang? Some of them would have sliced you up before we could have taken a step towards helping you."

I just looked at him and wondered the same. Someone really didn't want me around anymore. It was less than two hours but it was intense and coming after being attacked it felt like a whole day. No, not a whole day—the whole two hundred years. From amidships thrust into the Napoleonic Wars to Chicago and a concussion followed by a jailhouse fight. My family history was brought to mind vividly and the only thing that made sense to me was that it must have something to do with that crushing pain in the back of my head.

We exited the jailhouse into the harsh summer sunlight of downtown Chicago. They motioned towards the squad car and off we went. No flashing lights but we were going faster than most of the rest of the traffic and certainly faster than my head could focus on the passing streets.

"What was that all about?" I asked.

"Pride, your guess is as good as ours. I think you have upset someone, but as luck would have it you are free and clear. She was dead long before you arrived. Her killer must have been waiting for you. The only reason he didn't finish off what he started off with you is that he was scared away when the night watchman made his rounds."

We made the rest of the trip in silence. I was happy to let my head relax as I closed my eyes and tried to lessen the throbbing headache.

"I learned this, at least, by my experiment: that if one advances confidently in the direction of his dreams, and endeavors to live the life which he has imagined, he will meet with a success unexpected in common hours."

Henry David Thoreau

CHAPTER 10

Meeting steamers do not dread.
When you see three lights ahead,
Starboard wheel and show your red.

Green to green or red to red,
Perfect safety, go ahead.

When to starboard red is near,
"Tis your duty to keep clear;
Act as judgment says is proper,
Port or starboard back or stop her.

But when upon your port is seen
A steamer's starboard light of green,
There's not so much for you to do,
For green to port gives way to you.

HIGH IN THE SKY on the way back to Seattle I finally relaxed. Closed my eyes and without realizing it, drifted into a deep sleep.

Back to 1811, back to my family. It had been a few days since we had been able to sleep a full shift. Most of us had been transferred from the H.M. Ship *Russell* to the H.M.S. *Minden*. We had just returned to Bombay Harbor from an exhausting tour of the French coastline. The *Russell* had been put up and I had just been promoted to able seaman. In my sleep I could feel my tired arms. We had been getting everything shipshape and I was having trouble lifting my arms. I could feel a tingling in my shoulders and my hands were just raw from overwork. Sleep would be welcome. But first we would be headed over to the *Minden*.

Days later, we were on our shakedown tour. The *Minden* was a brand new ship, still third rate and with seventy-four guns but there the comparison stopped. This ship was a pleasure to be part of—everything new, lots of teak, and now with my new-found promotion to able seaman I would have a few more challenges as well as a couple of well fought liberties. She had been built right here in Bombay and we had been able to see her progress when we returned from patrols. Our Captain Edward Wallis Hoare had picked most of the crew from the *Russell* and now with our new battle orders we were off to Java.

The next few months passed by in a blur—I realized I was dreaming but I could see and smell everything going on around me. From the initial excitement of being part of a large invasion force of over 12,000 and twenty-four other ships, I now really knew what war was all about. We were there for the Siege of Fort Cornelis and brought aboard many of the wounded. The smell of war was everywhere. I could smell the blood and cannon fire. I saw comrades fall with arms and legs blown off. I was there for their last breaths. They said there were 630 British casualties and many more enemy dead. Suddenly war was not the thrill that we had started with, it was becoming the terror of the dead and almost dead. All around were the living wounded and some of them were friends.

Gregor was still with us. "Pride, we are among the living."

"Yes we are, but by the grace of God we survived. There were several times in the battle that I thought all was lost. I hear you are up for a promotion."

"You would be too, Pride. I just happened to be in the right place when our Lieutenant was injured. I don't know how we survived but here we are."

"I just heard that we are headed back to England."

I awoke with a start, back to the present. My brain was having trouble refocusing. Two centuries in the flick of a switch. What a switch; I would have to try to understand why I was having such vivid dreams. Whatever the reason, the dreams were becoming even more vivid. In some ways the dream was clearer than the present. In the present my brain felt foggy, not quite in focus, not quite the way it used to be. The dream was clear, without pain, with no distractions.

Misty had bailed me out and I narrowly avoided being charged with murder. It didn't make any sense but evidently Dave had found me and thought I had something to do with the dead body–our Cargill employee's cousin, Christine Duforth. All I knew was she had been pushed to her death and I was knocked out at the scene.

We were off the case and Dave said they had it under control. He was sure it was a few local people and they would have them rounded up in days. My contacts at the FBI had ensured that I was able to leave town but the possible charge would remain over my head.

Now I had a real personal stake in the investigation and yet I was not allowed to participate. Cargill would certainly not want to listen to my ideas anymore. They had decided to go with Dave's original idea, pay the ransom and hope the FBI could stop the violence.

"I never want to see the inside of a prison cell," I said to Misty. "There was a short period of time where I could almost see the end of my life. If you ever have to spend an afternoon behind bars make sure you aren't wearing your best clothes. I am sure some of them thought I was really a lawyer or a cop."

"I know the feeling," Misty said. "Remember I spent a day in jail and I was a cop. Try that for fun."

"Sorry, I forgot about your all too personal experience, Misty."

Thirty one thousand feet up, letting someone else do the flying, with two beers underway and ready for a solution. Not enough booze to impair the thought process but just enough to give me the impression of creative juices flowing. Actually, I wasn't more creative but I still felt the need to produce an answer. Everyone had questions and I needed to help solve the problem of how to flush out the terrorists and still keep us alive.

Let's see—one email with no answer. Two missed chances with the FBI intercepts. We were getting no closer. But I knew from the bottom of my heart, that place where I kept my dreams and desires, that I could crack the case.

What did I really have? One terrorist act, two counting the small one in Vancouver, a murder in Chicago I almost got nailed with, and an early retirement plan from the FBI. If I had any chance of solving the case I would have to move quickly.

My saving grace was my continuing relationship with the RCMP. At least Cam believed I was innocent. Thanks for old Scotch drinking friends. My father had a theory that real friends are made when the two of you have at least two things in common. It was not enough to share an experience or just be friends from school or work. You need to bond in at least two ways, perhaps school and war, or work and charity. Whatever, the combination of enjoying a good Scotch as well as experiencing the trill of the hunt with Cam had ensured we were truly friends. When he heard of my problems in Chicago, he was the first one to step in with the FBI and I heard later it was his personal guarantee that ensured I was released without charges.

I called Cam from the airplane phone. I wasn't expecting anything but perhaps he would be able to shed some light on the problem.

"How is the Vancouver weather?"

"A little overcast with some drizzle but warm none-the-less," Cam responded. "How goes the hunt?"

"We are at a stalemate and as you know I am off the payroll."

"What can I help with or are you just calling to talk about the weather?" Cam asked.

"I need another set of eyes to review the problem. I'm sure the FBI is headed up the wrong path and my resources are suddenly limited. What I really need is the ability to flush these guys out into the open."

"What do you have in mind? I am not sure the RCMP can help but we can give it the old college try. Not that we want to show up our friends at the FBI but any day we can help solve a terrorist crime is a good day."

I explained what I had done so far and he did have a couple of good suggestions. After a few minutes we decided to redirect the attack through the local Humans for Untouched and Unmodified Foods branch. Cam would see if he could get Standler to plant the needed seed.

After explaining Cam's side of the conversation to Misty, she asked, "What's the next step, John?"

"While on the inside, I received an interesting email. I just pulled it down on my laptop. Take a look at it."

To: John Pride

From: Anonymous Friend

Subject: GMO Research

I understand you are looking to unravel the latest anti-GMO bombing case. I will lead you to the answer if you meet me in Puget Sound. I will be off Whidbey Island tonight at midnight. Come alone and unarmed. I will propose an exchange of information for money.

"You aren't planning on meeting him on the water?" Misty asked. "You don't know what you are getting involved with and this is not your area of expertise. Let the FBI finish the case and catch whoever it is."

"This is something I have to see through myself. I got myself into this mess and perhaps this will help."

That evening as I left the dock slowly I was still thinking of Misty's pain. She wouldn't open up to me and she didn't want to talk to anyone about it. I tried to put it out of my mind as I headed north. The sunset was to my port side and I enjoyed the splash of bright reds and oranges as the sun dropped below the distant islands.

I liked boating at night. It was a combination of usually being alone on the ocean with my thoughts along with the need to have all my senses keenly ready for anything the dark might bring. I remembered other nights when passing pods of whales had joined my passage, and one night I had seen, just for a few moments, the fluorescent glow of hundreds of fish swimming along side the boat.

I knew Misty and I would have to broach her pain again. It was affecting her relationship with the FBI and it was starting to change the way we worked together. I wondered what had really started her spiral of misery that drove her from the police force. I would have thought her good work and commendations would have helped her ride out most career problems.

As the stars started to appear I focused on the horizon. I would be traveling about fourteen nautical miles or approximately sixteen regular or statute miles. I had the local chart at hand and my global positioning system or GPS was operating. My reference point was the mass of land to my right in the distance. I couldn't see my destination but I knew they would be waiting for me deep within the hidden channel.

Unlike traveling at day, when you would have to deal with weekend boaters and tourist yachters, at night most of the boats would know the rules of the water and I could assume if they were out here they knew how to handle a boat.

I didn't use the VHF radio. I wanted silence. Silence to plan my next moves and silence to think. The water was calm and the moon was giving enough light to see the difference between the black of the water and the black of the tree lined islands.

I had been watching a light move off to the right. The red light showed they had the right of way but they were running quite a distance off and I put it out of mind. Suddenly I realized the boat was closer than I thought and I was getting close to the channel.

A bright light played across the water and I veered behind a small island and shut the engine off.

I waited. I didn't have to wait long. A Swiftsure speedboat slowly rounded the island and I could make out four men quietly conferring. Right now they wouldn't be able to see my boat's silhouette against the shoreline but I knew they would when they got closer.

The moonlight was dancing through the clouds and for a minute it became dark and I moved towards the Swiftsure. When I was within hailing distance I called out, "This is Pride, where are you going?"

They appeared shocked I had appeared from behind them.

The engine shut off and it was silent for a minute. A long minute as we both drifted. I was about to say something when one of them stood up. "I know who is involved in the explosion and want to help you stop them."

Three of the boaters looked like local fishermen and the talker looked like a university student. I don't know who I was expecting but it certainly wasn't this crew. This looked like some of the locals from around here. I was momentarily lost for words but the university kid spoke up. "The whole plan was to extort money from Cargill and I think it has gone wrong. There was no plan to hurt anyone."

"This is my son," said one of the fishermen. "Stan is a good lad but he has been hanging out with some weird characters. He came to me yesterday and told me what he had gotten involved in and I suggested he talk to you."

"How did you know to contact me?"

"I talked to the local FBI and just told them we had some information about the bombing. I didn't want to identify myself but I knew I had to do something without getting in more trouble. After talking to them for a few minutes they suggested emailing my information to you. Dad said he knew the Prides and if you were one of them I could talk to you in confidence."

"I knew your grandfather Alex Pride," said the father. "We used to fish together and he told me great stories about the prohibition years and running whiskey down from Canada. There was a story about using some of these islands as a staging point for the transfers. I figured you might know how to keep Stan out of trouble."

He was right about the islands. If they could talk they would have some great stories, and my grandfather had some great tales about playing hide and seek with the law on both sides of the international border.

"Stan, what do you know?"

"I was approached several months ago when the group was looking for someone who could help them with international finance. I am taking business courses at the university and I guess someone knew I had worked with a bank over the summer."

I let my boat drift closer and could see Stan was young. He couldn't have been more than nineteen and had the start of a scraggly beard. I could remember when I was young and foolhardy. I could almost see myself reflected back across the years and made a conscious decision to try to work with him.

"The plan was to demand a payment from Cargill and I would set up a Caribbean bank transfer. Once we had received the money we would stop protesting against Cargill and genetically modified foods. I was promised it would just be a one-time thing."

"What changed the plan?" I asked.

"I don't know. All I heard was that there was someone else pulling the strings. We never did receive any money and someone decided we should show them we really meant business."

"You know you are in real trouble when the FBI gets ahold of you."

"Yes, but I have been thinking about this and I think I can lead you to the killers," Stan said. "I know the arrangements for the funds transfer and I think they have used the same scheme with several universities and research facilities. Perhaps you can trap them."

"What did you mean by your email saying you would exchange information for money?"

His father replied for him, "Stan is through with them. Forget about the money comment. He just wants to come clean."

"Okay, Stan, what do you have for us?"

"Just keep me out of it. If they find out I gave them up I'm sure they will come after me."

Stan gave me the contact information and although I gave him no promises I did tell him this might help him when everything was finished. As I watched the Swiftsure disappeared down the coast and I thought we might now have a chance against the terrorists.

Late at night, nothing to do but go to sleep.

 My dream never did get back to England, but I was there in person as we transferred over to the H.M. Brig-Sloop *Curlew*. It was 1812 and Gregor and I were off to North America for the time being, away from the heat of battle. It was a rough sleep, or perhaps just a rough voyage. We were headed across the Atlantic Ocean towards Halifax and a change of scenery. We had been told that we were going to patrol the American Coast and perhaps head as far south as Bermuda. It sounded a little warmer. Under Commander Michael Head we sailed in August of 1812 and by the fall we joined the *Shannon* when she captured the privateer brig *Thorn*. That was a big prize—with a crew of a hundred and forty. I must have awakened several times during the night. Awake I was in a fog; asleep everything

was clear. We fought up and down the American coast. We fought and captured more prizes, and by this time I do mean we because it was me doing the fighting in my dream, not my long ago relative. We captured the schooner *Enterprise*; the sloop *Endeavor*; the fishing vessel *The Gennet* and finally headed back to Halifax; back to the place where I might be able to make a clear start on my life.

The Song of the Exile
Cast off the anchor and unfurl the sail,
Drown the cry of the gull in the pibroch's sad wail.
Farewell to our mountains, adieu to our glen,
We, our children, will never see Scotland again.
For we're bound o'er the ocean, cast off on the deep,
Our land taken from us to feed England's sheep.
We're sentenced and outcast; condemned, dispossessed,
Torn away from our homeland and shipped to the West.

We are lost now, and frightened, cut off from our dreams,
From our mountains and moor lands and swift-running streams;
From our loved ones and families, our proud Celtic past,
Cast adrift on the ocean, to settle at last
In some country unsettled and savage and wild,
Where we'll have to build shelter for mother and child
From the wind and the weather, the frost and the snow.
God, grant us the strength to stand tall where we go!

There's a land men call Canada, somewhere out there,
With a beauty, they tell me, no man can compare.
But will we be able to carve out our mark
In a country whose history is shrouded in dark?

How far must we wander? How far must we roam?
How long will it take us to build a new home?
Will this Canada let us grow strong and stand free?
Dear God, that's in Thy future, for no man to see.

Jack Whyte

> *"What lies behind us and what lies ahead of us are tiny matters compared to what lives within us."*
>
> *Henry David Thoreau*

CHAPTER 11

"You have to think anyway, so why not think big?"

Donald Trump

A NIGHT TO SLEEP on my plan and a quick meeting with Misty and then I was out the door and on the way to Sea-Tac airport. I wasn't sure which plan was the more important one. In my dream it was starting again without the pain of battle and the British Navy. Some nights the long-ago naval battles felt pretty real, but in my real life the plan was to continue with the case. Or was the real plan to fight my daemons?

Misty didn't like my plan but she was prepared to go along with it. I needed her help on this end to make it work. We were closer to finding out what was at the bottom of the case but we still had to have some luck.

I arrived in the British Virgin Islands (BVIs) after flying into Puerto Rico and then transferring onto a small plane. We flew in low past a few smaller islands and I could see sailboats dotting the bathtub calm waters below.

I remembered back to a happier time when I was half of a newly wed couple enjoying a week on a sailboat with another couple along with a captain and cook. The best part of the vacation was having a cook take care of most of the meals. If she wasn't taking care of us we were off to one of her recommended restaurants run by someone she knew. All of her recommendations were excellent and I can still remember her meals as some of the highlights of that trip. We learned how to sail through the islands and after an afternoon of exploring or just lying around, there was always something delicious to take care of our appetites. The captain was important because he showed us how to quickly learn how to sail but after three days of lessons he left and we decided to keep the cook. Good choice as I remember.

I stepped off the small plane. No real terminal, just an old aircraft hanger with a wooden porch on the front. It looked like it dated from the Second World War with its original paint fading in the constant sunshine. The warm Caribbean breeze and a beautiful smile met me.

"Would you like a welcome rum drink?" the smile said.

The smile was attached to a young woman in a bright green and yellow dress with several rum punch drinks on a tray. I took one and relaxed. I hadn't been in the Caribbean since the accident. It always seems as if the Caribbean journeys marked the turning points of my life. I wondered what this trip would bring.

"Can you tell me where to find a car and trustworthy driver?" I asked the smile.

"Come with me."

Out of the shade it was hotter and as usual I knew it would take me a day and night to get used to it. And then I wouldn't want to leave. We walked up to an open-air car. It had no roof, no doors and it looked like no future. It did have a couple of serviceable seats in the front and a place for my one carryon suitcase.

"Ricardo, this gentleman is looking for transport," the smile stated.

She left us to negotiate and within minutes we were off to town. Ricardo talked non-stop and filled me in on all the changes since I had been to Road Town last. He explained his family had some of the original Carib blood and he was proud of his native background.

"How did you get as far north?" I asked.

"Our history says we are from South America and used primitive boats to sail to Dominica. My grandfather took a more modern mode of transport. He served in the navy during the war and disembarked here. He liked what he saw and more importantly he liked a particular woman he met here. The rest is history, or at least my history."

I looked around. Although I had been here several times I was noticing some subtle and not so subtle changes. "Is this all from the hurricane?"

"Yes, as you can see the hurricane changed many of the beaches and caused much damage to the marinas and businesses along the shore. But we now have a movie theatre in town. Will you be going anywhere this evening? I can show you the nightclubs."

"I need to check in and we can head down to the bank," I said. "Then I will be headed for my favorite bar in the Caribbean for dinner with an old friend. I didn't tell him that my old friend was a bottle of rum. Pusser's Extra Dark Rum if I had my choice. What is life for if you can't have old friends!

Half an hour later I was at the bank. Its brickwork was red and yellow, leftover from when it was unloaded as ballast on ships from Europe. It was a small branch but I knew it was one of the most profitable operations for its banking parent. Barclays Bank was one of the first to enjoy success in the Caribbean and was the banker of choice when it came to transactions that needed to be completed quickly, safely and privately. The tax-free status on the islands probably had something to do with their popularity.

As I entered the bank I went back a few generations. Everyone was dressed in white and in island formal with dresses for the women and linen suits and white hats for the men. I caught the eye of one of the men in a private cubicle and he rose and walked towards me.

"What can we do for you today, sir?"

"I would like to meet with Mr. Livingston"

"Is he expecting you, sir?" he asked.

"Please tell him John Pride is here to see him. I'm sure he will be expecting me."

I sat under the breeze from a mechanical series of fans. Six large fans whirled above me. I tried to see how the fans were being run but all I could see was a long fan belt connecting all the fans. As I pondered this great mystery of the universe, a senior banker joined me.

"Mr. Pride, it is an honor to meet you. I am Ben Livingston, the manager here. Your colleagues called yesterday about your visit. Please join me in my office. Sam, please bring us some tea"

We talked about the island for a minute until the tea arrived and then he said, "I am afraid that your visit may be for nothing. As you know we have strict privacy laws on the islands and I am not at liberty to tell you anything about our clients' transactions."

He poured the two of us our tea.

"I just need some background information about a group you may have some contact with," I said. "We believe you have been the banker of record for several non-profit organizations in Europe and the US. We need to be able to get in contact with a few people who may work with these organizations. Any information you can pass on to us will be held in confidence."

"What group are you talking about?" Ben asked.

"Humans for Untouched and Unmodified Foods," I said.

"The name sounds familiar. Let me check our files."

A few minutes later he returned. "Yes, we have banking arrangements with them. We deal with a bank in France for all of our transactions. The only thing I can give you is a contact at the French bank."

I stood up feeling like the trip had been a waste of time.

"There is one other strange thing about this account," Ben offered. "It has an FBI notation. Every time we do anything with the file a notation is made to the FBI."

"Is that a regular occurrence, having the FBI involved?"

"No, the only other times I can remember Barclays working with the FBI was when it was proven that an account had been used for money laundering. But this notation is different. We are just to email them with details if anyone inquires about the account. And then take no action."

"That has been of help," I answered. I had almost forgotten the second reason I was at the bank. When Misty found that investors in the Web Shadow Personals Website were tied to an account in the BVIs I said I would try to get some information while I was here. "There is one additional thing you may be able to help us with."

"Ask away."

"I do have another case we are trying to solve." I showed him the names and company information we were tracking.

He looked at it and turned to do what looked like a quick search on his computer. I patiently waited, just enjoying the cool breeze.

"This is interesting. I don't have much information but we have dealt with at least one of these men for some time. His company is registered in the BVIs but they do not have an account here. I have no problem telling you what I know. He has been involved in several companies in the past which have had complaints lodged against them. Nothing ever seems to come from the complaints but I do remember hearing that the authorities were interested in closing his activities down. Let me know if you get any further information and perhaps I can direct you on how to get satisfaction."

As I left the bank I had the feeling this would become a dead end part of the terrorism investigation. Without a real lever to use with the bank I didn't think I would get anywhere with them. Someone within the FBI already had the account under surveillance. It bothered me I hadn't been given this information directly by the FBI. I guess they thought that what I didn't know wouldn't hurt the investigation. At least the meeting was not a complete failure. I felt I had some new information for the Web Shadow case.

Ricardo picked me up and dropped me off for dinner at a small restaurant overlooking the bay. I had eaten here before and was expecting an excellent meal. Besides I knew my old friend would be waiting for me at the bar. I had just ordered and was enjoying a Painkiller made with Pusser's Rum when I was joined by the smile.

"Remember me from the airport? Ricardo told me you would be here."

"Yes, of course, you introduced me." The smile had evening clothes on and if possible she looked even more beautiful. Her dress was light and I could see her curves outlined beneath the material as the sunlight streamed through the windows.

"I have someone who wants to meet you. James works at the bank and he may be able to help you with your enquiries."

"Then join me. I haven't decided what to order."

The smile looked into my eyes and said, "Don't worry about dinner. I will order for the two of us. They have a specially prepared fish you will love."

The smile sat down and joined me for dinner, which was as promised, while she told me her story. We were to meet her friend James on the beach later. For now I was enjoying a surprisingly pleasant talk with Suzanne. I never did figure out what type of fish it was but it was definitely excellent. And it did go well with the rum drinks.

She told me her parents had been killed when she was fifteen and she had spent the past twelve years raising her two brothers and sister. She had been working at the airport for the past few years and had saved enough money to build her own small house near the beach.

"You have the nicest eyes but I sense sadness behind your eyes," the smile said. Even though I knew her name was Suzanne, I was still mentally referring to her by her smile.

"I haven't been back to the Caribbean for several years and whenever I think of the pleasure I have known here, I also think about my past." I don't know why I am telling her this but there is something about this place and the atmosphere and her laughing which makes me want to spend time with her.

"Tonight we will see the green flash."

"I have been coming to these islands for many years and although everyone talks about the green flash I am not sure it is real," I said skeptically.

"Oh, it is definitely real. If you are in love and on the right beach at the right time when the sun goes down, you will experience the flash."

"So how does this famous green flash work?" I asked.

"You have to see it to believe it, and it happens quickly. It is the change of the yellow rim of the setting sun into a green flash. It occurs when the refraction or bending of the light rays scatters most of the light from the sun leaving for a few brief seconds the remaining green flash."

"How often have you seen it?"

"Only when I have been in love," the smile reached up and pulled me down for a kiss. I should have been surprised, but I wasn't. It felt like the most natural thing in the world. I looked into her eyes and we broke contact, my first kiss in a long while.

"It reminds me that we have the Northern Lights. And you need to be cold and far north to enjoy them. If you are really lucky you might even hear them. I'll show you them once you show me your green flash."

I paid the bill and two smiles joined Ricardo for a quick ride to the beach. He looked at me with a knowing look when he saw us holding hands like a couple of school children.

The beach was deserted as I walked away from the car. Ricardo and Suzanne were to wait while I met with James. I could see someone sitting on a boulder near the shore. The waves were slight and although the sun had been down for over an hour, it was still not dark. Far out on the almost calm ocean I could see movement. It could be dolphins playing at the end of the day.

"Hello, I'm Pride."

"I understand you are looking for information on one of our clients," James said. "Normally I wouldn't divulge information but I understand what they have done and if you can keep the bank out of this we would like to see the terrorism stopped. This group has received several wire transfers over the past year and three relatively small withdrawals. In total there have been six transfers into the account and the account is set up for personal withdrawals only."

"What does that mean?" I asked. "Personal withdrawals only–I thought you could transfer money at will from offshore accounts."

"Normally offshore accounts are set up with nominee agents and a board of directors comprised of local lawyers or bankers. Quite often we don't even know the power behind the account and just deal with a local stockbroker or lawyer when making transfers. For some reason this account will accept wire transfers in but will only accept withdrawals in person."

"Who can make withdrawals?"

"I don't know his name but I met him twice and looking at the withdrawals he appeared to come to the islands regularly. The balance is $4.5 million and $250,000 has been withdrawn in total."

I was surprised at the sums involved. I knew about the attempted $100,000 from Cargill but obviously the account had been used for quite a while.

"One other thing you might find of help, there is one Gold MasterCard associated with this account. We find many of our clients take advantage of an offshore credit card to pay for some of their stateside expenses. There is no name associated with the card other than the corporate name and the user can make purchases without authorities tracing the purchases."

"MasterCard allows this?" I asked.

"Yes and so does Visa. After we open your account we can automatically issue you a corporate card and do all the accounting. I don't know whether this will help you but here is a printout with all the purchases that have come through the card. The only other thing I might be able to help you with is to inform you when the next withdrawal takes place."

I walked back towards the open-air car and tried to plan my next moves. If we could track the purchases to the group we might have something to work with. I would have to fax the list to Misty.

The car was gone but the smile remained. My mind jumped back to other evenings on other Caribbean beaches. The thoughts were all pleasant.

> *"There was a smile you gave me*
> *That was native to the land*
> *Of wide and tossing oceans*
> *And of silver sifted sand…"*
> Alfred Goldsworthy Bailey "Micheline on the Saguenay" 1927

CHAPTER 12

"Life consists of what a man is thinking about all day."
Ralph Waldo Emerson

"I TOLD RICARDO THAT I would take care of you."

We walked along the beach. For one night I could try to forget about the past and the case. Tomorrow would wait.

"This is my house."

We were in front of my dream. I had been dreaming about a place in the Caribbean sun for years. The palm trees framed a smart looking house painted white with turquoise shutters. There was a large veranda complete with two hammocks. Twenty steps to the water and backing onto a steep cliff, it was in its own private world. On the beach there was a dugout canoe with outriggers.

The smile took me by the hand and introduced me to the dream.

We sat on the veranda in one of the large hammocks. I looked out over the reef and then looked back to see her dress slide down her creamy shoulders. She looked into my eyes and I reached for her. Her breasts were firm and her nipples hard. In the moonlight I could see her desire and could feel my need.

I gave myself to pleasure. It had been too long.

Much later we swam in the ocean and fell asleep on the beach. I awoke to the smile and a new day.

"That was beautiful," I told my smile. "What happened?"

"You have been looking for last night for a long time," she explained. "I could tell we were meant to spend some time together. We fit together like old lovers."

"Great fit and I love the way you smell." I reached over and kissed her neck.

I remembered the second time, after we had dried off and after the quick swim. She looked into my eyes and kissed me with a passion I had been searching for. She lay on the beach and spread her long legs as I kissed her neck and marveled at her combination of innocence and thirst. We made love under the stars for hours and when we finally fell asleep it was more dreamlike than I can ever remember. I was so relaxed I slept soundly throughout the balance of the night. I awoke slowly, realizing that there had been no dreams of ships or war.

"What's next?" I asked, wanting today to last forever.

"First is breakfast. We have fresh coconut along with local eggs. You can learn how to cut open a coconut while I prepare the eggs."

"Smile, are you all full of surprises or are you just what the doctor ordered?"

"I am your Caribbean dream. In your sleep last night you kept saying Caribbean dream over and over," the smile smiled.

"After breakfast we should go out to the reef before I head to the airport and back to civilization," I said.

"First the coconut. Take one of these and quickly hack off the top end. Once you have a big enough opening, turn it over, drain the milk and then split it. I'll show you what to do once the coconut meat is visible."

After a few minutes I finally had my first coconut opened and she took over rendering it into bite sized hard pieces that were extremely tasty. We never made it to the airport that day. We spent the day in and out of the water. In and out - and then in and out again. I had my first dinner of conch fritters and island potato soup. After dinner we retired to the hammock. We came up for air long enough to watch the pelicans fly by.

"We need the tonic of wildness… At the same time that we are earnest to explore and learn all things, we require that all things be mysterious and unexplorable, that land and sea be indefinitely

wild, unsurveyed and unfathomed by us because unfathomable.
We can never have enough of nature."

Henry David Thoreau

The next morning I awoke relaxed alone. Realizing that the smile had left my side, I quickly slid into my shorts and sandals and joined her in the kitchen.

"Good morning, John. I assume you slept the sleep of the satisfied," she inquired.

"Yes, and the morning is even more spectacular than yesterday and certainly better than I remember from the last time down here."

"What are the plans for today?" I asked.

"After breakfast we are heading over the other side of the island and I want to show you where the pirates of old came ashore."

"I didn't know pirates actually came to the BVIs."

"They spent more time elsewhere but there were several cases of Spanish pirate vessels attacking Tortola and in fact there was treasure buried on Norman Island. Planters recovered that treasure, and it took the Lieutenant Governor and a British warship to recover it. So, you don't have to look far to find adventure and piracy."

After a superb breakfast of fresh fruit we headed out to what I assumed would be a relaxing day enjoying each other's company. She was driving today and as I watched the island pass by I thought that this was the life. How could I rearrange my life to make sure this remained an important part of it?

It wasn't long before we slowed down and left the main road and bumped up a narrow mountain trail. After a few minutes we were far away from what little civilization there was on the island. We hadn't even seen a goat on the way up and there certainly weren't any people waiting to serve up a cold beer.

"Are you ready for a short hike?" the smile asked.

"I will follow you anywhere today."

"Good, because this trail should be interesting for you. My father used to bring me here when I was young. We would pack a small lunch and head down the cliff."

We had been hiking for twenty minutes when I realized I had completely forgotten about the case. I was completely enthralled with watching the smile in front of me and just letting the day wash over us. We passed mango and fig trees, and a few bay rum trees. Then we came out on a clearing and I could see the many stone-terraced walls, which used to separate the sugar cane plantations. It wasn't until we got near the water that I could see the real attraction of this particular area. As we came around the final decent I could see a small bay that was completely protected by cliffs all around. No sand beaches here.

"Watch where you are stepping, it gets even steeper for the next few feet," the smile cautioned. We were heading almost straight down on an old rock trail.

When we reached the water I looked around to the north and was amazed to see a perfect little cave you would never see from the sea. The smile beckoned me to join her.

"I haven't been here for years but it has always been special." We bent down and entered the dark cave but as we moved deeper I could see there was another opening far above. Light was filtering downward and was giving us just enough light to maneuver with. The smile stopped and without a word started to remove her clothes. Not wanting to be the last one fully clothed I took off my backpack and started to take off my shirt.

"Wait here until I call you," she said.

Not more than two minutes later a diffused glow reached my eyes and she beckoned.

I slowly got down on my hands and knees and moved farther into the cave. I could barely make my way. As I crawled past the small opening I could see there was a slightly larger area ahead. I was surprised to see candlelight and water. The smile was lying in a small pool of water and there were two small lights illuminating the area. Her breasts were glistening with droplets of water and she looked like a golden statue. The candlelight was lighting both her and the surrounding grotto.

"Join me."

As I entered the pool I was surprised both that the water was almost too hot to enter and that it was fresh water.

"This is my present to you, John." The smile didn't move.

"Great present, fantastic surroundings."

As I moved towards my living dream she opened her arms and pulled me in. Her warmth and the recuperating warmth of the water were doing wonders on me.

"My father brought us here on Sundays. We packed a small picnic and after our soak here we talked about our futures. He was always able to encourage us to think big and follow our dreams."

Her family had used the cave for years and she told me the local history of the area. There had been a shipwreck near here and when the survivors had swum ashore this cave had been their salvation. This was one of the few places on this side of the island where fresh water could be found. After several weeks of recuperation, the survivors hiked overland and found the local natives willing to help them until the next ship came calling.

A fantastic afternoon was had by all. By the time we got back to her cottage the sun was starting to set and we were ready for a relaxing evening.

The next morning we enjoyed breakfast on the veranda and then took the canoe for a quick trip out to the reef. Her strokes were strong and we were well matched as we paddled in silence. Although we said nothing, she turned and pointed out various landmarks. We arrived at the reef and the snorkeling was great. I was able to see many fish I thought only existed in a painter's fantasy world. Thousands of brightly colored fish parted as we swam around the reef. Several larger fish joined us and by the time we climbed aboard the canoe again I was sold on the area. This was where I would return for my retirement.

Hours later I was in the air northward bound. My Caribbean trip seemed so far away, yet the memory of the smile was strong and constant. We parted at the airport without saying a word. In the whole time we had been together neither of us had talked about the future or whether we would see each other again. We just looked into each other's eyes and knew there was a future.

In the air I sent her an email:

To: Suzanne (the smile)

From: John Pride

Subject: Save the green flash for me –

I'll be back.

Actually I didn't send the email because I didn't even know if she had a computer connection and if she did, I certainly didn't have her email address. An email address would normally have been the first thing learned when I met a new friend or business contact. This time it was just the smile and I didn't think addressing the email to smile@bvi.com would reach her.

> *"Give me…one glance of langour and longing*
> *That I may sleep at peace with the golden dawning."*
>
> *A G Bailey*

CHAPTER 13

"There ain't no rules around here.
We're trying to accomplish something."
Thomas Edison, Inventor

MISTY MET ME AT Sea-Tac airport. The weather was overcast with a light Pacific Northwest drizzle in the air. I never use an umbrella because I always say that it takes too much effort to remember to take one and besides you never really get wet. I always laugh when I see how much time and energy some people use to try to eliminate a little water on their head. I found that if it was really raining, and it does downpour some days, a good hat does the trick.

"There have been several new developments," Misty started. "Why are you looking at me like that? You look different."

"I am just relaxed and ready to get back to work."

"No, really, what is different? You have the look of someone who has been on vacation for months."

"I found some good information on our terrorists and I think I am ready to retire," I explained.

"Retire! You just got back to work, and I'm not ready to do all the hard work by myself."

"What have you found out while I have been hard at work in the Caribbean?" I asked.

"My contacts at the FBI aren't sure Dave has a real good grasp on the case. Evidently you still have some backers in Washington. Dave is really trying to pull you down saying you blew his big chance to catch them in the act."

"What are they proposing?" I asked.

"I wasn't able to get any more info."

The phone was ringing as we entered the cottage.

"John, what the hell were you doing in the BVIs?" Dave's voice was loud enough for Misty to hear him in the next room. "I thought I told you that you were off the case and now I hear you have been snooping around the Caribbean Islands trying to round up the terrorists."

"Just doing a little personal research," I yelled back.

"Well, stay off the case or I'll have you arrested for interfering with a federal investigation. I have half a mind to come out there and arrest you myself. Maybe I will arrest Misty at the same time."

"Half a mind is all you have, Dave."

"Goodbye and watch your back from now on." Dave hung up on me.

Later Misty joined me for a cold beer on the deck while we watched the sun go down.

"I know you would rather be in the BVIs but we should get some progress on the personals case," Misty said.

"What is new?"

"Not much but I have an interesting date lined up."

"Not with one of the fraudsters I hope. We agreed you were not going to be put in that kind of direct danger," I said.

"I thought with all the excitement you have had over the past week, the very least I could do was to move the case forward. I am joining my new friend for a trip to Belize. This could be the break we have been looking for."

"What?" I shouted as I strode to the end of the dock and Freedom looked up at me.

"Don't get mad, John. I contacted Phil Gravenheart by email and after several phone messages I agreed to meet him. You were away and I thought at least I could try to see if he was involved. When he suggested a trip to Belize I knew I was on the right track. Perhaps we can close down the fraud."

"I don't like it. I don't like it at all. We were going to let the RCMP take it from here. Why can't they send someone?"

She looked at me sheepishly.

"I know why," I suggested. "You have already met him, haven't you?"

"Yes, and he is a real charmer unlike you," Misty said.

"I'm sorry I have been so involved with the GMO case and haven't been here for you. What do we do next?"

"Cam is getting his team ready to back me up in Belize."

It was quiet for a few minutes, almost too quiet.

"Misty, you are relaxed aren't you?" I asked.

"Yes, what do you want, John?"

"We have never talked about Seattle. What really happened, and why'd you stop your fight. You know you had a few of us who believed in you and would do anything to support you."

"I know," she replied.

"So why did you just quit the force without a real fight?"

"I don't want to say you wouldn't understand, but you have to live though an experience like that to really be able to grasp the feelings I was going through. I felt that my whole world had shifted and in fact had fallen away from me. And no one really was there for me. No one really understood what I was going through at the time. It was me and the rest of the bad guys against everything I believed in. I felt that all of a sudden I had shifted positions and was looking at reality from a new perspective. And nobody else was by my side supporting me."

I offered her another beer knowing she would drink it. Then for good measure I grabbed one for myself. Just so she wouldn't be drinking alone! I took a deep swallow and the two of us toasted the sunset.

"You know I was there for you," I said. "I tried to help you but you fenced yourself in for weeks at a time. Nobody could help you."

"Pride, nobody could help me. I was all on my own and I knew it. I made some mistakes and I certainly shouldn't have acted alone without support from my superiors. And perhaps I should have told you what was happening, but at the time I thought I could take care of my problem myself. At the time I thought I knew everything and could fix it up quickly."

"Sorry, I should have pushed myself into your problems," I replied.

She reached over and rubbed my shoulders. I closed my eyes and said, "You know I have always loved you but I was hesitant to tell you because I didn't want to change our friendship."

"Thanks, John, but I am not the only one with problems and secrets. Ever since the accident you have been a little withdrawn. Who have you talked to and who knows the real story?"

"Misty, Misty, I just haven't been ready to talk about my problems. Not problems really. I used to think it was a problem but now I just think it is a part of my past that I'm not ready to share with anyone."

We were silent. The moon was bright and our beers were still cool. What else could we ask for? Sometimes it isn't until you feel really comfortable being silent, no words, no need for conversation, no need for small talk that you really know you are in the presence of a real friendship. I can still remember the drive with my father when I realized that some times true love or friendship can be expressed without words. Long periods of time can be spent without talking, just being together, just enjoying being close to each other. The only other way to explain it is the similar feeling you get when you are with other people who are striving for the same outcome. Like a group of canoeists paddling hard for a distant shore, or a small group of hikers headed for a snow-covered summit, or a couple of cyclists up against the hills and wind. I am sure it is the same for any small group working together for a common goal.

"Sorry, Misty, I know I should be able to talk to you about my problems. And someday I will. But it is still too raw and I still feel like I am losing an important part of me if I bring it up."

"John, we both have many miles to go and we both need to confide in each other. Soon, maybe."

We didn't say anything else. Finishing our beers we headed up to our separate bedrooms in the cottage.

The next morning we spent a couple of quiet minutes down on the dock before heading back to the mainland.

I dropped her off at the ferry and watched it pull away. I loved her and didn't want to send her off alone. I knew she wouldn't be alone once Cam joined her in Belize but I was still worried about her. I should have gone with her but she suggested I should let her take the next step alone. She could handle anything this case would throw her way. Now if only she could get past her feeling of having to prove something to everyone. Perhaps she just had to realize she didn't have anything left to prove. But I knew she would have to find that out for herself. I wouldn't be able to tell her how to feel. Hell, I had enough of my own problems without having to fix hers.

> *"The tragedy in a man's life is what dies inside of him while he lives."*
>
> *Thoreau*

CHAPTER 14

"There is nothing – absolutely nothing – half so much worth doing
as simply messing about in boats."
Ratty said to Mole in Kenneth Grahame's 1908 classic,
The Wind in the Willows

AN AFTERNOON ALONE, I had a few things I could do on the personals case but they could wait until Misty was back in a few days. I would just sail.

I spent the afternoon on the water. It was times like this that allowed me to relax and, after several hours tacking back and forth around the island, quite often a solution to one of my problems would come to me. This was not one of those times. I just sailed. Freedom raised his head once in a while as if to say, "What's next, boss?"

We cruised along through the islands, nowhere in mind to head. I was thinking about what Misty had said. I needed to talk to someone about my problem. Keeping it bottled inside was not the answer. I pulled back on the throttle and slowed the boat down to a trolling speed. I wasn't planning on fishing today but I did want to see if I could see anything on the depth sounder. I spent the next half hour watching the display and could see there was a good run of salmon in the area. Tomorrow should be good fishing.

I finally shut the engine down and joined Freedom in a leisurely swim. That is one thing about tollers—they love the water. I left Freedom in the water after my swim and finally had to call him back to the boat.

It was early evening by the time we got back into the cottage. I poured myself a generous helping of single malt Scotch and got a block of ice out of the walk-in freezer. I brought the block of ice outside and placed it by the hot tub. I stripped down and slowly slid my tired body into the hot water and looked out on the Sound. Closing my eyes all I could see was the smile. I reached out for a big drink and let the image dissolve.

I had lost my biggest client. The FBI would never want to work with me again. Perhaps I should just go back to teaching and leave the detective work to the experts. At least that is what Dave was suggesting.

Maybe I should just pack my bags and move to the BVIs permanently.

The block of ice was starting to melt and I jammed my fishing knife deep into the block and broke another large chip for my drink. I dropped another part of the block into the hot tub and watched it dissolve as I savored the Scotch. I am not sure what came first, the realization I had at least one too many drinks or the telephone call.

All I know is that I slipped as I exited the hot tub and sprawled on the deck. The ice block was completely melted. The Scotch was gone. The phone continued to ring. I slowly got up and answered the persistent caller.

"Pride here."

"John, it's Rob. Are you on for an early morning of fishing tomorrow?" Rob LeBlanc often called the night before. He and Doug Marshall were two of my best friends and almost always ready to take a morning off to go fishing. They were local entrepreneurs involved in the booming real estate development business.

"Salmon or cod?" I replied. I could feel that start of a soreness deep within my head. I tried to concentrate on what Rob was saying.

"Let's go deep and see what's biting," Rob answered.

"I'll meet you at the pier before the sun is up. It's your turn to bring the lunch."

I headed back to the hot tub and thought about a last drink for the end of the evening. One look at the now cooling water was enough to make me decide to head off to bed. I was asleep shortly and deep into the battle. The battle that seemed to keep going on in my head every chance it got to find my tired brain.

Now it was 1813 and we had just returned from Bermuda. A great trip with no sign of American ships. We had this part of the Caribbean all to ourselves. No war, no battles and no bloodshed. The past year I had seen enough war and blood to last my lifetime. I was there when the *HMS Shannon* transferred prisoners to our ship. They had just fought the *USS Chesapeake* and we watched when they brought the wounded back to Halifax.

I stood at the rail with Gregor. "What does this war have in store for us?"

"I don't know, Pride, but I am not long for the navy."

I waited for him to continue. He looked at me with a faraway look. We had talked about our love for our home and the loss we both felt. Neither of us thought we would ever walk the highlands of Scotland again. If war didn't take us, then we would stay in the new world when the war was over.

"Pride, I don't think this war will ever end, and I have some living to do. When we dock in Halifax I am gone for the hills."

I looked at him with what must have been astonishment. We had never talked about running. Both of us knew what it meant if a deserter was caught. Some had been executed and others sent to Australia. Either way, we would never see our family again.

"If we do this, we do it together."

"Agreed, Pride."

"How does this get us closer to home?"

Gregor thought for a moment, "It might not, but we would be free at last. Do you want to spend the rest of your life sailing and fighting?"

Free—I thought about that. What I would do for a little freedom. I hadn't felt real freedom since roaming the hills of home. The navy kept us enslaved to the ship and even when we earned shore leave we were never alone. There were always marines with us, ensuring that our conduct didn't stray too far. And the ever-present threat was loss of privileges or a real flogging if we disobeyed the Captain's orders.

We didn't say another word. We didn't have to. We both knew that at the first chance we would act on our desire to be free. The battle was still to be fought and I realized that the pounding in my head was growing greater. I shook my head, groggy and full of alcohol. And I drifted off into a dreamless night, or at least the balance of the night was without the War of 1812.

"Some god took compasses;
With centre moon, and radius infinite,
Described an arc of mist upon the sky.
Near by
Three points of light
Burned bright,
A triangle isosceles and tall.
They all
Patterned upon the night—
The moon, the mist, the stars—
Gold bars
And silver schemes of light."

A G Bailey

The next morning Freedom and I were underway before the sun came up. The sea was glassy and the fish were waiting. We were on the Cabo, my thirty-six foot fishing machine. She has a tuna tower, a solid glass bottom and a great forward stateroom with an island style double bed. With a pair of big diesel 422 horsepower engines that would power us at forty-six knots, we picked up Rob and Doug at the Bremerton pier and were trolling before long.

"We haven't seen you for a while. Are you too busy to get out fishing with your buddies?" Doug asked.

"I have two cases that don't seem to be going anywhere except towards trouble," I explained. I started to tell them about my week from hell.

"Enough talk about work," Rob said. "Who is going to get the first hit?"

Doug quickly answered him, "Well, we know who it won't be. I can't remember the last time Pride actually brought a fish into the boat."

Rob popped up from below with three beers. "Breakfast anyone?"

I had been thinking about what I was going to say to my first beer of the day. And as much as I knew it would help me get over the excess alcohol from last night, I also knew I had to cut back some day. "Actually, I'm on the wagon today."

"Pride, that is a first. I'm impressed. Don't tell me you have given up drinking for good."

"Actually, it is a combination of drinking too much last night and finally deciding that perhaps I should think about trying to go a few days without the booze."

Doug looked at Rob and raised his beer. "We toast you. And give you twenty-four hours, or at least until you catch a good fish."

"Thanks for the support, guys."

Rob added, "What makes you think you are drinking too much?"

"Because every morning, after the night before, I wake up and wonder why, oh why, did I have that last drink? I know at the time it went down really well, so why does it feel so bad in the morning?"

"Pride, answer that question and you answer that which no man has ever had an answer for."

"Okay, who is taking the helm first while we start fishing?" I asked.

"Rob's Rules for deciding," Doug added. "He came up with a great new addition for the rock, paper, scissors game we used to play as kids. Now we add a bomb that beats the rock and the paper. Scissors cut the fuse that is sticking up out of the bomb."

Rob started us off, "One, two, three." And we all showed our hands. Nobody had scissors and Doug had the bomb so he won which left Rob and I for the second round. "One, two, three." Rob had paper and I had rock so that meant I was the captain for the first half hour or so.

"Okay, trivia for everyone. Who knows who the first fishermen were around here?" Doug asked.

"If I remember my history lessons the first white explorers were the Spanish who claimed land for Spain around the Quinault River in 1775," Rob claimed.

"Good for two points but the natives were the first fishermen around here and they started to trade with the settlers in Neah Bay in 1792," Doug said.

Not to be outdone I joined in, "Did you know Mount Olympus was named after the mythical home of the Greek Gods in 1788 by the English sea captain John Meares? And George Vancouver referred to the range as the Olympic Mountains."

"Fish on!" Rob was up and at his reel as the line screamed out.

"It's a keeper!"

And so it went for the next while. I thought that this could be a good time to discuss my reoccurring dreams. I needed someone to listen to my theory about why I was dreaming of my long ago relative. I didn't want to have to explain everything to a professional. I just wanted someone to listen and help me try to understand what it meant. Dreaming of the past, not mine but my family's Scottish past, meant to me that I was avoiding the recent past. I knew that I would have to come to terms with what had occurred in my past but it just seemed to hold too much pain for me to deal with. I knew Rob and Doug would listen and I almost started talking. But the moment passed and no discussion.

Two hours later with six salmon in the box we headed home. Just what the doctor ordered—a relaxing morning on the water with friends. Work had been left behind. Perhaps I didn't need to confront the past. Perhaps the future was all I needed.

Rob broke my quiet contemplation. "Misty called and told me about your run-in with the federals. Is there anything we can do?"

"No, I just need some time," I said.

"Just remember you need your job to keep you sane. We don't want to hear any more talk of you retiring. A morning every once in a while to go fishing is great, but the rest of your life without anything to do would be a life sentence for you."

Doug added, "Not to mention that if you were retired you would probably learn to fish like a real fisherman and then we wouldn't have anyone to rib on the seas."

"Great guys," I replied. "What better friends could I ask for? Two guys who always think they can do everything better than I can and don't worry about telling me so every chance they get. And don't forget that I did catch one of the salmon. Before I forget, say hello to your beautiful wives. We should get together for a BBQ soon."

After dropping them off at the pier, with promises to meet again soon, I headed north. I had nowhere in particular in mind but I had a couple of hours to kill and it was a beautiful day on the water. As they say, and I have always wondered who 'they' really are, a terrible day spent on the water is better than any day spent behind an office desk. To add to it, this was not a terrible day on the water. I would try to enjoy the rest of what had started out to be a special day.

I opened up the throttle and the two of us, Freedom and I, just cruised for an hour. I wanted to explore a few islands just over the border. I had an idea about that staging area I had discussed with Stan's father. Our grandfather had alluded to a stopover years ago and perhaps they were talking about the same thing.

We finally stopped at one of the smaller islands. Anchoring the Cabo in a sheltered bay, Freedom and I both dove off over the transom and swan ashore. I quickly made my way to shore and Freedom took the long way by swimming in a long circle and finding several small logs to play with on the way. When he finally tired of the water he joined me on the beach for a short walk around the island. I didn't find what I was looking for but I did see a few things on the adjacent island that I would have to check out the next time we headed north.

"Come on, Freedom. One last swim and then we head home."

He wasn't as fast a swimmer as I but I bet he would outlast me in a long distance swim. Freedom splashed on long after I pulled myself back onboard. Eventually he saw a pair of ducks not far off and made a short-lived dash or splash towards them. They took flight and he returned to the boat happy to accept my lift onboard. We both headed home happy and content for the day. It didn't take much to put a smile on my face and I am sure Freedom would have a contented sleep as well.

> *"You are capable of more than you know. Choose a goal that seems right for you and strive to be the best, however hard the path. Aim high. Behave honorably. Prepare to be alone at times, and to endure failure. Persist! The world needs all you can give."*
>
> E O Wilson

CHAPTER 15

"Ships that pass in the night, and speak each other in passing;
Only a signal shown and a distant voice in the darkness;
So on the ocean of life we pass and speak one another,
Only a look and a voice; then darkness again and a silence."
                                        Henry Wadsworth Longfellow

THAT NIGHT I GOT a call. "John Pride, this is Harry Poindexter from Starbucks."

I was sitting on the deck watching the sunset. It was almost a perfect evening after a great day on the water. I wasn't drinking and now I had to talk to someone whom I couldn't help. "Before you go any further you should know I'm not on the case anymore." I was almost ready for retirement, perhaps not for real but at least for a few months until I got over the past few weeks.

The voice continued, "That is exactly why I am calling you. I am the President and CEO of Starbucks International and I need your help. I think you may be able to help us. We are having some problems at several of our coffee shops and have had an attempted extortion."

"The FBI is investigating your problem and my small part in the investigation is finished," I explained. "I can't do anything for you."

"Please hear me out. If you can't help me I will understand but I have to explain our situation. Starbucks has had problems in the past with demonstrations against certain of our policies but we have never had to deal with terrorist actions. The rare group protested the type of milk we used, or the price we paid for coffee beans, or tried to unionize a few locations but never violence."

I nodded my acceptance and looked for my drink. Not an alcoholic drink, but an iced tea for a change. I didn't miss the alcohol today and that was unusual. Finally I realized Poindexter was waiting for me to say something.

New drink in hand, still non-alcoholic, I offered nothing. "I can't promise you anything but you have my attention. I agree you need help but I am not sure I am the best one to provide it."

"Thanks, we have been trying to decide what to do for the past forty-eight hours. The original boycott against our stores was manageable. We thought that making some changes to the way we do business and eliminating some of the GMO foods would be enough to satisfy them. Evidently we have a bigger problem. The FBI thinks they have solved the problem but we want to ensure we really get the culprits. We need someone who can work on our problem and get a quick solution."

"What has the FBI found out?"

"They are sure that this was an isolated incident and we won't hear from them again."

"Do you believe that?" I asked.

"No, and that is why we would like to talk to you. Can you come to Seattle tomorrow morning and discuss this in private at our office?"

"I have a better idea. I will be tied up early tomorrow and then I was planning to go boating in the afternoon. Can you meet me at the pier and we can talk in private on the water?"

We talked for a few minutes and I agreed to meet him at Pike's Market and see if I could help him.

What a great day. A few hours on the water with friends, a couple of fresh salmon in the fridge and a potential new client for the books. Now all I needed to round out the picture was someone to share my life with. On cue Freedom jumped up on the couch and snuggled in for an ear scratch. What more could I ask for? What about that retirement I was so looking forward to a few short minutes ago?

I started to get up and head over to the bar to make myself a drink when I remembered the damage that had been done to the Scotch bottle last night. Perhaps I could have at least one night without a drink. If that worked then I could consider extending it to two nights. I did tell Doug and Rob that I was cutting back and that probably means more than saying no to a couple of beers on the boat. But if I remembered correctly, that fishing trip was probably the first one I had enjoyed without a beer or two in hand. And I did catch a salmon, even without a drink.

Instead of a drink I decided to do a little research on Starbucks. After spending an hour on the Internet I quickly came to the conclusion that despite the millions of coffee drinkers who love Starbucks, there were a few people who had a problem with Starbucks' way of doing business. In particular there were some lobbying against the way Starbucks approached fair trade. They wanted more support for fair trade in other commodities in addition to coffee such as tea and cocoa.

I retired for the night. The last thing I was thinking about was the fact that I was glad I hadn't been drinking coffee or Scotch all evening. Actually just before I drifted into sleep I realized how I could eliminate the slippery deck the next time I decided to have an evening of Scotch and ice. What I needed was a portable refrigerated beer fridge and bar. It could be moved around and hold the cold beer and ice with a super cold aluminum trench to rest your beer or Scotch glass. This would eliminate the need for ice cubes and would keep the glasses cold while you were otherwise occupied, like for example in the hot tub with friends. The last picture before I slipped into a great sleep was two glasses of Scotch in my new invention—the Scotch cooler.

When I woke up I needed a drink. It was midnight and I didn't usually start drinking so late in a day so I made up my mind that instead I was actually starting really early in the day. I don't know whether it was thinking about the Scotch cooler or the fact I really hadn't had a good drink for more than twenty-four hours. And I thought I could stretch not drinking into a couple of days!

I did make myself a snack a little later. I think it was between my fourth and fifth beer. Or it could have been later when I switched to Scotch. Either way I didn't get much work done. I blamed the alcohol but in reality it was a combination of just needing some time away from the case. I finally fell asleep on the couch. I think Freedom was nearby but I could be mistaken. He could have been the smart one and left me for bed earlier in the night. Either way I fell asleep. No worries and no dreams to remember—certainly no smile to snuggle up to.

"I find it wholesome to be alone the greater part of the time. To be in company, even with the best, is soon wearisome and dissipating. I love to be alone. I never found the companion that was so companionable as solitude."

Henry David Thoreau "Walden"

CHAPTER 16

"The difficulty lies not so much in developing new ideas as in escaping from the old ones."

John Maynard Keynes

A GREAT SLEEP, I awoke with no hangover. I learned a long time ago that the secret to waking up with a clear head was to limit the amount of alcohol consumed. I always had a problem remembering that secret after a few - okay more than a few - drinks. So I learned a better secret—just sleep in. It was 11 a.m. by the time my feet hit the floor and although Freedom had already been up and around for hours he was back on the floor by my bed by the time I awoke.

"Up and at 'em boy, let's not sleep the day away."

He looked at me with that superior look. For once I had to agree with him. He was the smart one. He had gone to bed early and he had avoided all the booze. And to top all that, he had already had his early morning run.

I made myself a quick breakfast. Actually it was just coffee and Danish but don't tell anyone. I am trying to eat better. Mum always said that breakfast was the most important meal of the day. But she probably didn't mean eating it just before noon.

We were on the pier in Seattle within the hour and I found Poindexter sitting at a small table next to Pike's Market at the arranged time. Freedom remained guarding the boat. The last time I saw him he was trying to catch a fly. He always got the easy job.

"Poindexter, I'm John Pride. I don't know what you know about me but

I'm not sure I can help you. The FBI is working on this and they should be able to resolve it without my further assistance."

We headed down to the boat as he said, "I can understand your reluctance to stay involved but we need someone private to get results fast. This is bigger than the media realizes and as soon as it gets out, we are going to have serious problems at our stores."

I didn't say anything.

"John, I am running a multinational company with operations all over the world. The last thing I need to worry about is some terrorist who wants to blow up some coffee drinkers. I need to find a solution and find it fast. I understand you were getting close to them before you were pulled from the case. Can you find them for us?"

"I think the work I have done so far might be useful, but I don't know whether I have the resources to get the job done."

Poindexter replied, "From what I have heard from our contacts I have confidence you can do a good job for us, but what I am really interested in is whether you think you can keep this confidential."

"That is always a priority with me. Let's do it this way—let's head out in my boat and I'll try to outline a plan of attack."

There was no sign of the fly when we boarded the boat. Freedom either had an early snack or had chased it away. Freedom gave Poindexter the once over and then went back to sleeping. I powered the Cabo up and we headed out. Sunshine, clear sky—why is everyone always talking about the rainy coast?

"John, we need someone with your expertise to get a quick solution to our problem. I understand that you have had some success dealing with people demanding cash payments over the Internet. We are prepared to pay these people but we need to know that the terrorism stops. The last thing we need is for an explosion like the one at the university. The minute someone ties the two actions together we are going to see our coffee drinkers avoid Starbucks."

"Let me be clear," I explained. "I can't promise any solutions but I do know how to track these people and I know how to ensure we capture them at the end. What contact have you had with them so far?"

He leaned back. "When we first started to have demonstrations we thought we could just ignore them and eventually the individuals would get tied of picketing in front of a few of our stores. But then it quickly escalated into demands for money."

I looked out starboard and pulled the throttle back and eased us closer to the nearly island. We would drift for a few minutes. "And did you pay any money?"

"No, we didn't get the chance. Before we even had an opportunity to give it more than a cursory review, the explosion in Vancouver happened and we knew we had a more serious problem."

Poindexter brought out a thick file and we went through the sequence of events that led to the small explosion in Vancouver. It had started with the boycott and although I wasn't sure there was any connection, it continued to the original emails, the explosion and a final email that he showed me.

> From: Humans for Untouched and Unmodified Foods
>
> To: Poindexter, President & CEO, Starbucks
>
> Subject: Coffee Fee
>
> Further to our original demands we want a payment of ten cents for every cup of coffee Starbucks sells. This payment will be sent to our BVIs account. Acknowledge your agreement and we will send you banking details. If you do not agree with our demand, we will publicize our demands and set off ten additional explosions.

"We believe they are serious and what was an irritating boycott may be turning into a business nightmare. I understand from Cam that in the past you have been able to set up traps for Internet fraudsters. This is a little different but if this is the same group which was involved with the threats to Cargill and the universities perhaps you can use what you have learned to set up a trap for them."

"I would like to help you, but the FBI has taken me off the case."

"We understand that. Any agreement we come to would be as an individual person. We have told the FBI we will work with them but they seem to think the explosion was a harmless copycat at work. They are concentrating on the Cargill end. We can't afford to take the chance that they are wrong."

I explained to him why I believed that the explosion was not the result of a copycat. Even if someone had access to the same pens and knew the specifics of the university explosion, there were too many similarities for it not to be related. I also explained my involvement would have to be kept confidential.

"I will give you the full support of the Starbucks organization," Poindexter promised.

"What can you tell me about the threats and do you think it is related to the boycott?"

"We are pretty sure the two are unrelated. The boycott is an irritant we think we have under control. The threat and the small explosion have a different tone to them and I feel it is definitely from a new group. I had my security officer do some preliminary work on the threat when it came in but he was unable to gather any additional info."

"I'll look into it as long as we can keep my involvement a secret," I said. "As you can imagine, I don't want to further screw up my working relationship with the FBI. If I take on the case, I will be working alone. No one at Starbucks will be in the loop."

Poindexter agreed to my terms and we talked about next steps as we powered back to Seattle. Freedom walked him to the end of the pier as I refilled the diesel tanks. I quickly headed up to the market and bought enough fresh vegetables for the coming week and enjoyed a short beer. Okay, it wasn't a short beer but it was just one.

On the way back to the island I thought about the value of work and the importance of having a strong sense of worth. I have always known I could get whatever job done that was put in front of me. It has always been the challenges that have brought out the best in me. This would be a real challenge. I didn't know which would be the greater challenge–finding the terrorists or staying one step ahead of the FBI.

Tonight was a quiet night. No Scotch and no ice blocks. After a dinner of stir-fries and one glass of wine I got on the Internet and started to work with the known factors. If I was going to capture a terrorist I would have to set up a trap that not only he would fall for but one that would look real to the FBI as well. I could not afford blowing the investigation by worrying what the FBI would do when they realized I was back on the trail.

One last call—I tried to contact Misty. By now she would be at the Belize resort and I hoped Cam would have her activities well covered. He had mentioned he was bringing a team of three operatives and would be joined by a number of Belizean police. From what I knew about policing in Belize I believed that it was modeled after the old British colonial policing system. Cam would fit right in.

The front desk of the resort put my call through to her room. The phone rang on, unanswered—still no answer in Misty's room so I left a message on the resort's phone system.

I headed up to the spire with the best of intentions to get an hour of work done. But I couldn't get Misty and her present situation out of my mine. I finally gave up and set out for an evening walk with Freedom.

We walked along the shore. No swimming for Freedom tonight. He just explored the rocky shoreline while I tried to decide what to do next with Misty. Our relationship was built on trust but we just couldn't seem to trust each other to give each other what we really needed. And I didn't know what she needed—just that she wasn't getting it. Before long we had made our way to the memorial bench and I stopped for a rest. Freedom lay at my feet and I stared up at the clear sky. Millions of stars tonight and no city lights to ruin the sky view. I tried to clear my mind and concentrate on other matters. Nothing seemed to work—it was all Misty and her problems.

Freedom looked up, and I scratched his head and behind his ears. Not a care in the world. Why couldn't I follow his lead?

Finally we headed home. No answers but I felt a bit more relaxed. Now if I would just hear from Misty I would feel a little better.

"Not until we are lost do we begin to understand ourselves."
Henry David Thoreau

CHAPTER 17

"Probable northeast to southwest winds, varying to the northward and westward and eastward and points between. High and low barometer swapping around from place to place, probably areas of rain, snow, hail, and drought, proceeded or preceded by earthquakes with thunder and lightning."

Mark Twain

I WAS IN THE middle of a long sexual climax when the room exploded. The smile floated away and there was coffee all over the room, coming in the window and under the door. The phone rang again and I finally realized I had been jarred from the middle of one of the weirdest dreams I can remember—love, coffee and explosions. That will serve me right, going to bed completely sober.

"John, I love you."

Now if you are going to be woken up from a fantastic dream this is the way to do it.

"Misty, thanks for calling. How's the trip going?"

"I can't talk long. I just got back from a quick meeting with Cam. He has everything set up here and it looks like he knows what he is doing. My date hasn't tried to get me interested in resort property but tomorrow we are going on a boat tour and maybe I'll learn something then."

"A boat tour? Is Cam joining you on the boat? You know what I think of you spending time alone with that character."

"No, John, and I think I can deal with a fraudster without a lot of backup."

"So, do you know where you are headed?"

Misty replied, "Yes, and I've talked about it with Cam. Surprisingly he too wanted to be with me when we head out on the water. What is it with you men? Every time the situation starts to get a little sticky you want to jump in and ride shotgun. I explained to him and I will do the same to you that it would be pretty hard to introduce a new investor at the last moment."

"Okay, okay, you've made your point. You are probably right but that doesn't mean we can't worry about you."

"Thanks, Pride, now back to work."

"Can I do anything for you from here?" I really wanted to be close to her.

"No, I think we have everything under control. Cam and his team are close by and I will keep in touch with them as it goes down. I just wanted to talk to you. I do have one question for you. I am not quite sure what I should be looking out for if the developer starts giving me the gears. How do I know what is important to watch out for?"

"The key things to watch out for are promises. If he starts promising you guaranteed revenues and returns for your investment that is a sure sign there may be problems down the road. He may show you some great tax deductions for the first year and then some aggressive assumptions for rental revenues for the early years. They might even make some assumptions about the rate of inflation and use that to cover the future costs. The only way you should feel some comfort with the proposed investment is if he can show you past investments he has been involved in. Don't jump at the first proposal he makes. Let him work for your money. Or I should say, work for the government's money. You will need as many details as you can get if we are to nail him."

"And how will I know if the development is legitimate?"

"It will be hard for you to be certain, but in Belize I would be careful if you can't actually see some of the development started. You shouldn't have to invest when all you can see is the bare undeveloped property. You might not even be able to find out who actually owns the land so be extra careful if he wants you to immediately put up some good-faith money without real security. If it was your money I would tell you to make sure you have a lawyer you can work with to review the contracts and ensure all the paperwork is done properly."

"So, would I be buying a vacation home on the beach or part of a resort?"

"It depends on how they put the deal together but I would guess he will be offering you a part of the resort. You may find you don't really own any assets and only get the partial use of one unit in the resort. The new popular way to sell resorts is with the sale of a quarter ownership in a suite or unit. What that means, Misty, is you pay for the capital costs to buy part of the suite and then take responsibility for the costs of maintaining the suite. The partnership group will undertake to rent out your suite and will promise to share any generated revenue. That is where many of the deals fall down. They don't have the needed expertise to market the vacation property and the costs soon outrun the revenues. Then you are on the hook for cash calls and can find your sure thing investment turning into a very expensive purchase."

"But I still get to use the suite. Isn't that worth a lot? I keep hearing this is one way to guarantee you have a low cost vacation forever."

"Well, just remember you have to put the money upfront. When you are thinking about investing try to put the emotion of the moment aside and think how much money you would have each year to vacation if you just put the money into a good financial investment. And don't forget, if you want to use the suite you won't be getting any revenue from renting it out to someone else. Finally you will have to pay some sort of condo or maintenance fee."

"Pride, you make it sound so easy."

"Don't get me wrong, there are lots of excellent vacation properties out there but we want to shut the bad guys down when we get the chance. They give the rest of the industry a bad image."

"Thanks, John."

"So where is your date now?" I asked, not without some curiosity.

"He just went down to the bar and I told him I was making myself comfortable for his return. Do you want to know what I am wearing, John?"

This was a game Misty and I had played in the past. Even though we had decided to keep our relationship on a more or less professional level, she thought it funny when she could make me sweat or squirm. Maybe she still wanted to get closer to me. Little did she know how easy it would be to get me to join her fantasy.

"John, are you still there? I am slipping out of my dress and guess what? I am wearing nothing now."

"Misty, you never give up."

"I need to give this guy the impression I only have eyes for him. Why don't you talk to me for a few minutes and get me hot and then later I'll think of you?" she sexily purred.

"Misty, I can imagine being there and letting my eyes explore your great body but do you really want me to talk to you now?"

"I am lying on the bed looking out at the moonlight on the ocean."

"We could imagine we are together. I can see the moon here and although I'm sure your view is different than mine, at least I can see the water." I could get into this.

"Slip over here and put your big, strong arms around me. I need you now."

"Coming, Misty, at your service."

"John, he is coming back and I want you to know the next time I kiss someone it will be you in my mind." With that she hung up and I was left there literally hanging.

Why did I seem to be missing the great climaxes? Then I remembered the smile and revised my thought. Why then were all the great climaxes on other islands? I knew I wasn't going to fall right back to sleep. I retired to the deck and lay on the hammock remembering the last time I fell asleep on a hammock looking out over the ocean. In some ways the smile felt so close. I could feel her hands all over me and could see her lips when I closed my eyes. On the other hand she was in another world with her green flash. She was probably long asleep.

Gregor called me out of my daydream, "Pride, Pride, I have been thinking of leaving the navy since we were pressed into service. This is not what wanted and we certainly didn't sign up for this. Do you remember what I said when we were in Bermuda? I said the two of us were destined for greatness. We just didn't know what it would be. Battles and glory are for the officers. All we are going to get from the navy is blood and injury, perhaps even death. You can be sure that no one will really miss us, and our families are still where we left them."

I looked at him. "You know what really bothers me Gregor? The fact that although we have been sending a portion of our pay homeward, there really is no chance of ever seeing home again. And why is that so important? Perhaps we can restart our lives here."

He looked at me and if he said anything in return it was lost in the mists of time. My foggy brain just drifted away and before I knew it I was back on the Sound. I must have been tossing and turning because the sheets were all over the place.

"Yet if a cairn were put upon his bosum's sward it could teach the mummers something for a day of international mourning, marking the count of time, to point a finger at the sign-manual of the common dream, lost by men whose counsels failed..."

A G Bailey "Border River" 1952

PANB Ole Larson fonds: P6-261

CHAPTER 18

"He is the best sailor who can steer within fewest points of the wind, and exact a motive power out of the greatest obstacles."
Henry David Thoreau

I AWOKE TO A new mystery. The cottage front door was wide open and Freedom was nowhere to be seen. This in itself was not unusual. Most mornings Freedom was up and out the door early but he came back for breakfast. He didn't miss many meals.

I didn't think much of it until I was back on the dock. I had taken the rowboat out for some early morning exercise. I had been promising myself I would get back in shape and my resolve hadn't been up to my actual participation. Twenty minutes in a rowboat and I felt like I had been worked over by a boxer. My larms were burning.

No Freedom. After calling him I was worried. This was very unusual. I headed up island to look for him. The main trail is well used, meandering through the rock outcropping. Some of the rocks reminded me of long-ago canoe trips through the Precambrian Shield in Northern Canada. Fir, spruce and eucalyptus trees blocked my view so I couldn't see far down the trail but I looked down the various side trails and couldn't see any sign of Freedom. If he were just hunting for squirrels he should have come back when I called.

"Freedom, Freedom."

I finally made my way to the island's crest and could see for miles in all directions. The distant mountain ranges were visible and closer in could make out the various islands and islets between here and Seattle. Looking down in the north bay, what we called Homesteader Bay after the ill fated and short lived attempt by the original owners of the island, I saw a strange boat. It looked like a double-masted sailboat at anchor.

Occasionally we get an overnight visitor but not this late in the season. By now most of the boaters who are out for a week in the Sound or heading up to Desolation Sound in British Columbia have come and gone. The local boaters don't spend much time around Lumsden Island because the fishing and beaches are better elsewhere.

As I hiked down to Homesteader Bay I passed the old orchard and what is left of the small barn overlooking the bay. Before modern conveniences this would have been a forlorn place to spend the winter all alone with the closest neighbor more than ten miles away. You would have spent most of the winter without access to the outside as there were no supply boats to service this part of the Sound. Unless you had a reliable boat you would have to rely on your outdoor skills to maintain a barely comfortable log cabin or cottage.

When I arrived at the shoreline I could see the sailboat was anchored in an unsafe place. A few more hours and it would be aground. Low tide was coming and it was obvious the captain was unknowledgeable about the local waters. I swam over to the boat and was surprised to see Freedom pop his head over the transom as I climbed up the sea ladder.

"Freedom, what are you doing?"

I looked around and although the cabin was empty I could see it was well provisioned. A full chart table included an operating GPS mapping system and all radios were in operation. Full boat and no crew, I wondered what was up.

Freedom had made himself at home and had been eating from a dog bowl. It looked like he belonged.

The least I could do for the captain was to ensure the safety of the boat. I fired up the small engine and moved it about fifty feet farther out in the bay, where it would be safe from the tides. The two of us swam back to shore and I sat down to think about this mystery.

Suddenly I heard a small boat engine coming around the point. A black zodiac with a forty horsepower engine was rapidly approaching the sailboat and when the driver saw me she changed direction and made a beautiful landing on the rocky shore just feet away from us.

"Hello and welcome to Lumsden Island," I said.

"Hello. I have been enjoying your island and just brought in some fresh rock crabs for breakfast." She jumped out of the zodiac with the practice of one who has been around boats for a long time. "I met your dog earlier this morning and he stayed aboard when I headed off. I hope you don't mind."

"John, John Pride, and I don't mind. Freedom has the run of the island and is in charge of making newcomers welcome. I moved your boat to avoid the rocks. The tide is heading out and it wouldn't be long before your boat would be in trouble. You should be safer here or you can come around the island and take advantage of the dock in front of my cottage."

"Glad to meet you, John. I have been sailing by myself for the past two weeks and haven't had a chance to enjoy human company. I am Susan Ciscos. Thanks for helping me with the sailboat and I would be glad to take you up on the dock offer."

I offered to crew with her around the island and show her the hidden dangers in the rocks and unmarked ledges.

As we sailed out of the bay and around the island I took a closer look at Susan. She was looking forward while the anchor came up and I could see she was a few years older than I had originally guessed.

Susan commented, "This is a beautiful island. Have you been here long? I am looking for a private island to put some roots down."

"Years and years. Our family bought the island long before the high prices started. It is hard to find a reasonably priced island anymore."

She offered me a beer and when I accepted she suggested I grab two of them from the galley. Below I couldn't help but notice that the boat had a well stocked bar. In addition to the beer there was a good selection of Scotch whisky—a woman after my own heart. While looking over her bar I noticed an interesting book lying on the sideboard. It was a book I had referred to in the past, *Puget Sound Pioneers*.

Back on deck I mentioned the pioneers whom she was reading about could be found in the old buildings still scattered around the islands. "And if you look closely you will see some of the pioneer attitude in many of the locals."

Later, with our beers in hand, I showed her how to safely come around the point and alongside the dock.

"Thanks for the beer. Feel free to make yourself at home. There's a hot tub up on the deck and if you want to join us for dinner, come as you are after five."

"I would love to take you up on the offer and I'll bring the wine," Susan said.

I left her on her boat as I headed up the dock alone. Freedom had decided to remain onboard. I guess he had a good sense that Susan might pay him more attention than I usually did when working.

My immediate problem was how to turn the promise I had made to Poindexter into real progress. It wouldn't be easy to catch the terrorists and I wasn't convinced we would be able to make enough progress to catch them before they escalated their terror into something new. Normally I would be trying to trick them into contacting me but in this case it looked as if they were more interested in money than their message. And that meant I would have to track the money before I would be able to get close to the real terrorists.

I called a few friends to try and get a handle on what to do next. I knew what we needed was a way to track the money but I still didn't have a solution that would work with the terrorists' demands. They were looking for the money to be deposited into the Caribbean bank account and I was pretty sure that once it was there it would be gone within minutes. It could be transferred to an anonymous bank account almost anywhere in the world and then withdrawn before action was taken. What I really needed was a way to track the terrorists before they received their money.

I knew by the time the terrorists started the transfer of money it would be too late. The real goal would be to find where they were going to transfer the money and be ready for it when it arrived. Perhaps we could intercept the final transfer or redirect the funds once they arrived. The US government had been tracking the transfer of terrorism funds for years and this had become public knowledge with a series of newspaper articles soon after 9/11.

The Treasury Department and the CIA had access to the SWIFT (Society for Worldwide Interbank Financial Telecommunications) transaction database. Based in Belgium, SWIFT was set up to standardize worldwide financial transactions. They also operated the financial messaging network that facilitates the transfer of funds around the world. They don't do the actual funds transfer but they provide the information which allows the banking system to communicate. The network carries millions of messages daily and these messages include the names and accounts of banking customers. Utilizing their access to SWIFT information, the CIA was able to capture several al-Qaeda operatives.

The US government claimed that because this tool was now public knowledge it would become harder to track the terrorists and prevent terrorist attacks. The bad guys would start using other methods of getting funds into the hands of the terrorists. I could only hope our terrorists were still going to continue to use the banking system.

Our problem was that we needed to catch them in the act. We needed a way to combine the SWIFT info with a way to quickly monitor the transferred funds. Through my FBI contacts I was able to get three final destination banks for the previous university transactions. Now I had to decide where to go next.

My first idea was to try to add a final funds transfer to each of the three in the hope one of them would be used one last time. If we could do this we might be able to stall them long enough to get a handle on where they were. They might be flushed out looking for their money.

> *"Beauty is where it is perceived. When I see the sun shinning on the woods across the pond, I think this side the richer which sees it."*
>
> *Thoreau*

CHAPTER 19

"I find the great thing in this world is not so much where we stand, as in what direction we are moving – we must sail sometimes with the wind and sometimes against it – but we must sail, and not drift, nor lie at anchor."

Oliver W. Holmes

AFTER SPENDING THE AFTERNOON on the computer I had almost forgotten about the morning adventure with Susan. There was a holler from the deck and there she was.

"I brought a Californian cabernet and if you are in the mood I need some advice about real estate around here," Susan said.

"Relax and we can enjoy the late afternoon view from the deck," I said.

We settled in to enjoy the afternoon looking out at the beautiful Sound. "You mentioned you had just come back from some time in the BVIs, John. Are you doing work there?"

"Yes, but it wasn't very fulfilling. I didn't get anywhere on my latest assignment. It was frustrating to go all that way and not really achieve anything." I didn't know why I was unloading to her other than the fact she was easy to talk to and I felt like talking today. I told her a bit about what I had been doing.

"What are you going to do now?"

"I think we are going to concentrate on the scene here on the west coast. I have some ideas on how we can infiltrate the local group and perhaps that will lead back to the Caribbean."

After finishing our first glasses of wine she asked if the hot tub was warm.

"Feel free to enjoy it. I'll get dinner started."

I headed into the kitchen and thought it was nice to have someone other than Freedom to talk to. It didn't take long to get the BBQ up and running with dinner on and a fresh bottle of wine opened. This I would count a social drink. At least I wasn't drinking by myself. Perhaps that would be my new rule—no drinking by myself. I can remember the year after Dad died. Every time I had a drink, I poured a second glass of Scotch for him and put it above the bar. After I finished my first drink I would have his. I know he would have approved. It wasn't until a few years later that I learned that this was a tradition in some families—pouring a drink for the recently departed.

When I returned, she was deep in the hot tub with her eyes closed. Without opening her eyes she said, "I hope that is you, John, and not a wild animal."

"No wild animals here. Dinner is served. Follow me and don't worry about changing."

She opened her eyes and without taking them off me proceeded to give me the best show of someone exiting a hot tub I had ever seen. For someone, I would now guess was in her mid fifties, she had an incredible body and an attractive bikini, which just barely covered all the essentials.

"I have a shirt over there," Susan pointed. I grabbed it and tried to hand it to her. She just turned around, clearly expecting me to drape it over her tanned shoulders. As I did, she moved backward and brushed against me. I felt an immediate shock of attraction but said nothing.

We headed into the cottage and through the kitchen area to where I had laid out our dinner on the adjoining back deck. A fresh salmon and a few dozen prawns caught earlier were finishing on the BBQ and I had prepared a simple salad.

"Looks great, John. Do you eat like this every day?"

"I like getting out on the water at least once a week, and if I can, we have fresh fish twice a week when they are running."

She replied, "I could get used to this type of service."

It was hard to believe. After several years of no romantic interests, two attractive and desirable women in as many days.

"You mentioned you needed some real estate advice," I reminded her.

"Yes, I have decided that this is the place to spend more time. Can you recommend a good real estate agent?"

I told her I could give her several recommendations and spent a few minutes talking about the reality of living on an island.

"Our family has been in the Sound for years and we still meet locals who consider us newcomers. We are those Canadians from the North, just down for the season. And this is after I have been living here permanently for over ten years. You need to be prepared for the feeling of being an outsider."

"Well, I am prepared to work at being accepted and feel it is time I start to think about my leisure," she replied. "I have spent too many years living in the big city."

After dinner was over she quickly excused herself and told me she had an early start in the morning. "Thanks for the hot tub and dinner. I hope we meet again and perhaps by that time I will be a resident of the Sound."

I was happy to say, "Drop in any time. You will be a pleasant addition to the islands."

Freedom and I watched her walk down to the dock and board her sailboat. I think Freedom liked having her attention and I certainly had a relaxing evening. From the end of the dock she would be able to see the coming sunset. No green flash but none the less spectacular.

We went for a short walk and while Freedom completed his evening chores I realized I didn't even want another drink. That was good, or at least a start on my new slow drinking plan. Actually slow drinking was the wrong way to think about it. I did want to enjoy the occasional drink with friends and I did want to ratchet down the amount of booze I was drinking. So I would slowly try to change my drinking habits. And perhaps the first thing to change was to stop drinking when I was alone. Freedom wasn't going to start drinking so I wouldn't be able to count him as a drinking partner. And Dad had been gone for a while and I was no longer pouring him a drink. Now, when I toasted life I remembered him and his brothers, Wilson and Hugh. Gone but not forgotten.

It must have been the thoughts of Father. As soon as I got to bed I started dreaming of family. Not of long ago, but the family of more recent past. Dad had spent a lot of time in retirement tracing our family roots and we had spent many a happy evening discussing the various family roots—usually over a glass of good Scotch. We both enjoyed exploring family histories and the related documents. I can remember him telling me of the Wilsons who helped negroes on the last part of their voyage across the Great Lakes to freedom in Canada; and the Mordens who fought for the British in the War of Independence or as the British called it—The American Revolution; and the Secords–especially Laura Ingersoll Secord who helped the British; and Alex Pride's part in the War of 1812 with service in the British Navy off the American Coast.

And before I knew it—I was back onboard ship. We were outward bound to blockade the rebels and see if we couldn't keep their ships at home. No opportunity to slip away in Halifax, now we were in the midst of danger again. I had been promoted to quartermaster and Gregor and was now a boatswain. We were now an important part of the ship's operation and we were limeys. We didn't think of ourselves as limeys but when we were in the Caribbean that was what the natives called us—for the new habit of having fresh limes aboard. The navy had finally listened to reason and eliminated the disease of scurvy.

"Pride, this is it. Glory or death for me."

I looked at Gregor, not knowing whether to laugh or just join the rest of the crew in this ratcheting up of emotions. We were getting second and third rations of rum and it looked like we would soon be seeing battle. We could see four ships headed out of the harbor, and although we were battle-hardened we knew this would be a close battle. Our Captain had given us the orders. We were to blockade the Boston harbor and ensure no ship entered or left. It was, as some might say, a good day to die. The sun was high, and there was a good southeasterly wind. Some would say they were ready to fight for glory or death, but I had seen enough of death and battle to know that neither was much fun. And I certainly didn't think death would get me any closer to my goals of starting over.

A second ship joined us as we arrived to start our blockade. The slightly smaller *H.M.S. Shannon* was a thirty-eight-gun frigate with about three hundred aboard, and she was prepared to remain offshore for an extended tour of duty. After a few weeks of little action the *Curlew* headed back toward Halifax and missed the real action when the *U.S.S. Chesapeake* sailed out of Boston harbor to challenge the *Shannon*. I was there when the wounded were offloaded. There were twenty-three killed and fifty-six wounded on the *Shannon*, with about sixty killed on the *Chesapeake* for a total of two hundred and twenty-eight dead or wounded between the two ships' companies. I learned afterward that it was a furious and fast battle lasting all of fifteen minutes ending with the death of the American Captain Lawrence and the boarding of his ship led by *Shannon's* Captain Broke.

Tom Haliburton wrote what he saw: "The coils and folds of rope were steeped in gore as if in a slaughterhouse. She was a fir-built ship and her splinters had wounded nearly as many as the Shannon's shot. Pieces of skin and pendant hair were adhering to the sides of the ship, and in one place I noticed fingers protruding as if thrust through the outer wall of the frigate; while several sailors, to whom liquor had evidently been handed through the ports by visitors in boats, were lying asleep on the bloody floor as if they had fallen in action and expired where they lay."

The next morning Gregor and I watched as the British buried Captain Lawrence with full military honors. There were six British naval officers as pallbearers. "That is the end for me," Gregor said.

I looked at him but said nothing. I didn't need to. We both knew what needed to happen. This was our plan. We had just needed the occasion to make the plan successful. The two of us headed towards the edge of town and then without even looking back we were off. I felt a slight breeze

on my face, but what I really noticed was a lifting of a heavy
load off my mind.

"The sachem voices cloven out of the hills
spat teeth in the sea like nails
before the spruce were combed to soughing peace.

Hurdling a hump of whales they juddered east,
and there were horse-faced leaders whipped the breath
from bodies panting on the intervals.

The lights were planets going out for good
as the rancor of a cloud broke and fell
into the back of town and foundered there."

A G Bailey

CHAPTER 20

"I was like a boy playing on the sea-shore, and diverting myself now and then finding a smoother pebble or a prettier shell than ordinary, whilst the great ocean of truth lay all undiscovered before me."

Isaac Newton

ANOTHER MORNING AND ANOTHER day in paradise, at least that is how I look at life after the accident. Every day I wake up is a day I can enjoy and a day that I can consider a bonus. Plus, I had a clear head to enjoy the day. I thought back to my dream. This was one of the first times in recent memory that I had awakened with a clear mind. No headaches and certainly no hangover.

After you have been through a life-altering accident you tend to look at life differently. Even everyday routine actions take on a special meaning. The key was to put the past aside and concentrate on the future. I still had my health or at least most of it. And it looked like Freedom and I had met a great new friend. It was a good day to be alive.

Speaking of Freedom, my favorite toller came around the corner with a hungry look in his eyes, and a friendly swish of his bushy tail. He was a beast of habit and expected breakfast as soon as I was up. It didn't seem to bother him that he sometimes had to go for hours without a first meal as he explored the island early. But once I made an appearance he expected his needs to be taken care of immediately. I quickly laid out his meal and then turned thoughts to my breakfast. Perhaps I should head down the dock and see if Susan wanted to join us.

The phone rang.

"John, things are happening quickly," Misty said. "I am in the middle of this fraud and have met another woman on the tour. Joan is from Los Angeles and has been persuaded she should be interested in buying property. I spent the day with Phil, the developer, and Joan and her date who I assume is also in on the fraud."

"Do you have a good handle on Phil?" I asked, just a little curious about the previous evening.

"Phil and I spent the last day together and he is extremely slick. He didn't even mention the real estate property until we reached the beach yesterday afternoon. We were being treated like royalty. He had laid on cold cervezas and fresh coconut. We spent a couple of hours snorkeling and lying on the beach and then he started into his sales pitch. The other guy who is calling himself Donny started to get really interested in the idea. Donny jumped on the idea right away and made like it was the best deal he had ever heard about. It wasn't until last night in the bar that Joan mentioned to me she might be interested in investing here."

"How did they get her interested? Aren't the two of you just there for a vacation?"

"They are playing on our emotions. They seem to think they can get us caught up in the excitement of the day and then Phil starts going on about the opportunity of locking in our costs for vacations and never having to pay high prices for hotel and resort rooms."

It didn't take much to think about that. "And how does he justify the high cost of the properties he is promoting?"

"He is comparing them to resorts in Mexico, Hawai'i and California which have gone up in the past few years. He is telling us that Belize is ready to take off and by buying now we will be ahead of the coming vacation boom down here."

"So, has he persuaded you?"

"No, but Joan sure seems interested. All she can talk about is the chance to own part of a resort and how often she would come down."

"How is the undercover work going, Misty?"

"Covers, what covers? It is so warm here we are hardly wearing anything and certainly no covers at night!" Misty laughed. "You just want to know whether I spent the night with Phil. Admit it, Pride," Misty said. "You can't have it both ways. Wanting us to stay less than close and then getting jealous every time I see someone."

"Hey, I was just asking about work. What you do with your personal life is your choice. I am concerned about you." Actually, I did have special feelings for Misty but didn't want our professional and personal lives to be connected any more than they were already. And I really wasn't ready for more personal commitments.

"Thanks! Now for your interest, this guy is a criminal and definitely not my type. I thought I told you I was looking for someone like you," Misty said. "Back to work, Cam and I feel we should let the investigation run its course and not try to arrest the developers right now."

"That sounds good and on my side I have a new angle I am working on that may bare some fruit. Plus I am going to be busy with the GMO case. We are going to be doing some work directly with Starbucks." I explained what I would be doing.

"Take care, John. We don't want to have the FBI come down on us again," Misty said. "Why don't you just quit working with them and join me in Belize?"

"Thanks, but I can't quit now. I really feel I can make some good progress."

"Okay, but remember what I offered." And with that she said goodbye and promised to make contact with me before the day was out.

I looked out at the now empty dock and realized my dinner date really had left early. It was quiet.

Over breakfast I asked Freedom, "Do you have enough energy for a quick hike to the summit?" He just wagged his tail. Freedom never turns down a hike. He headed for the door as I cleaned up the breakfast remains.

Out the door, I realized that my clear mind had continued past the early morning. This was a real treat. Perhaps there was something to be said for resolving your problems through dreams. I was free in my dream, having slipped the bounds of the British Navy, and now I felt free as we head up island.

Freedom and I hiked up towards the summit and along the way my clear mind started to formulate a plan. If I was to have any success with the Starbucks case I would need to buckle down and try to get a solution before any more explosions took place.

Before long we reached the summit and looked east towards Seattle. It was one of those rare days—completely clear and sunny. My day was cut out for me. I would spend the morning trying to track down the Starbucks terrorist. If I was able to find some sort of lead I might be able to put aside my lack of progress in the Caribbean. The computer and I needed to have some quality time.

The afternoon would be set aside for some detective work. My thoughts were to concentrate on the Seattle area and let the FBI take the larger picture. I still think they are missing something. I just don't know what it is.

We headed back down and as we walked Freedom ran ahead and then circled back. He must get at least three times as much exercise as I do on a simple walk. He is always off chasing imaginary squirrels. As we arrived back on the front deck Freedom presented me with his favorite stick. I thought I would get way with a few throws but after retrieving it the second time he ran down to the dock and dove off the end into the cool ocean water. An Olympic diver couldn't have done any better. This diver was now waiting for me so I headed down to the end of the dock and threw the stick. We spent twenty minutes, with Freedom getting most of the exercise. All I was doing was reaching down and accepting the stick when he swam back to the end of the dock. He would do this all day if I humored him.

Finally, I headed back to the cottage leaving him swimming around and around in a big circle, splashing the water and just having a grand old time. He finally rejoined me on the deck and I threw the stick several more times before he lay down and guarded his part of the deck. I envied him. He was getting his morning nap and I was back on the job.

> *"I went to the woods because I wished to live deliberately, to front only the essential facts of life, and see if I could not learn what it had to teach, and not, when I came to die, discover that I had not lived."*
>
> *Thoreau*

CHAPTER 21

"Nothing limits achievement like small thinking; nothing expands possibilities like unleashed thinking."

William Arthur Ward

BY THE TIME I opened up my email program I had already thought of several new ideas which needed following up.

Forty-four new messages—with most of them from two contacts who were trying to help me track down the terrorists. My main idea is to set a trap but I knew it would need to be a step above my usual standard.

I called one of the contacts. "Tango 1, this is the Eagle."

"Pride, I recognize that voice anywhere. Have I ever told you that you have a perfect face for radio?"

"Ha, ha, that's what Dad always said."

"It has been at least two weeks since we have trapped one of the bad guys. What do you have in mind for me?"

"Dale, we need to turn it up a notch for these guys. You have all the background info I sent you but what you don't have is the latest developments. We now have to create a trap that will not only get the terrorists excited enough to let their guard down, but also be good enough to trick the FBI."

"What? I thought we were working for them," Dale asked.

"We are all working towards the same goal or at least similar goals but for the time being we are off the case officially. The good news is that we still have a paying client. Starbucks wants us to quickly catch the local bad guys."

"I think with the assistance of a colleague of mine we can get the job done," Dale said. "We will need to set up some Internet redirects. Hold while I get Hans on the line."

As the call was being made I thought back to what Whit would tell me, "Give me the details, John, I need the details."

"Hans, this is Dale and I have John Pride on the line with me."

"Hello all, to what do I owe this honor?"

"Hans, John has been doing some work with the FBI but he needs to quickly do some Internet redirects without them knowing what he is doing. They will be monitoring his Internet access and John needs some privacy for the next few days. Do you have any ideas that will be able to mask what he is doing?"

"As the two of you know, whatever we come up with is usually only one or two steps ahead of the major security companies and maybe not even that far ahead of the US government, but I think I can help you for a short period."

"What do you need from me?" I asked.

"Just get me the list of your normal website traffic and I will develop a plan to redirect anyone who is watching you."

After a detailed conversation between the three of us we decided on the best course of action. If we can set an interesting trap, the terrorists should lower their guard. Hans was going to develop a bug to monitor the terrorists' Internet activity and I was going to get the FBI involved. Even if they didn't know they were involved.

My part of the deal was to develop the series of emails we would send to them. Part of the trap was to get the FBI involved without them knowing what we were doing. This would give us a real air of authenticity.

I called the FBI to help set up our trap. Not to trap the FBI but to unwillingly make them part of the trap we were setting for the terrorists.

"Dean, this is Pride."

"Good to hear from you. I heard you are off the case. I am not sure what happened, it was probably just agency bureaucracy."

"I have finished writing a report on the work I have been doing for you on the GMO Incident. You can expect an email with the report in the next twenty-four hours. I hope you will be able to do something with this information. Thanks for all your help."

"And again, John, thank you. Sorry it couldn't work out better for you. I'll let you know if we need anything further."

That went well. Now we would be able to send the FBI an email and ensure the terrorists received it. With any luck or just hard work we would ensure the terrorists would think they were receiving it by accident. After working on the emails for over two hours I reviewed my progress with Dale and Hans. We agreed that we were ready to send out the first email.

To: Dean Bronfman

GMO Taskforce, FBI

From: John Pride

Subject: Final Report on GMO Incident.

Further to our conversation, please accept this email as my final report on this project. Attached you will find my detailed analysis of the email accounts for the alleged terrorist group. I have been able to determine one additional member you may be able to turn to your advantage.

I agree with your analysis that this group appears to be grossly incompetent and recommend you continue with our agreed course of action. Corrective action should include the full force of law to ensure you capture the responsible terrorists.

If you require any further assistance please let me know.

Attachment: Final Analysis of GMO Group

We sent this email to Hans through the anonymous email address set up to look like a real FBI account. We also sent a copy to the group making it look like it was sent to them by accident. I was sure that the comment about having found someone who might be prepared to help the FBI would attract their attention.

Imbedded in the Analysis Spreadsheet was a computer bug, which would ensure that within the hour we would be monitoring all their email. The program would also keep track of all keyboard action of any of the computers that received and opened the email. And we ensured that once the email attachment was opened, it would replicate itself and silently send the bug to any computers that received email from the group. With any luck we were well on our way to finding out where the terrorists were. And we might need luck to stop them before they had a chance to do any additional damage.

The next step would be the tricky one. We would have to keep the terrorists interested in what we were offering and at the same time bring the FBI back into the case. That was the part I was not looking forward to. And I was sure that they would need to be an important component of the solution, but they would not be happy I had deceived them. Well I would let that problem rest for a day or two.

The phone rang. I answered it and my life changed forever, just when I was trying to decide whether I was happier being back at work or would rather be retired and lying on a hammock. It looked like I would have to be resigned to solving at least two cases for the next while. Life was calling again. And I suddenly had the brain fog back with a vengeance, just when I was finally looking forward to never feeling it again.

> *"Truth strikes us from behind and in the dark, as well as from before and in broad daylight."*
>
> *Thoreau*

CHAPTER 22

"I wish to have no connection with any ship that does not sail fast for I intend to go in harm's way."

John Paul Jones

"PRIDE, IT'S CAM. HAVE you heard from Misty?"

I could tell Cam was upset. "Not since early this morning. What's up, Cam?" My brain was starting to throb, no pain but just an uncomfortable dull feeling of dread.

"Misty and I were to meet an hour ago to plan how we were going to resolve the personals case. She never returned to the resort and isn't answering her phone. I am worried about her and it isn't like her not to check in if she was planning to be late. We have a team ready and now we don't know what to do."

"Cam, she mentioned that she was meeting with the developer and her other new friends," I said. "Have you seen any of them?"

"I talked to one of the women and she said the last time she saw Misty was earlier in the day when they made plans to go out later. The planned time has come and gone and she hasn't heard anything either."

"I'm coming down," I said. "Misty needs me and I want to be there if she is in trouble."

"John, we can handle it from this end. I'll contact you if I hear anything new," Cam suggested.

I replied, "If you were handling it Misty wouldn't be in this trouble. She never should have been on her own."

"Pride, that's not exactly fair. You know she is part of a good team. We just couldn't get anyone else to be with her."

I didn't say anything. Cam continued, "I'll let you know as soon as we know anything."

Off the phone I walked down to the end of the dock with Freedom. We sat and watched the waves lap up on the shore for all of a few minutes. Normally this would be enough to start to relax me, but not today. I couldn't just sit up here while Misty was in trouble. I knew that if I was in trouble she wouldn't think twice before coming to my rescue.

Back inside I used the Internet connection to make my flight arrangements from Seattle south. Then I phoned Cam back.

"John, I told you we can handle it."

"No, I'm on the way. After we talked I thought about what Misty and I have been though and I need to be there. I have confirmed a flight and should be on the ground late this evening. I'll call you when I arrive and we can coordinate our next steps."

"Good luck, John. I guess Misty would feel better knowing you were around if she needs help."

It took me all of fifteen minutes to make arrangements for Freedom, grab my carryon bag and pack the necessary computer equipment.

Times like this made me appreciative of my travel options. I needed to get to Sea-Tac airport as soon as possible to make my flight connections. Normally I would take the seaplane but I had been planning for an opportunity like this. Today we would be going in boating style.

Not just any fast seagoing boat like my Cabo, but my personally designed *Rum-Runner Pride*. Named after the rum running boats, which brought liquor south from Canada during Prohibition days, it was a well-designed super fast speedboat.

Rum-Runner Pride has several advantages over the speedboats made popular by Don Johnson in the TV series Miami Vice. My *Rum-Runner* had been designed to go fast and handle the uncertain weather in the Pacific Northwest. The key feature was its ability to slice through the waves and keep its occupants virtually dry. It also had a slightly wider beam, which gave it a little more stability and room down below. I had been working with a local Seattle-based boat builder and it was the first in what I was sure would be a long series of Pride built boats. Today I would be giving it a good workout.

After leaving Freedom at the dock I put the boat through its paces and beat my previously best time to the mainland. There weren't any large waves but I did have to handle some ferry traffic and wake. Cruising through the wake I started to relax, realizing that my head was starting to feel better again. Perhaps just being in control was what the doctor ordered. I had radioed ahead to alert the harbormaster I had an emergency and would need immediate assistance once I reached the airport marina.

A fast driver and someone to take care of *Rum-Runner* were awaiting me. "Tie her up and I'll be back in a couple of days." I was lucky they knew me and would take good care of her. Anyone else would have a hard time finding good moorage at the last minute and certainly wouldn't be able to get the harbormaster to jump so quickly. My government work came in handy once again.

The fast driver was fast and with just minutes to spare I was through security and made the noon flight south. I started to review what I knew about Misty's predicament.

We both might have underestimated the fraudsters. I knew Misty was resourceful. And I knew Cam would provide any and all support if he could. I just hoped she hadn't got herself into a situation she couldn't handle. Misty was known for being extremely confident—sometimes to her detriment. But I was also confident of her abilities. Perhaps she was just in an area where she couldn't make phone contact—perhaps, but not likely.

The flight attendant leaned over and asked me what I wanted to drink. I just asked for a water and then closed my eyes and tried to rest as we winged our way south.

Back in New Brunswick, off the east coast of Canada, in my dream I was alone, having left Gregor to his own devises a couple of days ago. We both realized that together we would be targets for roving navy marines looking for deserters. I was looking for something or someone, I just wasn't sure what it was yet. I knew that I needed to start a clean new life but it wasn't clear what form my new life would take. I had heard that there was some shipbuilding going on in Saint John and perhaps my time onboard could come in handy. Saint John was far away from Halifax that it might allow me to start a new life. Or at least give me some breathing room until I came up with a plan to make my way home to Scotland. That had been our goal, Gregor and I, to make enough money to book passage homeward bound. But first we had to maintain our freedom.

Walking the wharves I could see how I might fit in among the various ship builders. Although these ships were different from the ones I had sailed on, the construction techniques were similar and all of us had some experience repairing ships. I looked for an inn to get a meal, a pint or two, and perhaps some information.

An hour later, settled in with my third pint and deep in discussion with a few new friends, my plan was starting to gel. Or perhaps it was just the beer taking hold.

What a weird discussion. We had been talking about the jobs available for a seaman, and although there were several I might find agreeable I was starting to have second doubts. I wasn't sure whether this was going to get me closer to home. What was my real goal? Did I really want to go home or did I want to start a new home? Although through all the years of the war and fighting my goal had always been to return home, now that I was free I wasn't sure where this new freedom was leading.

I wanted another pint and with that thought along with the question of what my real goal would be—I woke up with a start as we began to start final decent toward a different century.

"The winter mill will not return this
often
a granary for months of ill at
ease
Nor will the thaw engage to round and
soften

the burden of its coffin; from the
knee
To thigh and upwards cold as any fish
hook
will it look to sweep a mist from sunken
eyes,
Nor gather to its heart its cherished
april."

AG Bailey "The Winter Mill" in Border River 1952

McCord Museum I-76319.2

CHAPTER 23

"Good thoughts and actions can never produce bad results; bad thoughts and actions can never produce good results."

James Allen

CAM MET ME AT the same airport I had so recently left in high spirits. Actually it was a different airport and a different country, but a lot of the Caribbean airports look alike to me. It was another of those small open-air reception areas. Again there were drinks waiting for all, all as in everyone except yours truly. I was working today and although I occasionally have been known to have a drink or two when working, I never drank when lives were at risk.

It was hard to remember that only days ago I was flying home from the Caribbean with visions of the smile in my mind. Now all I could think of was Misty and how to help her. She had certainly come to my rescue often enough. Now was my chance to help her.

"No news, Pride." I climbed into Cam's agency issued Ford. It was a black sedan with four doors. Now we would stand out like sore thumbs. Almost all the other cars leaving the airport were brightly colored Jeeps or old trucks and we were in a car that would look at home commuting in any big North American city. Why didn't they just give us a big black SUV with US government written all over it? It never failed to amaze me how much the agency could screw up the small details.

"Any chance we can get a more suitable vehicle?"

"Sorry about that, Pride. This was all that was available on short notice. We don't have a lot of assets down here."

"Never mind cars, do we have any plans?" I asked Cam.

"We have been trying to find out exactly where the group was yesterday. We are also trying to get an intercept program working if she calls us. We should have that system up and running within minutes and then we will be live," Cam replied.

"How did she happen to disappear?

"We have these guys pegged as pretty low risk," Cam explained. "This is a white collar crime and from what we know they have no history of violence. They are looking for money. We just hope they haven't upped the stakes or discovered Misty's true identity. The only real thing we know about them is that they appear not to have criminal records. Other than that they are a blank slate and we were going on that to give us some comfort."

I answered, "My feeling is most white collar criminals don't really care what we think. They don't really think they are vulnerable. They never think they will be caught and they certainly don't think their marks or victims will turn against them. So we really don't know what they will do if they find out Misty is one of the good guys. They might just believe they can get away with helping her disappear."

We settled into an uncomfortable silence as we wound our way across the landscape. All around me I could see the countryside becoming more rugged. We had passed several sugarcane plantations on the way up but the terrain was pretty rough now. The road narrowed and the forest grew right to the road. This is where a Jeep would have come in handy.

Cam's phone rang.

I couldn't hear the other side of the conversation. "Yes, yes. We're almost there. Wait for us before you do anything," Cam ordered.

"My team has located the fraudsters and it looks like Misty is with them."

"What are we doing?" I asked.

"We have a helicopter in the sky and they have a boat sighted heading towards the same beach Misty was on yesterday. We are meeting several of the team on the government pier at St Pierre. We will try and intercept the boat before it gets to the island."

We drove in silence. We had reached the height of land and could see the sea again. We headed down. After numerous sharp curves, and having to slow for goats on the road, we reached the end of the road.

Cam brought the Ford to an abrupt stop by the pier and we tumbled out into the hot afternoon sun. Where was my hat when I really needed it? There was scarcely a cloud in the sky and it was going to get hotter. We ran down to the boat and hopped aboard.

Introductions were made after we were underway. This was a government issued boat. Made for inspecting cruise liners and visiting yachts, it had some speed and we made good headway. Cam spent the little time we had in quiet discussion with his team. I just looked out on the horizon with my eyes peeled for an early view of Misty.

We came up on the fraudster's boat on the lea of a small islet and three of us went below while Cam and the driver approached them. The idea was to check out Misty and see if the situation warranted immediate action. She knew Cam and if she played along we would be able to pretend that this was a routine inspection.

Cam spoke on the loud hailer, "Pleasure boat please come about for inspection."

They slowed as we came up on their port side.

"We are inspecting fish catches today. Have you had any luck?" Cam asked.

The man who I had come to know as Phil responded, "We are just out for an afternoon cruise, no fishing today."

I could see Misty through the cabin window from my perch in the V-berth. She appeared okay.

She spoke up, "We are headed back to a beach we visited yesterday. I think I left my purse there yesterday."

"Have a good day." Cam waved them on.

Several minutes later I explained I wasn't sure what the problem was, but I was sure Misty was trying to tell us something. Misty never carried a purse and she must have been trying to tell Cam that something was wrong.

"Misty recognized you but she wouldn't have known I was here," I said. "She couldn't be too concerned or she would have made a move to come aboard."

"I agree, John. We will let them get a good head start and then follow them using the radar. I'll let them get just far enough away so they don't see us."

Half an hour later Cam spoke up, "It looks like we are going to have company. Watch the radar, the blip straight ahead is our friend's boat. Coming in from the ocean is a larger vessel. It is going slow and is on a course which will take them directly to the area where Misty and her friends are going."

We watched as the two blips converged.

"Cam, we have to do something," I stated. "I am not sure what we have to do, but we certainly have to do it!"

"Pride, all we can do is wait and see what is happening. If my guess is right, we are going to catch some bigger fish before this day is done."

"I am only concerned with Misty."

Cam tried to make me feel better about her predicament. "If she really thought she was in imminent danger she would have acted when she saw me. Once we know what is happening we will be able to make some decisions."

I asked him, "So what do we know about them?"

"Unfortunately we don't have a lot more information to add to what Misty told you. The only useful detail that I was able to gather this morning is the fact that they have done this before. And we are still pretty certain these guys are not violent. The only time they have come up on our radar was a resort they were trying to finance up north of Seattle. In that case they were able to collect at least $2 million in deposits from more than twenty potential investors. Then they disappeared, leaving the investors and a few local contractors empty, and this is the first we have seen or heard of them for over a year."

"So you have been watching them."

Cam replied, "Not exactly. We were building a case against them but we couldn't get enough real evidence to go forward. We had planned on running surveillance on them but other priorities came up. And again, they don't have any history of violence in the earlier case."

"So I don't understand how Misty got involved."

"We had a team of agents on the original case and when this one came up we didn't put the two of them together. Using the Internet personals is a new angle for them. So Misty was contacted to help up run the new case and there we are. But now we are giving it a high priority."

"I hope that is good enough for Misty and her safety."

Cam didn't say anything. He knew anything he said would be tempered by our mutual concern for Misty's welfare. We could second-guess the case as much as we wanted but that didn't change the fact Misty was in harm's way.

We waited. The sun tracked across the clear sky. We were without words. All we could do was wait. I was starting to feel that doing anything would be better than just drifting here doing nothing.

An hour passed and still the two blips stayed together. We finally decided to move forward and see if we could see anything. Moving slowly against the hot sun we stained our vision trying to make out when the boats would first pop up in our field of view. We had decided to cruise in and take the zodiac when we got within a short distance.

Cam looked over at me trying to read my mood, but I stayed quiet. Misty and family, that was what I was thinking about but I didn't want to mention any of my thoughts to Cam. New Brunswick family, Puget Sound, Seattle family and now Caribbean family all connected one way or the other. I didn't know where this was headed personally but I wasn't prepared to drop any of my family—real or imagined.

We eventually motored close enough. We thought it best to try to surprise them and not show up in the same government boat again. So the smaller boat with just the two of us it would be.

> *"In the love of narrow souls I make many short voyages but in vain—I find no sea room—but in great souls I sail before the wind without a watch, and never reach the shore."*
>
> *Thoreau*

CHAPTER 24

"When anyone asks me how I can best describe my experience in nearly forty years at sea, I merely say, uneventful. Of course there have been winter gales, and storms and fog and the like. But in all my experience, I have never been in any accident...or any sort worth speaking about. I have seen but one vessel in distress in all my years at sea. I never saw a wreck and never have been wrecked nor was I ever in any predicament that threatened to end in disaster of any sort."

E.J. Smith, 1907–Captain, RMS Titanic

CAM AND I LOWERED the zodiac and headed towards the blips. There was a small island to our port and clear water starboard. Minutes later we could see our target. The beach was sand with palm trees dotting the shoreline and the two boats were anchored close to shore. I couldn't see anyone around. They must all be below in one or both of the boats.

As we got close the big boat started up and quickly pulled away from its mooring. The smaller boat joined in the exit and headed in a different direction. Now we would have to guess where Misty had ended up. This did not look good and I did not like our odds. We were about to take chase when I noticed movement.

At the head of the island someone was waving towards us. Binoculars in hand I took a quick look. It was Misty, all alone.

We quickly headed ashore and received a warm welcome.

"It's good to see you guys. I wasn't sure what was happening but I was starting to get a bad feeling about my situation."

After we had Misty comfortably seated, I asked, "What was that all about?"

"I think the developer, or I should say fraudster, was starting to get suspicious of my real intentions. Early this morning he called and said we were going for a short cruise back to the property, but when I got down to the boat I was the only one to join him and his buddy."

I looked at her with disbelief. "What were you thinking of, Misty? Why did you go with them?"

"Well, you know how it goes. One thing led to another. Phil said we were supposed to meet the others on the way. They were going to be at the main town pier and we would pick them up there. When we cruised over there we could see no one and by that time we were settled in and it did look like a good day for a cruise. By the time you stopped us we were all relaxed and I didn't think there was any danger. After you stopped we met up with that larger boat and I think they were still okay until someone noticed you coming up on them fast. I think they started to wonder about the coincidence of meeting the law on the water. They were whispering together and I think they decided to leave quickly. That was when they dropped me off and took off. The last thing Phil said was they had a private meeting and they would meet back at the resort before the wire transfer. They said they would arrange a water taxi."

"We're just glad to have you on board," I said.

"We will have to think about the next steps," Cam said.

By this time both boats were well out of range and we headed back. We would have to make contact with our fraudsters another way.

After docking Misty and I headed back to the resort. Cam and Misty had agreed earlier he would set up surveillance at the bank in preparation for the expected wire transfer and pickup. With any luck they would get their man at that time.

Misty still wanted to go through with the planned sting. So we waited by the pool for a call from Phil.

"We have only been here two hours," I said, trying to ease the tension.

"I know, but I can't stop feeling we are doing this the wrong way. Tell me again why we are doing this and not leaving it all for the RCMP?" Misty asked.

"You know that time is not in our favor and it certainly looks like we aren't going to get a second chance to catch these crooks. You are the one with the personal connection. Don't you want to put them away?"

"Of course I do, John. I guess I had been too close to the case. I thought we could bring them in peacefully. I never once thought they were involved in anything violent."

"I am still not sure there would have been any violence if we hadn't so-called rescued you this afternoon." I tried to calm her concerns.

Cam finally called and we explained that we had heard nothing. He persuaded us we should call it off for the time being.

The rest of the day was spent trying to decide what to do next. From my point of view I would have limited involvement and by the end of the afternoon could see my time would be put to better use back at home.

The next day I woke with a start. It was light outside but the sun had not yet risen. It was the period of the morning when everything was still and quiet. I quickly got up and headed down to the beach.

Nobody in sight.

Misty joined me by the water. "Hi, John. I woke up thinking of our last time on this beach," she referred to a romantic time long ago.

"I thought you had forgotten about that," I said.

"No, I am always looking for love in all the wrong places and that was one of the few which was almost right."

"Misty, you deserve to be happy and I'm sure love will find you. Or if not love at least great lust." I gave her a hug.

"Thanks, I needed that." Misty looked like she was close to tears.

Ten minutes passed and we just watched the orange sun finally catch up with our morning and start to rise over the ocean horizon. The rest of the team joined us. Nothing was said as we headed north up the beach.

Later that day Misty and I flew back to Seattle together. She was quieter than usual.

"Cam said he would keep us posted," I said.

"I know. I just have the feeling I should have played my cards differently. I'm sure we will never see them again," Misty pouted.

"I am sure it will work out. Just be happy your cover wasn't blown."

Misty looked at me. "I'm still not certain it wasn't."

We spent the rest of the flight in silence.

Back home and reconnected with Freedom we had a quiet evening. This was a refreshing change and we took advantage of the great weather to spend our time outside. Neither of us seemed to need a walk so we spent some time around the boathouse. There were several windows that I had been planning on refinishing and perhaps now would be a good time to get a start on the work. When Grandfather built the boathouse he had used some scavenged lumber and a few stained glass windows from an old church on the island. It had fallen into disrepair over the years and the recycled material had blended in with the rest of the cottage and outbuildings.

I thought about removing the old paint from the windows but a drink was calling.

"The only remedy for love is to love more."

Thoreau

CHAPTER 25

*"For all at last returns to the sea – to Oceanus, the ocean river, like
the ever-flowing stream of time, the beginning and the end."*
                                                            Rachel Carson

BACK ON MY ISLAND. Finally on the deck by myself, alone with a large tumbler
of Scotch and the ocean beckoning—a less than satisfying couple of days.
We were now no closer to solving the personals crime and I had just wasted
a couple of days, which could have been used to work on uncovering the
terrorists.

I guess the time wasn't really wasted. After all Misty was safe and sound.
That was the important thing. And I did have one of my best friends here with
me now—Mr Scotch, as in glass of. Not that I really wanted to give it much
thought but I realized that when it came to cutting down on my drinking I
wasn't exactly doing an outstanding job. I was trying to justify my actions by
reminding myself it would have been next to impossible not to drink with all
the friends around for the boating weekend. And if I was going to be drinking
all weekend why not get a head start tonight?

Tomorrow would be busy with friends and family arriving for the race.
Tonight would be my night to put the past few days into perspective. Not much
closer to the terrorists, and certainly hadn't caught the Internet fraudsters, but
we had one beautiful woman saved. What else could I ask for?

I know—it would be nice if a beautiful woman threw herself at my feet.
Oh well, that only happens in the movies, or my dreams.

Freedom looked up but seemed content to lie at my feet. I closed my eyes and saw the sunny Caribbean and the smile again. I hoped she was having a good week. I missed her. Several hours later I was still on the deck and the evening had disappeared.

I gathered up what was left of the Scotch and headed inside. Actually there wasn't much of the Scotch left but it had tasted good and for once I didn't feel like I had overindulged. Freedom stayed in the night air while I shuffled off to bed alone.

In the middle of the night I awoke to the reoccurring dream, only this time it had a satisfactory ending with dangers overcome. I felt as if finally there was some small sense of calm in my life.

I must have fallen back to an immediate deep sleep because the next thing I knew Freedom was jumping on the bed and morning was streaming into the house. It was starting out as a bright sunny day.

"Okay, boy. I'm up and at-em." This would be a busy day. After a quick breakfast I headed down to the dock to await my guests. Normally I would be headed into Seattle to pick up some of them but this year because I had been so busy I had made arrangements for everyone without boats to be met and transported to Lumsden Island by water taxi.

My brother Whit was one of the first to arrive. A reporter with the New York Times, he looked forward to his time on the island. He always gave me a run in the sponge race.

"Welcome to Lumsden Island, brother."

"Good to be home, John," Whit returned. He was loaded down with his travelling bag and laptop case. It sounded as if he was still loaded with the cares of the world. That would melt away after a few hours on the water. It always took him till then to put aside whatever new story he was working on.

"Good to see you too. How is the big apple?"

"New York is still New York. I think we have finally recovered from 9/11. We have our confidence back again and it is as busy as ever. I won't say we have forgotten what happened to us but at least now it doesn't start every conversation."

I asked, "When are you going to move back here? I know I ask that every year but it would be nice to have you closer more often."

"John, you will be the first to know. I have always thought I would move back west and work in San Francisco or Seattle but the right opportunity hasn't come along yet."

"Well keep up the good work and make sure you return at least a couple of times a year."

"Don't worry about that. This is still my favorite place in the world and I'm still planning on retiring here."

"Retiring—that will be the day. I can't see you retiring."

"I'll unload, quickly change and meet you on the water. Let's see if you can be more of a challenge than last year."

"Ha, you know you got lucky. If it weren't for the last sponge I would have won by a long way," I said.

"Just give me some competition and I'll be happy," Whit said.

"It will be my pleasure, and by the way don't forget to check the wine cellar on the way up to your room. You can have the honor of picking the wines tonight."

"See you on the water. May the best sailor win," Whit replied.

He headed up to the cottage and I started getting the sailboats ready. Once on the water I could concentrate on sailing. Or I should say, I could stop concentrating on everything else and just let my sailing instincts take over.

I should explain the sailboat race because to my knowledge it is a one of a kind race. There is no formal course—just the first boat around the island and past the dock wins. But we incorporated an interesting twist into the race. Each boat is equipped with three sponges. At anytime during the race, when close to another boat, you are allowed and even encouraged to throw a wet sponge at another boat. If you miss the boat, you have to come around and pick up the sponge losing time. However if you hit the other boat, or more likely the boaters, you score a hit and can continue. It is the hit boat's job to return the sponge as quickly as possible. All boats with more than three sponges onboard move into the runner up race.

As I prepared the Hobie Cats, I planned my strategy. I had organized a picnic buffet on the dock before the race and we were just settling in to enjoy some cold BBQ chicken along with all the fixings and a cold beer or two when I noticed a late entry approaching the dock.

According to my reckoning everyone I was expecting was already here. It was with interest I watched the tall woman beautifully maneuver her Hobie

Cat into a slow coast to the dock. Whoever it was, she would be welcome. Quite often one of the neighbors would drop over at the last minute.

"Now comes good sailing."

Thoreau

CHAPTER 26

"The sail, the play of its pulse so like our own lives: so thin and yet so full of life, so noiseless when it labors hardest, so noisy and impatient when least effective."

Henry David Thoreau

"Ahoy, Lumsden Island. Permission to land."

I was surprised to see our new sailor was none other than the mystery woman from last week. "I thought you had headed home."

She brought her boat smartly alongside the dock and stepped out. "I spent the past few days looking at real estate in the Sound and remembered you had mentioned the race. I hope you don't mind the fact I just dropped in. It sounded like a great day on the water," Susan said. "My real estate agent lent me her Hobie Cat."

"Not at all, the more the merrier. In fact you are just in time for lunch and then we will be starting the races."

I introduced Susan to the assembled gang and showed her the way to lunch.

Whit had fired up the charcoal BBQ and was grilling some of his special Lumsden hamburgers with some local cheese and veggies as toppings. Cold beer added to the festivities and before long everyone was in a party mood.

"Excellent meal, Whit," Susan said.

"My pleasure, and tell me how you came to be on our islands?"

"As I explained to your brother, I am looking for an island to move to.

John was telling me about this island and some of the history of the Puget Sound. You certainly have a slice of paradise."

I added, "Whit and I have always looked at this area as our retreat away from the pressures of life. When we get on the water and leave the city behind we are able to relax and do what is really important."

Whit asked, "Like drink and lose sailboat races, John?"

"This year I am going to give you a real run for your money. And with the new participants there might be a whole new group of winners."

An hour later all racers were assembled in their boats and we were ready to head around the island. The starting loon call was sounded from the end of the dock and we were off. My usual strategy was to get as close to the start line but not real close to the dock. I can remember several times when Whit had closely tacked towards me and caused me to drop well back in order to avoid hitting the dock. It wouldn't do to have the host hit the dock right off. I would let someone else have that honor.

A quarter of the way around the island I looked across my port beam and could see Whit and Russ tacking back and forth trading sponges. It was hard to see who was ahead but I wanted to avoid them at all costs. I cut behind the islet looking for some favorable wind.

As I came around, there were Whit and Russ. It appeared as if they had finished with the sponges and were going to pick on me. Before I had any time to do anything I was in the middle of a battle. Sponges and paddles were creating a real water fight and I had to come about several times just to retrieve my sponges.

All in all at the end of the battle I was up one sponge and just slightly behind the two of them. I threw one of the sponges hitting Whit. He returned it but missed me forcing him to come around for it. Russ was making a break for it and I would have to see if I could catch him before the turn at the island's end.

Half an hour later, after several more sponge battles and much shouting, we crossed the finish line. Of the eight sailboats, Freedom and I came in third. Whit was first and would get the honor of deciding tomorrow's course. I was in the winner's group of four with Whit, Russ and Susan. In addition to coming first, Whit ended up with only one sponge. I had my usual three!

Freedom took a celebratory jump into the water and swam towards land. He knew there was food waiting for us on land.

As I pulled up to the dock I looked over to the beach and was surprised to see someone whom I would never have expected. The smile was smiling directly at me and I quickly tied up the boat and jumped ashore and into her arms.

She looked at me and before I could say anything she kissed me and gave me the type of long hug I had been missing for years. During a short walk down to the water she explained how she came to be on the island. I had invited her up for the race but she had told me she couldn't get away right then. After I left the islands she had reconsidered and decided to take me up on the offer. Instead of calling, she planned to surprise me and had arranged to use the water taxi from the airport.

"What made you decide to come north?"

"After you left I remembered something and instead of calling I wanted to talk to you in person," the smile said.

"This is much better than a postcard or a call," I agreed.

"I didn't want you to think that I was intentionally misleading you by leaving out important information. I think I may know one of the people you are looking for—a man who flies in and out on a regular basis and stays out on the coral reef islands."

"What makes you think he might have something to do with the case I have been working on?" I asked.

"The last time he was on the island he asked me about farms on the island. He said he was involved with research and wanted to work with farmers who were growing coffee beans. I thought it strange because he didn't strike me as the farming type. He looked as if he should be off running a small criminal operation somewhere," she said.

"Did you give him any answers?"

"I mentioned a family friend who manages one of the largest independent growers on the island and he seemed happy."

"Thanks."

"Is this a private party or can anyone join?" I turned around and saw that Susan had joined us.

"Susan, Suzanne," I said, realizing for the first time the similarity in names as well as their ability to affect my emotions."

"Susan has been looking for real estate in these parts. Suzanne is my special friend from the Caribbean. This is her first visit to Lumsden Island and our part of the world," I explained.

I felt a little awkward but I told myself I didn't have any real reason to squirm.

Susan excused herself and said she would see us later.

We just sat quietly looking out on the Sound. I would have to return south and was afraid I was bringing the case to a head much too close to the smile's home. It was peaceful both here and there and it was going to change very quickly.

A great time was had by all that afternoon and into the evening.

After dinner we all sat around the hot tub on the deck and talked about past parties and how we had all changed in the past few years.

"Most of us have been here for this weekend for at least ten years," I mentioned. "Susan and Suzanne are the only newcomers. Have you ever thought where you will be in another ten or twenty years?"

"We will be right here," Whit answered.

"We could all be here," Suzanne said.

"That would make for an interesting weekend," Susan replied.

"What I am thinking about is that we should plan for a special reunion in twenty years. Let each of us put $1,000 per year into a reunion account and we can meet for an extra special weekend with our earnings."

"Maybe we should just spend some of the money and let the rest accumulate," Susan said.

"And then after twenty or thirty years as we become older the last one around can take the balance of the funds and have a memorial round the world cruise," Whit added.

"I can just see it," I said. "We will be meeting here and planning how to knock off each other. How about a swim through the narrows? Or a midnight walk up island?"

Whit added, "And every time we cook a new meal it will be: What is that almond flavoring? Is it really almonds or is it arsenic? Everyone would be plotting to knock off the rest of the group and be the last one standing. Then he or she would get all the money. Are you sure you want to spend the next twenty years worrying about whether your friends really had your best interests at heart?"

"Okay, maybe that was a bad idea, but I think we should plan a big twenty-year reunion and everyone can keep their money in their own bank account," I finished.

It was still early in the evening as Suzanne and I strolled down past the dock and onto our small sand beach. The sun was just starting to set as we both looked down at Freedom. He was trying to decide between an evening swim or a quick digging exercise. We sat on the sand as he finally decided to dig. Like many tollers he liked playing on the shore. I explained to the smile, "I told you earlier about the tollers' ability to retrieve ducks and other waterfowl but their unique talent is to attract them. They are called tollers because that is what they do. They toll or run along the shore and swim in the water, and to the ducks they look like red foxes. I think they come close because the fox is their enemy and is known to eat their eggs. Perhaps they think with their group they have a chance to drive off the fox. Once they get close, the hunter has a chance to shoot them and the toller swims out to retrieve."

"Impressive, have you ever seen Freedom in action?"

"No, but he is trained and ready to go. And he certainly can retrieve and as you can see, he likes to toll whenever he gets close to the shore."

We watched Freedom in silence. He was doing all the work and getting a good workout. I finally stood up and threw a good-sized log for him to retrieve. After several times having him retrieve it for me, I let him just swim. He paddled around in a circle and every once in a while he splashed the surface snapping at the resultant waterspout.

I was going to ask Suzanne a question but thought better of it. We were enjoying the present and she didn't seem to have any need to talk about our future.

Freedom rejoined us and lay at our feet. I rubbed his ears and he looked up at us with a contented look on his face. Then the moment was broken and Freedom was up sniffing along the shore, off searching for new adventure. Silently we headed back up the path and rejoined the rest of the crew.

Whit had started a fire and the guests appeared to be enjoying a few drinks. Whit asked, "Drinks for either of you?"

The smile said she was okay and I decided I didn't really need a drink. Shortly afterwards we headed off to bed and left the rest to the embers and talk of what they would be doing tomorrow.

"Love must be as much a light as it is a flame."

Thoreau

CHAPTER 27

"There is a tide in the affairs of men,
Which taken at the flood, leads on to fortune;
Omitted, all the voyage of their life is
bound in shallows and in miseries."
Shakespeare - Julius Caesar

I FELL INTO A deep sleep and in the early hours of the morning I started to dream of her. We were on the hammock in front of her Caribbean home. The sun was high in the sky and the music was soft. She was suggesting something I seemed to be in the mood for and for once I wasn't thinking of getting up to get a drink. Perhaps my time with the smile would reduce the need for so much drinking on my part. I hadn't really thought about it but it was easier to get up in the morning when I hadn't spent half the evening downing Scotches. Maybe this was the time I would really be able to reduce my drinking. Maybe...

I awoke with a fast heart. I was throbbing with excitement and not alone. Moonlight cascaded into the room and I could see her straddling me. I had enjoyed some exciting dreams before, but this was the first time I actually had a dream turn into reality.

It was the smile and she looked like she was happy to see me. I was certainly happy, and extremely excited to see and feel her.

"Are you starting without me?"

"Shush. Lie back and enjoy the moment," the smile suggested.

"Don't stop, I'm enjoying the view." And I was, and I had forgotten all about my internal discussion about my drinking habits.

Much later, I felt contented. She looked contented. We both were exhausted. I was glad I still realized the value of a good balanced exercise program. Just enough exercise to allow oneself the ability and interest in good sex. Isn't that what it is all about, or at least what I thought it was all about when starting a new relationship.

I awoke with a start. It was still dark but something had changed. The smile was still beside me but all was not as we had left it a few short hours ago. I quietly left the warmth of the smile's side and walked to the window. Outside the moon was lighting the beach and I could see the dock and boathouse. It took me a minute to realize what had changed. It wasn't my surroundings that had changed, but my resolve to protect the smile from whatever dangers that appeared to be headed our way. Perhaps this is what I had been looking for to lessen the after-effects of the accident. Perhaps I should talk to the smile about it.

I headed back to bed slightly more relaxed, comfortable with my new resolve to see a solution that would include our safety. And I would have to give some more thought to my reducing drinking idea.

The third time I woke up was much different. She was asleep with one arm gently draped over my chest. It was still night and because of clouds the room was dark.

Why was I awake? I usually slept soundly. And certainly after all the afternoon and evening exercise I had no reason to want to wake up early.

I looked over at Freedom. As usual he was sleeping not five feet from the bed, curled up with his tail over his nose. Whatever woke me didn't seem to bother him. I lay back ready to go to sleep.

There it was again. The reason for me awakening from a sound sleep was a strange noise. I couldn't place the sound. A creaking noise but not like a cottage door, more like an old barn door, and we didn't have any of those around here. I shouldn't be surprised to hear different noises tonight. What with all the invited guests who were here today there were an additional four people staying overnight. Whit my brother, the Hamiltons who lived on one of the outer islands and would head back early in the morning, and my first surprise visitor, Susan the mystery sailor.

I got up and decided to get a glass of water while awake and see what was making the noise. While downstairs the noise appeared to be gone. Whatever it was, I couldn't hear it anymore.

I walked outside and down to the dock. I turned around to see Freedom joining me on my nocturnal walk. He was a light sleeper and didn't want to miss anything.

We walked back up the dock and for a short distance along the beach. It was quiet, almost too quiet with all the guests. I looked back at the cottage. All the lights were out, complete darkness and quiet. We headed in.

On the way up the stairs the noise started again. That was strange. Freedom looked at me but didn't show any sign of distress. Whatever it was, it was okay with him.

It wasn't until I was back into my bedroom that I realized what the noise was. It was coming from the spire. Someone had just closed the bookcase entrance. That must be making the noise I had heard. I had never heard the noise from up here because I was always downstairs when I activated the entrance. Whit must be looking for a good book to put him back to sleep.

I cuddled back into Suzanne's back and quickly fell back to the sleep of the contented.

"Sometimes, in a summer morning having taken my accustomed bath, I sat in my sunny doorway from sunrise till noon, rapt in a revery, amidst the pines and hickories and sumachs, in undisturbed solitude and stillness, while the birds sing around or flitted noiseless through the house, until by the sun falling in at my west window, or the noise of some traveller's wagon on the distant highway, I was reminded of the lapse of time. I grew in those seasons like corn in the night, and they were far better than any work of the hands would have been. They were not time subtracted from my life, but so much over and above my usual allowance."

Henry David Thoreau "Walden"

CHAPTER 28

"If one does not know to which port one is sailing, no wind is favorable.
Seneca (the Younger)

AROUND THE BREAKFAST TABLE we were one short. As we sat down for a big early meal Susan had not appeared. The smile reported Susan wasn't in her room so we went ahead without her.

"She must have gone for an early stroll," I suggested.

It wasn't until after we had finished breakfast and washed the dishes that I realized Susan was gone.

Whit and I were down on the dock and I asked, "Whit, did you check all the sailboats last night?"

"Yes, most of them were pulled up on shore and the three that were still on the dock were well tied up."

"Well, it looks like Susan is an early riser. Both she and her Hobie Cat are gone," I said to Whit.

"She didn't say anything to me, but she was talking about looking at more real estate," Whit said. "Perhaps she had an early appointment with a real estate agent."

"You talked to her last night, Whit. What do you think of her?"

"She is interesting, and not what I am used to meeting around here."

"Whit, can you put a new chore on our cottage to-do list? We need to either oil the bookcase door or get a quieter set of hinges. When you were up in the spire late last night it woke me up."

Whit looked at me with a strange look. "I wasn't up there last night."

We turned and ran up the dock, into the cottage and over to the bookcase. I moved the bookcase and quickly bounded up the stairs two steps at a time. I wouldn't have done that if I had spent the previous evening drinking too much.

The room was as I had left it. We hadn't felt any need to lock the room late last night and everyone had been up to see the sunset so they all certainly knew what was here.

Nothing looked out of place but I was still curious as to who had felt the urge to do some late night exploring. My first guess was Susan. She was becoming more and more surprising as time went on. When we met next I would have some new questions for her.

After a few minutes of rummaging through my office stuff I decided I wouldn't be able to get a quick answer to the question of whether anything was missing.

"What do you have up here that would be of interest to any of our guests?" asked Whit. "Start with that and you may find your answer."

"Thanks, brother, do you have your journalistic hat on today? You may be able to help me."

"What can I help you with?"

I explained what I had been working on for the past week. "I think we may get a bite with our email trap but I would like to cover all the bases," I finished.

Whit suggested, "When I am trying to land a difficult interview I always try to get them to try to sell the interview to me. If you can get them working for you and wanting something only you can provide, then you have a real chance of getting something special. When you are simply chasing them, they will be next to impossible to get."

"How would that work with terrorists?" I asked.

"Same concept, ask yourself what they really want and try to provide it, or at least act like you are going to provide it to them. In my limited experience, almost all kooks are looking either for publicity or for someone to agree with their way of thinking. Give them a forum in which they can express their views and you will have them."

"Good idea, Whit."

"We could pretend the New York Times is writing an exposé on the mistakes the FBI is making with local terrorists.

"That part is certainly realistic enough," I agreed. "Just in this one case they have acted like they don't really want to catch them."

Whit continued, "Slant it towards the fact that there is some limited support for the views of this group. Get them to make a comment for the record. Perhaps we can even arrange a meeting with them."

"How would we do that?"

"You mentioned you had contact with one of the university students and he might be willing to give you some additional help."

"Perhaps we can use Stan," Misty suggested. I turned around to see my partner standing in the doorway.

"Great idea, let's see if he has the ability to lead us to the terrorists," I agreed. "By the way, Misty, I never did ask you yesterday, what made you decide to join us?"

"I was sitting at home all alone and doing nothing except mopping around and waiting for a call from Cam. I finally decided I might as well as do something constructive and see if you were making any headway with the terrorists."

"Misty, did you meet Suzanne on the way up to the spire?" I asked. It was getting crowded around here with all the sexual tension and I certainly didn't want Misty to go off half-cocked if I could avoid it.

"If you mean the green eyes Caribbean beauty on your dick, I mean deck. Sorry, Freudian slip," Misty laughed. "Yes I introduced myself as your business associate. She seems nice enough."

"Funny, Misty," I replied. "Seriously, I do have a problem. Now that you are here I'll tell you what Whit and I have been talking about. Someone was searching through the spire and I'd like to find out what they found interesting."

"Now you mention it, I did hear something strange last night," Misty said. "As I drifted off to a great sleep I thought I heard one of you down on the docks near the boathouse. I just assumed you were putting away some of the boating equipment and didn't think anything more about it."

I needed to head over to the boathouse. It couldn't wait. Whit joined me.

> *"If a man does not keep pace with his companions, perhaps it is because he hears a different drummer."*
>
> *Thoreau*

CHAPTER 29

First Rule of Sailing: Keep the ocean out of the boat.

AN INTERESTING STORY—OUR FAMILY boathouse. It was built by our Grandfather, the first Whit, known as Alex to many. He was a builder by trade but his real occupation was rum-running and that was how we came to afford a whole island in the middle of what was then nowhere. Whit didn't like the water, in fact he was afraid of it, but he knew an opportunity when it presented itself. When the American government brought in prohibition in 1917, and finally started enforcing it in 1920, Whit saw a huge opportunity and he wasn't prepared to let a little fear of the water step in his way. Or let his wife Mamie stop him. And that must have made for some interesting dinner table conversations because she was the local head of the temperance movement. So he got in the rum-running trade.

Just so you know, he wasn't a criminal. In Canada there was nothing illegal with loading your boat with booze and heading out for an afternoon or early, real early cruise down the coast. Where the illegal part came in was if he was caught by the American Coast Guard. And he never was, so what he did was okay. Or at least so my brother and I say. Father never did talk about what his father did but it was common knowledge around here when we were growing up.

The boathouse—yes, the boathouse was built to service the family business and it is probably the best example of a classic cottage boathouse this side of the Rocky Mountains. It was built like the ones he had known on the eastern seaboard. Rough-hewn with exposed rafters, the boathouse had the accumulation of our generations of boaters. As I swung the heavy fir doors open I could see the early sailboats high above. The walls were lined with mostly obsolete boating equipment—some real old life jackets, paddles, oars and an assortment of running gear. There was a colorful display of nautical signal flags, which hung from an almost forgotten mast.

I walked past the sunfish sailboats to the other side where *Rum-Runner* was kept when it was not in the water. I can remember going for a quick ride with Grandfather. If he was in a good mood he would talk about his days on the water.

I needed to check to see if everything was as I had left it. I reached down over the gunnels and into a place I knew like the back of my hand. Yes, it was there. Whatever they had been looking for last night, they were not successful in finding *The Book*.

"John, what are you doing?" I jumped as Whit came alongside me. I looked at him and one of those generational shifts happened. Just for a second I could see our father. He would have loved to be here for the weekend. He always enjoyed family get-togethers and nothing pleased him more than seeing the two of us working on a common problem.

"I didn't hear you. I was just thinking about last night and wondering what they were looking for," I told him. "I got to thinking about Grandfather and what he told us about his book and what it meant. I just wanted to make sure it was still here."

"You know we have never been able to figure out what his code was and what he might have stashed out there," Whit said.

Years ago after Grandfather Whit had died and we inherited *The Book* we spent a summer on the water up and down the coast looking for what we assumed was a hidden treasure trove. There had been a rumor Grandfather had made a lot of money during prohibition and not all of it had made it into the local bank. When we first saw *The Book* with all of its journal entries for the runs down the coast we thought we could finally solve the mystery. Grandfather had admitted he had a couple of surprises for us but he always said we would have to find them for ourselves.

"I can still remember that summer with fond memories," Whit reminisced.

"Yes, and I almost wonder if the treasure wasn't just the time we spent together searching. If it wasn't for the clear note mentioning stashing one of his boats with a full load of Canadian rye and the proceeds of a month's worth of runs, we wouldn't have started the search," I said.

"If you ever get any new ideas I can always spare a couple of days on the water," Whit replied.

We headed back to the cottage and joined the others for an early drink on the dock. I made a pitcher of iced tea and surprised myself by staying with the tea while the smile and I watched the rest of the day float by. I don't think any of us did anything productive but when I think back on the day it brings fond memories to mind. Why is it when you are relaxing with friends on a hot summer day you never really need a goal. We drifted into a friendly series of bocce ball games and finally headed up to the cottage for dinner.

I don't remember any of the dinner conversation but I do remember that no one talked about work.

> "I have spent many an hour, when I was younger, floating over its surface… having paddled my boat to the middle, and lying on my back across the seats, in a summer forenoon, dreaming awake, until I was aroused by the boat touching the sand, and I arose to see what shore my fates had impelled me to; days when idleness was the most attractive and productive industry."
>
> Thoreau

CHAPTER 30

"Sunset and evening star,
And one clear call for me!
And may there be no moaning of the bar,
When I put out to sea,
But such a tide as moving seems asleep,
Too full for sound and foam,
When that which drew from out the boundless deep
Turns again home.
Twilight and evening bell,
And after that the dark!
And may there be no sadness of farewell,
When I embark;
For though from out our bourne of Time and Place
The flood may bear me far,
I hope to see my Pilot face to face
When I have crossed the bar."

Alfred, Lord Tennyson

WE WERE UP EARLY and at Sea-Tac airport before noon. I had decided to join the smile on the way back to the BVIs.

We didn't talk much but I guess we didn't really feel the need for talk. I think both of us realized we had a special relationship. I just don't think we were ready to verbalize exactly what that relationship was or where it was headed. All I knew for sure was that we were headed for her hammock and a few relaxing days in the sun. Or at least that was what I had in mind.

After arriving in Tortola we spent a short evening on her veranda and then retired to the hammock.

Early the next morning we got up with good intentions of spending the whole day in the water. We had a short swim and then the hammock beckoned. It turned into most of the day in the hammock and by the time I remembered my original plans it was well after lunch.

I headed into the bank again. Why, I don't know but I thought as long as I was here I had better see if there had been any further action in the terrorists' bank account. I couldn't get out of my mind the nagging thought I was missing an important part of the case.

"Good to see you again, Mr. Pride," my friendly bank manager greeted me.

"Thanks for seeing me on such short notice, Ben. I am still interested in that account and wondered if it has had any further activity."

"You must have a crystal ball. You just missed the owner of the account. I just got off the phone from informing the FBI of the activity," Ben replied.

"What happened?"

"When we opened this morning a gentleman was waiting for me. He wanted to see his safety deposit box and then he made a small withdrawal, or at least a small withdrawal in terms of the money in that account. He withdrew $10,000."

"Thanks for the info," I said as I got up.

On the way out the door, thinking this was still a major unknown but probably best left to the FBI, I turned around as Ben started to say something. "There was something unusual. I made the usual notation to the FBI and within minutes they were on the phone with questions."

"What were they interested in?" I asked.

"They were insistent I had given the money to an unauthorized individual. I explained our procedure of needing an account number and then a confirming password," Ben explained.

"No passport or other ID?" I was surprised.

"No, as I explained to the FBI we never ask for ID. He seemed to think we should have and in fact it seems strange that he was so insistent we had made a mistake. Although I had never met the owner of the account he had the required info to gain access," Ben continued. "Then he wanted to know what the account holder looked like."

"How did you describe him?"

"He looked like an out of country businessman just down for the day or two. His only distinguishing characteristic was that he had a slight limp."

I strolled down the almost deserted beach and watched the last tourists heading home. I could see a couple of racing canoes out beyond the breaking surf and thought about my last big canoe race. Whit and I had joined several of the locals to put on a good show. We almost won.

I was under the boardwalk. To the north I could see the surfers, to the south miles of deserted beach. And straight ahead were the timbers of the boardwalk. It was relatively quiet here. Other than the breaking waves I was alone with my thoughts. Where I had expected more people even at this late time in the afternoon, I was now confronted with the fear I was vulnerable and if I met our 'friend' I would be in a position of weakness.

Three more steps and a real feeling of being alone, seeing nothing ahead I retraced my steps and a few minutes later in the warmth of the Caribbean sun I thought my feelings of threat had been unjustified.

As I reached the cottage I could see the lights were out and although the smile was not expecting me until later, I thought she would be home by now.

"Hello, anyone at home," I called.

What was I thinking about?—the sun was about to set and a cold beer was calling me, and all I could think about was work. Time to put the world's troubles aside and let the soothing evening pleasures work their magic on me.

I thought I would start on dinner and be ready with a drink for the smile when she returned. As I entered the cottage I was thinking of next steps, next steps in both the case and in our relationship. Surprised, I realized the smile was in the cottage. I could hear her rustling around in her bedroom. I called out her name and moved towards the dark room.

Barrel-chested, dark and angry she headed straight for me. Actually I could tell quickly he wasn't a she and certainly not my smile. I could see I would have little chance in a fair fight and he didn't look like he was interested in a long discussion. As a matter of fact I wasn't even sure he was capable of a long discussion.

I turned, looking like I was going to flee, and as he lunged at me with the metal bar, I turned around and before he knew what was happening I cold cocked him in the stomach and then I got out of there.

He wasn't as fast as I am and I could see I would be able to make it out of the cottage as long as I didn't slip and fall.

I slipped and fell.

Much later the doctor was explaining something to me. It took several times but I finally understood him to say fourteen, not fifteen and certainly not any less than fourteen. That is what my new friend, the doctor, told me. My attacker's fists had hit me fourteen times; he had mapped them out on my aching body. I watched as the doctor pointed out what he was sure happened. He explained the punches to my kidney, my chest, and the side of my face. After the explanation the only thing I was completely sure of was that I had been beaten up and I was still in a lot of pain. At least I could feel the pain.

This was starting to become a painful habit. One that I was prepared to quit at any time.

"You will need to stay here for observation for at least two days." My friend, the doctor, was explaining his plans for my future.

"Thanks for the opinion but I am ready to hit the road, places to go and people to see," I thought. When he left the room I decided to head out before anyone else had suggestions for my foreseeable future. The one thing I was sure of was that staying in the hospital would not get me any closer to a solution and I was not sure if I was really safe here. Getting dressed was easier said than done. Every step of the way was painful; it felt like stabbing knives every time I moved. After several tries at dressing I finally got myself together. At least the brain fog was gone, replaced by all the new pain, but now my mind was far from clear. I almost wanted the fog to return. At least I knew what it was all about—the uncertainty over my future. This new pain was unasked for, and not needed, but it might help me focus on what I really needed to do.

Without signing myself out, I slipped out of the hospital. I was in no shape to argue with anyone over my physical health, never mind my mental health. I knew I needed rest but I didn't see that occurring while the case was weighing down on my mental state.

> *"The trouble is not in dying for a friend, but in finding a friend worth dying for."*
>
> *Mark Twain*

CHAPTER 31

"For the truth is that I already know as much about my fate as I need to know. The day will come when I will die. So the only matter of consequence before me is what I will do with my allotted time. I can remain on shore, paralyzed with fear, or I can raise my sails and dip and soar in the breeze."

Richard Bode – First You Have to Row a Little Boat

"WHAT HAPPENED TO YOU?" Misty asked over the phone.

"I am not sure but I do know that we are getting close to something." The smile was attending to my injuries while I tried to marshal some resources. The pain hadn't subsided at all but at least I was getting some attention.

"I am staying down here until I find out what is happening. I'll try to get the local police force to get working on the scene and if the FBI finally comes around to our idea we might be able to get some traction in this case."

"Good luck, John. I'll be working with Blake," Misty said. "He still believes in you and the last thing he said before I called you was that he thinks he may be able to get some new resources from the FBI."

"See if he can find anyone local who might be able to help."

"Will do, Pride. Now try to get some rest."

I drifted back to sleep—the sleep of the wounded. It was short and when I awoke the smile was cooling my forehead with a damp facecloth. That felt good, but it was the only part of my body I was having good thoughts about.

"Why don't you head back to the States?"

"I can't do that until I find out who was in your cottage last night. I am sure it has something to do with the case and not just a simple house break-in that went wrong."

An hour later I was seated at the bank again. This time joining us was the local police with a composite sketch of the person who made the withdrawal. "Sorry, I can't identify anyone. The only thing I know is that someone was inside the cottage and whoever that was gave me a real beating."

"Well, for what it's worth, we have a positive identification from a couple of workers at the next cottage," the officer stated. "They saw the same person hanging around the beach several hours before your attack. We will keep a watch out on the islands for him. We have posted his picture at the airport and if he tries to leave we should be able to detain him."

I asked, "What do you know about him?"

"He is an unknown to us but we will try to get a handle on him in the next few days."

"What can I do? I would really like to understand his involvement. Can you let me know if you find anything?"

"Of course, Pride, but don't expect miracles."

I headed back to the smile's beach and dialed a number. "Have you had any luck tracking the calls?" I asked Misty anxiously. I was waiting for the smile to arrive. I wanted to ensure she was out of harm's way while we tracked the terrorists. Standing on the smile's beach talking to Misty was not going to get her protection. I had to get a handle on how to get some local support.

"No, and I think you should be back here," Misty replied.

"Fine, I'll rejoin you in my old life. Talk to you tomorrow."

Everyone seemed to want me to leave the islands.

The smile came down the beach and we were in each other's arms, kissing.

She led me to the hammock. I started to ease myself in and the pain of a hundred knives hit my back. I stood back up and the pain reduced marginally. She came around behind me and helped ease me into the hammock. That felt better.

"Thanks, I didn't think this would hurt as much as it does."

"Just relax." She left me for a few minutes and when she returned she had a couple of drinks and a big smile. "Is it too early for a drink?"

"No, and I don't think I have had enough painkillers to worry about a reaction."

"I told you I would be back." We were lying on her hammock and I was holding her tightly, as if I thought she would leave any moment.

"I knew you would return to continue your dream." The smile looked into my eyes.

"I just headed down to the bank to find out if they knew anything. The locals have a good idea what the terrorist looks like but it sure doesn't look anything like the character who attacked me last night. I don't feel right leaving you alone."

"I won't be alone. My brother is moving in until things settle down. You are needed stateside and besides you will never be able to solve this mystery lying around my hammock, as much as I'd like you to stay here," the smile stated.

The drink seemed to be doing its magic. The pain's edge was reducing and as I drifted into sleep I could hear her saying, "Just relax and let me take care of you…"

"Life isn't about finding yourself; it's about creating yourself. So live the life you imagined."

Thoreau

The dream was different tonight. The focus was there but something had changed. I was still in Saint John but I knew my mind's goal had changed. Family was in my future but it had shifted. I could see the highlands and my youth. I could see my Mum and Dad. But I could also see a different future. It was beside me, and as I looked around I realized I was pain free. The sun was up and I was strolling with a young lady. Instantly I knew who she was—my future wife, the mother of our children, all of this and we had just met. Emotions poured over me, no brain fog here.

Mary looked up at me. "Tell me more about your adventures, Alex." We had spent a couple of afternoons together and I had obviously been regaling her with some version of my heroic times on the high seas. We had spent most of the time talking. She told me of her father, Benjamin Bailey, born in England who came to the Americas and then up to New Brunswick as a loyalist in 1783. The family had been part of the big migration after the American War of Independence. Her mother, Susanna, was the daughter of local Judge Wanty and I soon learned, the sister of Benjamin Wanty who was in the British Navy. I realized that this family was one that would not take kindly to someone running from naval service. When I met them I would have to have a good story in hand. And meet them I would, according to Mary's plans. Although we had said little, our thoughts were apparent in our eyes. We both knew that there was a future, and I realized that my future was changing. No longer was the immediate draw of Scotland the most important goal. Now I needed to reinvent myself and become part of the new wilderness in this new country. I thought that this might be a more important goal for us. And us it was, because now I could see a real future, not just some vague idea of returning home to...to what?... that really was the question. If I returned I wanted to be returning with an accomplishment, and not just returning home with a price on my head always wondering whether the next day would be my last day of freedom. I could see a future working the land, bringing up children and becoming someone whom my relatives would respect.

All of this passed so fast, as fast as the time in which Mary took to tell me of her past, and tell me of her present. Now I could see my future, but not the next few years, now I could see my present situation. As we sat on the banks of the Saint John River I could clearly see myself lying in that hammock in the Caribbean. I knew that the next step would take me directly home to the smile or it would lead back to an uncertain future in the highlands. That alternative future would not be my remembered past, but would be some completely new future.

She was talking on, and I listened with a new understanding. She was describing her home farther north on Grand Lake in Queen County. Mary was just visiting her mother's family in Saint John and would soon be travelling up river with a couple of her brothers.

I looked at her, and felt a time shift. I knew that this was what was meant to happen. She must have realized my feelings because she stopped in mid sentence, "What, what are you thinking, Alex?"

I reached for her hand and said, "Please call me Edward."

"He clambered aboard the rocking boat while the waves
like the bright fins of fabulous fish kept slapping
the planks of the dock.
The rich water rewarded him as he climbed in the sail,
and away in the cloak of the gale he wrapped his thanks
as trim as a clock
geared, and unhampered as halyards, by the trim hand
held and felt."

A G Bailey "North West Passage"

CHAPTER 32

"Monsanto should not have to vouchsafe the safety of biotech food. Our interest is in selling as much of it as possible. Assuring its safety is the F.D.A.'s [Food and Drug Administration] job."

Phil Angell
Monsanto's director of corporate communications
Interview with the New York Times Sunday Magazine

THE NEXT DAY I was headed back to Seattle, back almost two centuries from the Saint John riverbank. Whatever happened in 1813, I knew that it had led to today. Whatever was happening now I would be able to deal with. No movement from the FBI. No missing attacker. No closer to the terrorists. It was time for me to take some action.

I had arranged to meet Misty on the dock and she was captaining the Cabo back to the island while I nursed my injuries. As I relaxed and let her get underway I could see Mount Olympus almost eight thousand feet above me. The snow-covered top was on my right and I remembered a late summer climb. I could also see Mount Rainier at over fourteen thousand feet. It was eighty-seven miles from Seattle and was the highest volcanic peak in the Cascades. My mind was drifting. It must be the painkillers. Remind me to get off them as soon as possible. Scotch was one thing but the last crutch I needed was some prescription drug.

Back to the mountains, what was I thinking? Oh yeah, the hiking trip with Whit just after high school. We had hiked all the way along the mountain range from Mount Garibaldi in British Columbia to Lassen Peak in California. I can still remember passing Mount Saint Helens fifty miles southwest of Mount Rainier. The 1980 eruption was still visible and I can remember Whit giving me the details, "…composite volcano made from sluggish, intermittent lava flows and explosive eruptions of ash and rock."

Eruptions—then back to the future, or at least back to the present with Misty talking at me.

"John, are you sure we should be involved in this case anymore?" Misty sounded more than just concerned.

"You know as well as I do that without our input this case would still be at the starting gate. We need to stay ahead of everyone."

"What are we going to do next? Our so-called friends in the FBI have shown no interest in following our lead and I'm not sure we can solve it on our own."

"Misty, I know you want to help but with your work on the personals case I'm not sure you have any energy to spare."

"Things are on hold until the fraudsters make their next move. I'm not sure if anyone wants me to be involved anymore. I guess we are both on the outside looking in," Misty said.

"So, it is just the two of us against the world. Maybe we can do something to find the terrorists. I was just thinking about eruptions and explosions. I still think the money trail will lead us to the terrorists. Let's leave these explosions to the FBI."

"By the way," Misty said. "Whit's article appeared in the New York Times and was syndicated out here. This is the most recent Seattle newspaper."

I quickly read Whit's words. Great, if anything would get the FBI even madder at me this would be it. *A reliable source tells this journalist that the FBI has made several major errors in its investigation. They are not giving any serious weight to the theory that these acts are just the beginning of a larger threat. In fact the FBI appears to think the organization which is behind the terrorists activities is just a small band of disorganized thugs.* Reading further down the page I came to the quote from our local member, Stan, *"A Seattle student is quoted as saying that even without publicity the group will not fade away. He believed they posed a major threat and it was their way of attracting students and people interested in fringe causes. In fact his interest in maintaining any connection to the group was extinguished with the loss of life but he believed many new people would be attracted to them."*

"Strong words," I said.

"Did you get down to the part about this being a new-wave terrorist group—one with a cause which many North Americans may support?"

"What a load of bunk," I replied. "But at least that should get some response."

I finished the article. The thrust of the piece was that the FBI was not giving the threat sufficient priority. They certainly weren't putting many agents into the field to solve the case. One of the more interesting quotes Whit had found was from my old FBI friend Dave, *We at the Federal Bureau of Investigation believe the case is almost closed. The immediate threat has been dealt with and we are mopping up the rest of the team. We believe that there is no threat to the American public.*

Talk about minimizing the threat. I thought after 9/11 the US government understood the need for not underestimating terrorists. Perhaps this was just Dave and not the whole FBI.

"John, I know not everyone in the FBI believes this threat is over. My contacts are taking it very seriously."

"What are we going to do next?"

"I'll call Whit and see if he has received any feedback." We were arriving back on Lumsden Island and I would have to maneuver my way up the dock and into the cottage.

"Misty, can you give me a hand getting back on firm ground? I am starting to feel a little dizzy with all the motion."

"Come with me sailor." She helped support me as we walked up the dock and back on the island. I could still feel the punches from yesterday but at least I would be resting at home.

Finally back in the spire and seated at my desk, I called Whit.

"Sorry to hear about the attack on you," Whit was saying. "Are you sure you want to keep the pressure up?"

"Of course, when have you ever known us to quit when the going got hard?"

"Good point and it looks like I wouldn't be able to stop what we started. Last night I received a mysterious call from someone claiming to be a part of the group. He said I had some good points in the article but I was missing the big picture. He claimed that they weren't the real terrorists. It was those who were in charge of world corporate domination. He sounded like a real brainwasher. He was definitely not one of the meek recruits. He was a real believer and wanted to make me one. He also tried to sell me a bill of goods by saying someone was framing them. He claimed they haven't been involved in the actual bombings."

"Where do you go from here?" I asked.

"My editor wants me to do an immediate follow-up piece this weekend and I think we may be able to set up a meeting with the guy I spoke to on the phone."

We discussed what we would do in the case of actually setting up a meeting and then I left it to Whit to get on with the hard work.

Misty and I spent the afternoon trying to get me to do some work. I finally took myself off the painkillers and my brain started to clear. It was later in the evening when I was finally starting to think about the case again. Even with a meeting we would not be able to crack the case by ourselves. And bringing in the FBI at this point would just scare off our only good lead. We would have to work smart and see if we could leverage the meeting into something that we could actually use to stop the group.

"What are you thinking about, John?"

"I'm worried about bringing my brother into this case. He's anxious to help but I'm not sure if he can really deal with meeting this contact face to face."

"He deals with contacts all the time and I am sure you will provide any needed protection," Misty said.

"That's not what I'm worried about; it's just that we've never worked together off the island. I'm not sure we will be able to work together."

"The two of you will get along well together. Put your energy into planning our next steps."

"Thanks Misty—you work on your contacts with the Seattle police and I will try to concentrate on how to solve this case. Try to find out if they have any new leads which may help us."

Two hours later and Misty had come up with nothing. I, on the other hand, had been productive. "I think I can work with Whit. I now have a good idea about how to use our work with the FBI to work to our advantage with this terrorism group."

"Well, I hope your idea is better than my lack of success with my old cop buddies."

"It is indeed, and by the way why are your old buddies not your buddies?"

Misty gave me a stern look. "John, we have had this conversation twenty times. My past is in the past, and talking about it is not going to change it."

"I know but that doesn't mean I don't want to fix it for you."

"Thanks, I appreciate your concern but I still don't want to discuss it. I tried to find someone who knew something about the Starbucks problem but all I got was snide comments about joining them for a coffee and a donut or is that coke and a donut. Now what is your idea?"

"I thought you would never ask," I replied. "This is brilliant if you ask me, and since you did ask me, here it is. I think that although the FBI is discounting the seriousness of the Starbucks problem, we can use the overall heightened awareness of terrorism to work to our advantage. By publicizing the threat and using the newspaper to cover our story we might be able to flush out more of the terrorists. If we can keep them talking perhaps that will keep them away from action."

"So what exactly do you have in mind?"

"I think Whit can take the information we are getting from this Washington-based terrorist group and imply through a news article that the FBI are discounting the seriousness of their threats. That could help us flush out the real terrorists."

The next morning Whit called. "It is arranged and I will be in Seattle early tomorrow."

I still had my reservations about the meeting but kept them to myself. "It sounds like he is going to make you travel to see him."

"Yes, and he is very uptight about security. He went into details about where we would meet. When I mentioned that my brother was joining us he didn't have a problem with it."

I arrived at Sea-Tac airport first and met Whit's flight.

"Thanks for coming, John. Together the two of us can really have a chance to solve this."

My concerns were starting to disappear. "I wouldn't miss this for the world," I replied. "This is where we prove Dave is really wrong. And strike one for the good guys."

The deal was to head south until we reached Narada Falls along the road between Longmire and Paradise. We would get a call then.

We drove south taking the curves fast, probably too fast, but after the past week I needed a release from the pressures of the case. I replayed the last few days and tried to see if there was anything I should have done differently. After several minutes of thoughtful thinking, okay maybe not thoughtful but at least half-hearted academic, the only improvement I could come up with was a larger team. That made sense and I would need to ensure more resources were available to us before going ahead. How we would persuade the FBI that we were part of the solution I didn't know, but that would come later.

We passed Paradise River and I could see it cascading over a rocky ledge. I remember taking the short but steep trail to the bottom of the falls for a breathtaking view. From there you could see Mount Rainier and Nisqually Glacier with its icefall jumble of truck sized ice blocks. In happier times I recollected having afternoon tea in the Paradise Inn. It was a massive wooden lodge and the huge lobby had peeled log-ceiling beams. We had spent many an afternoon enjoying the view near one of the two opposing stone fireplaces.

We got the call to watch out for a red Ford Mustang. We were pulled over to the side of the road waiting. Three sets of car lights passed before the car came into view. I knew it was our man by the way he was driving. If I didn't know better I would have thought that he had no cares in the world. He was driving slowly, almost too slow and certainly slowly enough to warrant a second look by any cop driving by.

We pulled out behind him and once he saw me, his pace picked up. Minutes later we were both doing more than sixty mph and on this road that seemed way too fast.

I didn't know what bothered me more—the fact we were driving dangerously on this narrow, winding road or the fact I didn't seem to care anymore.

We headed up the mountain, expecting to meet the enemy anytime. Whit looked over at me and although no words passed we both knew what the other was thinking.

This was war, or at least our small version of it. It was here we would meet our enemy.

"Watch out for signs he has reinforcements up here," Whit said.

"I haven't seen any signs of civilization since we left the woods," I replied. "We will need to think about what we are going to tell the FBI after we leave him. You aren't expecting to take him on by ourselves."

He just stared at me.

Minutes later we came out in a clearing. The trees had thinned out and we were now surrounded on both sides of the road by a massive boulder field. I could see an old cabin in the distance. It looked like a miner's cabin and I could see the remains of what were probably chicken pens. The other car was parked beside the cabin. We rolled to a stop and got out.

Our agreement was to come without weapons or tape recorder. He said once we parked our car he would join us. We didn't know where he was or where we were supposed to walk to. We didn't have to wait long.

Behind us his voice rang out loud and clear. "Over here." I wasn't expecting him to be behind us. We turned and noticed he must have been there all along. He was standing beside one of the large boulders dressed head to foot in army fatigues. A large menacing gun was slung over his left shoulder and he had military looking things hanging from his belt.

As we walked over to join him I glanced around but I could see no one else. Maybe it was just the three of us. Whit looked at me with that confident look he gets when he is ready for a situation. I felt somewhat less confident and was starting to get second thoughts. Why did I always seem to be the one who was put into harm's way?

Whit started the dialogue. "Thanks for agreeing to meet us. As you know I am interested in finding out as much as I can about the real reasons for your group's actions."

"The only reason I agreed to meet you was that it looks like you have an almost balanced viewpoint about GMO food and the problems that global corporations are forcing on us."

"The only thing I don't agree with is your use of violence," Whit said.

"We didn't have anything to do with the explosions. We certainly never planned to hurt anyone and we still don't think of ourselves as terrorists. Someone else outside our group is using our name."

"Can you explain what you think you can achieve now?" Whit asked.

"We have been trying to make a difference and ensure that companies take a second look before they jump into the GMO marketplace. We were trying to add a prohibitive barrier to entry for any new companies," our terrorist said trying to justify the unjustifiable.

"Why are you going after the universities? What do think you can achieve by blackmailing them?" Whit asked.

"We aren't blackmailing them. We are just trying to get them to see our viewpoints."

"Do you call terrorist activities viewpoints?"

"I tried to explain that we didn't start out that way. It was only after we didn't get any response from our demands."

"And are you going to continue with the bombs?"

"Unfortunately we are on that path and it looks like we will continue to press our views. The explosions are one way to generate publicity. And it works. Look at yourself. If the explosions hadn't occurred, your newspaper would never have covered this issue."

"We are never going to agree," I joined in.

"You are right but at least we are trying to do something about the worsening food supply situation."

"If it is really publicity and change that you are after, why did you extort so much money from the universities?" I asked.

"We needed cash to fund our operations," he said.

"Millions? Don't you think you could have raised money some other way?

"Millions! All we received was a few thousands. And even that was a fluke. We never intended to go after the universities for cash."

I couldn't hold my cool any longer. "I saw your bank account. More than two million dollars and still climbing, so don't try to justify your actions when it looks like all you are is an ordinary terrorist who is looking for a cause that gives you some credibility."

"What are you talking about?"

I looked at Whit. He didn't know everything I knew about the BVIs bank account. I had something only the extortionist would know about.

"Why did you open an offshore account?"

"Offshore, I can't move offshore. I can't even get a passport because of my previous legal problems."

I decided not to mention my attack. If they really didn't have anything to do with the BVIs account then they probably weren't the ones behind my injuries. I was starting to see that we were missing even more pieces.

"So what do you want from us?"

He seemed to relax, but I noticed he was still carrying his gun, "We just want to set the record straight. We want the public to know we are not the bad guys. We are only trying to get our message out about what the universities are researching. And we want everyone to know they are working for the big multinationals."

Whit looked at him. "So how does the violence come into it? That is what we really want to stop."

"The only thing I can say is that although we didn't start the violence, we do appreciate the media attention. Perhaps someone who has been watching us is trying to give us a bad reputation."

I asked, "So if you are against violence, why the fatigues and gun?"

"That is just to keep you honest. I didn't know if you would come armed and ready to attack me."

Whit asked again, "So you really didn't have anything to do with what happened at the university or at Starbucks?"

"No, and I can see that whatever happens we are not going to be able to change the minds of the university if we are associated with the violence. We promised violence but never planned on actually carrying through with our threats. I can't promise that we are going to melt away but I do believe we can achieve our goals without the use of bombs."

"Thanks for meeting with us. You haven't answered all our questions but at least we now have a better idea of what you are about." Whit gave me a meaningful look and I decided not to say anything more.

Later, on the drive back to Seattle I told Whit I believed our young misguided terrorist about the money. "He was really surprised when we mentioned the amount of money in the account. I don't think he could have fooled us on that detail."

"I agree," Whit nodded. "But where does that put us? If they aren't behind the real extortion perhaps there is some truth to what he is saying."

"It is just one more mystery to add to an already trying case. And we are not even supposed to be involved anymore."

"I thoroughly disapprove of duels. If a man should challenge me, I would take him kindly and forgivingly by the hand and lead him to a quiet place and kill him."

Mark Twain

CHAPTER 33

"Rowing harder doesn't help if the boat is headed in the wrong direction."

Kenichi Ohmae

WE WERE SITTING ON the deck reviewing the day. I remembered back to the sunny summer day when my Father and I built the new deck. We called it the new deck because it replaced the original one built by Grandfather. Looking back now I can see that the hard work that weekend was what I had needed to take my mind off my troubles. Working with Father, stopping only when Mum brought up lunch or joined us for a beer, allowed me to refocus my life. Now if we could just focus again and develop a real plan. I explained what Misty and I had discussed. "Perhaps we can use your article as a way to flush out the real terrorists. Write that we met one of the terrorists and explain why we don't think they are really worth worrying about. If it looks like someone is impersonating them we may get them to make a move."

That was our plan and Whit had agreed to send me his draft article later in the day. But before that happened, something changed our plans. And when I say changed, I mean really changed. We never could have foreseen the completely different course our investigation would take.

The phone rang. "Pride, I am coming for you."

I quickly realized my caller expected me to respond to his threat. "It sounds like you know me."

"I understand you are trying to find out about our organization. We want you to stop immediately. In fact we demand you drop all connections with us or Starbucks. We are only interested in having our demands met."

"What is it that you really want?" I asked the voice.

"We want Starbucks to recognize that we are serious and we want them to agree to pay us now."

I looked across to Whit and could see he was hanging on my every word. "And how do you think I can help you?"

"We understand that you have been talking to Starbucks and may be able to talk some sense into them."

"I don't think my kind of sense would mean much to your group."

"Pass on this message—they have two days to meet our demands and then we act." With that the line went dead.

"Whit, I think things are starting to unravel in their group and I'm not sure how we can take advantage of it," I said.

"All I can think of is that we have a fractured terrorist group," Whit replied.

"Perhaps we can leverage the fact the FBI is ready to move."

We spent the afternoon talking to Poindexter at Starbucks. He wasn't keen on meeting with the terrorists but he did want to ensure the violence stopped. Finally he agreed to let us set up a meeting and use his name to get some action. It would be a step in the right direction.

I called Dave, my old friend from the FBI who wanted us to have nothing more to do with the terrorists.

"Dave, John Pride in Seattle."

"I hope this doesn't have anything to do with our friends."

"Afraid so, but I think I can get out of your hair forever." I tried to promise.

"What is it?"

"The terrorists have made contact with me again and it looks like they are in a hurry to take action."

"And what does that have to do with you? And why should we be talking to you again?" Dave demanded.

"They want me to arrange a meeting between a couple of them and someone from Starbucks. They intend to fulfill their threats if they don't receive some money soon."

We talked about what was needed and I volunteered the use of *Rum-*

Runner. Dave agreed to meet the next day and I emailed the terrorist contact. He wasn't happy I was still involved but he certainly didn't seem to want to see anything happen without his involvement. Later that night I received a call inviting us to a meet out in the Sound.

The next morning Dave, Misty and I were onboard running hard out in the Sound. This was not the day to be out on the ocean but we had a meeting to complete. *Rum-Runner* was taking the waves head on and I knew my passengers would not be able to take much more of the pounding. They were below and couldn't see the waves. As much as I wanted to get them up above, I knew the benefits of being inside out of the weather outweighed the benefit of having their stomachs know when we were going up and down.

An hour later when I was sure the worst of the storm was past, I called out for Misty and Dave to join me. Misty looked okay but Dave definitely had a green tinge to his face.

"Dave is ready for land," Misty said.

"I'll be putting ashore in a few minutes and I think we have arrived first."

"No one could have beaten us in this storm. Now we can implement The Plan," Dave added.

"The Plan?" I asked looking at the two of them.

"While you where pretending to be Captain Bligh, we developed an excellent way to ensure the outcome we need," Misty volunteered. "Because Dave is still under the weather I'll explain it to you."

Several minutes later we arrived at the dock and I felt we at least had a good chance of achieving our goals. Tied up and sheltered by the lea of the island *Rum-Runner* looked protected as we hiked inland.

"Watch your step," I cautioned. "The way will be slippery and it will be awhile before we can change into dry clothes if you slip."

"We are going to wait up ahead until we hear from Seattle and know for sure that the boys are on their way," Misty said. "The last thing we want to do is barge into a problem and not have backup on the way."

It was still raining. I felt dry but I knew it was just a matter of time before we started to get clammy.

"Hold up while I contact Seattle again," Misty said.

After her call we headed to the top of the outcropping and found a dry place to sit and watch the cabin in the next bay. We knew if someone came up today, they would be approaching from the other end of the island and wouldn't see our boat.

I could see the front deck and the approach all the way down to the small rickety wooden dock. Last night Misty's team had secured listening devices throughout the cabin and now with our great line of sight and good headphones we would be able to see and hear what happened in the cabin.

Things started to happen much faster than any of us had anticipated. When they arrived it was in two boats, not the one we had planned for. And there were eight of them, more than the three or four we had been expecting.

"Does this change anything?" I asked.

"Not really," Dave replied. "But it emphasizes the fact we will have to wait for reinforcements before we take any direct action."

We had been listening to the group for about thirty minutes when we heard, "Chicago has lost control of what is happening on the West Coast and I don't like it."

"What are you going to do about it?"

"It's not what I'm going to do that is important, but what we have to do to protect ourselves. I don't think anyone else has our best interests at heart and I'm sure there are going to be some serious problems for most of us in the coming days and weeks."

"Okay, let's concentrate on how to get what we want. It appears as if someone has been using our somewhat less than good name as a cover for some even nastier business. And we are getting the blame for it."

Misty started to move closer to the cabin and Dave ran down the slope to join her. I stayed with the communications center and the relative dryness under the trees. Someone needed to be up here dry when the reinforcements arrived.

"John, I'm going to see if I can see into the back of the cabin," Misty checked in.

"Dave, back me up."

I continued to monitor the radio. "We picked a good night for this. At least no one else will be out on the water. We should pick our destination and then quickly get the explosives planted."

"I thought we were in this to change the way Starbucks brewed their coffee. Now it appears like our group is just out for the money."

"You know that is not true. It is the other group that has been extorting money. But that obviously takes away from any public sympathy we may have gathered. We are being tied into the university bombing and deaths. Now we just have to make a last statement and hope we get some good from the whole exercise."

"I would like to suggest we all lie low for a couple of years after tonight is finished. I for one don't want to end up doing hard time in jail for someone else's deeds."

"We'll all second that. Now are we agreed? One last communiqué and then we'll vanish into the forest."

"Yes," from all.

Half an hour later Misty and Dave rejoined me at the top of our hill.

"I couldn't get a good look at who was doing all the talking, but at least we have enough to hold them," Misty explained.

Ten minutes later I could see a boat rapidly approaching the dock where we left *Rum-Runner*. A few minutes after that we were joined by ten of Seattle's finest.

I wanted to be part of the rush on the cabin but I knew I would never be able to persuade anyone to let me join in. And Misty was certainly not welcome. I had decided that if Misty was to remain a significant part of my team we would have to put her problem with the police in Seattle behind us. I knew she hadn't been completely blameless but I did think she had been treated badly. It was important she regain her reputation if the two of us were to get the respect we needed to really run this case.

Things happened so fast that I still can't clearly see all the action. What I do know is within ten minutes the cabin had been stormed and everyone had been rounded up with no shots fired or injuries on either side of the law.

During the ride back to Lumsden Island we were quiet. We knew this wasn't the end of our adventure. In fact this was probably just the start of our real work. We still had to figure out who was behind the explosions and I still didn't think we were any closer.

The three of us knew the ones who were just arrested were not the dangerous terrorists but we had no way to prove it. And we certainly didn't have a good handle on who the real terrorists were, or what they were going to do next.

> *"And now that we have returned to the desultory life of the plain, let us endeavor to import a little of that mountain grandeur into it. We will remember within what walls we lie, and understand that this level life too has its summit, and why from the mountain-top the deepest valleys have a tinge of blue; that there is elevation in every hour, as no part of the earth is so low that the heavens may not be seen from, and we have only to stand on the summit of our hour to command an uninterrupted horizon."*
>
> *Thoreau*

CHAPTER 34

Red Right Returning

WE SAW DAVE OFF. He was unbelievably thankful for the day's outcome. He still seemed to think that this would be the end of the terrorists and their attempts at extortion. I thought otherwise.

Misty and I enjoyed a drink on the deck and Freedom was happy to have us all to himself. He was sleeping. After dinner Misty got a call and she was back on track with the personals case. She was scheduled to head south to Belize in the morning and I persuaded her that I should come along this time. I called Cam to get him onside and he insisted on involving Dave. The next morning we had an uneventful trip south and while I checked into the resort hotel, she got busy.

As agreed she headed down to the bank to be ready for the wire transfer. She had sent the fraudsters an email agreeing to buy one of the properties on the island and was going to make the first deposit today. We were to meet Dave and a few of his FBI colleagues. If everything went as planned, by nightfall the fraudsters would be behind bars. Another twenty minutes and then I made the call to Cam. The deal was for Misty to confirm the wire transfer and then travel with Phil out to the project site. We were planning to arrive onsite early and arrest the fraudster.

In order to be ready for Dave, I walked down the dock and readied the boat for action. He should be here by now and I would wait for another few minutes. I hadn't really wanted Dave to be part of this but I really didn't want to be totally responsible for everything that was going to happen on the water.

Our plans were not going as planned. Dave had still not arrived and we needed to head out soon. I called Cam. "Misty still hasn't made contact with Phil but she has headed down to the bank and I am getting a bad feeling about our ability to bring enough manpower to bear. When are you expecting your backup team to arrive on the island?"

"Still two more hours," Cam said. "We are on our own for now. It looks like we will have to do this without any FBI help."

"I'm going to call Dave one last time and then head down to the bank."

No answer and although Cam was sure the FBI would be there to assist us, I was starting to agree with Misty and ready to write Dave off. Not only did he seem to be against everything we suggested, but he also was constantly late. We needed help now. By now Misty would be at the bank but we were maintaining phone silence.

Misty and I had agreed we needed the assistance of the RCMP if we were to solve the case. Cam and I had been talking for a few minutes and I think I was close to getting his agreement.

"Can you help us?"

"I'll get our group to see if we can find anything for you, and I will personally contact our banking people and see if they can help," Cam offered.

I decided to head out on the water and assume Dave would catch up to me if he ever did make an appearance. It was a warm day and although I was concerned about Misty, I was able to enjoy the afternoon on the water. I just wanted this to be over and wasn't sure how Misty was going to handle her end. Especially now she knew Dave would be involved.

I had been drifting offshore in the rental boat. Waiting for Dave and his crew. I shifted down into neutral and coasted close to the dock. I was going to let it drift in quietly and get on the dock before anyone knew we were there. About ten feet from the end of the dock, just as I was readying myself for the step onto the dock with our lines, something starboard caught my attention—black, sleek and large; two, maybe more and heading directly into our path. I was just about to shift into reverse and give them a chance when I realized they were scuba divers.

"Get ready for evasive action," I cautioned. "We have company."

As the first diver came alongside I relaxed as soon as he raised his mask and I could see it was Cam.

"You gave me quite a jolt," I said. "I thought we were being boarded."

"If we had meant you harm you wouldn't have seen us coming, Pride."

He came aboard but the others stayed in the water alongside the boat. Now I could see Cam had left at least three more professionals in the water, and they all looked ready for action.

"John, we are going to have to move fast. I think our window of opportunity is closing fast. We intercepted several wire transfers last night and although we were able to give the appearance of a completed money transfer we will need to have results today or the money will really leave our hands."

"What can I do?" I asked. I was glad Cam was taking control of the situation.

"Keep on the lookout for any of them but don't do anything else to put them on guard."

The hundred and fifty-five mile coastline has over two hundred cayes or islands and we were headed for one of the most beautiful. East of the barrier reef were three atoll reefs separated by deep trenches. The mangroves help keep Belize's coastline intact. Black, red, white and buttonwood mangroves, with their intertwined root systems, line the coast. We could see locals at work uprooting large numbers of the mangroves.

Heading north of Caye Caulker we passed the Split. We could see the brightly colored small houses perched near the beach up on stilts. This is the channel that was created by Hurricane Hattie in 1961. We can see the effect of more recent Hurricane Iris, which hit the coast in 2001. And I was remembering that seventeen Scuba divers were killed not far from here when Hurricane Iris capsized their boat.

San Pedro on Ambergris Caye has a small pier and once past we headed by the airport and towards the resort. I looked ashore and saw the main road, or trail as I called it, a narrow track no more than sand covered. Ambergris Caye, twenty miles long and one mile wide has a reef along its entire length and the waves were breeching the lagoon. We could see many of the favored diving spots but no diving boats today. It was too rough for pleasure and I was starting to wonder why we were chancing the elements.

Five minutes later I was fully equipped and had dropped over the side of the boat and was afloat in another world. I descended into a coral canyon and immediately was surrounded by thousands of small blue and yellow fish. As I adjusted to the surrounding I could see tarpon, red snappers, yellow jacks, groupers, and hundreds of parrot-fish. I swam downward until I could see a tunnel directly below me. The last thing I wanted to do was enter a cave but here I was and there was no turning back at this point. I checked my buoyancy and drifted closer before giving a few quick kicks and sliding through the opening. I was surprised to see a large cavern beyond. A moray eel quickly moved deeper into the cavern as I advanced.

Misty and the resort developer were meeting on the other side of the islet and we wanted to surprise them by coming in through the cavern. I looked to my left and could see four black shapes sliding through the clear water—my friends from the RCMP. Now where were Dave and the FBI? Knowing him, he would be front and center when the fraudsters were caught.

Cam motioned for me to approach him. "Pride, stay here and we'll approach."

"Call when you need me." I didn't want to be left out of the action but I certainly had learned the hard way that I didn't want to get too close while they were making an arrest.

Twenty minutes later the cavern erupted with all sorts of action. It was hard to tell what was happening but I could hear Cam shouting at someone. "Police, stop before you get near the water."

"Whoever it was didn't stop. In fact they dove right in and before I really knew what was happening, I was in the middle of a water fight. And I don't mean just splashing water at each other. I think he was even more surprised to find me waiting for him. I was joined by Cam and in a few short minutes the two of us manhandled the fraudster onto the beach and into the waiting arms of the law.

Cam explained he got there just in time to hear the fraudster explain to Misty how the rest of the deal needed to go. And then he moved in to arrest him. That was when I got involved after our friend Phil tried to get away.

All in all an eventful couple of days, and at least one successful conclusion to a case we had been spending our time on.

"John, thanks for your help," Cam said. "We might not have found this fraudster without your original computer work."

"And I got to spend some quality time on the beach," Misty added.

"Now we have to find out what happened to Dave."

"John, I'll take care of that," Cam suggested.

It was too late to catch a flight by the time we arrived back on the dock. After dropping off the fraudster in the local jail, we headed out for a well-deserved meal. And who do we bump into, but Dave.

"Enjoying the view?" I asked Dave.

"Not that you care, but we were delayed getting down here. And I hear you accomplished what you needed to," Dave replied. "You have had a busy few days."

Cam stepped in, "I told John you could help us and I guess things just progressed too fast today."

"To tell you the truth, we were surprised at the airport when we had to declare our weapons and by the time we straightened that out you were long gone," Dave told us.

Dave and a couple of the FBI guys asked us to join them for dinner and by the time we had finished the meal and a few rum drinks I was almost ready to forgive Dave for his past errors. At least everyone seemed to be on the same team and Misty was enjoying the company.

After dinner I walked Misty back to the resort. "Thanks for being part of this, John."

"Glad to be of service lady," I joked. "I always wanted to be part of a big criminal takedown. I just didn't expect to be involved in two in as many days."

"Now, maybe I can focus my attention to helping you find the real terrorists in your case," Misty volunteered.

Quiet evening, alone in my room, I thought back to the dream and wondered how it was going to progress. Moving from the action of a fighting sailor during the Napoleonic Wars and War of 1812 to the relative calm of Saint John settlement times I realized that this period in our family's past was our pivotal turning point. It was this arrival in Saint John, New Brunswick, as a recent sailor on the run that had brushed our family with a combination of military service along with an unwillingness to meekly go along with the plans of their current military or political master. I knew from my Father's research into our family's Ontario history that it was Alexander Pride's son who fought against the family compact and the British Army. John Pride had sided with William Lyon Mackenzie and his reformers when they met at Montgomery's Tavern and marched down Yonge Street during the Rebellion of 1837. There was a family streak against authority, and it was no wonder I was now butting my head against the FBI!

I considered my relative's next steps. I knew he had married Mary Bailey but had little details of their time in New Brunswick. I finished removing the paint as the sun was starting to set. One last glance at our work and we headed up to the spire. Maybe I would try to take my mind off the case and do a little family history sleuthing.

I knew they had ten children and what I recently found out about her family's history may have colored my recent dreams. Over the years we had researched the land title records but hadn't found any family residences. We knew from family history that we had lived in a few places but I had no idea why Alex ended up moving north to the Grand Lake area. I would have thought he would stay near the boat building area around Saint John.

Originally we thought that Alex had married and then headed upland, but now it looked like he was married in the Gagetown area and now I had a good idea of why he headed there in the first place. We had the sequence of events all wrong. After an hour researching some Bailey family records I found the missing pieces. It wasn't Pride marrying a young city girl and taking her to the wilderness—it was a woman from the wilds of northern New Brunswick whose parents had moved north as Loyalists. Her Father, Benjamin, was born in England, immigrated to Maryland and was a Loyalist who supported the British when the American Revolution started in 1776. After the war he came to New Brunswick settling on Grand Lake with a land grant from the British government.

Unless Alexander colored his past it must have made for interesting dinner table conversations when they learned that he was on the run from the British Navy. I assume he changed his name to Edward and never told the in-laws the whole story.

It didn't take long to fall asleep and when I did…

My dream started where my last thought ended. I had been deep in thought about how to find the missing records to show where we had lived in New Brunswick. "Edward, I thought you were Alex or Alexander?" Mary looked thoughtfully.

I took her hand and as we strolled down the lane I replied, "I am starting over and from now on I will go by Edward. You know I am on leave from the navy but if I go back I will never see you again. I have had enough of sea life. So Edward it is and I want to continue to see you. I will be coming to visit you and your family in Grand Lake, if you will have me."

Mary didn't say anything. She just smiled and on we walked. It started to rain, which was interesting because in the dream we didn't get wet but we sure could feel the rain.

"Love is an attempt to change a piece of a dream-world into a reality."

Thoreau

"Pride, don't daydream up here." I looked over at Mary's brother, John Bailey. Then I looked down, way down, over a hundred and fifty feet. It appears as if I had made my way high up a white pine and was holding one half of a saw. We were part way through topping this magnificent tree and John was explaining something to me.

"When we arrived in 1783 with a group of Loyalists bound from Maryland this area was picked because a group of early settlers arrived from Massachusetts and received a whole township land grant around an area they called Maugerville. Father and Mother already had a couple of children and the rest of us followed shortly afterwards."

"Tell me again, what are we doing?" I could see for miles. The day was clear and the sun was warm on my face. It was just like being high in the ship's rigging. I felt at home here. To the south I could see the Saint John River and still felt the sense of amazement when I had set out in the small riverboat from the Bay of Fundy harbor. The tide was over twenty feet and still over two feet when we arrived at Maugerville. That was a first for me—to boat over seventy miles on a rising tide upstream. I could see my voyage, now in reverse, down the Salmon River over the portage to the Miramishi and the Jemseg and into the Saint John. There are highlands surrounding us, not unlike the Scottish ones but here much more covered with trees, and little sign of settlement.

"Pride, these tall timbers are sold to the British Navy and will be masts for the new ships being built in Saint John and Grand Manan. I understand that the only reason we are able to sell them is that Napoleon has blockaded the British from the Balkans. And you, my man, are made for these parts. It must be your naval experience that allows you to climb so quickly. You will earn yourself a steady job if you wish."

"I'd like that, John. Tell me more about the Bailey family. There seem to be a lot of you."

"Yes, in addition to Mary and I, there are seven other of Benjamin and Susannah. And don't get me started on the cousins. Mum's side, the Wanty family, has been in New Brunswick even longer than the Baileys and you will find them all over the place. The Judge, her Father, is still living in Saint John and you may meet her brother Benjamin who serves in the British Navy."

I had a nagging question I just had to ask, "And what do you do for the law around here?" I still had a concern about someone recognizing me.

We were almost through the last cut so we finished that and watched as the top twenty feet crashed to the forest floor. As we headed down John replied, "We take care of most of the small legal issues quickly and locally. I am a Lieutenant Colonel in the local militia and help out from time to time. We haven't had much that we have had to refer to Saint John."

I thought about that for a minute or two. Edward it was, and no one would be looking for him.

Later that day we were all having a late evening meal outside, not far from Mary's homestead. We were sitting down, over thirty of us, all at one long table under the trees. After the food arrived and we said grace, Benjamin stood and proposed a toast, "To friends present and friends absent, and to new and old friends all." I could taste the ale going down, I could even smell it. I looked over at Mary's mother. She was sitting off to the side, the only one not under the trees. Quietly she was just watching, and I felt her taking my measure. Again, there was a slight mist as we finished the meal.

After I woke up that was the overriding remembrance from the dream—rain but no water. I never felt the mist or the water.

"Let whales wake and sleep in their
own water,
the muskrat in his.
His bliss, like an emulsion, injects
his veins and arteries, a whale's
capillaries and accommodate a liquor
immense and sedate.
Dignity and industry lend size to the muskrat.
His size is his own, and mete.
The whale may think his dignity is greater.
The muskrat would be able, if the
thought struck him,
To prove his own title to this quality
sooner or later.

A G Bailey
"The Muskrat and the Whale" Thanks for a Drowned Island 1973

PANB Cercle culturel et historique Hilarion Cyr Inc. Collection: P51-38

CHAPTER 35

"The winds and waves are always on the side of the ablest navigators."

Edward Gibbon

THE PHONE RANG. "PRIDE here."

"John, we have a break in the case," Misty's welcome voice pulled me out of the pleasant dream. I would have to wait to find out what Mary and the now Edward were going to do.

"What are we looking at?"

"The FBI is ready to back your ideas and I think we are going to get some real results."

"I thought you had decided you never wanted to work with the federals again," I replied.

"I still have my doubts but at least they seem prepared to give our theories some muscle," Misty said.

"I'll meet you for breakfast in an hour and we can make plans."

Last evening I had explained to Misty why I thought we hadn't really caught all the terrorists. She had listened attentively and from time to time had offered some useful insight. She agreed she would email the FBI and see where we could go.

We met over breakfast by the pool. I watched her as she made her way over to my table. I could see Misty was dressed for work today. She had a skimpy two-piece bathing suit, which wasn't leaving much to my imagination.

"Reporting for work, Misty?"

"No reason we can't combine pleasure with business," she purred.

"And what type of pleasure did you have in mind Misty?"

"As usual, Pride, you are having a hard time keeping your mind on business. And all I want is a little sun with my business."

"Right you are, and how did you get someone to take us seriously?"

"I finally realized that as much as Dave is our new best friend, we are not going to get anywhere with him. We need to take a new tack."

"And that is?" I asked.

"I contacted one of my old bosses from Seattle and he put me in touch with someone on the force who has worked with the money laundering branch of the FBI. He was quite interested in what you have been doing and didn't know why the FBI couldn't help you. Something is definitely not adding up. It is almost as if within the FBI there are competing divisions."

"That is interesting."

"Yes, and wait until you hear the rest. The guy I was talking to is based in Washington and said they have had several cases that have had banking connections in the Caribbean. They are starting to take that part of the world seriously. He told me that there are strong indications drug money is involved in most of that area's criminal activities."

"Was he able to give you any ideas?"

"He wants us to keep in touch with him and said he would get back to me in a day or two once he checked out something. He didn't say what it was but did say he thought there might be a connection to something they have been working on."

"Are the two of you on vacation permanently now?" I looked up to see Dave approaching us.

He joined us and I said, "Not really, we are still working on finding the rest of the coffee and GMO terrorists."

"I thought I told you to stay away from my case," he screamed at me. "Your help was appreciated but the case is solved and we don't need your help anymore."

I stood up. "Where is this coming from, Dave?"

Dave got even closer and I could see help arriving from the corner of my eye. Misty stepped between the two of us. "Dave, I don't know what is bothering you but take it somewhere else. All we are trying to do is help and you don't seem to want our help."

"You, of all people, should understand why. Neither of you are real cops and the last thing I want to have to do is deal with you."

Misty asked, "Why, Dave, just tell us why and we will leave you alone."

"Never mind, just stay away from me and stay off this case. We don't need your help anymore."

With that he stormed off leaving Misty and I dumbfounded. "I thought we were all friends again," Misty questioned.

"Obviously not. I guess we don't have to worry about his cooperation. Tell me what the rest of the FBI is prepared to do for this case."

"When I was on the phone this morning my contact said the FBI has been concerned about money laundering through the BVIs for years. It seems just when they are close to making headway everything just disappears."

"What do you mean?"

"He wasn't prepared to give me details but he did say on several occasions it was almost if someone on the inside was feeding the bad guys information. He thought it might be coming from within the banking system."

I looked up and a well-dressed gentleman walked by. He nodded at us and all of a sudden I realized I was missing something. I didn't know what it was but in the back of my mind I had a feeling something was unexplained. Suddenly I realized what I should have followed up on. The gentleman had a slight limp and was using a cane. I didn't notice the limp until he was almost out of range and it was then I remembered the smile's comment on the Lumsden Island dock, "The last time he was on the island he asked me about farms on the island. He said he was involved with research and wanted to work with farmers who were growing coffee beans. I thought it strange because he didn't strike me as the farming type. He looked like he should be off running a small criminal operation somewhere." She was talking about the man with the limp. And I was sure he was the same man who had taken money out of the terrorists' Barclays bank account. Why hadn't I followed up on him and talked to the farmer?

"We have to go back to the BVIs, Misty. I think I know a way to smoke out the man behind the extortion. In the meantime I have to talk to Cam."

"There's one way to find out if a man is honest; ask him; if he says yes, you know he's crooked,"

Mark Twain

CHAPTER 36

"The greater difficulty, the more glory in surmounting it.
Skillful pilots gain their reputation from storms and tempests."
Epicures BC 341–270

CAM RETURNED MY MESSAGE. "Pride, are you still on the beach enjoying the view with Misty? Or should I say the view of Misty?"

"Yes and yes. But enough about beauty, have you had any further information from your man Standler?"

"Standler hasn't been able to get any more useful intelligence," Cam said. "Their group is unsure about the direction of the protests. All they know is that this has taken on a life of its own. Their contacts don't know what is going to happen next."

"That's too bad, but I might have a way to get right inside the real heart of this group."

"We are all ears," Cam replied. "The FBI seems to be at a standstill and I don't have any brilliant ideas."

I explained my idea about the BVIs coffee grower and the man with the limp. "If we could put pressure on the coffee grower we might be able to get our man out in the open. And Misty has finally got part of the FBI to be open-minded about our ideas. Dave for one is still against us having any continuing involvement in the case but we have some limited support for my idea from Misty's new contact in the FBI."

"Be careful about how you work with the FBI," Cam coached. "My experience with their inner working is that all you need is one person against you and your credibility is shot. Don't be surprised if you find people turning against you again."

A day later Misty and I found ourselves bouncing over dusty narrow tracks on the way to locating our coffee grower. I was back in the BVIs, hot and sunny with no cloud cover, but with a partner. This time we were driving ourselves and we had a suitable vehicle. It was an old pickup truck with a four-wheel drive. And it seemed to have more than enough power for what we were doing.

"Remind me what we found out about this character."

"The FBI didn't have much other than a general impression some of his dealing are less than upfront," Misty explained. "When I talked to our new FBI contact he said they hadn't had any direct dealing with him but they did get some information from the locals. It appears he had some union problems last year. There was a group of laborers who were trying to improve conditions. I didn't get all the details but the gist of it was the union was never formed and he ended up hiring a new group of workers."

"It doesn't sound like someone who would be involved with Starbucks."

"No, and what's the connection to our case," Misty wondered.

I must have been paying less than full attention to the road because before I knew it, we had arrived. I was not prepared for what lay ahead of us. My impression of a coffee grower was a small plantation high in the hills or deep in the jungle with donkeys and hand drawn carts. The reality of this organization was one of mass production and not an animal in sight. We had arrived in a large clearing with several modern steel buildings and a couple of new trucks parked outside. We could see several locals heading into one of the buildings driving small tractors pulling trailers loaded with beans.

"Let's see if we can find the owner," I suggested.

We knew his name was Franklin Olivine and when I asked for him at the office we were asked to wait while he was paged. It wasn't more than five minutes before Franklin joined us.

"Good afternoon, what brings you to our establishment?"

We had agreed Misty would do the talking until we got to the point of talking about the man with the limp. "We are working with Starbucks and looking for local growers who might be interested in providing long term supplies."

"That is interesting because we have had talks with them in the past and they weren't interested in doing business with us. We were told they didn't like the way we did business. Apparently we don't treat our workers the way they treat theirs in Seattle."

"Actually it is more complicated than a simple business relationship. We believe we may be able to work with you if we can change two things. And at the same time ensure that you continue on here in your slice of paradise," Misty continued.

"What are you talking about?" Franklin asked. "What does Starbucks have to do about my organization?"

I decided this was where I needed to step in. "The FBI knows about your relationship with a group of terrorists who have been harassing Starbucks. We are here to see if we can make a deal with you."

"I don't know what you are talking about. I'm just a coffee bean grower."

"The authorities know about your relationship with this man." I showed him a composite sketch of the man with a limp the FBI had provided after I gave them the information from Barclays Bank and the smile.

There was a long moment of silence. I almost continued with my bluff and then he said, "I knew someday this would come out. I really don't have anything important to do with any group. The only thing I provide is expertise in growing coffee beans."

"Tell us what your actual involvement is," I asked.

He motioned towards a grouping of comfortable looking wicker chairs on the veranda. As we settled in, I looked around and realized this plantation could be a front for any number of illegal operations.

"For the past two years I have been providing information on our operation to a man who said he was going to compete with Starbucks. When Starbucks originally approached us we signed a confidentiality contract and they provided us with all sorts of information on what they required. When we reached the point where we realized there was going to be no deal I thought that at least I could get some money for my inside knowledge. Little did I know it would lead to the point where we are now dealing on a monthly basis."

"What does he want from you?"

"Originally all he wanted was background information on how Starbucks dealt with the plantations. Then once he had me hooked and I had already broken the confidentiality contract he started to ask for small favors. Nothing big at first but then he started to impersonate a Starbuck's buyer and before I knew it I was really involved in his business. He wanted to use our banking arrangements to accept foreign deposits and then we were buying property for him. I don't know his full involvement in the area but if and when he decides to get into the coffee growing business he could be one of the area's biggest producers."

I glanced at Misty. This was not what we came prepared for. "And so you have been demanding money from Starbucks and others?"

"No, of course not. I don't know what you are talking about. My only involvement with Starbucks is to pass on how they do business down here. I know the man you are interested in is not on the up and up but I have nothing to do with him other than buying land."

"How often do you meet with him?" I asked.

"He usually meets me here at least once a month to tour the potential land purchases. When we started I was showing him all sorts of land and thought he would be interested in long-term land leases. But he is only interested in existing plantations that have the ability to be expanded. And he always wants to own the land."

"Do you have any idea how much land he controls?" I asked.

"Let me give you an idea. My business is 2,500 acres and he has already bought more than 180,000 acres. And I am pretty sure he has bought some directly because I haven't seen any money transferred into my bank for over six months. He must have his own banking arrangements now." This matched with what we knew had happened at the Barclays Bank.

I asked, "How much money did you see flow through your account?"

"Over two million dollars," he replied. "But that all stopped as I said over six months ago." Misty and I looked at each other with the realization this was bigger than we had already discovered.

I spent some time telling him we had no interest in arresting him for his role. What we needed was a way to reach his contact.

"I never know when to expect him," Franklin explained. "The last time he was here was two weeks ago and I usually see him at least once a month. He bought some land last time and he was extremely interested in seeing bigger parcels the next time. I got the impression he was expecting to be able to purchase even more land than usual. He was starting to look at the larger producers on the islands and he never did that when he started."

We agreed to stay in contact and made a deal he would contact us when he next heard from the man with a limp. Misty and I headed back towards town and the smile.

As we retraced our trip, we were deep into our private thoughts. We were trying to come up with a new plan of action. Or at least I was. Misty asked me, "John, tell me what is up with you and Suzanne. Is this serious or just an island fling?"

"I am not sure, Misty, but the two of us seem to have a connection I have been missing since my accident."

"Do you want to talk about her, or your accident?"

"No, but I am able to think about both and when we have a few hours back home I should be able to discuss them with you. Thanks for asking."

"No problem, John. I just want you to be happy. And the one thing you haven't been in the past few years is happy."

The rest of the ride was in silence. I realized that my mind was clear, one of those rare days when I didn't have that dull pain covering all my thoughts.

> *"Life does not consist mainly, or even largely, of facts or happenings.*
> *It consist mainly of the storm of thoughts that is forever flowing*
> *through one's head."*
>
> *Mark Twain*

CHAPTER 37

"Whoever commands the sea, commands the trade, whoever commands the trade of the world, commands the riches of the world, and consequently the world itself."

Sir Walter Raleigh

WE DROPPED INTO BARCLAYS Bank for a quick visit with my favorite banker to ensure he was still onside. Then I left Misty at the airport and arranged to call her tomorrow. She was going to try to get the FBI to take some of our new intelligence and find out who was really behind the terrorists.

The hard work being done for the day I decided to surprise the smile. I owed her one good surprise after she had landed on the Lumsden Island dock without calling.

I parked our rental truck near the beach and walked towards her cottage. It seems so long since I had spent that first night with her in the hammock. So much had changed, and yet so much was still unresolved. We hadn't talked about the future and we surely hadn't talked enough about the past. Especially my past and why it would be impacting any future the two of us might enjoy.

I could see the hammock gently moving as I approached. She looked up like she was expecting me. "Hello, John, what took you so long?"

"May I join you?" as I climbed in with her.

"You are always welcome in my hammock." I lay back, closed my eyes and relaxed.

I finally told her why I was on the island and thanked her for the lead that had led to our coffee grower. Then we said nothing. Just being together was what both of us needed. Or at least what I needed. We made love as the sun went down and then went inside and worked together on a simple dinner. She filleted a fresh yellowtail snapper while I made a salad.

"This fish looks excellent."

"My cousin caught it this morning, and after we lightly season it I will quickly sear it and then let it simmer in some broth while you tell me what you have planned for tomorrow," the smile explained. "I assume you didn't drop in just to have your way with me."

"No, this is just an added benefit, but one that is more pleasurable every time we meet. Actually the real reason we are back on the islands is because of the comment you made about the man with the limp. We need to find him. Misty and I headed up island yesterday and talked to one of the coffee growers who had dealings with him but won't see him again for a few weeks. We need to find him soon."

Suzanne looked at me and between thoughts we prepared dinner and sat down to what was an excellent main course.

"John, as you may have figured out, this island is small, not only in size but also because everyone's business is known by many. I think I can put you in touch with someone who might be able to help you. Can you trust me alone for a few hours tomorrow morning?"

"Okay, but be careful. Don't get into any trouble on my behalf."

We finished the fish and salad and took a stroll along the beach before bed. Bed—how could I be thinking of bed or hammock when I really should be working harder to solve the case?

Asleep I was snuggled up to the smile but was talking to Mary. "I told you I would follow you." I had been here for a couple of days, just off the riverboat that had taken the trip up the Saint John River to the Maugerville and Grand Lake area. I had met some of Mary's family, and had been out for a day of logging with her brother. Now she was telling me about her family. "Your experience in the navy will go a long way to winning them over. My uncle was in the navy and Father's military experience although brief gave him an understanding of the training you must have undergone."

I remember the evening after the dinner. I know I met more of the family. Every time I turned around there was someone new to meet and people were coming and going all the time. This area was a booming area and I could see how I might fit in. Several relatives had already mentioned that my sailing experience might come in handy during the fall log runs. And I could see that Mary was trying to make me feel right at home.

"Let's go for a short walk. I want to show you something," Mary said quietly.

We excused ourselves from the table and I thanked her mother for the great meal. Even in the dream I was hungry and could taste the homemade bread and fresh fish. We strolled hand in hand for a few minutes, nothing said. We weren't far from her homestead but we might have been in a different part of the world as we walked through the dense forest. Not too far off the sun was starting to set and we could see the evening sunrays playing across the forest floor. We broke through the forest to a clearing leading to a bare hilltop. It took us another few minutes to climb the short distance to the top and when I turned around my breath was shallow and slightly labored. The view took what little was left of my senses and knocked my reality for a bit of a tailspin. I was looking out on the view from my Scottish roots and it took a minute to recover and realize that although close it was not quite the same view.

"It is funny how your mind plays tricks," I said to Mary. "This is as close to the view I remember from home as any I have seen since I left Scotland. Thanks for bringing me here."

"This is mine, Edward."

I looked at her, not quite fully comprehending her meaning. She was smiling and leaned over to give me a short kiss.

"My father has promised me this piece of paradise and I have been planning my home for years."

I understood and replied, "Then we shouldn't disappoint him. Let's get started." She just smiled but we both knew what was coming next.

"She grew more love than he could
bear.
She went to trim his morning
heart.
She quickened all his little
leaves.
His railings fell and left him
bare."

A G Bailey "Isobel" 1952

The next morning I awoke early without the need of an alarm clock. Suzanne was still asleep and I got up without rousing her. Walking outside I realized again—just a few hours here was enough to lift my spirits. I knew it was a combination of paradise and the smile but I knew that just being with her was having the greater influence on my mind. Even without talking about our future, and perhaps not talking was the important point; we both realized our futures were entwined. She joined me on the deck. "Where are you headed from here?"

"I plan to spend a few days here and with any luck we will be able to wrap up our case before long."

"Do you still want me to help?"

"I have been thinking about your involvement and it is probably a good idea if we limit it from here on in," I replied. "I don't want you in any danger."

"John, I have been involved since that first day on the beach. When we met I knew you had a problem and without really thinking, I reached out to you. I want to help you to solve this problem and want to help rid our islands of this corruption."

"Thanks."

We lay in the hammock while I contemplated our next step. I felt the only way to really bring the situation to a head was to confront the leader of the terrorists. Although I thought we were getting closer to understanding what was going on, I really didn't think that we had enough information to persuade the FBI to move on foreign soil. And I certainly didn't think that local authorities would be ready to act solely on my say so. It kept coming back to the problem of not really having detailed information linking all the various participants.

I awoke alone. This hammock idea was starting to grow on me. I could learn to love the breeze in the evening and the ability to sleep under the stars. I still hadn't seen the green flash but I figured with the amount of time I was spending on this beach it was just a matter of time before I had that pleasure as well.

I went inside but still no smile. True to her word, she had gone out alone.

The phone rang, and rang again. After about ten rings it stopped. I wasn't going to get in the habit of answering her phone, especially if she wasn't at hand. I walked around not yet missing her but wondering where she had gone. She had mentioned earlier that we should head out and do some shopping for dinner. The phone rang again, and this time it didn't stop until I finally answered it after about twenty rings.

"Pride, we have your friend and she is staying with us until you leave the island and promise never to come back."

"Who is this and what do you want from us?" I replied.

"Never mind the details, just leave," the voice said. "We will be watching you and if you want to see your friend again you need to be off the island tomorrow."

"How do I know that you won't hurt Suzanne?"

"Don't worry about us, just make sure you are off the island tomorrow." He was starting to sound like a broken record. I felt that I would be getting nothing more from him.

"Let me speak to her."

"Concentrate on getting off the island, Pride, then nobody gets hurt." The line went dead.

I headed out walking. Walking west along the beach. The same beach the two of us had enjoyed so recently. I didn't know where I was headed but I knew that I had to do something. We felt we were getting close. And the last thing I wanted to do was leave Suzanne's life in the hands of some terrorists.

Although I didn't have a plan I did have some friends. Or at least Suzanne had some friends in town. And if they really weren't my friends, they would soon become friends in arms. So the first thing I did was head into the bank. My friend Ben was in his office and within minutes had invited me back into his inner sanctum.

"Ben, I don't know what you can do to help but whatever I have been doing on your island, it has led to a real problem for Suzanne. What can I do to ensure her safety?"

"John, when I said the bank can't help you I meant it," Ben replied. "But, at the same time that you have made some enemies you also have some resources you can call upon. Not officially of course, but there are members of this bank who have some experience with this type of situation. I am going to leave you here for a few minutes and won't be seeing you again today. Listen to the advice of my colleague and perhaps he can assist you."

The next two minutes seemed to last forever. Finally the door opened again and my friend from the beach joined me. "Don't say anything, just follow me."

We headed to what I assumed was going to be the back door, and although I had never left a bank by the back, I could see the wisdom in doing so. Although if anyone had actually seen me head into the bank they might wonder where I disappeared to. James grabbed my elbow and instead of heading out of the bank we moved past the back of the vault and down some of the oldest stone stairs I had ever seen. "How old are these stairs?" I asked.

"They were here before this bank and part of the first bank in town," James replied. "When this new bank was built about sixty years ago they kept the lower floor and a few special surprises."

We reached the bottom of the stairs and after a sharp right we went through what looked like a new metal door. It closed behind us with a solid thud and the two of us were alone in what looked like a set for a dungeon. There was what I assumed bank storage boxes piled against all the walls. James motioned to me to follow. He headed to the far end of the dungeon-like basement. It was dark and I could hardly see the floor as I joined him at what looked like a dead end corner. James pushed something and before I could see what really happened I was looking at the top of an additional set of stone stairs heading downward again. These stairs had been carved into rock and the lighting was just enough to see that the stairs had been worn deep with footsteps over the years.

"The first bank had been built over the original prison on this spot some three hundred years ago. Now you are going to see why I think we can help you. Sorry about the setting but you will see that it has its advantages." James moved over to what I assumed was a closed whiteboard against the wall. He opened the cabinet and before us was an elaborate wall of electronics. He stood and motioned to one of two chairs facing the electronic wall ten feet away. I sat. I could see he didn't want me to hear what he was saying.

"Give me a few minutes and I think we might be able to help you." James got up and moved over to a small table against the old stone-wall. He was making a telephone call.

I couldn't hear what he was saying, but after three calls he joined me at the table. "John, I think we know who you are dealing with."

"When you say *we*, I assume you aren't talking about the bank anymore."

He just smiled at me. "My employer finds the bank a good partner for its activities in this area of the globe. Now back to your problem, or as I should now point out, our problem. It appears that you have shaken more than one bad guy out of their hiding place."

"Tell me how we can find Suzanne."

"We are going to assign two of our agents to work with you on the understanding that this is never revealed to anyone."

"What do you mean by agents?"

"Just wait here and you will see soon enough."

"I had not lived there a week before my feet wore a path from my door to the pond-side; and though it is five or six years since I trod it, it is still quite distinct. It is true, I fear that others may have fallen into it, and so helped to keep it open. The surface of the earth is soft and impressible by the feet of men; and so with the paths which the mind travels. How worn and dusty, then, must be the highways of the world, how deep the ruts of tradition and conformity."

Henry David Thoreau

CHAPTER 38

"Anyone can hold the helm when the sea is calm."

Publilius Syrus (~100 BC)

JAMES DISAPPEARED AND I waited. At least I felt I wasn't alone anymore. I looked around the room, every few seconds I could see one or other of the electronic displays lighting up. Other than that, the room was static. No noise, no humming, no voices. In fact I hadn't noticed before but it was so quiet that it was eerie. James had told me that this used to be the old prison, and I would have thought the age of it would have meant sound would percolate through the walls. They must have insulated the whole room because I really couldn't hear anything.

"Hello, anyone here?" I was talking to myself after a few minutes. I wonder what I would be doing if I had been a real prisoner here two hundred years ago.

I remember Dad telling us about our ancestor, the first Alexander Pride, who had been pressed into service with the British Navy. He had been born in Bo'ness, Scotland in 1790 and had served during the Napoleonic Wars in the Indian Ocean and finally off the American Coast during the War of 1812. I wondered if he ever got this far south. If he had he might have offloaded prisoners into this very prison. And if he had got this far south and had enough of naval life on the seas he might have even jumped ship. And then I would perhaps have been born in the Caribbean and we all know what that would have led to. Rum and not Scotch—why does almost everything in my life seem to lead to booze or at least the thought of booze?

I got up and walked around. This was obviously an operations room, but I could see nothing with the written word. No books, no papers and no reports, just the wall of electronic gismos. Many of them looked familiar but even more were foreign to me. I could only guess what they did and how they did it.

"Hello, John." I jumped. One moment, complete silence and then without warning and from behind came a new voice. I turned and two colleagues now joined James.

"John, I would like to introduce you to two men you'll never see or talk to again." They looked as British as James, but these two had spent a lot of time working out in a tough gym or perhaps they had just spent a few decades fighting for the flag. "For your purposes today refer to them as Strider and Flint. Strider is on your left and will be in command. Flint is our counter-terrorism expert in the islands. Both of them come highly recommended and I think they will be able to help you."

Strider sat down at the table, Flint remained standing and James headed back to banking, leaving the three of us alone in the old prison. "John, what do you know about the money laundering operation at the coffee plantation?" Strider asked.

I told him what I had learned from Franklin Olivine, and the little I knew about the man with the limp. Strider looked at me, almost with a look that said he had been there before. Then a screen lit up and a picture of a man getting out of a car somewhere in Europe appeared. This was followed quickly by two more pictures of the same man seated at a coffee table still somewhere in Europe. If I had to guess, I would say it was in the south of France. The setting looked exotic but the man just looked all business-like.

"This is Francois-Henri Gaucher. He is your man with the limp, and is on Interpol's most wanted list. Flint and I are part of the Caribbean Financial Action Task Force working on countermeasures to address the problem of money laundering. Although it is not common knowledge, we have had some excellent results working in the islands. But we have not been able to get close to Francois-Henri. We believe him to be involved in some of the largest laundering operations but he is extremely secretive. Every time we think that we are getting closer to him, he melts away and we are at the beginning again."

Flint added, "We know there is some connection between Francois-Henri and some terrorist groups in Europe but we have not been able to connect him to anything. The fact that you seem to have a North American connection is of great interest to us. That is a new angle."

"How can I help? How is this connected to Suzanne's disappearance?"

"Suzanne has nothing to do with this. She is just involved because you are evidently getting too close to something. We need to know what that is," Strider said.

"I'm sure that it is something Suzanne mentioned to someone this morning. And that must be related to Francois-Henri. I am prepared to do anything in order to get her back safely."

"Why do you think it was this morning?"

"Because when she headed out I know she was going to try find out some information that would help me."

"Good, now this is what we think might work," Strider said. "We don't know who she was talking to, but we do know that it hit a real nerve. And that might be because you were getting close. Can you send some emails to the terrorist group with something that mentions Francois-Henri and the money that they are expecting from Starbucks?"

"That will be easy, but how is that going to get Suzanne back? And remember they want me off the island tomorrow. You can't expect results that fast."

"Don't worry about the speed of the results. We are sure if you can flush out Francois-Henri, he will lead us to Suzanne. What we would like in the email is some comment about timing with Starbucks. I think we can get him to move and then we can begin to find out what is really happening."

We discussed a few more logistics and then I was left alone in the old dungeon, alone with my thoughts and access to a laptop computer. After a few minutes thinking how to create the email, I went to work. I knew Suzanne's safety was dependant on my ability to get to Francois-Henry. With that in mind I was motivated to come up with a persuasive and luring email.

"In the long run, men hit only what they aim at.
Therefore, they had better aim at something high."

Henry David Thoreau

CHAPTER 39

"Only two sailors, in my experience, never ran aground.
One never left port and the other was an atrocious liar."

Don Bamford

QUIET—THIS TIME I DIDN'T mind the quiet and lack of other distractions. Just knowing Suzanne was in danger because of my actions was enough to keep me focused.

I knew whatever I came up with, it had to be good enough to trick the terrorists. And it had to be good enough the first time because we would not get a second opportunity.

After a few false starts I finally felt I was headed in the right direction. What was needed was a clean message to the terrorists, something that wasn't connected to Suzanne's present danger. I was going to route the email to the coffee plantation owner with a blind copy to the terrorists on the west coast. I was sure it would catch the attention of Francois-Henri.

To: Franklin Olivine

From: John Pride

Subject: Starbucks and Land Purchases

Thanks for the helpful information you gave us about Starbucks' operations on the islands. We think we can provide you what you need in order to find suitable land for them. Although you were dealing with someone else in the

> past, we are prepared to work with you and Starbucks to set up a Caribbean operation.
>
> We will be heading up to see you tomorrow to finalize details. In the meantime please pull together the banking details on our individual of interest. Once Starbucks can prove he received proprietary information about their operation we should be able to put him out of business. In return for your cooperation Starbucks is prepared to overlook your role in this affair. In fact, they are extremely interested in working with you again.

I felt a little bad about involving Franklin in my entrapment but he, in the first place, had provided Francois-Henri with Starbucks' operational details. Why not use him to catch the bad guy and free Suzanne?

Flint rejoined me and I detailed what I had in mind. "We have to flush out Francois-Henri and get him to lead us to Suzanne. He will want to stop Franklin from giving us any banking info on his land dealings. From what you have told me he might resort to violence to ensure his past stays hidden. You will have to protect Franklin."

"Great, John. Send the email out and we will put our own trace on where it goes."

"I am anticipating that if Francois-Henri heads up the mountain we will be able to follow him back to where he has Suzanne," I said.

"Yes," replied Flint. "And as long as we are prepared before he tries to meet with Franklin, we should be able to help avoid any injuries. The only touchy point will be following him back to Suzanne."

After sending out the email we prepared for our visit to the coffee plantation. We were not expecting Francois-Henri to bring a large army of men with him so Flint suggested driving up this afternoon. We were soon underway. Just the three of us—it was Flint, Strider and yours truly against the bad guys. We were expecting to get Franklin out of the way, watch Francois-Henri come and go, and then follow him back to what I was anticipating would be a joyful reunion with Suzanne. We thought it would be simple. And it would have been if Francois-Henri played along with our plan.

We got up to the plantation in good order and explained to Franklin what we had in mind. After a few minutes of stubborn resistance to our ideas, he came around.

"I don't appreciate the fact that you used me like this, but I do like the idea of getting Francois-Henri out of the Caribbean. Perhaps with him gone the price of raw land will return to a more realistic value and I can once again resume my expansion."

Strider explained, "We need to get you out of here for a few hours. He will probably be here later today or early tomorrow. How can you explain your disappearance and our being here?"

"I go away on a regular basis when I am checking in on coffee operations around the islands so that won't be a problem. And I can set Flint up as my assistant to meet with Francois-Henri and the two of you can listen from my private office."

It was almost as if Franklin relished the coming excitement. We promised to call him as soon as it was safe to return and with little commotion he was gone for a day or two.

"Let's see how we can set up our meeting," Flint said.

We discussed how to play it and in the end we decided to keep it simple. With Flint trying to keep Francois-Henri from becoming suspicious he would try to give enough details in order for Francois-Henri to feel comfortable about leaving to come back another day.

"We will monitor the conversation," Strider explained. "And then we can follow him down the mountain. With any luck and a little bit of skill we should be able to follow him straight to Suzanne."

A couple of hours later, just after we had talked about thinking of dinner, the quiet of the mountainside was disturbed by a surprising noise. Instead of an approaching car we heard a small helicopter coming from the other direction.

"This will make it more interesting," Flint commented. "Everyone to their positions."

"Good luck, Flint. We will be close by if you need help."

A couple of minutes later, Strider and I were safely hidden in Franklin's office looking out through the one-way mirror to the reception area and beyond to the deck. We could see the helicopter land and two men jump out. The pilot stayed aboard and I liked the odds if anything physical started.

Francois-Henri and the second man, a tall well-built guy who looked like a bodyguard, approached the desk and Flint got up to greet them.

"Where is Franklin? We have business to do today," Francois-Henri demanded.

"Mr. Olivine is away today up in the mountains. Can I help you? I am Mr. Olivine's assistant."

"We will wait. We need to talk to him today."

"I afraid Mr. Olivine won't be back for at least two days," Flint explained. "He is exploring some properties with a new client."

Although Francois-Henri was getting angry, he also looked like he didn't want to spend hours talking to someone who probably wouldn't be able to solve his problems. "Tell him I came looking for him and I'll be back in a couple of days. Is there a way to get in touch with him before he gets back here?"

"Not really." Flint was ready to sink the hook on our plan. "But the Starbucks guy he was with did leave me a satellite phone number that works in the mountains."

"Starbucks? I thought you weren't dealing with them anymore. What happened?"

"Something changed in the past few days. A couple of the Starbucks' guys returned and are anxious to get a presence here."

Flint gave Francois-Henri the number and then they were gone. I looked at Strider. "How are we going to track him now?"

"Don't worry about him. I have put out a tracking request on the helicopter and we will know where it goes. Anywhere in the island and it is ours now." Strider continued, "And if we can't find Suzanne today, we will be able to track Francois-Henri if he calls that number to set up a new meeting."

We headed back to town to monitor progress of the helicopter tracking. "No news yet, John, but we know they returned to the airport and haven't moved in the past hour," Strider said. "We have agents stationed around the airport waiting for something to happen. I'll let you know as soon as I hear something."

Waiting—with no personal action leading to a quick solution. Again this was a position that I had been put into I didn't like. Inaction weighed on me and I headed out to gather my thoughts. Walking through the main tourist part of town I thought back to the first time I met the smile. I certainly didn't think this is how it would turn out. And I didn't like the fact that I wasn't able to provide a solution. I walked down the hill towards Wickham's Cay and the harbor. Stopping at one of the restaurants the two of us had enjoyed,

I grabbed a quick meal of fresh fish washed down with a cold beer. Looking out on the ocean I waited for something to happen.

My phone rang. "Get back here, John. Things are happening fast," Flint yelled over the phone.

"I am down at the harbor and will be there in a couple of minutes."

"Wait there and we will pick you up. Meet us on the dingy dock. We are headed out on the water and it looks like we will be tracking the helicopter."

I paid for the quick but great lunch and walked down to the water. A minute later Flint and Strider jumped out of their truck and the three of us headed down the dock. Strider explained, "Shortly after you left, the helicopter took off and headed offshore. Based on its direction we think it's headed towards Jost Van Dyke. It's a small island only four miles long with a couple of bars, a few small places to stay and the customs office. It is a great place to hold Suzanne. We are going to try to find out where they are headed and rescue Suzanne if we can. The only thing we know for sure is that Francois-Henri is onboard and they aren't going far. We talked to the gas jockey at the airport and he confirmed they haven't refilled since their trip earlier. They only have enough fuel for about an hour's worth of flight."

"John, like we explained earlier, we want you to remain away from wherever Suzanne is held," Flint said. "We will provide the muscle."

"Fine, but remember I got her into this and I want to be part of the solution."

It took forty-five minutes to boat around the island and across towards Jost Van Dyke. It was a beautiful day on the water and we could see many tourists out on charter sailboats enjoying the mild breezes. We pulled into the customs dock and tied up.

Strider had been talking to someone. "The helicopter touched down at a private residence just down the beach from here. We are by ourselves and think we should move rather than wait for reinforcements."

"Wait here, Pride," Flint reminded me. They headed down the beach at a good clip while I watched. And waited for hours—actually it just felt like hours because I wasn't doing anything useful.

I looked down the beach and tried to decide what I was seeing. It was a commotion but I couldn't really make out what was happening. Whatever it was, it was happening fast and was coming this way. My heart skipped. It was Suzanne half running and half being dragged by Francois-Henri. And no sign of the good guys.

I could see Francois-Henri had a gun. I dropped over the side of the dock and waited. I was beside our boat slightly hidden and wet halfway up my legs. I would wait and see what was going to happen. Or I would attack Francois-Henri, rescue Suzanne and become the instant hero. No, I would wait!

"Hurry up and get in the red boat at the end of the dock," Francois-Henry was telling Suzanne.

"Why don't you just leave me here?"

"Not bloody likely. You are my ticket off these islands. Where I go, you go with me."

The two of them got into a boat about ten feet from where I was hiding. I submerged and quietly swam closer. Through the crystal clear water I could see Francois-Henri leaning over the transom preparing to start the engine. It was now or never. With a big spring of my legs against the ocean bottom I sprang out of the water and grabbed Francois-Henri. I don't know who was more surprised—me that it worked, or Francois-Henri when he found himself in the water and defenseless. A minute later I had him pinned to the sand beach with Suzanne, Flint and Strider all staring at the two of us. I noticed Flint had a gun pointed at Francois-Henri and I relaxed. Why hadn't I been provided with a gun? That surely would have been much easier.

"Congratulations, John. You appear to have done what the two of us failed to accomplish," Strider said. He let a small smile creep onto his face and I could tell he was enjoying the fact that I had a small role in the capture. Okay, let's call it a major role—I am after all trying to impress the island women. Or at least the one island woman I was really interested in. And speaking of impressing Suzannne, this was her cue. She threw her arms around me and pulled me away from Francois-Henri.

"How did you know what to do, John?" Suzanne asked. "I thought I was headed off for another ride."

Strider and Flint bundled up Francois-Henri and Strider explained what just happened. "The last you saw us we were headed up to intercept Francois-Henri, but we didn't count on him having a lookout waiting for us. Before we could do anything we were without weapons and being held in a locked room. By the time we figured out how to get free, you had solved the case."

"I am glad I was able to help." And with that we all headed back to town.

The ride back was uneventful other than I had to bear the burden of having Suzanne's head on my shoulder as she replayed how scared she had been. It was a burden I was more than happy to bear.

"If you want to be happy, be!"

Thoreau

CHAPTER 40

"A sailor without a destination cannot hope for a favorable wind."

Leon Tec, MD

I CALLED WHIT. "GOOD news brother. We finally cracked the case."

"Don't give me the details. I've a great idea on how to celebrate. Wait a couple of days and we can finally get that cruise up the coast."

"Great idea, I'll have a drink ready for you and *Rum-Runner* ready to head out. I have been giving our Grandfather's mystery some thought and I have some ideas I would like to try out on the water."

Two days later with a fully stocked *Rum-Runner* we were headed north to Canada. We had agreed to spend a few days out on the water recreating the last rum run just before prohibition ended. Grandfather had hinted he had a few secrets out on the water and he did tell the two of us that we should be able to figure out what he meant by that. When Whit and I were younger we had spent many a summer day exploring the Sound looking for evidence of the last run. The only details we had were in the book Grandfather left us. He had detailed all of his runs south and returns to Canada after successfully delivering booze. When locals asked us about the rumors about hidden booze money and wealthy Canadians we always laughed them off. We were used to telling the locals that all the money was accounted for and went into bringing up the family. But I knew there was more to it than that. Grandfather was shrewd with money. After all, he did buy this island and he was able to put all of us though university. And he always talked about taking Whit and I for that final cruise when he would show us where he had hidden the first *Rum-Runner*. The trip never happened and time passed without us discovering the truth. Whether there was any treasure was something that I wanted to put to rest.

We stopped overnight at a great bed and breakfast I had been to before and the next day we were out on the water early. A perfect day for exploring—a clear day, almost calm waterway with a goal in mind. We were going to have one more look for Grandfather's treasure.

Several hours later we pulled into shore for a quick lunch.

"Whit, look over at the island across the way."

"What do you see, John?"

"I see something we should explore. See that old tree? There is something about it that is worth a second look."

We motored over and Whit quickly saw what I had seen earlier. Behind the tree in a nook in the rock was an almost completely overgrown boathouse door. At least from here it looked like part of an old boathouse door. And unless I was mistaken, it was a close cousin to the door on our boathouse. The only difference was that this was a single door and it looked like it hadn't been opened for years. It was well hidden in the trees along the shore and had all its original metal hardware. The wood was unpainted cedar and it had weathered well and blended in so you couldn't see it until you were right up close.

It took us most of the rest of the afternoon to get the door open. We had to move a few trees and I can tell you that is not the easiest thing to do from a moving platform like a boat. Several times we almost ended up in the water. We knew we were on the verge of finding something special.

Whit had the honor of the final pull on the door and we were looking in at Grandfather's final run. Inside the specially designed boathouse was his *Rum-Runner*. It was just as he had promised— forty-five feet long, narrow beamed with nice mahogany and oak woodwork. It was raised out of the water with several slings and it still looked fast just sitting there. It would be fun getting it ship-shape again and out on the Sound.

I could see several small outboard engines on the wall, or I should say on the rock wall. One of them reminded me of the ancient engine I had on our first boat. A pull cord that took several pulls to get the sparks going.

Everywhere you looked you could see the tools of the trade. There were rows of liquor—all in old bottles and all full. It would take us a long time to drink our way through this treasure. At the back of the rock boathouse on a ledge high above the boat we found his roll-top desk. It was like he had just left it earlier in the week. A little dustier no doubt but still looking like a working desk. Whit went back to exploring the bottles as I looked through Grandfather's desk. The most interesting thing I could see was an old journal. I grabbed it and thought it would be interesting to read with a dram or two of whisky. It was a medium sized brown leather-bound journal, well worn and with the name *Pride* on the front.

I sat down in the old chair in front of the desk. This desk would have a place of honor in our cottage. I leaned back and thought for a minute, what a real pleasure to be here with Grandfather as he showed the two of us his treasures. I closed my eyes and thought of the last time I had seen Grandfather and the talk he had given to Whit and me. I can almost hear the words today. Grandfather had given us his famous words about the trip taken being worth much more than the actual prize at the end of the trip. I remembered a trip taken by ten-speed bicycle across Canada in my youth. And I thought of a trip being taken by one of his grandchildren right now, a canoe trip across Canada from Vancouver to New Brunswick, raising money for the Nature Conservancy and Heritage Rivers. That trip being taken by my cousin is one that Grandfather would have supported and I am sure he would have wanted to be there for some of the portages and some of the celebrations.

I looked up at the desk. It seemed to be out from the rock wall. I reached back past where I found the journal into what felt like a recessed hiding place. It was just made for my hand. I felt a bottle, then another. I brought out one, stood it up on the desk, sat down again and stared at the bottle. I reached in and pulled out another one, and then another. By the time I was finished Whit was standing behind me and we were both awestruck. These were Scotch bottles—and not just any Scotch bottle—they were the long lost *Graham Bell Scotch* bottles. Grandfather had talked about meeting the Bells and Grahams during the thirties. He had told us that he had taken them a case of his best Canadian rye and in return he had received a case of twenty-year-old Scotch from a small distillery in the hills of the border country. These bottles were now over a hundred-years old and if I was correct, nobody knew these existed. Certainly as far as I knew, nobody had tasted this Scotch for over fifty years.

Half an hour later we were back at the boat toasting our discovery. I know this was extravagant but we opened one of the *Graham Bell Scotch* bottles. It was great. I was reading to Whit. "This journal wasn't started by Grandfather, it was started by his grandfather. Do you mind old John Pride?"

"Yes, John, wasn't he the one with the large family back in Ontario? Two wives and eleven children."

"Listen to this. This starts as his journal back in 1837. Heady days they were, he is talking about his times with William Lyon Mackenzie and the Rebellion of 1837. Grandfather always hinted about a black sheep in the family. This is really interesting Whit. He talks about his time in America after their short attempted rebellion."

I read from the journal. "Mackenzie and about twenty of us spent the night discussing where we were headed now. The only thing decided was that we are now all members of the *Order of the Rebellion*. Yours truly is trusted with the responsibility of keeping track of the original members."

"*Order of the Rebellion*," Whit said. "I've never heard about this. This could be interesting. Just think, our great, great Grandfather on the run with Mackenzie. And you will remember from your history lessons that Mackenzie's grandson was William Lyon Mackenzie King, one of Canada's most illustrious Prime Ministers."

"Enough with the history lesson. We should promote this *Order of the Rebellion* within the family and perhaps share a bottle or two in honor of Grandfather and John Pride."

On the way back to Lumsden Island I thought back to where we had come from. Not the family, but the few of us that really believed that we could catch the terrorists. If we were to succeed we would need to redouble our efforts. We had a few of the minor players but still had no idea who was running the show.

"Thanks, Whit. I couldn't have done it without you."

"I enjoyed working with you, John. It was more interesting than my usual work at the paper. I think I am going to be doing some research on the asset backed securities that you have been hearing about lately."

"Wow," I said. "I can hardly wait until you try to explain why investors are investing in a security which is made up of mortgages written to homeowners who really shouldn't have qualified for a huge home in the first place. If you can explain that to your average reader you deserve the Pulitzer Prize."

"You will be the first to hear about it."

The next morning we boated back to Seattle so Whit could catch a flight back east.

"I'll call you after I talk to the FBI and let you know how they are wrapping up the case."

"What are you going to do with your free time now?" Whit asked.

"It is the twentieth anniversary of the hike I did with John Clarke. You remember him—the Coast Mountains mountaineer, conservationist and wilderness educator. He was the one who the First Nations called Mountain Goat."

"Wasn't that the hike to the top of Mount Elaho?"

"Yes, and I can remember him telling me about being on the Kitilope the day Randy Stoltmann died. He never did understand how it happened. John said he was right there when Randy skied past him and off the side of the mountain never to be seen alive again."

"Well, take care of yourself, don't overdo the hiking."

"I am going to head over to the west side of the Olympic Peninsula and do the North Wilderness Beach hike. I will meet my old friend, Rick Morden and his toller dogs. Maybe we'll spend a little time researching the Skokomish, Chehalis, Hoh, Quinault, Quileute, Makah, S'Klallam tribes. I still want to explore how they used potlatches back in the old days. Rick has some ideas about how the potlatches compare to some of his Scottish traditions. He thinks there is a similarity to the raiding parties of the Reivers of the Borders. Perhaps there is a story to be written."

"It sounds like you have your plans."

"Yes, we'll do the twenty miles and then probably stop for a few days at the Lake Quinault Lodge. I think Rick has a special plan for watching his favorite football team. His family is from Saskatchewan, up in Canada, and he cheers for the Roughriders. I must have watched at least thirty or more of their games with him and have to say that they are usually more entertaining than the NFL games. They play on a larger field and with only three downs it makes for an exciting game."

"Sounds like fun—football, beaches, tide pools, harbor seals, bald eagles and gray whales. Did you know that President Roosevelt planned the National Park while he stayed there?"

"Yes, and I might plan my retirement now this case is finished."

I said goodbye to Whit, headed back to Lumsden Island and awaited the arrival of the FBI to explain what we had accomplished.

What I didn't mention to Whit was that the main reason I wanted to head over to the west side was that now that I had a few days of leisure I might be able to do some work on a new case. I had been approached a month ago about trying to get some evidence on an owner of several marine resorts. I had been asked by a group of investors to try and to unravel the tangled business affairs of Vincent Michael. He along with several investors owned several popular resorts in the Puget Sound and Seattle area. The investors were certain Vincent was siphoning off money but didn't have enough to go to the authorities so I was going to try and get the goods on him. My first idea was to head out to his most secluded resorts and that would fit in with the story I had just given Whit.

I would be headed off after I heard from the FBI tomorrow. They were going to explain how they would wrap up the case. At least my small part in it was finished.

"The whole course of human history may depend on a change of heart in a single, solitary, even humble individual. For it is within the soul of the individual that the battle between good and evil is waged and ultimately won or lost."

Thoreau

CHAPTER 41

"The waters of the upper Niagara River are heavy this week with the dead land and the decay of a passing winter as they churn slowly toward the mighty gorge. And as they spill over they fall slowly, muddy and dark."
RHD Phillips, Canadian Press Staff Writer, April 24, 1957

IT WAS QUIET. VERY quiet, and I was not complaining. Whit should have stayed to hear directly from the FBI how the case was completed. Freedom nuzzled my legs and looked towards the back door and a potential walk. "Okay, old boy, let's stretch our legs while we wait. Let's go for a walk." Freedom perked up and we headed up the hill and picked some blackberries while we waited. I threw him a couple and after the first one, the next one bounced off his closed mouth. He was concentrating on something, and that was not the food at hand. I looked out on the sound and could see a small powerboat incoming. This must be the end to the case, the final explanation. I was looking forward to hearing what the FBI was doing to finish what I still thought was an unfinished case. It was early for them to be here. I had been told to expect them in the afternoon and had laid on some lunch.

We walked down to the dock and I was surprised to see that there was only one man aboard.

"Welcome to Lumsden Island—" I hesitated because I was surprised to see Dave. I thought he would be the last person the FBI would send to talk to me. Especially to congratulate me on a good job, well done—assuming that was what he was going to do.

"Hello, John. I guess you must be surprised to see me again." He jumped out and the two of us tied up his boat. It wasn't a government boat, and looked like a local rental. That was definitely odd because I knew the federal office had several excellent ocean-going boats that were available for agent use.

I didn't know what to say and in a minute it looked like I wouldn't need to say anything. I looked out on the Sound again and then—a gun comes out. Where did that come from and why is it pointing at me? I stare at it for a moment before realizing what was happening.

"Pride, you are smart but you never saw this coming, did you?"

"Dave, can I assume we are on different teams again?"

"Smart ass, you just couldn't stop pushing and sticking your nose in where it didn't belong."

I didn't think I really had anything to lose. It was only in the movies that the good guys arrived in the nick of time to save the hero. And I didn't feel like a hero right now. "So, Dave, it looks like you have some explaining to do."

"Not to you I don't, and when you are gone I rather doubt anyone else will be able to finish what you started. Start walking." He motioned up the hill to where he wanted me to head. I turned around and slowly walked north.

"You know, Dave, you don't have to stop me. This will still unravel if I am not around. Misty knows enough to keep investigating and my brother is still interested in a final piece for his newspaper."

"Thanks for telling me how to pick up the loose ends," Dave said. "I might have just stopped with you. Now you can go to your death knowing you are responsible for their demise. As a matter of fact I think the three of you should die together."

We reached the crest of the hill. The sun was high in the sky, and an eagle soared high above. It was almost a perfect day. We had solved a case, or at least we thought we had, and now Dave was ruining the day forever. I looked far out towards Seattle. Why was I almost always alone when I really needed someone to come to the rescue? It would be days before anyone thought to check up on me. If only I had seen through Dave's act and realized he must have had something to do with the terrorists.

"How did it work? All we could see was the two different groups. And the one who we had the most information on was the least important."

"I guess there is no reason why you can't know why you failed, Pride." Dave looked proud of being in a position of strength. "You couldn't see farther than the bad guys. The only problem I had was your continued interest in following the money. I knew eventually someone would see the discrepancies. The real threats were coming from the terrorists on the west coast, but the money was going somewhere else. I took advantage of seeing that they didn't seem to want large amounts of money. They just needed recognition. They really did just want to change the system, starting with how GMO research was being carried out, and carrying on to trying to influence Starbucks' operations. My brilliant addition was to up the financial stakes to take advantage of their actions for my own gain."

"But you must have known that someone would find out," I asked.

"No one was going to find out. If you hadn't confronted the guys out here and found out that there were no offshore accounts, no one would have been the wiser. The plan was to increase the demands and piggyback on the threats from the small town terrorists. No one would know I wasn't a real terrorist. And then I came up with a plan to get some serious money from Starbucks. And I would have if you hadn't come along and ruined it for me."

We continued along the ridge and I could see Dave was still trying to come up with a plan. We reached the old farm site and the derelict buildings. Dave motioned for me to sit down in front of the old log cabin and pulled out his cell phone. He pointed his gun at me and said, "Not a word, Pride. One word and I shoot your kneecap. And then just for fun I'll shoot your gut and see how you like dying in pain, all alone."

He walked a few steps, just far enough that I could hear his side of the conversation. But not too close to allow me to jump him.

"Misty, this is Dave. I think you should get over to Lumsden Island. I am here and can't find Pride. All I see is a little blood on the deck."

I was going to say something—just a few words to warn Misty. But somehow I knew that by the time I had a word or two out, it would be too late and Misty would be off the line and she would already be on her way to danger.

Dave sat down. It looked like neither of us was headed anywhere. I made myself comfortable in the shade. The sun moved slowly across the sky and I wondered where everyone had gone. Whit was on the way back east, and Freedom was off exploring.

"Put your hands behind your back," Dave demanded. He tightly bound my hands hard against my back and roughly pushed me back on the ground.

"Enjoy your last few hours. When Misty arrives the two of you are going to meet your timely demise." With that he headed back down the hill.

I lay down. Tried to concentrate. Failed. All I could think about was Misty boating directly into trouble. And I was going to be of no help. I couldn't even think of a plan that might work. I closed my eyes and tried to concentrate. All I could see was disaster. I opened my eyes and I could see that part of the afternoon had slipped away. I must have fallen asleep. No dreams today.

There was noise coming up the path. Misty and Dave. And Misty was not happy. "You are lower than a snake, you thieving federal agent," Misty screamed. "First you get me out here thinking that John was injured, and now I find out you're a slime ball of the lowest order. You think you can get away with this?"

She looked at me. "Are you okay, John?"

"Physically yes, but emotionally wrecked. This is my fault, Misty."

"Don't beat yourself up, John. Remember it was me that kept saying I didn't like having Dave involved. I should have known that there was more to his involvement."

"Okay, enough with the old times talk," Dave interjected. "The two of you are going for a short one-way boat ride. And I don't think either of you are going to like how it ends."

We both looked at each other, but said nothing. We headed back down the hill towards the dock. It was almost dusk when we arrived at *Rum-Runner*.

"Load the canoe aboard."

Misty and I maneuvered it onto the bow. Once aboard, Dave told me where to head. I was surprised. He wanted us to head towards the narrows. I wondered what he had in mind. Whatever he was thinking about it would have to look accidental, and would have to end up with him getting out safely. And that wasn't the easiest thing to do from a moving boat, especially in or around the narrows. Dave wouldn't know the history of the area—the many boaters who had drowned and the many people who just disappeared in the area. But who was I to complain. I am sure he had a plan, and we would be a big part of it soon enough.

"Whatever you have planned, Dave, it's not going to work."

"Shut up, Pride. Just drive and I'll take care of the planning."

When we got close to the narrows Dave pointed his gun at me. "Now it is time for you to get the canoe overboard."

I took a few minutes to get the canoe overboard and he tied it to the gunnels. "Sit back and enjoy the ride."

He headed off and the only thing we could do was watch Dave head towards the narrows. Just the way he was overcorrecting every time the boat hit a wave showed me that his experience in boats was minimal.

We were approaching Deception Pass, the rapids that separated Whidbey and Fidalgo Islands. I could see the two channels ahead with more water flowing through them than the combined flow from all the rivers emptying into the Sound, two million cubic feet per second and not rapids suitable for a novice boater. And although I was sure Dave could handle the boat in normal conditions, I just didn't have any idea what he had in mind. Whatever it was, it probably included Misty and me getting wet.

"John, the two of you are going to get off this joy ride and let me enjoy the rest of the trip without you." He forced us into the canoe, tied us with the rope and then we were away from him.

I could see what he had in mind. Now that we were upon the two channels he was piloting the boat close to the southern-most channel—the main Deception Pass. Not the one I would have recommended, but nobody was asking me. We always took Canoe Pass. Although Dave had throttled back, the current was starting to pick up. It was a high tide and I could see the flow was at least eight knots. We were moving by the shore at a good clip and I couldn't see how Dave was going to make land safely. I looked over to him and saw he was fixated on a point off the bow. He started to bring the boat around and—before he could compensate for the surging rapids the stern swung around. Dave had a quick decision to make. Either he could jump and get wet, or he could stay with the boat and enjoy the rapids.

"Don't jump, Dave. You will never make shore from here. The current is too strong and the eddies will pull you down."

"Give me a break, John. I'll take my chance."

He jumped. But not the way I thought he would. Not downstream towards what I would have thought would be safety. He jumped the other way—the closer to shore way, but upstream. *Rum-Runner* was free of him and I wished we were still aboard instead of in the canoe.

We could see him after he resurfaced. He was swimming. Or at least he was trying to swim. He was struggling to keep above water, and he certainly wasn't getting any closer to shore. He didn't seem to understand the physics of the rapids. Not only was he trying to swim against the current but he also had the combined tidal and hydraulic effects working against him. A few more strokes and even Dave could see he was getting nowhere. And we were floating farther away. He changed direction and tried to swim to a large boulder halfway to shore. I could see the eddies on the downstream side and tried to warn him, "Watch out for the undercurrent."

It was too late and I'm not sure he heard me. Before we had a chance to worry about our danger, he was gone from view.

"What are we going to do now?" Misty asked.

I could feel the rope was not going to be removed easily. And we only had a few minutes before the boat hit a rock and pinned us in with a certain death. This aluminum boat would stick onto any rocks and then I knew what would happen. It would capsize and with water flowing into the boat, it would bend around the rock. Nothing could stop that, and I for one did not want to be around to experience that again. I had been in an aluminum canoe when it took about twenty seconds for the force of that river to bend the canoe into an unrecognizable pretzel that would have killed me if I had remained.

"Misty, we have to get out of here. See those rocks below. We are not going to be able to get through without the boat going under. If we jump we should be able to do a three armed dog paddle."

"I don't know what you have in mind, but I always thought it was best to stay with the boat."

"Usually, but not when we can't pilot the boat, and certainly not in this case when I am pretty sure we are so far south in the narrows that we will hit at least one or two big rocks."

"Okay, let's take our chances in the water," Misty agreed.

We rolled off the stern and before we had a chance to think twice about what we had just done, we were in the middle of a class IV rapid.

"Don't try to go against the flow. We are not going to be able to swim to shore. Just keep your head up and go with the flow." We kept our feet out in front and tried to keep from swallowing too much water. It was hard coordinating our arms. At least our feet were free and we could kick them independently.

We were upstream from the canoe and could see it starting to bang off a series of barely-submerged rocks. Then the canoe caught a sharp rock and in a flash of an eye it had rolled and water was pouring over the gunnels. Thousands of pounds of water pressure—we could hear the water working on the canoe. It was bending metal and seconds later it exploded with sparks shooting skyward.

"That was close, but don't look now—here comes another series of rapids."

"Pull left hard." I recognized the voice. I looked over my shoulder and was more than pleasantly surprised to see Whit bearing down in a Zodiac. "Hang on and try to swim left of the rapids."

Whit had arrived just in time. "Hang tough, I'll get you." He threw us a line and in a matter of less than a minute Misty and I were onboard the Zodiac. Whit had hauled us in and we lay on the floorboards, wet and thankful.

"Am I glad to see you. We have to head upstream and see if we can rescue Dave."

"Don't waste your breath thinking about him. I saw what he was trying to do to the two of you. And I saw what happened to him. He went under the water in the eddy behind the rocks he was swimming towards. I headed close to him and when he resurfaced I told him to grab hold of a line that was tied onto the stern. He grabbed it but then he tried to pull himself onboard. I told him it was too dangerous to do that in the middle of the rapids but he wasn't listening to me. His eyes had a terrified look and as he was trying to get onboard he swung underneath. I think the prop got him and he didn't come back up."

"Yew, better him than us," Misty said.

"And look below the rapids," Whit said. I couldn't believe my eyes. *Rum-Runner* looked like it had come through unscathed. A few minutes later we made ourselves downstream and recaptured the long lost boat. Lashing the canoe and zodiac to the stern I looked over to Whit. "What made you come back?" I asked.

"After you dropped me at the dock I saw Dave when I was getting a cab for the airport," Whit explained. "It wasn't until I reached my flight that I finally realized what was bothering me. There was no reason for Dave to be back in Seattle. He would be the last person the FBI would send to congratulate you. I tried calling you but he must have met up with you by then. I tried to get

Misty on the phone but all I got was her answering machine. I didn't have any choice but to head out to the island and see for myself. By the time I arrived I could see the boat heading out so I stayed back until I figured out where you were going. It didn't take a rocket scientist to see that you were on the way to the narrows. The rest is history."

"And a nice future history thanks to you," Misty purred, giving Whit a well-deserved kiss and hug. I stood back and just gave him a light punch on his shoulder.

"I am not sure how you put it all together, Whit, but we are both in your debt." I looked out at the narrows, and could see the first of the emergency vehicles arriving—two coast guard boats, which would look for any signs of Dave. And if the sounds were correct, a few of Seattle's finest riding to the rescue. Or as Misty would tell them in a few minutes, "What took you so long, did you hear it was me in trouble?"

They never did find Dave. And I am not sure I would have wanted to see him after the narrows was through with him. I have seen people cut with a boat propeller and to have a mile of sharp rocks on top of that would not look pretty. One or two prop cuts can be stitched up. I know that from experience. And years later it is hard to see where the prop blades went in and went out. But I am sure you would never forget the feeling of falling out of a boat and being hit by a moving prop.

"Life in us is like the water in a river."

Thoreau

CHAPTER 42

"Now would I give a thousand furlongs of sea for an acre of barren ground."

Shakespeare "The Tempest"

Two hours later we were settled into a Scotch on the Lumsden Island deck. We had spent a few minutes with the police onshore and after Misty explained what had transpired, we headed back to the cottage. We were met by three of the FBI's finest. Anyone other than Dave was an improvement. Blake was there with Mike, one of his Washington operatives. And they had brought my old friend Francis. After bringing them up to speed we got down to business.

"We were coming here to congratulate you for all your help, John," started Blake. "But I think we had better rethink closing this case. Obviously we have been overlooking some important facts."

"Ah, the good Francis. You can help us capture Francois-Henri."

"Yes, perhaps now there really is a connection between Francois-Henri, Dave and our local terrorists," replied Francis.

"That is more like it. Ever since Dave got involved I have felt that the FBI was working against me, and now we know why."

"We hope you won't hold that against the agency," Mike replied. "We are headed back to Washington and will ensure that the full might of the agency is finally working with you to finish this case. In particular I think we should concentrate on the work you have done in the BVIs. I really think you were on

— 222 —

to something and if Dave hadn't been involved I'm sure we would be farther ahead by now."

"What's next?" Misty asked.

Francis jumped in, "I was out in Seattle and when Blake told me he was headed over here to see you, I invited myself along. And I am glad I did. Now we know we still have a long way to go, I think we can get CLEW involved. I can see you have some real proof that the bad guys have been using international transfers of money and that is all we need to throw the weight of our enforcement agency along side the FBI. Together we should be able to solve this. And we can work with your new friends on the Caribbean Financial Action Task Force. I'll get on the phone to Flint and see what assistance we can provide."

"I am going to recommend that we reconnect in the BVIs where we can finally find the real terrorists. You have given us some good leads and the local talent should be able to continue to help."

"Ahoy, permission to come onshore." The voice caught our attention.

I looked to the end of the dock and couldn't believe what I was seeing. Susan our mystery woman was mooring her sailboat next to the FBI boat. I walked down the dock. Slowly—trying to decide what to say to her—what to ask her first.

"Don't say anything, John. I have a lot of explaining to do. Let me tell you what happened."

The two of us walked together to join the others. "John doesn't know," Susan said to Blake.

I looked at Blake and said, "John doesn't know what?"

"Susan is one of us and was assigned to Dave to help him work on the terrorist case. I am not sure what happened but I am sure Susan can fill in some details."

Susan sat down and started to tell us her tale. And what a tale it was. It appears that she is a highly thought of FBI computer agent and when Dave saw that we were getting close to the BVIs connection he assigned Susan to try and find out what we really knew.

"I didn't know he was a rogue agent, John," Susan explained. "All he told me was that you were doing investigating into a case and were holding onto classified information that wasn't getting back to the FBI. He had me meet you to try and see what you were doing. I searched your office but I wasn't able to find anything that could help Dave. I told him that and he wanted me to go back to your cottage and break in. Things moved too fast for that and thankfully before we were able to really cause any hardship for you he acted himself. Sorry I had to deceive you."

"You were very convincing," I replied. "No need to apologize. But what was Dave looking for?"

"He kept talking about wire transfers of money from the BVIs and was sure you had learned something you were not sharing with him. Now it appears that he was just concerned you were getting close to him. We know he had been swindling money from universities for over three years."

"Blake, why didn't you tell me?" I asked him.

"John, I wasn't in the loop. And I don't think Dave would have wanted me to know because he knew that I thought highly of you and would have questioned any second-guessing of you. I didn't hear about this until yesterday and was on my way to see you when I heard about what transpired on the water. I grabbed a boat and here I am."

"Well what ends well—"

"Actually," started Blake. "We don't think this is the end either. Dave was an important part of the terrorist case but we now think he was just taking advantage of something that was started by others. Your ideas and evidence in the BVIs is strong reason to believe that we still haven't finished with this case."

"I should finish my story," Susan joined in. "What Dave really wanted me to do was search your computers but before I had a chance to do that you were up and around that night and I hid and then snuck out early the next morning. I thought someone had seen me up in the spire and didn't want to be confronted. That is what I told Dave and still he wanted me to break in and have a second go at looking at your computer files. Now I am glad it didn't get to that because he authorized me to destroy your computers if I could gain access. Then we would have lost the work you have been doing this past week."

"What do you mean?" I asked. "I haven't been able to gain any headway with my work and now with all this excitement I am even farther behind."

"Actually your work has been fruitful, you just don't know it. Your work to exclude the FBI was well done but when I reviewed the email you sent us I noticed your work. It took me a while to figure it out and take it from me, you are to be commended if your team can develop something that can fool not only the terrorists but also our counter-terrorist computer team. When we found out what you were doing we still assumed that you had something to do with the money transfers and were able to intercept the emails that you were trying to intercept. Did you follow that? What I am trying to say is that although you didn't know you were being successful, we have been able to gain a much better picture of the terrorists in the past few days."

"I knew it would work," I replied. "What is next and can you show me what has happened?"

"John, I think you should spend a couple of hours with Susan and her team in Seattle before heading to the BVIs," Blake mentioned. "She can bring you up to speed quickly and then you can work with the British agents."

We got to work in the office spire and Susan patched us through to her Seattle team. After reviewing the gathered info it was clear that Dave's part in the case was just a crime of opportunity. He saw the chance to take advantage of the situation the terrorists had created. Dave had been able to build on the universities' fear of research funding disruption and create a way to persuade them to pay monies to avoid terrorism. The real terrorists didn't understand what was happening and certainly didn't have any way to stop Dave.

Susan showed me some of the redirected emails. "What these show is that the main terrorists fell for your initial email with the FBI report. Not only did they read it but they forwarded to several main players and now we are in a better position to start to round them up. But the most interesting development is the role Francois-Henri has been playing over the past few years. Although we suspected him of involvement with terrorists, neither Interpol nor us could pin anything on him. But now, thanks to you, we have a direct link between Francois-Henri and the terrorists. And some of their money is being laundered through his land holdings in the BVIs."

"So, what are you suggesting?"

"John, you should try to get closer to Francois-Henri and persuade him that his best chance of avoiding prosecution is to work with the authorities to bring down the terrorists. We are not positive about his role but think it is limited to a financial one and not linked to the actual bombings. If so, we might be able to work with him to get rid of the real terrorists."

"But what about his involvement with the abduction of my friend

Suzanne? He could have really hurt her and he did have at least one gun when that happened."

"We know, but we think he can still help us with bigger fish."

"I don't like him, and the last time I saw him he was being led away by Strider and Flint."

"Yes, but when we realized what was happening we intervened and had him held in solitary confinement in the BVIs. I think you will find him ready to cooperate when you return."

It was starting to look like we were going to have to postpone our hike. I called Rick. "Morden, I have good news and bad news, but first the bad. I am unable to meet you for our hike this week."

Rick answered, "Don't tell me, you are off on another wild assignment."

"Actually, you are not far off. We thought we had that terrorist case wrapped up and it looks like we have just scratched the surface. Now I have to head back to the BVIs."

"And that is the bad news. I wish I got that type of bad news. What is the good news?"

"Rick, my hiking partner, this is your lucky day. We need your talents on the job. Get down to the islands and you can help us finish this."

"Which of my talents are you talking about?"

I said, "The FBI has an idea that if we can bring a real expert on GMO foods into the case we may be able to bring more of the bad guys out in the open."

We talked for a few more minutes but it didn't take much to persuade Rick to jump on board our adventure. We planned to meet in the islands.

The next morning we were in the air on the way to the smile again. Misty looked at me. "Why is it that you get that special look when you talk about Suzanne?"

"I think it is because I feel at home when I am around her. It doesn't matter where we are. We are just at home together. Do you know that feeling?"

"Not recently, and I don't think you have for a long while. Not since your accident, and you still don't want to talk about that, do you?"

"No." We both relaxed and enjoyed the quiet until it was time to get ready for landing.

I hadn't called the smile. I wanted her as far away from what we were going to do as possible. She would understand. Perhaps she wouldn't like being avoided but surely she would understand.

Misty and I exited the plane to the regularly boring sunny and warm Caribbean weather. I must remember to come here when we don't have to put in a regular workday.

My friends, the local British talent, met us at the airport. Our day would start to speed up, starting right now.

> *"I left the woods for as good a reason as I went there. Perhaps it seemed to me that I had several more lives to live, and could not spare any more time for that one."*
>
> *Thoreau*

CHAPTER 43

"It isn't that life ashore is distasteful to me.
But life at sea is better."

Sir Francis Drake

"THANKS FOR REJOINING US, John." Strider and Flint were walking towards us, Strider doing the talking, both considerably friendlier than when I first met them.

I introduced them to Misty and Rick. "This is my partner, Misty, who can help us finalize this case. Rick will be our GMO expert."

"Good to meet the two of you," Strider continued to talk for the two of them. "We hope the two enjoy your time in the islands. It should be interesting."

"Good to be back in the islands. I wish I were here on vacation. It just seems that every time I return, the case is more and more mysterious."

"Well," Strider answered. "Perhaps now we can get some real answers. We never did feel comfortable with Dave's role in all this. You were right to keep questioning the banking end. Now we understand that the FBI thinks we can use Francois-Henri to wrap up more of the bad guys."

"Do you have any ideas?"

"Keeping with the banking angle, we think there may be an opportunity to use the lure of a big financial payout as the means to get some of the main terrorists to travel here. As you know, your Internet intercept has given both the FBI and Interpol the opportunity to detail a good number of the terrorists. Several we had well documented, but it appears as if you have been able to flush out several additional ones. And the ones we knew about we were having trouble infiltrating. Now, if we play our cards right, we may be able to make a significant breakthrough in breaking the back of several terrorist organizations."

Flint added, "If we can persuade Francois-Henri that it is in his best interests, he should be able to give us an air of authenticity. The key will be to get him to see a real personal benefit. At the present time all we can charge him with is the kidnapping and weapons offences. As major as those are, they are minor in the scheme of things. We really would like to get his cooperation and think you would be helpful because of your knowledge."

I looked at Flint with a newfound level of respect. Up until now I had assumed that he was the muscle part of the British intelligence presence on the islands. "Let's get the show rolling."

We headed off to my favorite bank. Through the front doors, a nod to the bankers and then downstairs. Nothing had changed except the addition of Francois-Henri in the high tech intelligence room. I could see that he had seen better days. He was downcast and slouching in a metal chair. There were two big military looking guys in the room with him and they quietly left as we entered. On the large computer screens along the old brick walls were images of the past few days. It left nothing to the imagination as to how much the authorities knew about Francois-Henri's activities.

Francois-Henri glared at the three of us, but focused on me. "I suppose that you are here to gloat on my downfall."

"Actually no, we want to understand what your role is in the continuing terrorism operations of your associates," I replied. "We are more interested in catching them than punishing you."

He didn't change his demeanor immediately but I could see that he was interested in what I was saying. He did sit up straighter and I could see his eyes take a new focused appearance, and he seemed to gain a real sense of power. I really couldn't see that he was going to be able to give us what we wanted but was prepared to play along and see where it went.

Strider started in, "We need to stop the escalation of the bombing and we view your capture as an opportunity. If you play your cards right, you might find yourself able to walk away from your criminal problems. But don't think that you will be able to continue to associate with them. When we are finished here you will want to melt away and never come to the attention of Interpol or your pals again. We can help with that but you may not like what you will need to do to get our assistance with the rest of your life."

I just sat back and listened. I had already worked out a plan with Misty. If we could get Francois-Henri's cooperation we should be able to strike an enormous blow to several terrorist groups.

Francois-Henri looked back and forth and finally fixed on me. "What makes you think I want to work with you?"

"It is not a matter of wanting to work with us, but a way for you to save your hide. You really don't have a choice. As we see it, with all the money laundering charges that you are facing, your time outside of jail will be near nil. This is not only your best chance for some freedom but also your only chance. If you don't help us, they are going to know that you are talking to us and I don't relish your chances of staying alive behind bars. You need our help to make yourself disappear after you have helped us."

Strider said, "I'll tell you what we need from you. We are putting together a deal which should interest most of the terrorists. It will include promising not to involve Starbucks in any of their terrorism. The selling point is a $60 million payout to them and a promise not to include Starbucks' worldwide operations in any form of terrorism. And that would include the just-started campaign against Starbucks' use of GMO food items. We will provide the funding and your job is to ensure that as many as possible of the terrorists travel to the islands to participate in their expected payday."

"How am I going to do that? They are used to transactions taking place by untraceable wire transfers. Remember, these are people that are very security conscientious. How are you going to ensure they come?"

I explained what Misty and I had come up with, "Your job is to explain to the terrorists that the ownership of Starbucks is prepared to deal but only directly. They want to hand the money over directly to the key players and they want to receive direct confirmation that they are actually paying for protection. You will be here in the Caribbean to welcome them and will be with them when we swoop in and arrest everyone including you for the second time. If it goes according to plan they will not realize that you have set them up."

Francois-Henri thought for a few long minutes. I was thinking that this was a long shot and certainly would be harder to do without his direct assistance. I didn't think we would be able to lure very many of the terrorists to the bait without his assistance. "I can do it but it won't be easy. These terrorists can smell a trap thousands of miles away. How can you promise me that you can succeed?"

Strider answered him, "We know it won't be easy, but your freedom won't come easy or cheaply. We need to know whom we are dealing with and have to ensure we can trap as many of them at the same time. We will not get a second chance. And neither will you."

Rick spoke up for the first time, "This is the important hook for the terrorists. In order to really get them involved in the sting we need for them to think they have a real strong hand. It is not enough for them just to be muscle with a threat of violence against Starbucks. They need to think they have something that will terrify Starbucks."

Francois-Henri looked at Rick. "And what is that?"

"Starbucks has been dealing with the threat of boycotts over GMO items in their stores. This has been a thorn in their side for years but it really hasn't been something they have had to worry too much about. Think what they would face if the real threat was genetically modified coffee beans. What if you could threaten them with the potentially disastrous public relations nightmare of not knowing which coffee beans had been contaminated with GMO beans? Let the terrorists think that we can provide this and they will be prepared to do almost anything to be a part of your operation."

We spent the rest of the afternoon putting together the contact list and fine-tuning the approach to the terrorists. It would be initiated by an email from Francois-Henri and followed up with a personal telephone call to each of the terrorist leaders.

The email was the easy part:

To: Group of twelve

From: Francois-Henri

Subject: Starbucks' Protection

We have an opportunity to expand your protection business. Further to our discussions about Starbucks, they have gone farther than even we have dreamed. They are prepared to meet our demands and more. Instead of just a payment to stop the terrorism acts, they are prepared to make a larger one-time payment to each of you directly. They do not want to have me act as the middleman in this transaction. They want direct face-to-face confirmation from you that they are paying for protection. In order for us to complete this transaction, I need your confirmation. I will call you tomorrow to confirm your intentions and ensure travel arrangement that will meet this weekend's deadline.

"I can teach anybody how to get what they want out of life. The problem is that I can't find anybody who can tell me what they want."

Mark Twain

CHAPTER 44

"Land was provided to provide a place for boats to visit."
Brooks Atkinson

THE NEXT MORNING WAS a blur. I had thought about visiting the smile last evening but realized that seeing her would just misdirect my attention for the evening and I wanted to stay focused on the job at hand. Strider put me up in their safe house and after a quick dinner I headed off to an early sleep knowing the following day would be eventful.

We met at the bank and my British friends brought me up to date on what they had achieved. "You seem prepared," I said.

"I think we are ready for whatever comes our way," Strider confirmed. "Francois-Henri has commitments from all the terrorists and we have our navy friends gearing up for the weekend. Two days and we should know whether all this has led to success."

Flint added, "We are all heading to sea this afternoon and will be out of touch until the operation starts."

"Why are we headed out to sea so soon?" I asked.

"We are concerned that if we stay on land Francois-Henri will become a problem. The last thing we need is for one of the terrorists to try to find him and start questioning the arrangements. Better to have everything arranged and for Francois-Henri to tell all of them to keep radio silence until they all meet on the water. They will be out in international waters when they all meet aboard his yacht and by keeping silent we can reduce the uncertainties."

"Right you are," I agreed. Even though I did agree, I wasn't looking forward to spending the next two days on the water. The weather forecast was for rough weather and I knew Misty would need hand holding. She wouldn't want me to mention this but we both knew that her stomach started to soften up after a few hours of rough going on the water.

Right on clue Misty looked right at me, or I should say right through me, and any ideas of bringing up the suggestion that she should stay on land was quickly dropped. The last thing she wanted was to miss any of the action.

"Looking forward to a few days of boating," she confirmed.

Rick added, "This should be like old times. Adventure on the high seas—count me in."

We picked up Francois-Henri and headed down to the docks. I knew we were going out in his yacht but I guess I really wasn't reconciled to the grandeur of his ill-gotten gains. His black yacht must be at least ninety feet long, with a helicopter pad and several high-speed motor-launches thrown in for good measure. After settling in I compared details with Misty.

"My stateroom is forward and has room for at least three sailors," she mentioned.

"Is that in addition to you, and are they already there?"

"Funny, John." She playfully hit me on the left shoulder. "But seriously, I never did hear how Francois-Henri is going to explain the three of us to the terrorists."

"Our cover story is that I am the captain and you are the cook, and I think we can pull that off. Rick is going to be Francois-Henri's GMO expert. I just hope that when the time comes for action we can keep our heads down and stay out of harm's way. Our real role is to ensure Francois-Henri doesn't alert any of his friends once they are aboard. We won't be able to monitor all his conversations but the fact he knows the best of the Royal Navy is just a short distance away should eliminate any ideas he might have."

"For our sakes I hope so, John."

"Strider and Flint will be with us until just before the terrorists start to arrive and they will be able to get here quickly if anything happens before scheduled."

We headed up to the upper deck and joined Strider, Flint and Francois-Henri around the state-of-the-art command center. It was clear that neither of the British lads were boaters, but Francois-Henri was doing his best to explain some of the electronics. "You understand how the depth sounder works and this is our new radar. I am not sure what you have done with my system but it is not picking up any of the naval ships you tell me are lurking just past the horizon. I'll take your experts at their word when they say they can mask their approach. What I can say is that my system usually shows any vessel approaching within twelve nautical miles. And I assume you will be closer than that."

"We may not know our way around your yacht but yes, our ships are out there and once we are aboard we will stay out of visual sight but within easy access of you at all times," Strider explained. "We want to stay hidden for the next few hours until all of your friends are aboard. And as we have had no last minute changes and have passed the start period of radio silence, we can assume that eight of them will be coming out by boat after arriving by commercial airline, and four will be joining you by helicopter."

"John, do you have everything you need?" Flint asked.

"Yes, this is a little bigger than anything I have piloted but since we are staying offshore I shouldn't have any problems running this yacht. I'll be staying out of everyone's way so I should be able to keep my cover. My understanding of my role is one of being on board to ensure Francois-Henri doesn't bolt before the cavalry arrives."

"Good understanding, John. We want you and Misty to be here to make sure the yacht stays on course until we arrive," Strider confirmed. "And when we do arrive, the two of you can make yourself scarce until we have everyone rounded up."

We headed to the stern to get a good understanding of where the navy would be coming aboard. Most likely they would have small boats with lots of horsepower.

"I still don't understand how you are going to get aboard without the terrorists becoming alarmed," stated Misty.

"Our team has prepared for this type of operation for years," Flint explained out of Francois-Henri's hearing range. "We are planning to come aboard as soon as it gets dark. Francois-Henri is expecting us to wait until everyone is in bed and we don't want him to think otherwise. By arriving early we will counteract any of his thoughts about alerting any of his friends. He will think he has lots of time before we arrive. Your jobs are to ensure everything goes smoothly until we arrive."

As we reviewed the options for getting on board, a heavy Caribbean rain began to fall. Misty started to move into the cabin. "Don't worry about the rain," I told her. "As soon as it starts it will be finishing and before you know it, the hot air will dry you off." And a couple of minutes later while we were still talking about the best way for the navy to get aboard, the rain stopped and before long we were all dry.

"That was refreshing," Misty agreed. "I'm glad I didn't miss it. Is it always this quick?"

"Yes, do you like it better than the four months the rain always seems to last in Seattle?"

"Ha, aren't you the funny one, Pride."

Flint showed us on a chart where the navy would be in relation to the yacht. It looked close but I knew from experience that many things could go wrong in a few minutes and we would be without help until they actually arrived on the scene.

> *"I did not wish to take a cabin passage, but rather to go before the mast and on the deck of the world, for there I could best see the moonlight amid the mountains."*
>
> *Thoreau*

CHAPTER 45

"Out of sight of land the sailor feels safe.
It is the beach that worries him."

Charles G. Davis

WE SAT DOWN WITH Francois-Henri. Flint started, "Just so we are clear, we will be monitoring all conversations on your yacht and expect you to follow our plan to the letter."

"It is not like I can go anywhere and I do understand my options."

Strider added, "We aren't worried about you heading anywhere. We just want you to understand that in order for you to have any future that doesn't include a long time in Her Majesty's finest prison you need to act like nothing has changed. And we need lots of details discussed. The more evidence you help us get with our electronic monitoring, the better your future will be. It is imperative that you implicate as many of your terrorist friends and get them to talk about what they have done in the past. And if you can get them to lay out future plans that would be a big bonus."

Flint stared at Francois-Henri. "Are we clear?"

"Yes," Francois-Henri replied. "I know what I have to do and the last thing I want is to end up in prison with any of them. It won't take them long to figure out my role in their downfall."

"Good, at least we all understand that," Strider agreed. He finally had a smile on his face. "When we come aboard it will be before sunrise and long before anyone is up and about. Make sure you keep the wine and drinks flowing tonight. We don't want any sober terrorists shooting at us."

"How are you going to keep me safe?" Francois-Henri asked.

"When you hear the first shots, you hit the deck and don't move. If you do that, you will be safe. Move or help any of the terrorists and you will be considered an enemy combatant and we can't promise you anything."

Flint looked at me. "Your job, John, is to see that our man Francois-Henri doesn't pull any stunts. There aren't a lot of options but it doesn't hurt for him to know that we are just over the next wave and ready to punish any and all enemies."

After a few last minute items Misty, Rick and I were left alone with Francois-Henri. He looked at me and said, "I really do regret my role in this whole affair. If I had known what I was getting involved in I would never have had anything to do with them."

I replied, "How did you get involved?"

"It just went from one thing to another. I started out helping one of them purchase some small parcels of land and then before I knew it I was a respected go-between and I couldn't back out. And the money was great."

I left Misty with Francois-Henri to finalize the dinner plans and I headed forward to make myself comfortable with the controls. Rick was trying to get a football game on the satellite TV—some things never change.

All things considered I would rather be at the helm of *Rum-Runner Pride* or even more enjoyably in the two-man kayak with the smile. Enough of that nice thought, time to get back to the business at hand. Lots of fuel and I really wasn't worried about that since we were going to stay at a low-speed cruise. My real concern was to spend enough time moving around the helm so that if one of the terrorists came nosing around it would look like I belonged. And perhaps I should be ready and able to answer basic questions.

I had just finished glancing through the logbook when I heard the first terrorists arriving. I expected Misty would be busy in the galley but I thought one of us should join Francois-Henri.

Coming alongside was a thirty-two foot Boston Whaler with what looked like four fishermen and a guide. They had all the right fishing gear and even had a couple of good-sized marlin onboard. "Throw me a line and I'll secure your boat before you try to get aboard."

The skipper replied, "Great. I'll be heading back to shore right away and will be back before noon tomorrow."

One of the terrorists called to Francois-Henri, "Thanks for the recommendation about fishing. We had a great day. I can't wait to get back to the fishing."

Francois-Henri replied, "Don't worry, if you really have some energy left we can head out in a while and catch a few more fish. Perhaps I can even find you some turtles."

"That would be great. And is there any good snorkeling around here?"

"Yes, but we will have to wait until the rest of the gang arrives. There are just the three of us aboard."

I didn't like where this was heading. The last thing Strider wanted was for our new group to be separated and off in boats.

The four terrorists with their fishing bags and newly caught trophy fish stepped aboard and appeared the genuine article. Fishermen, not terrorists that is, but I expected there was firepower hidden in their baggage and if I didn't know better I would take their enthusiasm for the fishing as the real thing. But I wouldn't be caught off guard. Underneath the friendly attitudes they were all cold-hearted terrorists and killers. And if they started to head off in different directions we would have our hands full.

Ten minutes later we were joined by the sound of an approaching helicopter. It was a Bell 429 and held three terrorists, one of which was the pilot. It didn't take long to realize the biggest of these appeared to be the most senior terrorist. Everyone looked to him first and he was the first to talk once the helicopter was secured on deck.

"Francois-Henri, my friend, what have you got for us now?"

"Tony, nothing but the best opportunity to come our way for a long time." Francois-Henri appeared comfortable with him. "Tony, this is John, my captain. You will meet the cook, Misty, before dinner, and you know everyone else. We are just waiting for two more boats and in the meantime we have opened the bar."

"Thanks, let's hope the sun is over the yardarm somewhere. Is that the correct nautical expression?"

"Yes, Tony."

As they headed to the bar I could hear Tony ask Francois-Henri what the sun over the yardarm actually meant. I couldn't hear his response as I stayed aft to wait for our remaining guests but I remembered back to when Grandfather had explained to Whit and me what it meant: "Sun over the yardarm is an expression that was started in northern waters when the sun would rise above the upper yards, or the horizontal spars where the square sails were hung. This was at 11 am or so and that was when they dished out the first tot of rum." Now it usually refers to a time after 5 pm but I guess when you are on the water or on vacation you can revert back to the earlier time!

I was daydreaming. Thinking of earlier times with sailors on the high seas manning the tall ships headed for glory or death, I almost didn't hear the approaching Cabo. Now this was my kind of boat for fishing. It looked to be over thirty-five feet and like mine, it was well appointed for deep-sea fishing. As it came alongside I could see it was a forty-foot express. All of a sudden I was looking right at the ugliest man I had ever seen and to top that off he was attached to what looked like a huge rocket launcher. Or at least that is what it looked like when it is pointed right at you.

The rocket launcher spoke, "Where the hell is everyone? And who are you?" Actually it was the ugly guy with several knife scars running across his face that spoke but I was still trying to focus on him and not his weapon.

Pulling myself together I said, "Francois-Henri and the rest are at the bar. I'll help you come aboard. Please relax and throw me a line."

He seemed to take me at my word and I was surprised to see he actually knew how to maneuver the Cabo. After getting the four of them onboard I let about forty feet of line out so their boat would comfortably track behind the yacht.

I headed forward to the bar to see what was going on. We were still awaiting the last terrorist to bring the total to twelve plus Francois-Henri. As I entered the bar I could see Misty serving drinks.

She had just met Scarface and was explaining the options. "Some of your friends are drinking the local beer, Red Stripe, and I have a couple of pitchers of rum drinks—Nelson's Blood and Painkillers."

Scarface looked Misty up and down. "What are the rum drinks?"

"They are both made with Pusser's dark rum with Nelson's Blood being equal parts rum, cranberry, grapefruit and pineapple juice. The Painkiller is my favorite and it has two ounces of rum with four of pineapple juice alone with an ounce each of orange juice and cream of coconut."

"Give me two Painkillers—I need something to help my stomach."

I joined Misty behind the bar and looked for trouble. With this crowd it didn't look like it would take long to find trouble but Misty seemed to be handling herself well. "How goes the war?"

"So far, so good, John, the only problem we might have is running out of rum. Are they all aboard now?"

I told her we were still awaiting the last terrorist. Then I headed over to where Francois-Henri was telling a story to his terrorist friends. "...and so when I talked to Starbucks about the protection we could provide not just in the States but around the world they bit. They not only want to do business with us, but I think there may be some additional opportunities in the future."

"Other opportunities, what do you mean?" Scarface demanded.

"Their president made it clear he was not interested in repeat payments. This five million dollar payday for each of you would be the one and only time he wanted to pay anything. But he did say they are working all over the world and from time to time they get extortion attempts. We may be able to help them. I think some of you can dissuade other bad asses. What I need to tell them is how you can do that."

Tony stepped to the plate. "If it is happening in Italy or Spain I will know about it. Nothing of real importance happens without us knowing. Remember what we did to that grocery chain when they tried to come in and displace all the local mom and pop corner grocers? Three small bombs and two sons taken out in an afternoon and we never heard from them again. Protecting a few coffee shops would be child's play."

Scarface added, "That is nothing. When the British brewers faced competition from the Americans during the 80s we persuaded them it would not be a good idea to push their expansion plans. I am still drinking for free on that one."

Tony asked, "What do we have to do for our money?"

Francois-Henri started to address everyone, "They want the terrorist activities to stop and—"

"What terrorist activities?" Scarface asked. "All we are doing is making sure we protect our territories. If they paid when we asked them originally, none of this would have happened. And we weren't any part of what happened on the west coast of the States."

Francois-Henri continued, "I know we weren't but it worked out to our advantage and now Starbucks just wants to get on with business. They want to know that we will stop everything and work with them to discourage anyone else."

Tony stood up. "I'm in, and I think I can speak for everyone. We take the money and run. Let's have a drink to celebrate the future."

Misty brought around another two pitchers and then Francois-Henri started singing, *"Fifteen men on the dead man's chest. Yo-ho-ho, and a bottle of rum! Drink and the devil had done for the rest. Yo-ho-ho, and a bottle of rum."*

"So which of you pirates can tell me where that came from? No guesses. Well, it is suited to us, splitting up a real treasure from Starbucks. That used to be sung by sailors of old and Stevenson used it in his book, *Treasure Island.*"

"Great, Francois-Henri, now let's get out and catch some more fish like you promised," Tony demanded.

"Okay, who wants to join us? We'll take the Cabo and be back in time to welcome Hong Qu."

In a few short minutes it was sorted out that four of the terrorists along with Francois-Henri would be fishing while Misty maintained the bar and I remained to welcome the last terrorist. I didn't like the idea of letting Francois-Henri out of our view but assumed that Strider and Flint would keep them on radar.

"Time is but the stream I go a-fishing in."
Henry David Thoreau

CHAPTER 46

"For me, my craft is sailing on,
Through mists today, clear seas anon,
Whate'er the final harbor be
Tis good to sail upon the sea!"

John Kendrick Bangs

No sooner than the Cabo was off, I noticed the darkening skies to the east. Perhaps it would pass to the south. I headed back to the bar. As I entered the bar I saw Misty was serving drinks to the remaining terrorists and appeared to have them under control so I ducked out and continued to the helm. I knew Strider would be monitoring our conversations and would already know that one boat was out and about on the seas but I thought I should let him know who was in it. I looked over at the radar. Still no sight of the British ships but I could see the Cabo and it wasn't far away.

I quietly brought Strider up to date. "Francois-Henri and four are fishing, waiting for last one." I didn't expect a response but felt better now. I checked the weather forecast. No mention of storms in the immediate area so I looked farther afield and saw the start of a small hurricane which looks like it was gong to head northward and miss the British Virgin Islands. *Hurricane Bertha, 5am: 23.5N/56.5W, moving 305T@9k, sustained wind 65k, gusting 80k, pressure 987mb. During past 12hr / previous 12hr, Bertha moved 0.8 / 1/3 deg N Lat; 1.7 / 1.5 deg W Lon; wind decreased 10k / 30k; pressure rose 7mb / 25mb.*

I noticed a new blip on the radar. Coming in fast and most likely the last terrorist, I decided to head aft. I was surprised to see that it was an old boat and when it came alongside I could see it was a beautifully restored Egg Harbor. Now this was a great looking fishing boat. The only problem I could see was that it held five Chinese sport fishermen.

"I hope only one of you is getting off."

"Where is Tony? We're here and nobody's leaving. Move or we'll make you sorry you didn't get out of our way."

I assumed this was Hong Qu. Him we were expecting. Long hair and mustache that you could hide a few bird's nests in along with a brace of guns around his waist. His friends we were not expecting. And it appeared they were ready for war. They were completely sober and all armed as they trooped aboard the yacht. This would change the coming battle.

"Where is everyone? I asked you already."

"Tony and Francois-Henri with some of the rest are out fishing, the balance of your friends are forward in the bar."

Hong Qu yelled at me, "Those scum are not my friends. Get out of my way. Wang and Lei, stay here and wait for the rest. Lian, join me and we'll see who is in the bar."

We headed to the bar and I tried to make small talk, "Would you like a drink while you wait?"

"We will get what we want, just stay out of our way."

Misty looked up when we entered. "Drinks for the newcomers?"

Hong Qu looked at Misty. "Aren't you a pleasant surprise. Do you have any Kiran beer?"

"Coming up." Misty brought out a tray of cold beer to the now full table of terrorists.

Hong Qu was explaining why he had brought some firepower, "I know we were supposed to arrive alone, but I had to come all the way from Shenzhen and wasn't about to travel alone. And what was I going to do with my gang when I got to the islands? I couldn't very well leave them in town. They would have taken it apart by the time I returned for them. I can control them here."

One of the terrorists said, "I wonder what Tony will think of that?"

And with that all of a sudden we were thrown into war. We could hear shots being fired and everyone exited the bar and into the bright sunlight.

Hong Qu demanded, "Hold your fire." His men stopped firing as the remaining terrorists circled the yacht.

I yelled out to Francois-Henri, "It's alright to come aboard now."

Tony was not happy when he finally got his bearing on the yacht. He looked at me and then said to Hong Qu, "What the hell is going on and why did you bring your gong show?"

"This is who I am and you knew that when we started to work together. I do not need to apologize to anyone. You want me, you get my gang."

I decided to man the helm while they worked out their differences. The only good thing to happen so far was that the menacing dark clouds to the east had disappeared. No sooner had I started the engines and slowly headed westward when Misty joined me.

"Are we ready to serve dinner?" Misty asked.

"Yes, and let's get everyone relaxed. The minute the two of us can leave this situation I will feel better."

"Right you are, love. How are you doing?"

I replied, "Other than a few new terrorists, fine. It would be nice to know what Strider has planned and if he has to make changes now."

"Knowing Flint and Strider, they will be prepared. I'll meet you in the dining room in a few minutes. Can you tell the guests that we are ready for them?"

"Done and just relax."

Dinner went better than I expected. Tony and Hong Qu appeared to have settled their differences and the two of them were eating with Francois-Henri. The rest of the terrorists were seated at the big dining table overlooking the foredeck. They were close enough to hear what the three of them were saying but were obviously deferring and staying quiet.

Hong Qu was questioning Francois-Henri, "Correct me if I am wrong. What you are saying is that Starbucks needs my help in China. And they will pay me if I help them expand. And how do they know that I won't just take the money and run?"

"I think they are depending on our greed. By paying us upfront they seem to think we will help them. What they really have is an open-ended opportunity for us. They do not realize it but they will need us even more as time goes on. And when that happens, we will be able to go back to them and demand even more money."

Tony added, "When Francois-Henri was negotiating with Starbucks he alluded to your ability to instill loyalty from your gang."

"I don't know whether you would call it loyalty. It is more like fear. After a few of them lost both hands I never had even one of them leave me or join another triad."

Francois-Henri turned to Rick. "I think our friends like your threat of added GMO coffee beans to their supplies. That will solidify Starbucks' rush to pay for our protection."

Rick just nodded.

Hong Qu stood up. "A toast to the new plan. We work together on this. Ganbei."

"Ganbei," the rest responded. And Misty poured another round of drinks.

Tony got up and led the next cheers, "Alla Salute."

"Alla Salute," was heard around the room.

"They can do without architecture who have no olives nor wines in the cellar."

Thoreau

CHAPTER 47

"Faintly as tolls the evening chime,
Our voices keep tune and our oars keep time,
Soon as the woods on shore dim,
We'll sing at St.Ann's our parting hymn;
Row, brothers, row, the stream runs fast,
The rapids are near and the daylight's past."

Thomas Moore

AN HOUR LATER I was at the helm again and the sun was well set. "It is quiet on board and I think our friends are starting to settle in for the night," Misty said.

"It is quiet on the horizon," I added. "Why don't we head below?" I was thinking that action could be coming at any time and perhaps it would be better to get as far away as possible.

We were headed down the companionway when I noticed a light on in the bar. I thought everyone had cleared out but Francois-Henri and Tony were having one last drink. Tony motioned for me to join them.

"John, tell us what the morning brings!" Tony demanded with a menacing look.

"I have been tracking the hurricane and it looks like it is going to pass us by with little disruption."

"What does that mean?"

"We are going to get an increase in wave action over the next few hours and you may hear the wind, but by morning the storm should be past."

"So, it will be okay to head home in the morning?" Tony asked.

"Yes, as long as the airlines are flying."

"Good, as much as I enjoy everyone's company, I don't trust the seas. And I wish I didn't have to trust everyone on board. I like to control my future and there are a few too many people in this deal for my liking."

"Tony has been telling me that he doesn't trust some of his colleagues and wants me to set up a side deal for him," Francois-Henri explained.

"I just want to deal directly with the Starbucks guy."

"I told Tony you might be willing to take the yacht north once everyone else is gone. Then Tony and I could meet with Starbucks without any complications."

We could only hope Strider and company was listening. I didn't know whether this would change the plans but it would at the very least give them something to think about. If they delayed the attack until tomorrow they would be able to round up the remaining terrorists and then let Tony meet with Starbucks and perhaps build a better legal case.

"Whatever you want, the yacht is at your service. Perhaps the two of you want a nightcap and then off to your staterooms if you want an early start."

"Good plan, I think we can handle a last drink."

I knew Francois-Henri was thinking it would be hours before the attack began. He would be surprised if indeed Strider arrived early. In fact I wasn't really sure if he would wait or decide to go with the original plans. Either way I wanted to get some sleep, even if it was only a couple of hours. Hopefully by the time I awoke everything would be taken care of.

After pouring them a last drink I excused myself and checked that Misty had made it safely to her stateroom. "Captain to mate are you shipshape?"

"See you in the morning, John."

And so it was, in the middle of one of my coffee dreams. Only this time I was up to my neck in a huge cup of coffee about ready to be poured overboard. And then I awoke to the sound of gunfire and explosions and lights all over the place.

The door was yanked open and Strider was talking at me. "John, all hell has broken lose." As if he had to tell me.

"We have most of the terrorists but three have escaped. Can you help us round them up?"

I knew my plan for a quick sleep waking up to everything being wrapped up by the good guys was too good to be true. And now I would have to get wet in the middle of the night.

"Okay, let's go. What boat are they on and are they armed?"

"We don't know whether they are armed, but it is Hong Qu and it looks like he has most of his gang with him. We are assuming they are well armed. They left the yacht firing their weapons and almost hit two of our officers. They just have a few minutes head start on the Cabo."

"Great, they have the boat I wanted and we have what?"

"John, I think you will like it." We headed up to the aft deck and I could see that I would like it. But I wouldn't be the one piloting that craft. It was black and what I could see was all military and fast. I had never seen anything like it and wasn't sure why they needed me. I was looking at a flat metal surfaced boat with lots of hard lines. It was over eighty feet long and looked like it was still moving fast even though it was hard against the aft boarding platform.

"What am I supposed to add?"

"John, you are the only one around here that they know. We are going to track them and then with your assistance we should be able to trick them into surrendering peacefully."

"I don't know how I can help you accomplish that but let's get going."

We were underway. Misty, Rick and I were in the jump seats with Strider and Flint busy running the controls. I wasn't sure what all the controls did but whatever they did, they did fast. And fast we went. Flint showed me the radar and pointed out the Cabo. It had a great signature and we could see we were keeping pace.

"Stand by for acceleration," Strider cautioned us. Within twenty seconds we were up on plane and going faster than any of my boats. We headed off on a tangent to where the Cabo was heading and before long we were actually in front of it and headed the same bearing.

"Can you tell me what this is?"

"Strider, this the Navy's Mark V Special Operations Craft. We love it. It is fast at over fifty knots and can turn on a dime with its dual jet drives," Flint explained. "We can go five hundred nautical miles full out and can carry a payload of over six thousand pounds. You may have noticed some of our weapons topside. We carry Gatling guns, a stinger and several other classified guns."

"What are the plans?"

"We are going to keep them in our radar sight and let them get away for now. Once they have relaxed and think they are in the clear you come into the plans."

"Great," I replied, "That is what I was afraid of. Perhaps I can just find a quiet beach and a few beers and wait out your little war."

"No such luck, Pride," Strider said. "We think we still have a good chance to get them all in one piece. And that is the important part of this operation. The more of them we can capture, the bigger the bang we will have in rolling up their individual operations. In particular we are really interested in Hong Qu's Chinese operation. From what we have learned in the past few hours it is even more important to take him alive. That is why we didn't engage them on the high seas. We could have taken out the Cabo or tried to overpower them but both of those options would have had a high probability of loss of life."

"So what am I going to do?"

"This is the preliminary plan. We want to let Francois-Henri escape with you and make contact with Hong Qu. Once together we hope you can offer him safe passage off the islands in one of Francois-Henri's boats. If we can get him back in a more relaxed state of mind we might be able to capture him with no gunfire."

"It sounds like we are back to depending on Francois-Henri."

Flint responded, "We don't think anything has changed as far as his ability to work with the terrorists. In fact Hong Qu may feel he is in a stronger position now the other terrorists are captured. Well, Pride, are you in?"

"I don't see any other option. Let's keep Misty out of this." I looked over to her and could tell by her expression that she wasn't happy but I really believed that the fewer people involved, the greater the chance for success.

Misty was reading my mind. "John, you know how I feel about being on the sidelines, but you are probably right. Hong Qu is not going to want a lot of people around. The fewer he sees, the more comfortable he will be."

We all sat quietly watching the ocean go by fast. I could see the beginning of the sunrise and just start to make out the BVIs on our port. The Cabo was over the horizon but we could still see it on the screen.

I asked, "What next?"

Strider explained, "We think they will try to find a secluded anchorage and make their way inland. We are going to get Francois-Henri to call them and set up a meeting place before they get too far away. We will stay out of sight and the two of you will meet them near where they have the Cabo. If plans go as I think they will, you can transfer them to Francois-Henri's boat and be on your way later today. The navy will monitor your progress and when you get to the next islands we will move in."

"It sounds easy when you explain it like that!"

Rick added, "How do we know they won't just kill John as soon as they get onboard?"

Strider said, "They really want a deal with Starbucks and will do almost anything to get it. They know Francois-Henri is the contact and John is one of Francois-Henri's men. And I don't think that gang will think of John as a threat. He is the captain and that's all."

I put my head back and felt the action of the boat's prow slicing through the waves. I thought back to my first few days on the islands with the smile and wished I were back with her.

Misty looked over at me and said, "I bet you wish you were on a hammock somewhere." I just smiled. For the next half hour everyone kept their thoughts to themselves. I was looking forward to the end of this case and perhaps a case of Scotch. But that would be getting ahead of myself. And I was the last person to want to start a celebration before we finished the case. But now to think of it, a Scotch would taste good right about now.

"I believe that water is the only drink for a wise man."

Thoreau

CHAPTER 48

"The wonder is always new that any sane man can be a sailor."
Ralph Waldo Emerson

WE LANDED AROUND THE point from where the Cabo came ashore and a few minutes later a fast helicopter carrying Francois-Henri joined us. He looked none the worse for wear.

"We meet again," Strider said to Francois-Henri.

"Yes, and I hear you still need my assistance."

"Don't let it go to your head," Strider glared at him. "We wrapped up most of your friends. And now we need to get Hong Qu and his gang. Do you think he still trusts you?"

"Don't worry about Hong Qu. He wants to get a good deal and will work with us. He has a big ego and thinks he is invincible. It should be easy to convince him everything can work out better for him. Just leave him to me."

The morning came and went before Francois-Henri was able to make contact with Hong Qu. He had turned off his phone and was worried about the authorities tracing his calls. But eventually he must have realized that the longer he stayed put, the greater the chance of discovery. He needed assistance to leave the islands and when Francois-Henri called him he was more than ready to listen to any good idea.

"We are going to pick him up just after sunrise," Francois-Henri was explaining to me. Strider just nodded. The two of them had agreed on a course of action. "He has three of his gang with him and likes the idea of leaving the island under the cloak of darkness. He has contacts north of here that will help him get off another island.

Strider added, "We will intercept you when you are underway. With any luck they will be asleep or drugged when we arrive."

Misty told me she would spend the evening with Suzanne and make sure she understood what was happening. I had promised her that it would be long over by now and she would have started to worry. "We'll see you tomorrow and enjoy the islands and our success for a few days before we head back to Seattle."

"That sounds great, Misty. Thanks for taking care of talking to Suzanne."

We weren't going to use the yacht. It had a few bullet holes and that meant Francois-Henri was bringing in a favor from a boating friend and borrowing a new smaller but faster ocean-going yacht. It was just after dark when the two of us were motoring up the coast to the rendezvous point. I was curious. "How did you regain Hong Qu's trust?"

"I just told him that the navy looked at the two of us as the yacht owners and not part of the terrorists. He believed me when I explained we were just hired transportation help. And he really wants to get away from the BVIs."

We shut down the engines and coasted for a few minutes. Off the starboard I could just make out a small inflatable with what looked like a good sized outboard engine. It was slowly making way heading towards us. With the glow of the recent sunset behind the inflatable we could see the outlines of the four Chinese terrorists. A few minutes later they were coming alongside and we were scrambling to help them.

"Welcome aboard for the second time in twenty-four hours," Francois-Henri said.

"Just get us out of here and I'll be happy," Hong Qu snarled.

"Would you like to wait for a better taxi?" Francois-Henri asked. "Or can we make you comfortable for our short voyage?"

"Funny man, just get us off this island and I might even be in your debt."

The four of them were onboard when I released the inflatable to the ocean. I watched it drift away and we got underway. We didn't have room for it on deck and I certainly didn't want to tow it all the way across the ocean and back.

"I hope this adventure is all worth it at the end," Hong Qu spat. "I don't appreciate being shot at. If you ask my opinion I think it is Tony's fault that we almost got caught. His big mouth must have attracted some unneeded attention. It serves him right. I hope he rots in some terrible prison."

I thought that at least he was directing his suspicions in a way that was harmless to us. Now if we could only keep him focused on the future we might make it through the night.

"How long will it take to get somewhere safe?"

Francois-Henri answered, "As we discussed, I figure that after a four-hour cruise we should be close enough to your friends to be able to feel safe again. The real challenge will be to see if they can meet you."

"Don't worry about them," Hong Qu replied. "They are expecting us and as long as we don't have any problems they will be there to meet us."

"Good, so let's get underway once again," I said.

A few minutes later we were up to speed and leaving the islands. Leaving the islands—that seems to be my theme song. Every time I starting to enjoy myself here, I had to turn around and leave. Not that I was enjoying myself today, but I was leaving again.

We didn't have a full galley but I was able to serve up a small snack along with some strong drinks. The drinks were one of my rum concoctions and included a little surprise courtesy of Flint. His idea was to make them as groggy as possible without arousing suspicion. The real trick was to ensure the terrorists were the only ones getting the additions. I wasn't drinking, not that I didn't want to drink but I thought the driver should stay sober on this important night. We didn't mind if Francois-Henri became a little drowsy.

"Good drinks," Hong Qu said. I noticed that he of all the terrorists was not drinking very much. At least the rest of them were knocking back the alcohol. But he wasn't. I wouldn't worry about it but it was strange.

It would be at least two hours before contact with Strider and Flint and I knew I wouldn't be able to relax until well after that time. I glanced at the instrument panel and everything was as expected for now. I still enjoyed boating by moonlight. Tonight was a different joy. Although I was in the company of dreaded terrorists I was also enjoying the quiet ride. Up on the bridge I was alone with my thoughts. Scotch, beer, rum drinks, the smile–all things that I was not getting tonight, at least not in the next few hours.

I was thrust from my thoughts by the sound of commotion below. "What's going on, Francois-Henri?"

No answer, so I headed to the aft deck and saw what had started the terrorists yelling. Below us in the water we could see the outlines of at least four shark fins as they sliced through the water. One of the terrorists was leaning over the transom and Francois-Henri was throwing a life ring into the water. I watched it splash down and then realized we were one terrorist short. I could see a swimmer far back behind where the sharks and the now added life ring floated. If he had any chance we would have to circle around.

"Francois-Henri, keep your eye on him as I come around."

It was a long three minutes to get to where the terrorist was last seen. I was surprised to see he was still above the water. I was more than half expecting the sharks would have started their dinner plans. But no, it was the terrorist's lucky day. We didn't waste any time pulling him aboard and was he happy.

The one that wasn't happy was Hong Qu. "What the hell happened to you?"

Our wet terrorist looked up. "I don't know. I felt seasick and was leaning over the rail and then I was in the water."

"Well stay away from the side of the boat and get some rest, all of you. Tomorrow will be a busy day and it would be nice if one or two of you were ready for work."

I looked at Francois-Henri but couldn't read his expression. I knew that he knew the real cause of the seasickness was the drink addition. But what I really didn't know was how he would react once Hong Qu came to the realization that he had been broadsided. We needed Francois-Henri to stay on our side for the time being.

I helped get our wet terrorist warm again with a couple of heavy blankets and a hot coffee. I didn't want to sober him up too much so I spiked it again and hoped he wouldn't notice. With any luck he would be passed out soon.

By the time I got back on the bridge and had the yacht back to full power we had lost at least thirty minutes towards our planned rendezvous. I knew Strider would be able to adjust but it would mean that the booze and drugs would start to wear off.

And so it was while I was worrying about timing that everything started to come together. I glanced at the radar and noticed the naval ship approaching. I slowed down the yacht to about five knots and decided to head to the stateroom to see if I could stay out of harm's way. I was just about to where I thought I was safe when I heard what was definitely not Strider or Flint. "Hong Qu, we are here to take you away to safety."

And then a boat came alongside with a firm crash. By the time I got topsides again three men had thrown lines onboard and were making the two boats hard together. This was not the cavalry I was expecting. The good guys weren't the only ones that could plan to arrive early. My only hope was that the navy had some alert eyes that had seen the early arrival.

I realized my plan to head to the stateroom was going to be disrupted. "Pride, down here," Francois-Henri was calling for me.

When I arrived on the aft deck I could see that the plans were in fluid motion. Rather than the new terrorists coming aboard, they were waiting for Hong Qu and Francois-Henri to abandon ship. That was good. Perhaps they would want me to stay with the yacht and I might still avoid the coming fireworks.

I started to head back to the helm when Hong Qu yelled, "Where do you think you are heading? Over here and help us get off this cursed vessel."

I moved over towards the transom and that was the last thing I remember doing.

We were back in New Brunswick in 1813. We being Mary and I or at least Mary and my relative, Alexander or as he now called himself, Edward. "Edward are you up for some bridge building? Mary asked. "The old bridge over the creek is ready for a rebuild. You will get a chance to use your boat building skills. John and his crew could use someone to help with the timbers."

"I look forward to helping."

We headed overland to where a large number of men were already milling around. They all looked like they knew what to do. Some were squaring the large timbers and others were building rock cribbing in the creek. John and a few men were tackling the covered woodwork on the old bridge. I joined him.

"Welcome to our new bridge." John pointed to the site

of the new crossing. "We need a better bridge with all the new settlers arriving. And the old bridge only had a year or two left after this spring's flooding. We don't want to have to depend on the lower crossing. Can you help with the timber fitting?"

"Aye, I can. It would be good to get some manual exercise."

"If you can help the men working on the timbers it won't take you long to become part of their team."

He was right and the work seemed to work for me. We were using the horses to maneuver the long timbers over the stonework in the creek. My real value was in showing several of them how to save a few steps in the timber joinery. Swinging a short ax to trim the timber ends, I was able to eliminate some of the work and make short order of identifying which timbers to use where.

At one point I was working under the new bridge structure completing some of the supports when two of the men joined me. One asked me how to do what I was doing with the joinery and after a few quick lessons the two of them were happily putting into action my new way. It wasn't long before the rest of the crew noticed that we were getting our share of the work completed faster.

John joined me and commented, "You have a good way with the crew. That must be from your time in the navy."

"Yes, I know what it is like to work your way up in a job and if you can find a better way to do it then you should pass it on to others."

Several hours passed with lots of shouting and hard work by all. I didn't notice her arrival but as John called for a stop in the activities I looked upstream to see Mary. She along with a few other women had brought some food. I joined her.

"Edward, have you found any suitable work for the day?"

"Not only that but I showed them how to join the timbers in a manner that makes the joints stronger. And they are talking about covering the bridge when we are finished," I said.

Mary smiled at me. "John looks like he has already found a place for you."

We all enjoyed the hearty midday meal. Mary and I lay in the shade finishing off the food and I asked, "How is it that your family has such an understanding of their future in this place?"

"We have always had to work hard for what we wanted. And we know what is possible so we have always had strong beliefs and goals to lead us. But I think the most important thing that has always guided us–from our voyage from England to the new American settlements to our Loyalist journey here is our belief in family and our history. We have always worked together and remembered the sacrifices and achievements of our family."

As we enjoyed the summer afternoon I thought back to my Scottish family roots and wondered whether I would ever be able to see the old places again. Place seemed to play a strong role in both of our families. I could remember my family and could walk in my mind the highland trails that the Prides had hiked for hundreds of years. I could see the fields where we had herded our cattle and sheep. I could see the towns and villages around us, and I could still see my family around the kitchen table. Could I replace that with our own new place and how would that affect our future?

Bridges, hard work and future work–I knew this meant something but I just couldn't grasp it.

"When times grow small may men take heart from these."
A G Bailey

PANB Assorted Photo Acquisitions: P194-472

CHAPTER 49

"Thank God I have done my duty."

Admiral Horatio Nelson - last words

AGAIN I AWOKE IN a fog. Unfortunately the fog was in my head. I lay there, no motion and with my eyes closed. This was starting to become a bad habit. Perhaps I should go back to heavy drinking. At least when I woke up I knew who was to blame for the terrible feelings. Once again I had been hit in the back of the head. The concussion that I had been fighting for months was now back with a vengeance. Dizziness, a sense of nausea and a throbbing headache did not feel good. This was not what I wanted or needed. I needed a nurse, or at least the smile or Misty to administer some booze or at least a little tender attention. So I drifted away thinking about lying on a hammock on a beach somewhere. The boat was rocking from side to side. I was rolling around. Great, that really helped.

I could feel real motion. We were underway. "Why did we bring Pride?"

"He can help us find the Starbucks guy and I didn't want him to tell the authorities where we are headed."

This was a new opportunity for me—a new opportunity to get killed or worse. It was the worse that I was worried about. Unless Strider found us fast it would be me against Francois-Henri, Hong Qu and his gang. Especially if Francois-Henri turned again and told the terrorists who I really was and what the authorities had in mind for them. My only chances were to go along with the terrorists and try to think on my feet. Perhaps the timing would be right for Strider to come up with a new plan.

The motion was not helping me lose the fog so I decided to just stay put for now. Perhaps they would forget me and go ashore without me. We were headed back to the BVIs. That was a surprise but they felt that the yacht was being monitored. A big surprise that—obviously they weren't as slow as I thought. So they had engineered a swap of boats and were hoping the navy would miss the second boat. I still didn't quite understand what I was supposed to do for them once we arrived on shore but at least it gave me some value.

I finally fell back to sleep and when I awoke I was underwater. Or at least that is the way it felt. Someone was throwing water in my face. "Wake up, Pride. We are here. Let's go."

With some assistance I struggled to my feet and opened my eyes. Just the effort of getting up was painful. No pain, no gain. That should be my motto this year. Maybe I can change it for next year to no booze, no John working on the case. Oh, and make sure the case involves nothing more strenuous than working on the computer and walking outside to admire the view. Yes the view. As I finally focused on what was happening I didn't recognize anything here.

We loaded into a big SUV and headed up into the mountains. The sun was just starting to rise and it was now a few hours past when the navy was supposed to have completed their job. So a new day and it looked like I was going to have to come up with a new plan. I'd better start to pay attention to what was happening around me.

"John," Francois-Henri was looking at me. "I am going to try to get our Starbucks guy up here and then our friends can negotiate with him directly."

"So why did they have to knock me out? Didn't they think I would come along with them? Or did they think that I wanted to fight them, me against them and their guns and knives."

"No, I think that they thought it would be easier to handle you if you were out. And the big part of the plan was to make the switch quickly and have the yacht continue on with a new captain. They were planning that when the navy came down on the yacht we would be far away."

I was still wondering why me. "And my role is—?"

"Believe it or not, I persuaded them that you were indispensible to their plans. Actually when they knocked you out I think they were going to throw you overboard but I quickly explained that you had been the real contact between Starbucks and me. They bought it and now you are Mr. Coffee Expert so don't blow it for us."

"So it is a good thing that I am a quick study who remembers most of what I've learned in the past few weeks. I can just hope that most of it is still upstairs and not shaken loose with that last blow to my head."

"I think what Hong Qu really wants is a direct contact with Starbucks."

The next hour was spent quietly as we headed up and in, up the mountain and farther inland, away from any potential help and certainly further away from my retirement. Why was I thinking of retirement at this moment? I guess it was just a combination of pains in my head and the potential danger that was coming up.

"What are we to do now?"

"I am calling the Starbucks contact and I want you to persuade him to meet us up at a coffee plantation."

"Why am I calling him and what do I say?"

"The last time I talked to him everything was arranged. We need you to persuade him that you have something extra to offer."

"And what is that?" I wondered.

"You are going to tell him that you have been meeting with your Chinese friends and they are prepared to guarantee a successful expansion for Starbucks, not only for China but throughout the East."

"Why will that be what he wants to hear?"

"Because when he last talked to me we were talking about China and he said that he wanted to ensure he never had to talk to any of us again unless we could solve his larger problem with expansion in the countries bordering China. You are going to persuade him you have a new deal on the table and if he wants to accept it he has to meet us now."

I looked out the SUV's window and thought to myself that this was getting more and more complicated with every move. I knew I could probably get him to come to a meeting but I certainly didn't have a good feeling about how I would escape once I had provided my services.

"Yes, I can do it."

I had the phone in my hands and quickly thought about the next few hours while Francois-Henri dialed a number. It rang two times and was answered, "This had better be good. I told you not to contact me again. I was about an hour from throwing this phone away for good."

"We haven't talked but my name is John Pride and I have been working with Francois-Henri and some of his friends. We would like to meet with you and offer a new plan."

The man from Starbucks took a long time to reply and when he did it was in a quiet voice, "Tell your friends that I will meet with them this once and then that will be the last time I see any of you."

I handed the phone over to Francois-Henri and he gave him the directions. They hung up and then we drove in silence. After about thirty minutes on the road we turned off and headed up a steep mountain trail. It was more like a goat trail but we made good progress and before I even had a chance to really take in the changing scenery we had arrived at the coffee plantation. Exiting the SUV I was surprised to see it was much bigger than anything I had seen so far. The mountainside was covered with coffee plants as far as the eye could see. This was not like the other plantations I had visited with their forest cover. Here coffee plants had replaced all the forest and I could see this was a major operation with large new equipment and well outfitted staff. They all had green hats and white work clothes.

"The Starbucks guy is already here," Francois-Henri stated.

The three of us, Francois-Henri, Hong Qu and I, headed towards what looked like a screen house with a large desk with one man sitting behind it. The rest of Hong Qu's gang remained by the SUV.

The man stood but did not come out of the screen house. "I apologize but I can't stand the sun." He was wearing a big hat like the archaeologists of old.

We all pulled up chairs and Francois-Henri started, "Our plans have changed slightly and I thought it was important you meet my Chinese colleague. Hong Qu will be working with me to ensure your Chinese stores enjoy continuing success."

Hearing something directly behind me I turned around to see a nicely turned out staff member with a tray of cold drinks. "Iced tea for everyone," the Starbucks guy stated the obvious.

Hong Qu must have decided not to impair his thought process today because he surprised me and stayed with the ice tea. "We want to make a few changes to what has been discussed so far."

"Francois-Henri, I thought I made it clear that I didn't want any direct negotiations. I don't actually work directly for Starbucks but someone might think I do and that wouldn't help their public relations."

Francois-Henri replied, "Yes, I know but I think Hong Qu has some interesting ideas that you may be able to pass along to Starbucks."

Hong Qu put on his menacing look. "If you want to have success in the land of the dragon you will need to keep me happy."

I just sat back and tried to enjoy my iced tea. This would be a long morning and I still felt like my concussion was here to stay for a while. I closed my eyes and tried to follow the conversation.

"I think what Hong Qu is proposing is for a continuing payment to ensure Starbucks has clear sailing when operating in China."

"Actually, it is more than that. We see it as a business relationship. We have partnership in many Far East countries and can assist in sourcing new partners for Starbucks and ensure they perform. With our help, Starbucks will never have to worry about the quality of its beans. No worrying about whether GMO beans will make their way into your products."

The Starbucks guy looked at Hong Qu silently. A long minute passed and Hong Qu broke the silence, "We have the loyalty you need and can provide men on the street to keep the peace around your operations. But most importantly, we have the infrastructure to get your stores built, and the contacts within the governments to get the required construction and operating permits. We can also ensure that you receive your store supplies in a timely manner. Working with us will ensure continuing success. Not working with us virtually ensures you will have continuing troubles, real problems."

Again the Starbucks guy looked at us and said nothing. This was starting to unnerve me. I wasn't sure about Francois-Henri or Hong Qu, but I was starting to get an uneasy feeling about this meeting. The Starbucks guy didn't seem in any hurry to talk and he didn't seem intimidated by any of us. I stole a glance up the mountain, past the rows and rows of coffee plants and could see many of the plantation workers going about their daily tasks.

The Starbucks guy looked directly at me. "We are going to talk about this further after dinner. I have to see someone about plantation business and when I get back I want to hear what this is going to cost us. I want two numbers, a price for what we have already agreed and a new price for what you are now offering. I can't promise you anything today but if Starbucks is prepared to work with you I will get back to you soon. Before I leave I need to talk to Pride. From now on I don't want to talk to anyone else but him. He will be my conduit to the rest of you. If any of you or your friends ever contact me or anyone at Starbucks, the deal, if indeed we end up doing a deal, is off and we will take our chances by ourselves. We do not want to be involved with you but we will if that is what it takes in your part of the world. I am going to leave for a minute and when I come back I expect everyone to be gone except Pride."

I am not sure what I was expecting, but this was definitely not it. It appeared as if for some reason he wanted to work directly with me. But in the long run that might be a good idea and solidify my importance to the terrorists. At least ensure I stay alive to fight another day.

After the Starbucks guy left we sat in silence for all of twenty seconds. "What the?" Hong Qu started. "Why does he ignore me and direct his answers to this character?"

Francois-Henri answered for me, "I think he wants deniability. He thinks if he never talks to you he will never have to admit that what he is conspiring with us to do is against the law."

"Well, just don't get any inflated idea of your worth, Pride." Hong Qu looked like he was trying to decide if I actually had any worth to him at all.

"Don't worry about me, Hong Qu. When this is all over, you will never hear from me again."

"No, that is not how this is going to go down with me," Hong Qu was mad. "Listen to me, Pride. What you are going to do is get the best deal we can get from Starbucks. And then what you are going to do is make sure that you are always available to me. Your value to us is to continue to keep Starbucks satisfied and keep the money flowing."

I just looked at him and said nothing. Perhaps I could play the same hand as the Starbucks guy and stare him down. I was not optimistic but it was worth trying.

"Pride, do we understand each other?"

I finally replied, "Yes, I am not here to cause problems."

Then they gave me the proposal I was to present.

"Don't try to cut your own deal, Pride. We will be ready to deal with you if we find out you're not straight with us." Hong Qu stomped out with Francois-Henri in his wake.

"Any fool can make a rule, and every fool will mind it."
Thoreau

CHAPTER 50

"The joy is in creating, not maintaining."

Vince Lombardi

I SAT THERE BY myself just thinking of what I had gotten myself into. If I hadn't been so insistent about this case, I wouldn't be in this position now. If I hadn't argued that the case wasn't already wrapped up, I never would have wound up back on the islands with this crew of winners. I wandered outside and strolled uphill. The peak afternoon sun was finished but it was still hot enough. I found a shady spot under one of the few trees remaining on the hillside. Sitting against the tree, I must have quickly fallen asleep because I don't even remember closing my eyes.

Back to the woods of New Brunswick 1813.

Mary looked over at me. "What are you thinking of, Edward?"

I was just starting to get used to the shift from Alex Pride to Edward Phillips. "We should make sure your brother is ready to join us for dinner. He mentioned that he is ready to get started clearing your land. And I am itching to get our home built."

"Our land, Pride, and you will always be my Pride."

I could see her green eyes sparkle. "Aye, our land. That sounds mighty fine. Our land and our new home."

Mary smiled. "I like your ideas for the house. I can

picture us sitting at a table looking out across the valley. Can you really see us moving in before winter?"

"Aye, there are enough seasoned logs to build our home. It is just having the time and manpower to get it done before the snow falls."

"Don't worry, Pride. The way my family works we will have all of them together next week for a great house-raising. And...by spring there will be the sound of a young one to join us."

I looked over at her and...the dream disappeared.

"Pride, get up." I slowly came to and looked up at Francois-Henri. "Follow me, we don't have much time to talk."

We headed farther up the hill and looking back I could see Hong Qu and his men relaxing by the SUV. I couldn't see the Starbucks guy.

"I think this is going to work if we can get it done quickly and get out fast."

I looked at Francois-Henri. "What do we need to talk about? I thought all I was going to do was repeat the proposal and ensure he accepts it without any changes."

"That is what will happen if it goes like we want it but Hong Qu is worried Starbucks will want some major changes and he is not prepared to negotiate. So you have to ensure that it is a done deal. Can you make sure he understands that this is a take it or leave it deal? And if he leaves it they might as well leave the Far East."

"I will do my best. I can certainly explain what I know about Hong Qu's reputation."

We headed back down and just as we were headed over to the screen house Hong Qu headed us off. "What are the two of you talking about?"

"I was just telling Pride that he better make sure they accept the deal as he presents it."

Hong Qu just looked at the two of us and said, "Why do I get a bad feeling about having to depend on you?"

I didn't say anything. Francois-Henri and Hong Qu drifted back to the SUV and I waited for the Starbucks guy. I tried to relax in one of the screen house chairs but I couldn't make myself comfortable. All I could think about was having to deal with Hong Qu on a long-term basis. That was not a happy thought.

The Starbucks guy finally came back in. He looked at me. "I guess you are wondering why I picked you."

I decided to try his trick again and just looked at him without saying anything. This was starting to be a habit for me.

"You are the perfect person for us to work with. You appear smart and non-threatening. And you can help us maintain a distance from your friends—if indeed they are really your friends." And then he gave me what I thought was a meaningful look and continued on, "I want your deal and then I need for you to get your friends away from here as quickly as possible."

"They are prepared to give you what you want for an upfront fee of $15 million and an ongoing yearly fee of $3 million. They will never ask for more and they will ensure you have no problems. If problems occur, they will take care of them and you never have to talk to them again."

"Done," the Starbucks guy replied. "And for the record, I think you are in over your head. But I look forward to dealing with you and only you in the future. How do you want the money transferred?"

This was our chance to catch more of the terrorists. I could only hope that the navy was ready to monitor the transactions. "I have the details written down. They want to remain here until they can confirm the money has safely left the islands."

"Give me the details and you can wait while I make the calls." The Starbucks guy put out his hand and waited until I handed him the banking info.

I sat there and waited. I also listened to his call and was surprised that he didn't seem to have any problems with persuading the person on the other end of the phone. He was transferred several times and the last time all he said into the phone were the details the terrorists had given me.

"I hope your friends can deliver, Pride."

I just looked at him and left the screen house and headed back to the SUV. I slowly made my way, perhaps thinking the longer it took me to rejoin the rest of the gang the longer it would be before I would be back in harm's way. I was starting to think of myself again and I didn't like my odds. They were all ready to go. After I belted in and explained that the accepted deal, we headed out. I let out a sigh of relief and wondered how this was going to play out. If I could get out of their hands before the navy appeared I might stand a real chance to come out of this intact again. Well, at least I was starting to think positively again.

Hong Qu asked, "What happened, Pride?"

"The money is transferred. They agreed to everything you asked for."

"Pride, I don't know what just happened or why but you are now our man in North America. If we need to get a hold of Starbucks we will be contacting you. And if Starbucks needs anything you will be dealing with me," Hong Qu explained.

I wasn't looking forward to spending more than another hour with this character let alone working with him on a long-term basis. I was glad that this would be playing out fairly shortly. We drove down the mountain and back on the coastal road. By the time we arrived in the next town my heart had almost returned to normal and I was looking for a place to get out.

"We are taking a helicopter out and we will drop you off along the way, Pride," Francois-Henri stated. So much for leaving them early.

By the time we arrived at the place with the helicopter I had decided I really didn't want to leave the islands with them. "I am staying here. I will make my way overland back to the main part of the island and let the two of you head off."

"No chance, Pride. We came together, we leave together," Hong Qu shouted.

Francois-Henri added, "Hong Qu is going to drop the two of us off in the Bahamas and we can make our way home from there."

I looked around. The only thing I could see in addition to the helicopter was a small flight services shack. It had a metal roof with old wooden siding and a few dirty windows. We headed over there and in addition to what I assumed was the pilot was my friend Strider. Now this was a pleasant surprise.

"Welcome, your ride awaits," this came from the pilot. Strider just sat behind the desk while Hong Qu talked to the pilot and arranged our next leg of the voyage.

The pilot said, "Your flight plan is filled in and the helicopter is fully fueled. We are ready anytime you are."

We strolled out to the helicopter. Hong Qu's gang was waiting. They had guns out and ready for whatever might come. We walked up and I don't know how we all got aboard but in about a minute we were all buckled in, with the pilot going through her pre-flight list. I watched as she confidently went through the various checks and readied the helicopter for flight. I wondered what Strider had in mind. I hoped it didn't include anything with me in the air.

The pilot started the rotors and it looked like we were going to take off if Strider didn't do something soon. Before I knew what was happening we were skimming over the ocean. We weren't very far above the waves. I estimated it at about thirty feet and I asked the pilot, "Are we going to stay at this height for long?"

"It is part of special requirements to keep below radar notice."

Hong Qu added, "What's the problem, Pride? Are you seasick or just sick of us?"

I didn't say anything.

We came around the point of land just off the water. In front of us two black helicopters were coming fast, about a hundred feet apart. I was expecting to head up, but no, we headed down. The two helicopters came alongside and their rotor action stirred up wave spray and our whole world was white. Our pilot banked left and we started to lose elevation. The engine cut out and then we were spinning heading even lower. I could now see the waves below us cresting. We were only a few feet above the waves and then we were in the waves with the skids splashing through them. Before I could brace myself the helicopter was in the water and sinking fast. I took a big breath and looked around. The terrorists were all trying to get out of the sinking helicopter and the pilot and Strider were just sitting there doing nothing. That wasn't right.

Shots started to ring out and looking around I saw two round red holes appear on Hong Qu's and another terrorist's forehead. I looked over at Strider and saw him aim his gun again and that is when the weight of the incoming water hit me and knocked me to the side of the helicopter. By this time I had released the seat belt and started to feel myself float upwards. I hit the top of the cabin and that was it. Nowhere to go, behind me was blocked by the two dead terrorists.

Then the window shattered and I was in the ocean. Free and ready to head for the surface I could see just feet overhead. Then a hand came out and grabbed my legs and down I went. So close and yet so far—it looked like this was the end. If I were a character in a mystery novel it would be like my author was just playing with me and had decided that this would be a one-off book with no sequels. Great, the end of the line and I had so much to live for.

I tried struggling but whoever was holding on was much stronger than me. I was sinking fast and running out of air in my lungs. I could hold my breath for a few minutes but with all the struggling my lungs felt like they were ready to explode.

My vision started to blur and I was starting to lose focus about where I was. I knew I was underwater but I was starting to feel like I was just floating. I stopped fighting. I just looked straight ahead. All I could see was darkness, no fish and no sunlight breaking the surface of the water high above.

"You must live in the present, launch yourself on every wave, find your eternity in each moment."

Thoreau

CHAPTER 51

Mare's tails and mackerel scales mean strong winds and full sails.

The sharper the blast, the sooner 'tis past.

The winds of the daytime wrestle and fight
Longer and stronger than those of the night.

A backing wind means storms are nigh;
Veering winds will clear the sky.

When halo rings the moon or sun
Rain's approaching on the run.

Rainbow to windward: foul fall the day;
Rainbow to leeward: rain runs away.

THEN SOMETHING WENT OVER my mouth and I thought someone was going to either strangle me or break my neck. All this way for a stupid case and now it looks like I was going to die underwater alone. They say that your life flashes before you when you are dying, but all I saw was water, more water and no escape. But no, I could feel oxygen entering and looking down I recognized Flint and Misty swimming below. Flint was just below me holding the mouthpiece to a Scuba tank. That was the something that had gone over my mouth. Looking back I saw the swimmer I thought had been attacking me. He had released me and was moving away. I would have to find out who he was. He deserved a big thank you. I really don't know whether I would have made it out without his help.

Once relaxed, Flint motioned for me to head lower and we swam away from where the helicopter must have been. Looking around—swimming over a rock ledge I could see hundreds of fish. No, I could see thousands of them. Most of them were bright blue and I could see a few yellow ones and bigger green and white fish. There were a few fish I recognized—several groupers and a couple of small sharks. They didn't seem to be disturbed by our action.

Stopping, I looked up to see the helicopter and tried to figure out how far we were away. Flint tapped me on my left arm and we moved farther away just as the helicopter lost its last buoyancy and finally slid under the waves and headed our way. I could see it coming towards us but it looked like it was floating. The helicopter was certainly not falling fast, almost as if trying to decide whether it was going to continue to fall or just float under the ocean surface. Then it started to pick up speed just as we moved back. Flint again motioned for me to follow him and we headed along the ledge.

We stopped and although we were now away from the path of the helicopter my heart was still pounding. Misty joined me reaching out to touch my arm as the helicopter finally started to pick up speed. We watched it hit the ledge and as it teetered there I could see Hong Qu inside. He was one bad dude I would not be missing. Then the helicopter rocked once more and headed downward once again. I watched it for a minute and saw it start to plummet at the same time as I saw one of the terrorists pop out the side door. As the helicopter headed down the terrorist was floating upward. I couldn't see which one it was but he wasn't very lively. Flint motioned for me to follow him again.

It seemed like ages when we finally broke the surface and swam to shore. We had been underwater for about ten minutes and looking up the beach I could see Strider pulling two terrorists out of the water, and another Navy Seal taking care of what looked like the remaining gang member.

Strider looked at me. "Well, John, I guess you weren't expecting a quick swim were you?"

"No, and why didn't you take them out at the airport."

"We weren't sure that they would be there. After we realized they were switching yachts, we monitored all the ways off the islands and were watching for new charters of planes and helicopters. We didn't want to put all of our resources in one area so we kept the naval helicopters in a central place ready to pounce once we knew where you were. Both the pilot and I were trained in emergency water landing and we thought that would be safer than mounting a land-based operation. And it worked to perfection. No injuries for the good guys, Hong Qu taken out at the beginning and two of the remaining terrorists dead. We rounded up the remaining three with no resistance and can celebrate a successful operation. We couldn't have done it without the two of you. And just so you know, Francois-Henri was on our side to the end. I got him out of the helicopter safely and the pilot swam with him to shore."

I looked at Misty. "And how did you get in the water beneath me?"

She smiled. "That was Flint's idea. He didn't want me to miss the action and when they told me what was going to happen I told him I was qualified in underwater combat. We came in one of the naval helicopters and when you hit the water, your engine and fuel supply were already turned off so there was little chance of an explosion. We jumped together and grabbed you away from the sinking helicopter and the rest you know."

"Well, I guess I owe you both thanks."

"And the country owes you a debt of thanks. While we were waiting to get going Misty told me of her problems with the Seattle police department. I committed to her that once this was finished I would head back home with her and make it right once again. Now, if you can spare an hour or two, we have a few surprises ready for you."

I looked at Flint and said, "I don't think I can handle any more surprises today."

"You will like these." We got back into one of the black helicopters and headed offshore. I couldn't believe that I was actually back in the air. Misty was up front with Flint and the pilot, and I couldn't help but notice that the two of them seemed to be leaning awfully close for professionals who had just met. She was smiling up at him as he pointed out the waiting naval ship.

The next few minutes were a blur. We touched down and were welcomed aboard by the crew. We were led upstairs and along a short corridor and into the operations room. Everything was metal, the floor, the walls and all the furniture. I could see out over the ship's superstructure and noticed the ocean flowing by. Or at least it looked like we were moving along quickly. I was pleasantly surprised to see a row of coffee mugs filled with coffee. I could use a cup of coffee. Actually I could use a couple of Scotches but I didn't see anyone offering anything stronger than coffee. Rick was there and he looked like he had been relaxing while we were almost getting ourselves killed.

I asked, "Are you making yourself comfortable, Rick? I hope you are ready to hear about all of our excitement. We have been busy."

Rick said, "Welcome back, sorry I missed the action. I would like to be able to say that you missed a good football game but I wasn't able to get anything more exciting than the weather forecast. Yes, the crew has been doing their best to make me feel at home."

Before I could answer him there was a commotion behind us. "Congratulations, Pride." I turned around and almost blacked out. My right leg felt weak and for a second or two I thought I must be hallucinating. I was faint and not sure whether it was just the aftermath of all the action underwater, or the shock of seeing him. It was the Starbucks guy, just standing there, addressing me. I stepped back, somewhat taken aback. What was he doing here? The last time I saw him he was doing a deal with terrorists—albeit through me but nonetheless doing a deal. This definitely did not feel right.

The past few weeks my mind had been conditioned to think of him as one of the bad guys. I certainly wasn't expecting him to turn up onboard looking like part of the ship's team.

"The question is not what you look at, but what you see."
Thoreau

CHAPTER 52

"Starbucks represents something more than a cup of coffee."
Howard Schultz,
Founder, Chairman, President and
Chief Executive Officer, Starbucks Corporation

STRIDER INVITED US TO join us around the briefing table. "John, we are sorry to have kept you in the dark for so long. Starbucks has been onside with us from the beginning. When the first demands came in, they approached the FBI and let us know what they were up against."

"So I was the one in the dark."

Strider looked at me. "Yes, but we thought that was the only way we would be able to get you really into the case. We also needed Starbucks to play along with the terrorists in order to reel them in. You should formally meet the Starbucks guy–Henry Fallis."

The Starbucks guy added, "We couldn't have done it without your initial investigative work, Pride."

"I still can't believe that you are one of the good guys."

Henry said, "We have had so much negative press over GMOs that the last thing we need is to be associated with terrorists, especially since 9/11. We really didn't want to have a hands-on role but Strider persuaded us that we could lend a level of authenticity that was needed. It really didn't take much to get us onside once our president heard the details of the operation."

"So Starbucks never intended to work with any terrorists?"

The Starbucks guy replied, "No, but we did want to play a part in catching them. That was when you met with Harry Poindexter who runs our international operations. Even he was kept in the dark. All he knew was that Starbucks had to do something and you would be able to help us."

"But what about Starbucks in the British Virgin Islands? Was that all a farce?"

"Not at all. Starbucks has spent many years here and we are interested in supporting the local plantations. We found out someone was terrorizing them but couldn't make any headway into solving that part of the case until you got involved."

"And what about our favorite villain Dave, did he really mastermind everything on the islands?" I asked.

Flint answered, "That is the only easy answer, Pride. Dave really wasn't part of the terrorists. He just took advantage of the situation and built his own system of demanding payments. And he would have gotten away with it if you hadn't noticed what he was doing with the offshore accounts."

"Did he have anything to do with the explosions?" Misty asked.

"We don't think so. He might have encouraged the group but we haven't found any direct involvement in the bombings. It was started with the local group and then was supplemented by one of Hong Qu's men. He provided the explosive material and although the local group insisted on no deaths, he went ahead and set the university bomb where he knew it would do the most damage. The second one at Starbucks was already set in play before the university bomb went off. They had no way of stopping it."

"So what happens now?"

"Now we get down to work and round up the rest of the terrorists. Each of the groups represented at the meeting on the yacht is backed by many more back in their country. We had a good lead on all of those groups and believe that with the help of Interpol we should be able to round up many of them."

Strider added, "I just got off the phone. We received the SWIFT info and were able to match several of the money transfers. As we speak Interpol is ramping up to take down several organizations. We are confident that we should be able to get most if not all of them. And if we get the final transfers we should be able to roll up many more of the terrorists."

Misty looked over at me. "The best part of all is that it will all be accomplished while we lie on the beach relaxing."

I still had at least one more question that had been bothering me. "What about the fact that Francois-Henri is not going to pay the price for the wrongs he did?"

Strider laughed, "I knew you would never agree with us that we had to promise him safety in return for his assistance. But believe me when I say that was our only option. Without him we would never have been able to get close to the terrorists. We have found that in every terrorist group there is at least one person like Francois-Henri, someone who values his or her own life or liberty higher than the group's aims."

I turned around and looked at Strider. "That doesn't mean I like it."

"If it makes you feel any better, Pride," Flint added. "Francois-Henri will never be really free. For the next couple of years he will be under the close supervision of Interpol. He will be housed in a safe house in Belgium and will be at the beck and call of our senior intelligence operators there. He will have no freedom for many years and in the meantime we anticipate his help will assist us in capturing many terrorists."

The ship's commander spoke up, "I think the sun is over the yardarm. Is everyone ready for a toast? I have some good dark rum." He brought over the bottle and poured all of us a good measure. He raised his glass and toasted, "Here's one which was used by the British Navy during the Napoleonic Wars—confusion to the enemy."

I added, "That is great. Any day we can confuse the terrorists is a good day indeed."

Strider agreed, "I'll drink to that." And we did. And it felt good going down.

Flint and Misty toasted something over in the corner and I finally had a chance to have a private word with Strider, "I really want to know what you think about what is happening to the plantations on the islands. It appears as if all the small operations are being bought up and it won't be long before all that is left are the large corporate plantations. Tell me that Starbucks isn't helping that occur."

"Henry, come over here and join us."

Henry Fallis, the Starbucks guy, brought some fresh coffee and Strider repeated the question I had just asked him.

Henry answered us, "We are trying to encourage fair trade practices in the islands but it is not easy. A lot of the plantations are looking for an easy solution and that usually means they are prepared to sell to the first real buyer. Sometimes that is a large corporate plantation owner and sometimes it is someone looking to develop a resort. And it is our experience that when the plantations start to consolidate it makes it harder for us to find real coffee bean growers. We want to work with the long-time established plantations but when they consolidate they seem to lose the hands-on way of operating. We don't have an easy solution but we do want to offer a fair price."

"So how does the GMO situation impact Starbucks on the islands?"

"Well, John, we are all looking for better ways to grow coffee and one of the challenges is learning how to operate with less chemicals. We are working with a research team in Hawai'i to develop a decaffeinated coffee bean, and we have had some success promoting shade-grown and organic coffee. This is in addition to encouraging fair trade practices."

"So my coffee is changing," I replied.

"We like to think that it is getting better and more consistent. And we have a new commitment to origin, which is helping us ensure sustainability with many of the smaller growers. This will allow us to gain a long term supply of the beans we want and need."

Misty raised her coffee. "Well, I don't care how you make it or how you get it to me, I just want it hot and ready when I get to your storefront every morning."

I looked at her with a little surprise in my voice, "Give me a break, Misty. You are the first one to try to persuade us to buy organic. And you were the one to try to get the police department to go green and have a larger contingent of bicycle riding officers making the rounds."

"That is different, Pride. I think we should encourage good deeds. I just don't understand how we can influence what happens on a small coffee plantation all the way over here."

Fallis answered, "Now you have some idea of the problems we deal with every day. Most consumers want to do something for the environment and for sustainability but when it costs more for them they have a difficult time justifying the extra cost, especially if it makes their daily coffee more expensive. But one thing we will be doing here is to increase our small plantation support."

I added, "I am just happy that we were able to do our part. And I look forward to returning to the islands and seeing the improvements in the coffee plantation workers' lives. That will make it all worthwhile."

Strider said, "We can all agree with that."

"What I still don't understand was how our friend Dave got himself involved with international terrorists?"

"Pride, we think it just built on his initial idea of a few quick bucks from the universities. Once he was into the scheme of extorting money it wasn't far for him to start consorting with the thugs," Strider replied. "We found some email trails which indicated that he may have been pressured to increase his extortion. And when it comes right down to it, Dave had already started playing for the other team, he just couldn't stop being dragged further into the whole terrorist mess."

No further words were needed. I looked out on the ocean and thought about the past—the past few weeks, and the distant past. I wondered what Alexander Pride would have made of the activities, and how he would have handled them. I like to think that he would have risen to the challenge and enjoyed the adventure. Without both, life would be boring. But perhaps he too looked for an opportunity to step away from the dangers of the high sea during war and start to build a new life in a new country. He certainly must have changed his outlook on life a few times during his lifetime.

"Cowards suffer, heroes enjoy."

"If one advances confidently in the direction of his dreams, and endeavors to live the life which he has imagined, he will meet with a success unexpected in common hours. He will put some things behind, will pass an invisible boundary..."

Henry David Thoreau
"Where I Lived, and What I Lived For"

CHAPTER 53

"I pray to be like the ocean, with soft currents, maybe waves at times. More and more, I want the consistency rather than the highs and the lows."

Drew Barrymore, Actress

IT HAD BEEN AN extremely tiring day and both Misty and I were more than ready to do nothing for a while. After the briefing aboard the naval ship we got a quick ride on one of their fast auxiliary tenders. We were dropped off on a beach I recognized, a good length of sand with a few palms and no tourists. We walked over to a cottage I knew.

We were sitting there enjoying the view when I looked over at Misty and said, "This has been a busy case, much too busy if you ask me. Remind me to reconsider when the FBI comes calling again. I should have listened to you when you said you didn't like Dave."

"You should always listen to me, John."

"And I'm glad you and Flint are going to try and work out your problems in Seattle."

"Yes, he mentioned he worked with the chief when he was in the FBI and has already put in a good word for me."

"So what does that really mean? Are you sure you want anything to do with the Seattle police department again?"

Misty didn't immediately answer me and I didn't rush her. We both looked out at the ocean and when she finally answered it didn't surprise me. "John, I don't know where it will lead but I do know that I need some final resolution and I also know I'm not really ready for retirement. When I do retire I want it to be on my terms and certainly not on some phony made-up charges. I had a call from your friend Blake last night."

That caught my attention. I was expecting to hear from Blake but I had thought he would be calling me. Misty and Blake still had some issues and I wasn't sure they trusted each other. "What did Blake have to say and why would he be calling while we are out here?"

"Flint had a word with him and I guess Blake did some investigative work on my problems and is prepared to listen to my side of the story."

"That's great news, Misty. I'm glad you are finally getting that straightened around. I hope that doesn't mean you will be going back to work for the Seattle police department. I would miss your help."

"Not on your life, Pride. You have me for good."

I looked out on the ocean and asked, "When are you headed back?"

"Soon, John, soon."

A pair of hands slowly massaged my tender back. I felt myself start to relax. My concussion appeared to be gone for now but I still had a few kinks to be worked out. This felt good. Actually it felt better than good, it felt great.

I smiled and looked back into the smile's face. "Great end to a long week."

She just smiled as Misty got up without a word and headed down the beach.

> "Many men go fishing all of their lives without knowing that it is not fish they are after."
>
> Henry David Thoreau

CHAPTER 54

"Sunset and evening star,
And one clear call for me!
And may there be no moaning of the bar,
When I put out to sea."
Alfred, Lord Tennyson 1809-1892

WE HAD A QUICK swim out to the closest coral reef. Free diving, we just relaxed for a few minutes. No words passed between us, but none was needed. We were in the place where we both knew what was coming. Or at least in our own individual way we both thought we knew what came next. On the swim back to the beach I thought this was as close to retirement as I wanted to get. It really wasn't the final destination that was important but enjoying the voyage. This part of the voyage was sure to remain clear in my mind. As we reached shore I realized that the smile was looking at me with desire in her eyes—about time.

We walked over to the hammock. As we settled in I looked up to the most spectacular sunset. And there it was—one of the things I had been looking for—the *green flash* as the sun dropped below the horizon. It didn't last long but it was spectacular.

"In wilderness do we find the preservation of the world."
Thoreau

CHAPTER 55

"So we dream on. Thus we invent our lives...
We invent what we love and what we fear.
We dream on and on: the best hotel, the perfect family,
the resort life. And our dreams escape us almost as vividly as we
can imagine them...
That's what happens, like it or not.
And because that's what happens, this is what we need:
we need a good, smart bear...
Coach Bob knew it all along: you've got to get obsessed and stay
obsessed. You have to keep passing the open windows."
                    John Irving "The Hotel New Hampshire"

LOOKING OUT AT THE horizon my mind flashed a thought. I needed a new
goal and why couldn't I combine my love of the wilderness and special places
with my need to build a new home?

I knew that there were resort developers planning for major changes in
the islands and perhaps we could conserve this part of paradise. I had just
finished reading my favorite naturalist E.O. Wilson's novel *Anthill* and he had
some interesting passages:

> *Raff said, "Suppose we didn't make those habitats and species*
> *into obstacles that we put on the cost side of the ledger. Suppose*
> *we added them to the profit side. I've been checking. It's getting*
> *routine around the country for high-end retirement communities*

and second-home resorts to make an asset out of nature if they possibly can. As you can see…the trend started back in the sixties and it really began to climb in the nineties. It's now a national trend, and it's more or less recession-proof…two factors weigh high on profitability. The closer the development to a major center of population, the larger the per-acre profit, especially for homes at the high end. I think we're in a situation here where it would pay to build a smaller number of estates than we planned. Maybe have a row of relatively small lots…with a private gated road…there would be a community landing and boathouse… With that we add some nature trails but leave the rest…just as it is."

That brought me full circle. I thought back to Alexander Pride and Dad. Both of them always had a goal in mind or project on the go. I now had something to strive for, and could plan for the future.

"He knows that something somewhere has to break
He sees the family home now looming in the headlights
The pain upstairs that makes his eyeballs ache
Many miles away there's a shadow on the door of a cottage
on the shore of a dark Scottish lake."

Sting

"I had rather be shut up in a very modest cottage, with my books, my family, and a few old friends, dining on simple bacon, and letting the world roll on as it liked, than to occupy the most splendid post which any human power can give."

Thomas Jefferson

-30-

Afterword

"I'm headed to Cransley and the beach."
Sandy Phillips 2010

This is the first novel written by a new author writing under the pseudonym of Robert Alex Bell. My father was a journalist and writer, and one of the last things he recommended to me was to use the name Robert Alex for my novels. Those are my first two names and I am honored to follow his advice one last time and to be able to put those names to print.

When I started thinking about the subject matter for this novel I was heavily involved with a senior management position and put an initial story line to paper—220 words. It wasn't until over three years later that I found the time and motivation to start putting the story down on paper.

During the month of August 2001 I wrote 22,000 words, and when the tragedy of September 11, 2001 occurred the book was put on hold for two reasons. The first was that I was in the process of starting a new professional career that would entail a significant amount of international travel. The second and more important reason for putting this story on hold was the fact that I needed to evaluate how I was dealing with terrorism.

I finally realized although North Americans were now dealing with terrorism on a new level, there was still a place for a story that dealt with localized small-scale terrorist actions.

Robert Alex Bell
Calgary and Cransley 2013

The Green Flash

Yes, the Green Flash is real. It is a rare optical phenomenon caused by atmospheric refraction on the horizon. And this author, after many years of searching, finally saw it on two consecutive evenings on the Big Island of Hawai'i in 2007. The Green Flash is much smaller than the setting sun and occurs just as the sun sets. It is magnificent and well worth the wait.

International Finance and Future Investments

The world is changing. As I finished this novel I thought back to the recent financial crisis, which started with the US Sub-Prime Mortgage meltdown and its effects on world credit and stock markets. My working experience in investment banking and corporate finance started in the early 1980s at McLeod Young Weir - now ScotiaMcLeod - when interest rates spiked at over 20%, and I was in Toronto at Merrill Lynch when Bloody Monday happened on October 19, 1987. That day was the biggest daily percentage drop on the Dow Jones Industrial Average at over 22% and it was my first day licensed with Merrill Lynch. The previous Friday I had been in New York City on the world's largest trading floor when the crash started. There are always opportunities to make money in the markets but what I have learned is that it is far better to choose stocks in good companies and hold them for the long term.

Cargill, Starbucks, the US Navy and others

Although some corporate and government facts are used in the telling of this novel, reference to the GMO Research Group and management at Cargill, the management at Starbucks and all conversations and people identified are fictional, and bear no true relationship to any real person or organizations named.

Resort Developers and Sustainable Development

A final word on resort developers—I have spent much of the past twenty years consulting with corporate resort owners, and most of them are honorable and want to create something that will provide value for their investors and guests.

The rogues in this novel are the exception. But there are some places that should never be developed, and there are special places on the water that will always be home to me. Puget Sound in Washington State and the whole area from the border up to Desolation Sound in British Columbia has some of the world's best boating. Lumsden Beach, my experience of sustainable development, has been enjoyed by five generations of our family and remains virtually the same as when my grandparents, Whitman and Mamie, first brought their family to the cottage. And Cransley, what can I say about Cransley except that it is the future. Stay tuned for the next installment with Pride to learn more about how Cransley plays an important role in his future.

> *"Men and boys are learning all kinds of trades but how to make men of themselves. They learn to make houses; but they are not so well housed, they are not so contented in their houses, as the woodchucks in their holes. What is the use of a house if you haven't got a tolerable planet to put it on?"*
>
> *Thoreau*

Is it a Dock or a Pier?

Throughout this novel I used the word *dock* when I have been referring to that structure which boats are tied to and you walk out on. Technically a dock is something you do with a boat and when you bring your boat to shore you dock alongside a pier. That being said, I like the word dock and most non-boaters know what I am talking about. I just hope that the boaters out there - especially you Rob - forgive me and let me know if I got anything else wrong. I'll get it correct the next time Pride heads out on the Sound.

Rum Running and the Puget Sound

As far as I know my family had no connection to rum running but my grandmother - Mamie Wilson - was one of the leaders in the Temperance Movement in Regina and made her sons sign the non-drinkers pledge. I have my father's letters home to her during the Second World War and it is obvious that he found it hard to break the news that he was drinking and smoking.

More than once he asked his parents to send a few packs of cigarettes but they never did, and he quit smoking the pipe after being hounded by his sons. I have spent many pleasurable days and evenings exploring with friends the coves and inlets used by rum runners. All along the American and Canadian coasts, both Atlantic and Pacific, there are reminders of the not too distant past with numerous hiding spots named Smuggler Cove, Pirate Bay and Secret Cove.

Family History and the War of 1812

Our family enjoys genealogy and the following are some of the interesting facts about the family. The flashbacks to Alexander Pride's time in the British Navy are based on his actual naval records found in the ships' logs, which I held in my hands at The National Archives at Kew, just outside London. Conversations are fictionalized but the dates and places are real. Alexander was press ganged from Bo'ness, Scotland into the British Navy in 1809, sailed from Madras, India and saw service in Indonesia during the Anglo-Dutch Java War; in the Mediterranean and Atlantic Oceans during the Napoleonic Wars; and in the Caribbean and off the American coast during the War of 1812. He *ran from service* at Halifax, married Mary Bailey and they had 10 children. They lived in Maugerville, New Brunswick and Brougham, Ontario; and their descendants live in Ontario, Western Canada, the Puget Sound area and throughout the USA. Pride died in 1845 while helping to cut down a tree on his son's farm in Uxbridge, Ontario and if he had lived two more years he would have qualified for one of the first real British campaign medals—the Naval General Service Medal of 1847. His service at the qualifying action of the Invasion of Java would have won him the medal with the clasp of *30 July Boat Service 1811.*

Westerners

Did your ancestors pioneer this ground?
Can you trace your descent that far back?
Are you proud of your family background,
Of their success, despite what they lacked?

Well, remember, my friend, when you're tempted
To turn up your nose at hard work,
That the price of this land they preempted
Was sweat, by the gallon, and work.
...
For this land that we all take for granted
Was constructed by men wild and rough
At a time when you took what you wanted,
And if you couldn't handle it-tough!
For theirs was the law of the jungle
Where only the strong stayed alive
And the quitter who hollered out "Uncle"
Was a creature who couldn't survive.

Look around you, my friend, and remember
That this West's just a hundred years old,
That the ground won't produce in December
And a man has to battle the cold
Every bone-chilling day for a half-year
And sleep warm every long winter night,
And be honest, my friend, could you stay here
Had those ancestors not won their fight?

Jack Whyte -
National Bestselling Author of The Forest Laird, and the Templar Trilogy

Alfred Goldsworthy Bailey, OC FRSC 1905-1997
While I was researching my family history in New Brunswick I came upon the poetry of Alfred G Bailey, Canadian educator, poet, anthropologist, ethno-historian, and academic administrator. I have not confirmed that he is related to my Bailey family but they knew the same countryside. His poetry was published in five volumes... *and Northrop Frye declared him in the first ranks of Canadian poets. The Bailey family had connections with the New England family of Ralph Waldo Emerson... by choosing and starkly presenting a series of images of the contemporary Maritime scene Bailey evokes a deeply tragic*

sense of the decay of a once-proud culture. Desmond Pacey article appearing in
Canadian Literature Spring / Summer 1976.

"Here in the east the barns are empty of grass
and commerce has moved to the focal canals
and freight yards
of the smoking west.
From the muddy rims of the tidal estuaries
the wrecks of tugs stick out, a tourist's emblem,
graphs of decay and a kind of awakening.
Framed through the posts of a once-fenced field
our glaucous vision rest on rusted trash
thrown long ago.
The tons of timber buoyed on the bend of the teeming
river
are nothing now but a yellowed notation
in an archivist's scrapbook."

A G Bailey "Here in the East"

Henry David Thoreau, 1817-1862
Thoreau's Walden has always held a special place in my library. He was an early advocate of canoeing and hiking, private land conservation and the preservation of wilderness.

"Do not lose hold of your dreams or aspirations. For if you do, you
may still exist but you have ceased to live."

Thoreau

John Alexander Pride
When I wrote this novel I thought of John Pride having my middle name of Alexander, after my great Grandfather Alexander Bell and the original Alexander Pride. Although I didn't use it in this story, I thought of the

original as Sandy, the diminutive or Scottish family nickname for Alexander. I also realized when I was halfway through the writing process that there was another John Alexander, a family friend - John (Jack) Alexander Boan, PhD.

The End - 30 -
This is in honor of my father, RHD, the writer. When he worked as a newspaper journalist they used this -30- notation at the end of anything typed to signify the end of the final page.

> *"Books are the treasured wealth of the world and the fit inheritance of generations and nations. Books, the oldest and the best, stand naturally and rightfully on the shelves of every cottage."*
>
> Thoreau

Pride Family

Scotland to Canada   *England to Maryland to New Brunswick*

|

|

William Pride *1753* – Jean Smith   Benjamin Bailey – Susannah Wanty

|

|

Alexander Pride *British Navy, War of 1812* – Mary Bailey *New Brunswick*

|

John Pride *Rebellion of 1837* – Polly Sharrard *Loyalist*

|

Robert Seth *1855-1935* – Louantha McGregor *1855-1916*

|

Whitman Harold *1886-1969* – Mayme Wilson *1885-1951*

| Peter Bell *Cransley, Scotland* – Della Fallis

Robert Howard Daniel *1921-2005* – Tanyss Bell | Elizabeth Bell

|

Robert Alex Bell *Cransley*   John Pride   Whit Bell Pride